Karl Ove Knausgaard

My Struggle

Translated from the Norwegian by Don Bartlett

archipelago books

SECOND HARDCOVER PRINTING

First published as *Min kamp 1* by Forgalet Oktober in 2009.

Archipelago Books
232 3rd Street, Suite A111
Brooklyn, NY 11215
www.archipelagobooks.org

Library of Congress Cataloging-in-Publication Data
Knausgård, Karl Ove, 1968–
[Min kamp. English]
My struggle / Karl Ove Knausgaard ; translated from the Norwegian by Don Bartlett. – 1st Archipelago Books ed.
p. cm.
ISBN 978-0-914671-00-8 (alk. paper)
I. Bartlett, Don. II. Title.
PT8951.21.N38M5613 2012
839.82'37—dc23 2011048978

PRINTED IN THE UNITED STATES OF AMERICA

Distributed by Random House
www.randomhouse.com

Cover art: Anselm Kiefer

The publication of *My Struggle* was made possible with support from the Black Mountain Institute, Lannan Foundation, the National Endowment for the Arts, the New York State Council on the Arts, a state agency, NORLA (Norwegian Literature Abroad), and the New York City Department of Cultural Affairs.

Part 1

For the heart, life is simple: it beats for as long as it can. Then it stops. Sooner or later, one day, this pounding action will cease of its own accord, and the blood will begin to run towards the body's lowest point, where it will collect in a small pool, visible from outside as a dark, soft patch on ever whitening skin, as the temperature sinks, the limbs stiffen and the intestines drain. These changes in the first hours occur so slowly and take place with such inexorability that there is something almost ritualistic about them, as though life capitulates according to specific rules, a kind of gentleman's agreement to which the representatives of death also adhere, inasmuch as they always wait until life has retreated before they launch their invasion of the new landscape. By which point, however, the invasion is irrevocable. The enormous hordes of bacteria that begin to infiltrate the body's innards cannot be halted. Had they but tried a few hours earlier, they would have met with immediate resistance; however everything around them is quiet now, as they delve deeper and deeper into the moist darkness. They advance on the Havers Channels, the Crypts of Lieberkühn, the Isles of Langerhans. They proceed to Bowman's Capsule in the Renes, Clark's Column in the Spinalis, the black substance in the Mesencephalon. And they arrive at the heart. As yet, it is intact, but deprived of the activity to which end its whole construction has been designed, there is something strangely desolate about it, like a production plant that workers have been forced to flee in haste, or so it appears, the stationary vehicles shining yellow against the darkness of the forest, the huts deserted, a line of fully loaded cable- buckets stretching up the hillside.

The moment life departs the body, it belongs to death. At one with lamps, suitcases, carpets, door handles, windows. Fields, marshes, streams, mountains, clouds, the sky. None of these is alien to us. We are constantly surrounded by objects and phenomena from the realm of death. Nonetheless, there are few things that arouse in us greater distaste than to a see a human being caught up in it, at least if we are to judge by the efforts we make to keep corpses out of sight. In larger hospitals they are not only hidden away in discrete, inaccessible rooms, even the pathways there are concealed, with their own elevators and basement corridors, and should you stumble upon one of them, the dead bodies being wheeled by are always covered. When they have to be transported from the hospital it is through a dedicated exit, into vehicles with tinted glass; in the church grounds there is a separate, windowless room for them; during the funeral ceremony they lie in closed coffins until they are lowered into the earth or cremated in the oven. It is hard to imagine what practical purpose this procedure might serve. The uncovered bodies could be wheeled along the hospital corridors, for example, and thence be transported in an ordinary taxi without this posing a particular risk to anyone. The elderly man who dies during a cinema performance might just as well remain in his seat until the film is over, and during the next two for that matter. The teacher who has a heart attack in the school playground does not necessarily have to be driven away immediately; no damage is done by leaving him where he is until the caretaker has time to attend to him, even though that might not be until sometime in the late afternoon or evening. What difference would it make if a bird were to alight on him and take a peck? Would what awaits him in the grave be any better just because it is hidden? As long as the dead are not in the way there is no need for any rush, they cannot die a second time. Cold snaps in the winter should be particularly propitious in such circumstances. The homeless who freeze to death on benches and in doorways, the suicidal who jump off high buildings and bridges, elderly women who fall down staircases, traffic victims trapped in wrecked cars, the young man who, in a drunken stupor, falls into the lake after a night on the town, the small girl who ends up under the wheel of a bus, why all this haste to remove them from the public eye? Decency? What could be more decent than to allow the girl's mother and father to see her an hour or two later, lying in the snow at the site of the accident, in full view, her crushed head and the rest of her body, her blood-spattered hair and the spotless padded jacket? Visible to the whole world, no secrets, the way she was. But even this one hour in the snow is unthinkable. A town that does not keep its dead out of sight, that leaves people where they died, on highways and byways, in parks and parking lots, is not a town but a hell. The fact that this hell reflects our life experience in a more realistic and essentially truer way is of no consequence. We know this is how it is, but we do not want to face it. Hence the collective act of repression symbolized by the concealment of our dead.

What exactly it is that is being repressed, however, is not so easy to say. It cannot be death itself, for its presence in society is much too prominent. The number of deaths reported in newspapers or shown on the TV news every day varies slightly according to circumstances, but the annual average will presumably tend to be constant, and since it is spread over so many channels virtually impossible to avoid. Yet *that* kind of death does not seem threatening. Quite the contrary, it is something we are drawn to and will happily pay to see. Add the enormously high body count in fiction and it becomes even harder to understand the system that keeps death out of sight. If the phenomenon of death does not frighten us, why then this distaste for dead bodies? It must mean either that there are two kinds of death or that there is a disparity between our conception of death and death as it actually turns out to be, which in effect boils down to the same thing. What is significant here is that our conception of death is so strongly rooted in our consciousness that we are not only shaken when we see that reality deviates from it, but we also try to conceal this with all the means at our disposal. Not as a result of some form of conscious deliberation, as has been the case with funeral rites, the form and meaning of which are negotiable nowadays, and thus have shifted from the sphere of the irrational to the rational, from the collective to the individual – no, the way we remove bodies has never been the subject of debate, it has always been just something we have done, out of a necessity for which no one can state a reason but everyone feels: if your father dies on the lawn one windswept Sunday in autumn, you carry him indoors if you can, and if you can't, you at least cover him with a blanket. This impulse, however, is not the only one we have with regard to the dead. No less conspicuous than our hiding the corpses is the fact that we always lower them to ground level as fast as possible. A hospital that transports its bodies upward, that sites its cold chambers on the upper floors is practically inconceivable. The dead are stored as close to the ground as possible. And the same principle applies to the agencies that attend them; an insurance company may well have its offices on the eighth floor, but not a funeral parlor. All funeral parlors have their offices as close to street level as possible. Why this should be so is hard to say; one might be tempted to believe that it was based on some ancient convention that originally had a practical purpose, such as a cellar being cold and therefore best suited to storing corpses, and that this principle had been retained in our era of refrigerators and cold-storage rooms, had it not been for the notion that transporting bodies upward in buildings seems *contrary to the laws of nature*, as though height and death are mutually incompatible. As though we possessed some kind of chthonic instinct, something deep within us that urges us to move death down to the earth whence we came.

II

It might thus appear that death is relayed through two distinct systems. One is associated with concealment and gravity, earth and darkness, the other with openness and airiness, ether and light. A father and his child are killed as the father attempts to pull the child out of the line of fire in a town somewhere in the Middle East, and the image of them huddled together as the bullets thud into flesh, causing their bodies to shudder, as it were, is caught on camera, transmitted to one of the thousands of satellites orbiting the Earth and broadcast on TV sets around the world, from where it slips into our consciousness as yet another picture of death or dying. These images have no weight, no depth, no time, and no place, nor do they have any connection to the bodies that spawned them. They are nowhere and everywhere. Most of them just pass through us and are gone; for diverse reasons some linger and live on in the dark recesses of the brain. An off-piste skier falls and severs an artery in her thigh, blood streams out leaving a red trail down the white slope; she is dead even before her body comes to a halt. A plane takes off, flames shoot out from the engines as it climbs, the sky above the suburban houses is blue, the plane explodes in a ball of fire beneath. A fishing smack sinks off the coast of northern Norway one night, the crew of seven drown, next morning the event is described in all the newspapers, it is a so-called mystery, the weather was calm and no mayday call was sent from the boat, it just disappeared, a fact which the TV stations underline that evening by flying over the scene of the drama in a helicopter and showing pictures of the empty sea. The sky is overcast, the gray-green swell heavy but calm, as though possessing a different temperament from the choppy, white-flecked waves that burst forth here and there. I am sitting alone watching, it is some time in spring, I suppose, for my father is working in the garden. I stare at the surface of the sea without listening to what the reporter says, *and suddenly the outline of a face emerges*. I don't know how long it stays there, a few seconds perhaps, but long enough for it to have a huge impact on me. The moment the face disappears I get up to find someone I can tell. My mother is on the evening shift, my brother is playing soccer, and the other children on our block won't listen, so it has to be Dad, I think, and hurry down the stairs, jump into shoes, thread my arms through the sleeves of my jacket, open the door, and run around the house. We are not allowed to run in the garden, so just before I enter his line of vision, I slow down and start walking. He is standing at the rear of the house, down in what will be the vegetable plot, lunging at a boulder with a sledgehammer. Even though the hollow is only a few meters deep, the black soil he has dug up and is standing on together with the dense clump of rowan trees growing beyond the fence behind him cause the twilight to deepen. As he straightens up and turns to me, his face is almost completely shrouded in darkness.

Nevertheless I have more than enough information to know his mood. This is apparent not from his facial expressions but his physical posture, and you do not read it with your mind but with your intuition.

He puts down the sledgehammer and removes his gloves.

"Well?" he says.

"I've just seen a face in the sea on TV," I say, coming to a halt on the lawn above him. The neighbor had felled a pine tree earlier in the afternoon and the air is filled with the strong resin smell from the logs lying on the other side of the stone wall.

"A diver?" Dad says. He knows I am interested in divers, and I suppose he cannot imagine I would find anything else interesting enough to make me come out and tell him about it.

I shake my head.

"It wasn't a person. It was something I saw in the sea."

"Something you saw, eh," he says, taking the packet of cigarettes from his breast pocket.

I nod and turn to go.

"Wait a minute," he says.

He strikes a match and bends his head forward to light the cigarette. The flame carves out a small grotto of light in the gray dusk.

"Right," he says.

After taking a deep drag, he places one foot on the rock and stares in the direction of the forest on the other side of the road. Or perhaps he is staring at the sky above the trees.

"Was it Jesus you saw?" he asks, looking up at me. Had it not been for the friendly voice and the long pause before the question I would have thought he was poking fun at me. He finds it rather embarrassing that I am a Christian; all he wants of me is that I do not stand out from the other kids, and of all the teeming mass of kids on the estate no one other than his youngest son calls himself a Christian.

But he is really giving this some thought.

I feel a rush of happiness because he actually cares, while still feeling vaguely offended that he can underestimate me in this way.

I shake my head.

"It wasn't Jesus," I say.

"That's nice to hear," Dad says with a smile. Higher up on the hillside the faint whistle of bicycle tires on tarmac can be heard. The sound grows, and it is so quiet on the estate that the low singing tone at the heart of the whistle resonates loud and clear, and soon afterward the bicycle races past us on the road.

Dad takes another drag at the cigarette before tossing it half-smoked over the fence, then coughs a couple of times, pulls on his gloves, and grabs the sledgehammer again.

"Don't give it another thought," he says, glancing up at me.

I was eight years old that evening, my father thirty-two. Even though I still can't say that I understand him or know what kind of person he was, the fact that I am now seven years older than he was then makes it easier for me to grasp some things. For example, how great the difference was between our days. While my days were jam-packed with meaning, when each step opened a new opportunity, and when every opportunity filled me to the brim, in a way which now is actually incomprehensible, the meaning of his days was not concentrated in individual events but spread over such large areas that it was not possible to comprehend them in anything other than abstract terms. "Family" was one such term, "career" another. Few or no unforeseen opportunities at all can have presented themselves in the course of his days, he must always have known in broad outline what they would bring and how he would react. He had been married for twelve years, he had worked as a middle-school teacher for eight of them, he had two children, a house and a car. He had been elected onto the local council and appointed to the executive committee representing the Liberal Party. During the winter months he occupied himself with philately, not without some progress: inside a short space of time he had become one of the country's leading stamp collectors, while in the summer months gardening took up what leisure he had. What he was thinking on this spring evening I have no idea, nor even what perception he had of himself as he straightened up in the gloom with the sledgehammer in his hands, but I am fairly sure that there was some feeling inside him that he understood the surrounding world quite well. He knew who all the neighbors on the estate were and what social status they held in relation to himself, and I imagine he knew quite a bit about what they preferred to keep to themselves, as he taught their children and also because he had a good eye for others' weaknesses. Being a member of the new educated middle class he was also well-informed about the wider world, which came to him every day via the newspaper, radio, and television. He knew quite a lot about botany and zoology because he had been interested while he was growing up, and though not exactly conversant with other science subjects he did at least have some command of their basic principles from secondary school. He was better at history, which he had studied at university along with Norwegian and English. In other words, he was not an expert at anything, apart from maybe pedagogy, but he knew a bit about everything. In this respect he was a typical school teacher, though, from a time when secondary school teaching still carried some status. The neighbor who lived on the other side of the wall, Prestbakmo, worked as a teacher at the same school, as did the neighbor who lived on top of the tree-covered slope behind our house, Olsen, while one of the neighbors who lived at the far end of the ring road, Knudsen, was the head teacher of another middle school. So when my father raised the sledgehammer above his head and let it fall on the rock that spring evening in the mid 1970s, he was doing so in a world he knew and was familiar with. It was not until I myself reached the same age that I understood there was indeed a price to pay for this. As your perspective of the world increases not only is the pain it inflicts on you less but also its meaning. Understanding the world requires you to take a certain distance from it. Things that are too small to see with the naked eye, such as molecules and atoms, we magnify. Things that are too large, such as cloud formations, river deltas, constellations, we reduce. At length we bring it within the scope of our senses and we stabilize it with fixer. When it has been fixed we call it knowledge. Throughout our childhood and teenage years, we strive to attain the correct distance to objects and phenomena. We read, we learn, we experience, we make adjustments. Then one day we reach the point where all the necessary distances have been set, all the necessary systems have been put in place. That is when time begins to pick up speed. It no longer meets any obstacles, everything is set, time races through our lives, the days pass by in a flash and before we know what is happening we are forty, fifty, sixty . . . Meaning requires content, content requires time, time requires resistance. Knowledge is distance, knowledge is stasis and the enemy of meaning. My picture of my father on that evening in 1976 is, in other words, twofold: on the one hand I see him as I saw him at that time, through the eyes of an eight-year-old: unpredictable and frightening; on the other hand, I see him as a peer through whose life time is blowing and unremittingly sweeping large chunks of meaning along with it.

The crack of sledgehammer on rock resounded through the estate. A car came up the gentle slope from the main road and passed, its lights blazing. The door of the neighboring house opened, Prestbakmo paused on the doorstep, pulled on his work gloves, and seemed to sniff the clear night air before grabbing the wheelbarrow and trundling it across the lawn. There was a smell of gunpowder from the rock Dad was pounding, of pine from the logs behind the stone wall, freshly dug soil and forest, and in the gentle northerly breeze a whiff of salt. I thought of the face I had seen in the sea. Even though only a couple of minutes had passed since I last considered it, everything had changed. Now it was Dad's face I saw.

Down in the hollow he took a break from hammering at the rock.

"Are you still there, boy?"

I nodded.

"Get yourself inside."

I started to walk.

"And Karl Ove, remember," he said.

I paused, turned my head, puzzled.

"No running this time."

I stared at him. How could he know I had run?

"And shut your maw," he said. "You look like an idiot."

I did as he said, closed my mouth and walked slowly around the house. Reaching the front, I saw the road was full of children. The oldest stood in a group with their bikes, which in the dusk almost appeared as an extension of their bodies. The youngest were playing Kick-the-Can. The ones who had been tagged stood inside a chalk circle on the pavement; the others were hidden at various places in the forest down from the road, out of sight of the person guarding the can but visible to me.

The lights on the bridge masts glowed red above the black treetops. Another car came up the hill. The headlights illuminated the cyclists first, a brief glimpse of reflectors, metal, Puffa jackets, black eyes and white faces, then the children, who had taken no more than the one necessary step aside to allow the car to pass and were now standing like ghosts, gawking.

It was the Trollneses, the parents of Sverre, a boy in my class. He didn't seem to be with them.

I turned and followed the red taillights until they disappeared over the summit of the hill. Then I went in. For a while I tried to lie on my bed reading, but could not settle, and instead went into Yngve's room, from where I could see Dad. When I could see him I felt safer with him, and in a way that was what mattered most. I knew his moods and had learned how to predict them long ago, by means of a kind of subconscious categorization system, I have later come to realize, whereby the relationship between a few constants was enough to determine what was in store for me, allowing me to make my own preparations. A kind of metereology of the mind . . . The speed of the car up the gentle gradient to the house, the time it took him to switch off the engine, grab his things, and step out, the way he looked around as he locked the car, the subtle nuances of the various sounds that rose from the hall as he removed his coat – everything was a sign, everything could be interpreted. To this was added information about where he had been, and with whom, how long he had been away, before the conclusion, which was the only part of the process of which I was conscious, was drawn. So, what frightened me most was when he turned up *without warning* . . . when for some reason I had been *inattentive* . . .

How on earth did he know I had been running?

This was not the first time he had caught me out in a way I found incomprehensible. One evening that autumn, for example, I had hidden a bag of sweets under the duvet for the express reason that I had a hunch he would come into my room, and there was no way he would believe my explanation of how I had laid my hands on the money to buy them. When, sure enough, he did come in, he stood watching me for a few seconds.

"What have you got hidden in your bed?" he asked.

How could he possibly have known?

Outside, Prestbakmo switched on the powerful lamp that was mounted over the flagstones where he usually worked. The new island of light that emerged from the blackness displayed a whole array of objects that he stood stock-still ogling. Columns of paint cans, jars containing paintbrushes, logs, bits of planking, folded tarpaulins, car tires, a bicycle frame, some toolboxes, tins of screws and nails of all shapes and sizes, a tray of milk cartons with flower seedlings, sacks of lime, a rolled-up hose pipe, and leaning against the wall, a board on which every conceivable tool was outlined, presumably intended for the hobby room in the cellar.

Glancing outside at Dad again, I saw him crossing the lawn with the sledgehammer in one hand and a spade in the other. I took a couple of hasty steps backward. As I did so the front door burst open. It was Yngve. I looked at my watch. Twenty-eight minutes past eight. When, straight afterward, he came up the stairs with the familiar, slightly jerky, almost duck-like gait we had developed so as to be able to walk fast inside the house without making a sound, he was breathless and ruddy-cheeked.

"Where's Dad?" he asked as soon as he was in the room.

"In the garden," I said. "But you're not late. Look, it's half past eight *now*."

I showed him my watch.

He walked past me and pulled the chair from under the desk. He still smelled of outdoors. Cold air, forest, gravel, tarmac.

"Have you been messing with my cassettes?" he asked.

"No," I answered.

"What are you doing in my room then?"

"Nothing," I said.

"Can't you do nothing in your own room?"

Below us, the front door opened again. This time it was Dad's heavy footsteps traversing the floor downstairs. He had removed his boots outside, as usual, and was on his way to the washroom to change.

"I saw a face in the sea on the news tonight," I said. "Have you heard anything about it? Do you know if anyone else saw it?"

Yngve eyed me with a half-curious, half-dismissive expression.

"What are you babbling on about?"

"You know the fishing boat that sank?"

He gave a barely perceptible nod.

"When they were showing the place where it sank on the news I saw a face in the sea."

"A dead body?"

"No. It wasn't a real face. The sea had formed into the shape of a face."

For a moment he watched me without saying anything. Then he tapped a forefinger on his temple.

"Don't you believe me?" I said. "It's absolutely true."

"The truth is you're a waste of space."

At that moment Dad switched off the tap downstairs, and I decided it was best to go to my room now so that there was no chance of meeting him on the landing. But, I did not want Yngve to have the last word.

"You're the one who's a waste of space," I said.

He could not even be bothered to answer. Just turned his face toward me, stuck out his top teeth and blew air through them like a rabbit. The gesture was a reference to my protruding teeth. I broke away and made off before he could see my tears. As long as I was alone my crying didn't bother me. And this time it had worked, hadn't it? Because he hadn't seen me?

I paused inside the door of my room and wondered for moment whether to go to the bathroom. I could rinse my face with cold water and remove the telltale signs. But Dad was on his way up the stairs, so I made do with wiping my eyes on the sleeve of my sweater. The thin layer of moisture that the dry material spread across my eye made the surfaces and colors of the room blur as though it had suddenly sunk and was now under water, and so real was this perception that I raised my arms and made a few swimming strokes as I walked toward the writing desk. In my mind I was wearing a metal diver's helmet from the early days of diving, when they bestrode the seabed with leaden shoes and suits as thick as elephant skin, with an oxygen pipe attached to their heads like a kind of trunk. I wheezed through my mouth and staggered around for a while with the heavy, sluggish movements of divers from bygone days until the horror of the sensation slowly began to seep in like cold water.

A few months before, I had seen the TV series *The Mysterious Island*, based on Jules Verne's novel, and the story of those men who landed their air balloon on a deserted island in the Atlantic had made an enormous impact on me from the very first moment. Everything was electric. The air balloon, the storm, the men dressed in nineteenth-century clothing, the weather-beaten, barren island where they had been marooned, which apparently was not as deserted as they imagined, mysterious and inexplicable things were always happening around them . . . but in that case who were the others? The answer came without warning toward the end of one episode. There was someone in the underwater caves . . . a number of humanoid creatures . . . in the light from the lamps they were carrying they saw glimpses of smooth, masked heads . . . fins . . . they resembled a kind of lizard but walked upright . . . with containers on their backs . . . one turned, he had no eyes . . .

I did not scream when I saw these things, but the horror the images instilled would not go away; even in the bright light of day I could be struck with terror by the very thought of the frogmen in the cave. And now my thoughts were turning me into one of them. My wheezing became theirs, my footsteps theirs, my arms theirs, and closing my eyes, it was those eyeless faces of theirs I saw before me. The cave . . . the black water . . . the line of frogmen with lamps in their hands . . . it became so bad that opening my eyes again did not help. Even though I could see I was in my room, surrounded by familiar objects, the terror did not release its grip. I hardly dared blink for fear that something might happen. Stiffly, I sat down on the bed, reached for my satchel without looking at it, glanced at the school timetable, found Wednesday, read what it said, *math*, *orientation*, *music*, lifted the satchel onto my lap and mechanically flipped through the books inside. This done, I took the open book from the pillow, sat against the wall and began to read. The seconds between looking up soon became minutes, and when Dad shouted it was time for supper, nine o'clock on the dot, it was not horror that had me in its thrall but the book. Tearing myself away from it was quite an effort too.

We were not allowed to cut bread ourselves, nor were we allowed to use the stove, so it was always either Mom or Dad who made supper. If Mom was on the evening shift, Dad did everything: when we came into the kitchen there were two glasses of milk and two plates, each with four slices of bread plus toppings, waiting for us. As a rule, he had prepared the food beforehand, and then kept it in the fridge, and the fact that it was cold made it difficult to swallow, even when I liked the toppings he had chosen. If Mom was at home there was a selection of meats, cheeses, jars on the table, either hers or ours, and this small touch, which allowed us to choose what would be on the table or on our sandwiches, in addition to the bread being at room temperature, this was sufficient to engender a sense of freedom in us: if we could open the cupboard, take the plates, which always made a bit of a clatter when they knocked against each other, and laid them on the table; if we could open the cutlery drawer, which always rattled, and place the knives beside our plates; if we could set out the glasses, open the fridge, take the milk and pour it, then you could be sure we would open our mouths and speak. One thing led naturally to another when we had supper with Mom. We chatted away about anything that occurred to us, she was interested in what we had to say, and if we spilt a few drops of milk or forgot our manners and put the used tea bag on the tablecloth (for she made us tea as well) it was no huge drama. But if it was our participation in the meal that opened this sluice gate of freedom, it was the extent of my father's presence that regulated its impact. If he was outside the house or down in his study, we chatted as loudly and freely and with as many gesticulations as we liked; if he was on his way up the stairs we automatically lowered our voices and changed the topic of conversation, in case we were talking about something we assumed he might consider unseemly; if he came into the kitchen we stopped altogether, sat there as stiff as pokers, to all outward appearances sunk in concentration over the food; on the other hand, if he retired to the living room we continued to chat, but more warily and more subdued.

This evening, the plates with the four prepared slices awaited us as we entered the kitchen. One with brown goat's cheese, one with ordinary cheese, one with sardines in tomato sauce, one with clove cheese. I didn't like sardines and ate that slice first. I couldn't stand fish; boiled cod, which we had at least once a week, made me feel nauseous, as did the steam from the pan in which it was cooked, its taste and consistency. I felt the same about boiled pollock, boiled coley, boiled haddock, boiled flounder, boiled mackerel, and boiled rose fish. With sardines it wasn't the taste that was the worst part – I could swallow the tomato sauce by imagining it was ketchup – it was the consistency, and above all the small, slippery tails. They were disgusting. To minimize contact with them I generally bit them off, put them to the side of my plate, nudged some sauce toward the crust and buried the tails in the middle, then folded the bread over. In this way I was able to chew a couple of times without ever coming into contact with the tails, and then wash the whole thing down with milk. If Dad was not there, as was the case this evening, it was possible of course to stuff the tiny tails in my trouser pocket.

Yngve would frown and shake his head when I did that. Then he smiled. I returned the smile.

In the living room Dad stirred in his chair. There was the faint rustle of a box of matches, followed by the brief rasp of the sulfur head across the rough surface and the crackle as it burst into flame, which seemed to merge into the subsequent silence. When the smell of the cigarette seeped into the kitchen, a few seconds later, Yngve bent forward and opened the window as quietly as he could. The sounds that drifted in from the darkness outside transformed the whole atmosphere in the kitchen. All of a sudden it was a part of the country outside. *It's like we're sitting on a shelf*, I thought. The thought caused the hairs on my forearm to stand on end. The wind rose with a sough through the forest and swept over the rustling bushes and trees in the garden below. From the intersection came the sound of children, still crouched over their bikes, chatting. On the hill up to the bridge a motorbike changed gear. And, far off, as if raised above all else, was the drone of a boat on its way into the fjord.

Of course. He had heard me! My feet running on the shingle!

"Want to swap?" Yngve mumbled, pointing to the clove cheese.

"Alright," I said. Elated to have solved the riddle, I washed down the last bite of the sardine sandwich with a tiny sip of milk and started on the slice Yngve had put on my plate. The trick was to eke out the milk because if you came to the last and there was none left it was almost impossible to swallow. Best of all, of course, was to save a drop until everything was eaten, the milk never tasted as good as then, when it no longer had to fulfill a function, it ran down your throat in its own right, pure and uncontaminated, but unfortunately it was rare for me to manage this. The needs of the moment always trumped promises of the future, however enticing the latter.

But Yngve did manage it. He was a past master at economizing.

Up at Prestbakmo's, there was a click of bootheels on the doorstep. Then three short cries cut through the night.

"*Geir! Geir! Geir!*"

The response came from John Beck's drive after such a time lag that everyone who heard concluded that he had been considering it.

"*Right*," he shouted.

Straight after, there was the sound of his running feet. As they approached Gustavsen's wall, Dad got up in the living room. Something about the way he crossed the floor made me duck my head. Yngve ducked too. Dad came into the kitchen, walked over to the counter, leaned forward without a word, and closed the window with a bang.

"We keep the window closed at night," he said.

Yngve nodded.

Dad looked at us.

"Eat up now," he said.

Not until he was back in the living room did I meet Yngve's glance.

"Ha, ha," I whispered.

"Ha ha?" he whispered back. "He meant you as well."

He was two slices ahead of me and was soon able to leave the table and slip into his room, leaving me to chew for a few more minutes. I had been planning to see my father after supper and tell him they would probably be showing the story with the face in the sea on the late-night news, but under the circumstances it was probably best to ditch that plan.

Or was it?

I decided to play it by ear. After leaving the kitchen I usually stuck my head into the living room to say good night. If his voice was neutral or, if luck was with me, friendly even, I would mention it. Otherwise not.

Unfortunately he had chosen to sit on the sofa at the back of the room, and not in one of the two leather chairs in front of the TV, as was his wont. To gain eye contact I could not just poke my head in at the door and say good night, en passant, as it were, which I could have done if he had been sitting in one of the leather chairs, but would have had to take several steps into the room. That would obviously make him aware that I was after something. And that would defeat the whole purpose of playing things by ear. Whatever tone he replied in I would have to come clean.

It wasn't until I was out of the kitchen that I realized this and was caught in two minds. I came to a halt, all of a sudden I had no choice, for of course he heard me pause, and that was bound to have made him aware I wanted something from him. So I took the four steps to enter his field of vision.

He was sitting with his legs crossed, his elbows on the back of the sofa, head reclining, resting on his interlaced fingers. His gaze, which had been focused on the ceiling, directed itself at me.

"Good night, Dad," I said.

"Good night," he said.

"I'm sure they'll be showing it again on the news," I said. "Just thought I'd tell you. So that you and Mom can see it."

"Showing what?"

"The face." I said.

"The face?"

I must have been standing there with my mouth agape, because he suddenly dropped his jaw and gawked in a way I understood was supposed to be an imitation of me.

"The one I told you about," I said.

He closed his mouth and sat up straight without averting his eyes.

"Now let's not be hearing anymore about that face," he said.

"Alright," I said.

As I made my way down the corridor I could feel his glare relinquishing its hold on me. I brushed my teeth, undressed, got into pajamas, switched on the lamp above my bed, turned on the main light, settled down, and started reading.

I was only allowed to read for half an hour, until ten o'clock, but usually read until Mom came home at around half past ten. Tonight was no exception. When I heard the Beetle coming up the hill from the main road, I put the book on the floor, switched off the light, and lay in the dark listening for her: the car door slamming, the crunch across the gravel, the front door opening, her coat and scarf being removed, the footsteps up the stairs . . . The house seemed different then, when she was in it, and the strange thing was that I could *feel* it; if, for example, I had gone to sleep before she returned and I awoke in the middle of the night, I could sense she was there, something in the atmosphere had changed without my being able to put my finger on quite what it was, except to say that it had a reassuring effect. The same applied to those occasions when she had come home earlier than expected while I was out: the moment I set foot in the hall I knew she was home.

Of course I would have liked to speak to her, she of all people would have understood the face business, but it did not seem like a burning necessity. The important thing was that she was here. I heard her deposit her keys on the telephone table as she came up the stairs, open the sliding door, say something to Dad and close it behind her. Now and then, especially after evening shifts on the weekend, he would cook a meal for when she arrived. Then they might play records. Once in a while there was an empty bottle of wine on the counter, always the same label, a run-of-the-mill red, and on rare occasions, beer, again the same Vinmonopolet label, two or three bottles of pils from the Arendal brewery, the brown 0.7 liter one with the yellow sailing ship logo.

But not tonight. And I was glad. If they ate together they did not watch TV, and they would have to if I was to accomplish my plan, which was as simple as it was bold: at a few seconds to eleven I would sneak out of bed, tiptoe along the landing, open the sliding door a fraction, and watch the late news from there. I had never done anything like this before, nor even contemplated it. If I wasn't allowed to do something, I didn't do it. Ever. Not once, not if my father had said no. Not knowingly at any rate. But this was different since it was not about me, but about them. After all I had seen the image of the face in the sea, and did not need to see it again. I just wanted to find out if they could see what I had seen.

Such were my thoughts as I lay in the dark following the green hands of my alarm clock. When it was as quiet as it was now, I could hear cars driving past on the main road below. An acoustic racetrack that started as they came over the ridge by B-Max, the new supermarket, continued down the cutting by Holtet, past the road to Gamle Tybakken and up the hill to the bridge, where it finished as quietly as it had begun half a minute earlier.

At nine minutes to eleven the door of the house across the road opened. I knelt up in bed and peered out the window. It was Fru Gustavsen; she was walking across the drive with a garbage bag in her hand.

I only realized how rare a sight this was when I saw her. Fru Gustavsen hardly ever showed herself outside; either she was seen indoors or in the passenger seat of their blue Ford Taunus, but even though I knew that, the thought had never struck me before. But now, as she stood by the garbage can, removing the lid, chucking the bag in and closing the lid, all with that somewhat lazy grace that so many fat women possess, it did. She was never outdoors.

The streetlamp beyond our hedge cast its harsh light over her, but unlike the objects she was surrounded by – the garbage can, the white walls of the trailer, the paving slabs, the tarmac – which all reflected the cold, sharp light, her figure seemed to modulate and absorb it. Her bare arms gave off a matte gleam, the material of her white sweater shimmered, her mass of grayish-brown hair appeared almost golden.

For a while she stood looking around, first over at Prestbakmo's, then up at the Hansens', then down at the forest across the road.

A cat strutted down towards her, stopped and watched her for a moment. She ran one hand up her arm a few times. Then she turned and went inside.

I glanced at the clock again. Four minutes to eleven. I shivered and wondered briefly whether I should put on a sweater, but concluded that would make everything seem too calculated if I was caught. And it was not going to take very long.

I crept warily to the door and pressed my ear against it. The only real element of risk was that the toilet was on this side of the sliding door. Once there, I would be able to keep an eye on them and have a chance to retreat if they should get up, but if the sliding door was closed, and they came toward me, I wouldn't know until it was too late.

But in that case I could pretend I was going to the toilet!

Pleased with the solution, I cautiously opened the door and stepped into the passage. Everything was quiet. I tiptoed along the landing, felt the dry wall-to-wall carpeting against my sweaty soles, stopped by the sliding door, heard nothing, pulled it open a fraction, and peered in through the crack.

The TV was on in the corner. The two leather chairs were empty.

So they were on the sofa, both of them.

Perfect.

Then the globe with the N sign whirled round on the screen. I prayed to God they would show the same news report, so that Mom and Dad could see what I saw.

The newscaster started the program by talking about the missing fishing boat, and my heart was pounding in my chest. But the report they showed was different: instead of pictures of calm sea a local police officer was being interviewed on a quay, followed by a woman with a small child in her arms, then the reporter himself spoke against a background of billowing waves.

After the item was over there was the sound of my father's voice, and laughter. The shame that suffused my body was so strong that I was unable to think. My innards seemed to blanch. The force of the sudden shame was the sole feeling from my childhood that could measure in intensity against that of terror, next to sudden fury, of course, and common to all three was the sense that I *myself* was being erased. All that mattered was precisely *that* feeling. So as I turned and went back to my room, I noticed nothing. I know that the window in the stairwell must have been so dark that the hall was reflected in it, I know that the door to Yngve's bedroom must have been closed, the same as the one to my parents' bedroom and to the bathroom. I know that Mom's bunch of keys must have been splayed out on the telephone table, like some mythical beast at rest, with its head of leather and myriad metal legs, I know that the knee-high ceramic vase of dried flowers and straw must have been on the floor next to it, unreconciled, as it were, with the synthetic material of the wall-to-wall carpet. But I saw nothing, heard nothing, thought nothing. I went into my room, lay down on my bed, and switched off the light, and when the darkness closed itself around me, I took such a deep breath that it quivered, while the muscles in my stomach tightened and forced out whimpering noises that were so loud I had to direct them into the soft, and soon very wet, pillow. It helped, in much the same way that vomiting helps when you are nauseous. Long after the tears had stopped coming I lay sobbing. That had a soothing effect. When it too had worn itself out I lay on my stomach, rested my head against my arm, and closed my eyes to sleep.

■ ■ ■

As I sit here writing this, I recognize that more than thirty years have passed. In the window before me I can vaguely make out the reflection of my face. Apart from one eye, which is glistening, and the area immediately beneath, which dimly reflects a little light, the whole of the left side is in shadow. Two deep furrows divide my forehead, one deep furrow intersects each cheek, all of them as if filled with darkness, and with the eyes staring and serious, and the corners of the mouth drooping, it is impossible not to consider this face gloomy.

What has engraved itself in my face?

Today is the twenty-seventh of February. The time is 11:43 p.m. I, Karl Ove Knausgaard, was born in December 1968, and at the time of writing I am thirty-nine years old. I have three children – Vanja, Heidi, and John – and am in my second marriage, to Linda Boström Knausgaard. All four are asleep in the rooms around me, in an apartment in Malmö where we have lived for a year and a half. Apart from some parents of the children at Vanja and Heidi's nursery we do not know anyone here. This is not a loss, at any rate not for me, I don't get anything out of socializing anyway. I never say what I really think, what I really mean, but always more or less agree with whomever I am talking to at the time, pretend that what they say is of interest to me, except when

I am drinking, in which case more often than not I go too far the other way, and wake up to the fear of having overstepped the mark. This has become more pronounced over the years and can now last for weeks. When I drink I also have blackouts and completely lose control of my actions, which are generally desperate and stupid, but also on occasion desperate and dangerous. That is why I no longer drink. I do not want anyone to get close to me, I do not want anyone to see me, and this is the way things have developed: no one gets close and no one sees me. This is what must have engraved itself in my face, this is what must have made it so stiff and masklike and almost impossible to associate with myself whenever I happen to catch a glimpse of it in a shop window.

■ ■ ■

The only thing that does not age in a face is the eyes. They are no less bright the day we die as the day we are born. The blood vessels in them may burst, admittedly, and the corneas may be dulled, but the light in them never changes. There is, in London, a painting that moves me as much every time I go and see it. It is a self-portrait painted by the late Rembrandt. His later paintings are usually characterized by an extreme coarseness of stroke, rendering everything subordinate to the expression of the moment, at once shining and sacred, and still unsurpassed in art, with the possible exception of Hölderlin's later poems, however dissimilar and incomparable they may be – for where Hölderlin's light, evoked through language, is ethereal and celestial, Rembrandt's light, evoked through color, is earthy, metallic, and material – but this one painting which hangs in the National Gallery was painted in a slightly more classically realistic, lifelike style, more in the manner of the younger Rembrandt. But what the painting portrays is the older Rembrandt. Old age. All the facial detail is visible; all the traces life has left there are to be seen. The face is furrowed, wrinkled, sagging, ravaged by time. But the eyes are bright and, if not young, then somehow transcend the time that otherwise marks the face. It is as though someone else is looking at us, from somewhere inside the face, where everything is different. One can hardly be closer to another human soul. For as far as Rembrandt's person is concerned, his good habits and bad, his bodily sounds and smells, his voice and his language, his thoughts and his opinions, his behavior, his physical flaws and defects, all the things that constitute a person to others, are no longer there, the painting is more than four hundred years old, and Rembrandt died the same year it was painted, so what is depicted here, what Rembrandt painted, is this person's very being, that which he woke to every morning, that which immersed itself in thought, but which itself was not thought, that which immediately immersed itself in feelings, but which itself was not feeling, and that which he went to sleep to, in the end for good. That which, in a human, time does not touch and whence the light in the eyes springs. The difference between this painting and the others the late Rembrandt painted is the difference between seeing and being seen. That is, in this picture he sees himself seeing whilst also being seen, and no doubt it was only in the Baroque period with its penchant for mirrors within mirrors, the play within the play, staged scenes and a belief in the interdependence of all things, when moreover craftsmanship attained heights witnessed neither before nor since, that such a painting was possible. But it exists in our age, it sees for us.

■ ■ ■

The night Vanja was born she lay looking at us for several hours. Her eyes were like two black lanterns. Her body was covered in blood, her long hair plastered to her head, and when she stirred it was with the slow movements of a reptile. She looked like something from the forest lying there on Linda's stomach, staring at us. We could not get enough of her and her gaze. But what was it that lay in those eyes? Composure, gravity, darkness. I stuck out my tongue, a minute passed, then she stuck out her tongue. There has never been so much future in my life as at that time, never so much joy. Now she is four, and everything is different. Her eyes are alert, switch between jealousy and happiness at the drop of a hat, between sorrow and anger, she is already practiced in the ways of the world and can be so cheeky that I completely lose my head and sometimes shout at her or shake her until she starts crying. But usually she just laughs. The last time it happened, the last time I was so furious I shook her and she just laughed, I had a sudden inspiration and placed my hand on her chest.

Her heart was pounding. Oh, my, how it was pounding.

■ ■ ■

It is now a few minutes past eight o'clock in the morning. It is the fourth of March 2008. I am sitting in my office, surrounded by books from floor to ceiling, listening to the Swedish band Dungen and thinking about what I have written and where it is leading. Linda and John are asleep in the adjacent room, Vanja and Heidi are in the nursery, where I dropped them off half an hour ago. Outside, at the front of the enormous Hilton Hotel, which is still in shadow, the lifts glide up and down in three glass shafts. Next door there is a redbrick building which, judging by all the bay windows, dormers, and arches, must be from the end of the nineteenth century or early twentieth. Beyond that, there is a glimpse of a tiny stretch of Magistrat Park with its denuded trees and green grass, where a motley gray house in a seventies style breaks the view, and forces the eye up to the sky, which for the first time in several weeks is a clear blue.

Having lived here for a year and a half, I know this view and all its nuances over the days and the year, but I feel no attachment to it. Nothing of what I see here means anything to me. Perhaps that is precisely what I have been searching for, because there is something about this lack of attachment that I like, may even need. But it was not a conscious choice. Six years ago I was ensconced in Bergen writing, and while I had no intentions of living in the town for the rest of my life I certainly had no plans to leave the country, let alone the woman to whom I was married. On the contrary, we envisaged having children and maybe moving to Oslo where I would write a number of novels and she would keep working in radio and television. But of the future we shared, which actually was just an extension of the present with its daily routines and meals with friends and acquaintances, holiday trips, and visits to parents and in-laws, all enriched by the dream of having children, there was to be nothing. Something happened, and from one day to the next I moved to Stockholm, initially just to get away for a few weeks, and then all of a sudden it became my life. Not only did I change city and country, but also all the people. If this might seem strange, it is even stranger that I hardly ever reflect on it. How did I end up here? Why did things turn out like this?

Arriving in Stockholm, I knew two people, neither of them very well: Geir, whom I had met in Bergen and saw for a few weeks during the spring of 1990, so twelve years previously, and Linda, whom I had met at a debut writers' seminar in Biskops-Arnö in the spring of 1999. I emailed Geir and asked if I could stay with him until I had found a place of my own, he said yes, and then I phoned in a "Flat Wanted" ad to two Swedish newspapers. I received more than forty replies, from which I selected two. One was in Bastugatan, the other in Brännkyrkgatan. After viewing both, I opted for the latter, until in the hallway my eye fell on the list of tenants, which included Linda's name. What were the chances of that happening? Stockholm has more than one and a half million inhabitants. If the flat had come to me via friends and acquaintances the odds would not have been so slim, for all literary circles are relatively small, irrespective of the size of the town, but this had come about as a result of an anonymous advertisement, read by several hundred thousand people and, of course, the woman who responded knew neither Linda nor me. From one moment to the next I changed my mind, it would be better to take the other flat because if I were to take this one Linda might think I was pursuing her. But it was an omen. And one laden with meaning, it turned out, for now I am married to Linda and she is the mother of my three children. Now she is the woman with whom I share my life. The sole traces of my previous existence are the books and records I brought with me. Everything else I left behind. And while I spent a lot of time thinking about the past then, almost a morbid amount of time, I now realize, which meant that I not only read Marcel Proust's novel *À la recherche du temps perdu* but virtually imbibed it, the past is now barely present in my thoughts.

I believe the main reason for that is our children, since life with them in the here and now occupies all the space. They even squeeze out the most recent past: ask me what I did three days ago and I can't remember. Ask me what Vanja was like two years ago, Heidi two months ago, John two weeks ago, and I can't remember. A lot happens in our little everyday life, but it always happens within the same routine, and more than anything else it has changed my perspective of time. For, while previously I saw time as a stretch of terrain that had to be covered, with the future as a distant prospect, hopefully a bright one, and never boring at any rate, now it is interwoven with our life here and in a totally different way. Were I to portray this with a visual image it would have to be that of a boat in a lock: life is slowly and ineluctably raised by time seeping in from all sides. Apart from the details, everything is always the same. And with every passing day the desire grows for the moment when life will reach the top, for the moment when the sluice gates open and life finally moves on. At the same time I see that precisely this repetitiveness, this enclosedness, this unchangingness is necessary, it protects me. On the few occasions I have left it, all the old ills return. All of a sudden I am beset by every conceivable thought about what was said, what was seen, what was thought, hurled, as it were, into that uncontrollable, unproductive, often degrading, and ultimately destructive space where I lived for so many years. The yearning is as strong there as it is here, but the difference is that there the goal of my yearning is attainable, but not here. Here I have to find other goals and come to terms with them. The art of living is what I am talking about. On paper it is no problem, I can easily conjure up an image of Heidi, for example, clambering out of a bunk bed at five in the morning, the patter of little feet across the floor in the dark, her switching the light on and a second later standing in front of me – half asleep and squinting up at her – and then she says: "*Köket*. Kitchen!" Her Swedish is still idiosyncratic; her words carry a different meaning from what is usual, and "kitchen" means muesli with curdled blueberry milk. In the same way, candles are called "Happy birthday!" Heidi has large eyes, a large mouth, a big appetite, and she is a ravenous child in all senses, but the robust, unadulterated happiness she experienced in her first eighteen months has been overshadowed this year, since John's birth, by other hitherto unknown emotions. In the first months she took almost every opportunity to try to harm him. Scratch marks on his face were the rule rather than the exception. When I arrived home after a four-day trip to Frankfurt in the autumn, John looked as if he had been through a war. It was difficult because we didn't want to keep him away from her either, so we had to try to read her moods and regulate her access to him accordingly. But even when she was in high spirits her hand could shoot out in a flash and slap or claw him. Alongside this, she was beginning to have fits of rage, the ferocity of which I would never have considered her capable two months before. In addition, an equally hitherto unsuspected vulnerability surfaced: the slightest hint of severity in my voice or behavior and she would lower her head, shy away, and start to cry, as though wanting to show us her anger and hide her feelings. As I write, I am filled with tenderness for her. But this is on paper. In reality, when it really counts, and she is standing there in front of me, so early in the morning that the streets outside are still and not a sound can be heard in the house, she, raring to start a new day, I, summoning the will to get to my feet, putting on yesterday's clothes and following her into the kitchen, where the promised blueberry-flavored milk and the sugar-free muesli await her, it is not tenderness I feel, and if she goes beyond my limits, such as when she pesters and pesters me for a film, or tries to get into the room where John is sleeping, in short, every time she refuses to take no for an answer but drags things out ad infinitum, it is not uncommon for my irritation to mutate into anger, and when I then speak harshly to her, and her tears flow, and she bows her head and slinks off with slumped shoulders, I feel it serves her right. Not until the evening when they are asleep and I am sitting wondering what I am really doing is there any room for the insight that she is only two years old. But by then I am on the outside looking in. Inside, I don't have a chance. Inside, it is a question of getting through the morning, the three hours of diapers that have to be changed, clothes that have to be put on, breakfast that has to be served, faces that have to be washed, hair that has to be combed and pinned up, teeth that have to be brushed, squabbles that have to be nipped in the bud, slaps that have to be averted, rompers and boots that have to be wriggled into, before I, with the collapsible double stroller in one hand and nudging the two small girls forward with the other, step into the elevator, which as often as not resounds to the noise of shoving and shouting on its descent, and into the hall where I ease them into the stroller, put on their hats and mittens and emerge onto the street already crowded with people heading for work and deliver them to the nursery ten minutes later, whereupon I have the next five hours for writing until the mandatory routines for the children resume.

I have always had a great need for solitude. I require huge swathes of loneliness and when I do not have it, which has been the case for the last five years, my frustration can sometimes become almost panicked, or aggressive. And when what has kept me going for the whole of my adult life, the ambition to write something exceptional one day, is threatened in this way my one thought, which gnaws at me like a rat, is that I have to escape. Time is slipping away from me, running through my fingers like sand while I . . . do what? Clean floors, wash clothes, make dinner, wash up, go shopping, play with the children in the play areas, bring them home, undress them, bathe them, look after them until it is bedtime, tuck them in, hang some clothes to dry, fold others, and put them away, tidy up, wipe tables, chairs and cupboards. It is a struggle, and even though it is not heroic, I am up against a superior force, for no matter how much housework I do at home the rooms are littered with mess and junk, and the children, who are taken care of every waking minute, are more stubborn than I have ever known children to be, at times it is nothing less than bedlam here, perhaps we have never managed to find the necessary balance between distance and intimacy, which of course becomes increasingly important the more personality is involved. And there is a quite a bit of that here. When Vanja was around eight months old she began to have violent outbursts, like fits at times, and for a while it was impossible to reach her, she just screamed and screamed. All we could do was hold her until it had subsided. It is not easy to say what caused it, but it often occurred when she had had a great many impressions to absorb, such as when we had driven to her grandmother's in the country outside Stockholm, when she had spent too much time with other children, or we had been in town all day. Then, inconsolable and completely beside herself, she could scream at the top of her voice. Sensitivity and strength of will are not a simple combination. And matters were not made any easier when Heidi was born. I wish I could say I took everything in stride, but sad to say such was not the case because my anger and my feelings too were aroused in these situations, which then escalated, frequently in full public view: it was not unknown for me in my fury to snatch her up from the floor in one of the Stockholm malls, sling her over my shoulder like a sack of potatoes and carry her through town kicking and punching and howling as if possessed. Sometimes I reacted to her howls by shouting back, throwing her down on the bed and holding her tight until it passed, whatever it was that was tormenting her. She was not very old before she found out exactly what drove me wild, namely a particular variety of scream, not crying or sobbing or hysteria but focused, aggressive screams that, regardless of the situation, could make me totally lose control, jump up, and rush over to the poor girl, who was then shouted at or shaken until the screams turned to tears and her body went limp and she could at last be comforted.

Looking back on this, it is striking how she, scarcely two years old, could have such an effect on our lives. Because she did, for a while that was all that mattered. Of course, that says nothing about her, but everything about us. Both Linda and I live on the brink of chaos, or with the feeling of chaos, everything can fall apart at any moment and we have to force ourselves to come to terms with the demands of a life with small children. We do not plan. Having to shop for dinner comes as a surprise every day. Likewise, having to pay bills at the end of every month. Had it not been for some sporadic payments being made into my account, such as rights fees, book club sales, or a minor amount from schoolbook publications or, as this autumn, the second installment of some foreign income I had forgotten, things would have gone seriously wrong. However, this constant improvisation increases the significance of the moment, which of course then becomes extremely eventful since nothing about it is automatic and, if our lives feel good, which naturally they do at times, there is a great sense of togetherness and a correspondingly intense happiness. Oh, how we beam. All the children are full of life and are instinctively drawn to happiness, so that gives you extra energy and you are nice to them and they forget their defiance or anger in seconds. The corrosive part of course is the awareness that being nice to them is not of the slightest help when I am in the thick of it, dragged down into a quagmire of tears and frustration. And once in the quagmire each further action only serves to plunge me deeper. And at least as corrosive is the awareness that I am dealing with *children*. That it is *children* who are dragging me down. There is something deeply shameful about this. In such situations I am probably as far from the person I aspire to be as possible. I didn't have the faintest notion about any of this before I had children. I thought then that everything would be fine so long as I was kind to them. And that is actually more or less how it is, but nothing I had previously experienced warned me about the invasion into your life that having children entails. The immense intimacy you have with them, the way in which your own temperament and mood are, so to speak, woven into theirs, such that your own worst sides are no longer something you can keep to yourself, hidden, but seem to take shape outside you, and are then hurled back. The same of course applies to your best sides. For, apart from the most hectic periods, when first Heidi, then John, were born, and the emotional life of those who experienced them was dislocated in ways that can only be described as tantamount to a crisis, their life here is basically stable and secure, and even though I do occasionally lose my temper with them, they are still at ease with me and come to me whenever they feel the need. Their demands are very basic, there is nothing they like better than outings with the whole family, which are full of adventure: a trip to the Western Harbor on a sunny day, starting with a walk through the park, where a pile of logs is enough to keep them entertained for half an hour, then past the yachts in the marina, which really capture their attention, after that lunch on some steps by the sea, eating our panini from the Italian café, that a picnic didn't occur to us goes without saying, and afterward an hour or so to run around and play and laugh, Vanja with her characteristic lope, which she has had since she was eighteen months, Heidi with her enthusiastic toddle, always two meters behind her big sister, ready to receive the rare gift of companionship from her, then the same route back home. If Heidi sleeps in the car we go to a café with Vanja, who loves the moments she has alone with us and sits there with her lemonade asking us about everything under the sun: Is the sky fixed? Can anything stop autumn coming? Do monkeys have skeletons? Even if the feeling of happiness this gives me is not exactly a whirlwind but closer to satisfaction or serenity, it is happiness all the same. Perhaps even, at certain moments, joy. And isn't that enough? Isn't it enough? Yes, if joy had been the goal it would have been enough. But joy is not my goal, never has been, what good is joy to me? The family is not my goal either. If it had been, and I could have devoted all my energy to it, we would have had a fantastic time, of that I am sure. We could have lived somewhere in Norway, gone skiing and skating in winter, with packed lunches and a thermos flask in our backpacks, and boating in the summer, swimming, fishing, camping, holidays abroad with other families, we could have kept the house tidy, spent time making good food, being with our friends, we could have been blissfully happy. That may all sound like a caricature, but every day I see families who successfully organize their lives in this way. The children are clean, their clothes nice, the parents are happy and although once in a while they might raise their voices they never stand there like idiots bawling at them. They go on weekend trips, rent cottages in Normandy in the summer, and their fridges are never empty. They work in banks and hospitals, in IT companies or on the local council, in the theater or at universities. Why should the fact that I am a writer exclude me from that world? Why should the fact that I am a writer mean our strollers all look like junk we found on a junk heap? Why should the fact that I am a writer mean I turn up at the nursery with crazed eyes and a face stiffened into a mask of frustration? Why should the fact that I am a writer mean that our children do their utmost to get their own way, whatever the consequences? Where does all the mess in our lives come from? I know I can change all this, I know we too can become that kind of family, but then I would have to want it and in which case life would have to revolve around nothing else. And that is not what I want. I do everything I have to do for the family; that is my duty. The only thing I have learned from life is to endure it, never to question it, and to burn up the longing generated by this in writing. Where this ideal has come from I have no idea, and as I now see it before me, in black and white, it almost seems perverse: why duty before happiness? The question of happiness is banal, but the question that follows is not, the question of meaning. When I look at a beautiful painting I have tears in my eyes, but not when I look at my children. That does not mean I do not love them, because I do, with all my heart, it simply means that the meaning they produce is not sufficient to fulfill a whole life. Not mine at any rate. Soon I will be forty, and when I'm forty, it won't be long before I'm fifty. And when I'm fifty, it won't be long before I'm sixty. And when I'm sixty, it won't be long before I'm seventy. And that will be that. My epitaph might read: *Here lies a man who grinned and bore it. And in the end he perished for it.* Or perhaps better:

Here lies a man who never complained
A happy life he never gained
His last words before he died
And went to cross the great divide
Were: Oh, Lord, there's such a chill
Can someone send a happy pill?

Or perhaps better:

Here lies a man of letters
A noble man of Nordic birth
Alas, his hands were bound in fetters
Barring him from knowing mirth
Once he wrote with dash and wit
Now he's buried in a pit

Come on, worms, take your fill,
Taste some flesh, if you will
Try an eye
Or a thigh
He's croaked his last, have a thrill

But if I have thirty years left you cannot take it for *granted* that I will be the same. So perhaps something like this?

From all of us to you, dear God
Now you have him beneath the sod,
Karl Ove Knausgaard is finally dead
Long is the time since he ate bread
With his friends he broke ranks
For his book and his wanks
Wielded pen and dick but never well
Lacked the style but tried to excel
He took a cake, then took one more
He took a spud, then ate it raw
He cooked a pig, it took a while
He ate it up and belched a Heil!
I'm no Nazi, but I like brown shirts
I write Gothic script until it hurts!

Book not accepted, the man blew his top
He guzzled and belched and couldn't stop
His belly it grew, his belt got tight,
His eyes glared, his tongue alight
"I only wanted to write what was right!"

The fat it blocked his heart and vein
Till one day he screamed in pain:

Help me, help me, hear me wailing
Get me a donor, my heart is failing!
The doctor said no, I remember your book
You'll die like a fish, like a fish on a hook.
Do you feel much pain, are you near the end?
The stab in the heart, this is death, my friend!

Or perhaps, if I am lucky, a bit less personal?

Here lies a man who smoked in bed
With his wife he wound up dead
Truth to say
It is not they
Just some ashes, it is said

When my father was the same age as I am now, he gave up his old life and started afresh. I was sixteen years old at the time and in the first class at Kristiansand Cathedral School. At the beginning of the school year my parents were still married and although they were having problems I had no reason to suspect what was about to happen with their relationship. We were living in Tveit then, twenty kilometers outside Kristiansand, in an old house on the very edge of the built-up area in the valley. It was high in the mountains with the forest at our backs and a view of the river from the front. A large barn and an outhouse also belonged to the property. When we moved in, the summer I was thirteen, Mom and Dad had bought chickens, I think they lasted six months. Dad grew potatoes in a patch beside the lawn, and beyond that was a compost heap. One of the many occupations my father fantaszed about was becoming a gardener, and he did have a certain talent in that direction – the garden around the house in the small town we came from was magnificent, and not without exotic elements, such as the peach tree my father planted against the south-facing wall, and of which he was so proud when it actually bore fruit – so the move to the country was full of optimism and dreams of the future, where slowly but surely irony began to rear its head, for one of the few concrete things I can remember about my father's life there during those years is something he came out with as we sat at the garden table one summer evening barbecuing, he and Mom and I.

"Now we're living the life, aren't we, eh!"

The irony was plain, even I caught it, but also complicated because I did not understand the reason for it. For me an evening like the one we were having was living the life. What the irony implied ran like an undercurrent throughout the rest of the summer: we swam in the river from early morning, we played soccer on grass in the shade, we cycled to the Hamresanden campsite and swam and watched the girls, and in July we went to the Norway Cup, a youth soccer tournament, where I got drunk for the first time. Someone knew someone who had a flat, someone knew someone who could buy beer for us, and so I sat there drinking in an unfamiliar living room one summer afternoon, and it was like an explosion of happiness, nothing held any danger or fear anymore, I just laughed and laughed, and in the midst of all this, the unfamiliar furniture, the unfamiliar girls, the unfamiliar garden outside, I thought to myself, this was how I wanted things to be. Just like this. Laughing all the time, following whatever fancies took me. There are two photographs of me from that evening, in one I am lying under a bundle of bodies in the middle of the floor, holding a skull in one hand, my head apparently unconnected with the hands and feet protruding on the other side, my face contorted into a kind of euphoric grimace. The other photo is of me on my own, I am lying on a bed with a beer bottle in one hand and holding the skull over my groin in the other, I am wearing sunglasses, my mouth is wide open, roaring with laughter. That was the summer of 1984, I was fifteen years old and had just made a new discovery: drinking alcohol was fantastic.

For the next few weeks my childhood carried on as before, we lay on the cliffs beneath the waterfall and dozed, dived into the pool now and then, caught the bus into town on Saturday mornings, where we bought sweets and went round the record shops, while expectations of upper secondary school, the *gymnas*, which I was soon to start, loomed on the horizon. This was not the only change in the family: my mother had taken a sabbatical from her job at the nursing school, and was going to study that year in Bergen, where Yngve already lived. So the plan was that my father and I would live alone up there, and we did for the first few months, until he suggested, presumably to get me out of the way, that I could live in the house my grandparents owned on Elvegata, where Grandad had for many years had his accounting office. All my friends lived in Tveit, and I didn't think I knew the kids at my new school well enough to spend time with them after school, so when I wasn't at soccer training, which I had five times a week in those days, I sat on my own in the living room watching TV, did my homework at the desk in the loft, or lay on the bed next door reading and listening to music. Once in a while I popped up to Sannes, as our house was called, to pick up clothes or cassettes or books, sometimes I slept there as well, but I preferred the digs at my grandparents', a chill had settled over our house, I suppose because nothing went on there anymore, my father ate out for the most part, and did only a minimum of chores at home. This left its mark on the aura of the house which, as Christmas was approaching, had taken on an air of abandonment. Tiny, desiccated lumps of cat shit littered the sofa in front of the TV on the first floor, old unwashed dishes on the kitchen drainer, all the radiators, apart from an electric heater which he moved to the room where he was living, were turned off. As for him, his soul was in torment. One evening I went up to the house, it must have been at the beginning of December, and after depositing my bag in my ice-cold bedroom I bumped into him in the hall. He had come from the barn, the lower floor of which had been converted into a flat, his hair was unkempt, his eyes black.

"Can't we put on the heating?" I asked. "It's freezing in here."

"Fweezing?" he mimicked. "We're not putting on any heating, however fweezing it is."

I couldn't roll my "r"s, never had been able to say "r", it was one of the traumas of my late childhood. My father used to mimic me, sometimes to make me aware that I couldn't pronounce it, in a futile attempt to make me pull myself together and say "r" the way normal Sørland folk did, whenever something about me got on his nerves, like now.

I just turned and went back up the stairs. I did not want to give him the pleasure of seeing my moist eyes. The shame of being on the verge of tears at the age of fifteen, soon sixteen, was stronger than the ignominy of his mimicking me. I did not usually cry anymore, but my father had a hold on me that I never succeeded in breaking. But I was certainly capable of registering a protest. I went up to my room, grabbed some new cassettes, stuffed them in my bag and carried it down to the room beside the hall, where the wardrobe was, put a few sweaters in, went into the hall, put on my coat, slung the bag over my shoulder, and headed into the yard. The snow had formed a crust; the lights above the garage were reflected in the glistening snow which was all yellow below the streetlamps. The meadow down the road was also bright because it was a starry night and the almost full moon hung above the uplands on the other side of the river. I began to walk. My footsteps crunched in the ruts left by tires. I stopped by the mailbox. Perhaps I should have said that I was going. But that would have ruined everything. The whole point was to make him consider what he had done.

What was the time, I wondered?

I yanked the mitten half off my left hand, pulled up my sleeve and peered. Twenty to eight. There was a bus in half an hour. I still had time to go back.

But no. Not likely.

I slung the bag over my back again and continued down the hill. Glancing up at the house for a last time, I saw smoke rising from the chimney. He must have thought I was still in my room. Obviously he had felt remorse, carried in some wood, and lit the stove.

The ice on the river creaked. The sound seemed to ripple along and climb the gentle valley slopes.

Then there was a boom.

A thrill went down my spine. That sound always filled me with joy. I looked up at the sweep of stars. The moon hanging over the ridge. The car headlights on the other side of the river tearing deep gashes of light into the darkness. The trees, black and silent, though not hostile, stood dotted along the banks of the river. On the white surface, the two wooden water-level gauges, which the river covered in the autumn but now, at low water, were naked and shiny.

He had lit the fire. It was a way of saying he was sorry. So, leaving without a word no longer had any purpose.

I retraced my steps. Let myself in, began to unlace my boots. I heard his footsteps in the living room and straightened up. He opened the door, paused with his fingers on the handle, and looked at me.

"Going already?" he asked.

That I had already gone and come back was impossible to explain, so I just nodded.

"Reckon so," I said. "Start early tomorrow."

"Yes, of course," he said. "Think I'll pop by in the afternoon. Just so you know."

"Okay," I said.

He watched me for a few seconds. Then he closed the door and went back into the living room.

I opened it again.

"Dad?" I said.

He turned and looked at me without speaking.

"You know it's parents' evening tomorrow, don't you? At six."

"Is it?" he asked. "Well, I'd better go then."

He turned around and continued into the living room, whereupon I closed the door, laced up my boots, slung my bag over my shoulder, and set off for the bus stop, which I reached ten minutes later. Below me was the waterfall which had frozen in great arcs and arteries of ice, dimly illuminated by the light from the parquet factory. Behind it and behind me rose the uplands. They surrounded the scattered, illuminated habitation in the river valley with darkness and impersonality. The stars above seemed to be lying at the bottom of a frozen sea.

The bus rolled up, its lights sweeping the road, I showed my card to the driver and sat down one seat from the back on the left, which I always did if it was free. There wasn't much traffic, we zipped along Solsletta, Ryensletta, drove by the beach at Hamresanden, into the forest on the way to Timenes, out onto the E18, over Varodd Bridge, past the gymnas in Gimle, and into town.

The flat was down by the river. Grandad's office was on the left as you came in. The flat was on the right. Two living rooms, a kitchen, and a small bathroom. The first floor was also split into two, on one side there was a huge loft, on the other the room where I lived. I had a bed, a desk, a small sofa, and a coffee table, a cassette player, a cassette rack, a pile of schoolbooks, a few magazines including some music mags, and in the cupboard a heap of clothes.

The house was old, it had once belonged to my father's paternal grandmother, in other words, my great-grandmother, who had died there. As far as I had gathered, Dad had been close to her when he was growing up and spent a lot of time down here then. For me she was a kind of mythological figure, strong, authoritative, self-willed, mother of three sons, of whom my father's father was one. In the photographs I had seen she was always dressed in black buttoned-up dresses. Toward the end of her life, that began in the 1870s, she had been senile for almost an entire decade or had started to "unravel" as the family called it. That was all I knew about her.

I took off my boots and went up the staircase, steep as a ladder, and into my room. It was cold; I put on the fan heater. Switched on the cassette player. Echo and the Bunnymen, *Heaven Up Here*. Lay down on the bed and began to read. I was halfway through *Dracula* by Bram Stoker. I had already read it once, the year before, but it was just as intense and fantastic this time. The town outside, with its low, steady drone of cars and buildings, was absent from my consciousness, returning only in waves as though I were in motion. But I was not, I lay reading, completely motionless, until half past eleven when I brushed my teeth, undressed, and went to bed.

It was a very special feeling to wake up in the morning, all alone in a flat, it was as though emptiness were not only around me but also inside me. Until I started at the gymnas I had always woken to a house where Mom and Dad were already up and on their way to work with all that entailed, cigarette smoke, coffee drinking, listening to the radio, eating breakfast, and car engines warming up outside in the dark. This was something else, and I loved it. I also loved walking the kilometer or so through the old residential area to school, it always filled me with thoughts I liked, such as that I was someone. Most of the kids at school came from town or neighboring areas, it was only me and a handful of others who came from the country, and that was a huge disadvantage. It meant that all the others knew one another and met outside school hours, hung around together in cliques. These cliques were also operative during school hours, and you couldn't just tag along, not at all, so during every break there was a problem: where should I go? Where should I stand? I could sit in the library and read, or sit in the classroom and pretend to be going through homework, but that was tantamount to signaling I was one of the outsiders and was no good in the long run, so in October that year I started smoking. Not because I liked it, nor because it was cool, but because it gave me somewhere to be: now I could skulk around doorways with the other smokers in every break without anyone asking questions. When school was over and I was walking back to my place the problem ceased to exist. First of all, because I would usually go to Tveit to train or to meet Jan Vidar, my best pal from the last school, and secondly because no one saw me and therefore could not know that I sat on my own in the flat all those evenings that I did.

It was different in the lessons. I was in a class with three other boys and twenty-six girls, and I had a role, I had a place, I could speak there, answer questions, discuss, do schoolwork, be someone. I had been brought together with others, all of them had been, I had not forced myself on anyone and my being there was not questioned. I sat at the back in the corner, beside me was Bassen, before me Molle, at the front of the same row Pål, and the rest of the classroom was occupied by girls. Twenty-six sixteen-year-old girls. I liked some better than others, but none of them enough to say I was in love.

There was Monica, whose parents were Hungarian Jews, she was as sharp as a razor, knowledgeable, and doggedly defended Israel to the bitter end when we debated the Palestine conflict, a stance I could not understand, it was so obvious, Israel was a military state, Palestine a victim. And there was Hanne, an attractive girl from Vågsbygd, who sang in a choir, was a Christian and quite naïve, but someone whose appearance and presence cheered you up. Then there was Siv, blond, tanned, and long-legged who on one of the first days had said the area between the Cathedral School and the Business School was like an American campus, a statement which singled her out for me at first as she knew something I didn't, about a world of which I would have liked to be part. She had lived in Ghana for the last few years and boasted too much and laughed too loud. There was Benedicte too with sharp, almost fifties-like facial features, curly hair, clothes with a hint of class. And Tone, so graceful in her movements, dark-haired and serious, she sketched, and seemed more independent than the others. And Anne, who had braces on her teeth and whom I had made out with in Bassen's mother's hairdressing chair at a class party that autumn; there was Hilde, fair-haired and rosy-cheeked, firm of character but still somehow anonymous, who often turned around to me; and there was Irene, the girls' focal point, she had that attractiveness that can dazzle and wilt in the space of one glance; and there was Nina who had such a robust, masculine frame but also something fragile and bashful about her. And Mette, small, edgy, and scheming. She was the one who liked Bruce Springsteen and always wore denim, the one who was so small and laughed all the time, the one who dressed in clothes that were as provocative as they were vulgar and smelled of smoke, the one whose gums were visible every time she smiled, attractive apart from that, but her laughter, a kind of constant giggle that accompanied everything she said, and all the stupid things she came out with, and the fact that she had a slight lisp, detracted from her beauty, in a way, or invalidated it. I was in the midst of a deluge of girls, a torrent of bodies, a sea of breasts and thighs. Seeing them in formal surroundings alone, behind their desks, only made their presence stronger. In a way it gave my days meaning, I looked forward to entering the classroom, sitting where I was entitled to sit, together with all these girls.

That morning I went down to the canteen, bought a bun and a Coke, then took my place and consumed my snack while flicking through a book, as the classroom around me slowly filled with pupils, still sluggish in both movement and expression after a night's sleep. I exchanged a few words with Molle, he lived in Hamresanden; we had been in the same class at our old school. Then the teacher came, it was Berg, wearing a smock, we were going to have Norwegian. Besides history, this was my best subject, I was on the cusp between an A and an A plus, couldn't quite make the top grade, but I was determined to try for it at the exam. The natural sciences were of course my weakest subjects, in math I was getting a D, I never did any homework, and the teaching was already way above my head. The teachers we had for math and natural sciences were old-school, for math we had Vestby, he had lots of tics, one arm jiggled and writhed the whole time. In his lessons I sat with my feet on the table chatting to Bassen until Vestby, his compact, fleshy face ablaze, screeched out my name. Then I put my feet down, waited until he had turned and continued to chat. The science teacher, Nygaard, a small, thin, wizened man, with a satanic smile and childlike gestures, was approaching retirement age. He too had a number of tics, one eye kept blinking, his shoulders twitched, he tossed his head, he was a parody of a tormented teacher. He wore a light-colored suit in the summer months, a dark suit in the wintertime, and once I had seen him use the blackboard compasses as a gun: we were hunched over a test, he scanned the classroom, clapped the compasses together, put the instrument to his shoulder and sprayed the class with jerking motions, an evil smile on his face. I could not believe my own eyes, had he lost his senses? I chatted in his classes too, so much so that now I had to pay the penalty for whoever did any talking: Knausgaard, he said if he heard some mumbling somewhere, and raised his palm: that meant I had to stand beside my desk for the rest of the lesson. I was happy to do so because inside me I had a rebellious streak developing, I longed not to give a damn about anything, to start skipping classes, drinking, bossing people around. I was an anarchist, an atheist, and became more and more anti–middle class with every day that passed. I flirted with the idea of having my ears pierced and my head shaved. Natural sciences, what use was that to me? Math, what use was that to me? I wanted to play in a band, to be free, to live as I pleased, not as others pleased.

In this I was alone, in this I had no one with me, so for the time being it remained unrealized, it was a thing of the future and was as amorphous as all future things are.

Not doing any homework, not paying attention in class was part and parcel of the same attitude. I had always been among the best in every subject, I had always enjoyed showing it, but not anymore, now there was something shameful about good grades, it meant you sat at home doing your homework, you were a stick-in-the-mud, a loser. It was different with Norwegian, I associated that with writers and a bohemian lifestyle, besides you couldn't gut it out, it required something else, a feeling, a natural talent, personality.

I doodled my way through lessons, smoked outside the doorway in breaks, and this was the rhythm for the whole day, as the sky and the countryside beneath slowly brightened, until the bell rang for the last time at half past two, and I could make my way home to my digs. It was the fifth of December, the day before my birthday, my sixteenth, and Mom was coming home from Bergen. I was looking forward to seeing her. In many ways it was fine being alone with Dad, in the sense that he kept as far away as possible, stayed at Sannes when I stayed in town and vice versa. When Mom came this would end, we would all be living together up there until well into the new year, so the disadvantage of meeting Dad every day was almost completely outweighed by Mom's presence. She was someone I could talk to. I could talk to her about everything. I couldn't say anything to Dad. Nothing beyond purely practical things such as where I was going and when I was coming home.

When I arrived at the flat his car was outside. I went in, the hall reeked of frying; from the kitchen I could hear clattering noises and the radio.

I poked my head in.

"Hello," I said.

"Hello," he said. "Are you hungry?"

"Yes, quite. What are you making?"

"Chops. Take a seat, they're ready."

I went in and sat down at the round dining table. It was old, I assumed it had belonged to his grandmother.

Dad put two chops, three potatoes, and a small pile of fried onions on my plate. Sat down and heaped his plate.

"Well?" he said. "Anything new at school?"

I shook my head.

"You didn't learn anything today?"

"No."

"No, of course not."

We ate in silence.

I didn't want to hurt him, I didn't want him to think this was a failure, that he had a failed relationship with his son, so I sat wondering what I could say. But I couldn't come up with anything.

He wasn't in a bad mood. He wasn't angry. Just preoccupied.

"Have you been up to see Grandma and Grandad recently?" I asked.

He looked at me.

"Yes, I have," he said. "Dropped in yesterday afternoon. Why do you ask?"

"No special reason," I said, feeling my cheeks flushing. "Just wondered."

I had cut off all the meat I could with the knife. Now I put the bone in my mouth and began to gnaw. Dad did the same. I put down the bone and drank the water.

"Thanks for making me a meal," I said, and got up.

"Was the parents' evening at six, did you say?" he asked.

"Yes," I answered.

"Are you staying here?"

"Think so."

"Then I'll come and get you afterward and we can drive up to Sannes. Is that alright?"

"Yeah, course."

I was writing an essay about an advertisement for a sports drink when he came back. The door opening, the surge of sounds from the town, the thudding of footsteps on the hall floor. His voice.

"Karl Ove? Are you ready? Let's get going."

I had packed everything I would need in my bag and satchel, they were at bursting point because I was staying for a month and didn't quite know what I might need.

He watched me as I came downstairs. He shook his head. But he wasn't angry. There was something else.

"How did it go?" I asked without meeting his eyes, even though that was one of his bugbears.

"How did it go? Well, I'll tell you how it went. I was given an earful by your math teacher. That's how it went. Vestby, isn't it?'

"Yes."

"Why didn't you tell me? I had no idea. I was caught completely off-guard."

"So what did he say?" I asked and started to get dressed, infinitely relieved that Dad had kept his temper.

"He said you sat with your feet on the table in lessons, and that you were obstreperous and smart-alecky, and talked in class and you didn't do classwork or your homework. If this continues he will fail you. That's what he said. Is it true?"

"Yes, I suppose it is in a way," I said, straightening up, dressed and ready to go.

"He blamed me, you know. He went on at me for having such a lout as a son."

I cringed.

"What did you say to him?"

"I gave him an earful. Your behavior at school is his responsibility. Not mine. But it wasn't exactly pleasant. As I'm sure you understand."

"I do," I said. "Sorry."

"Fat lot of good that is. That's the last parents' evening I'll ever go to, that's for sure. Well then. Shall we go?"

We went out to the street, to the car. Dad got in, leaned over, and unlocked my side.

"Can you open up at the back as well?" I asked.

He didn't answer, just did it. I put the bag and the satchel in the trunk, closed the lid carefully so as not to rouse his ire, took a seat at the front, pulled the belt across my chest, and clicked the buckle into the locking mechanism.

"That was excruciatingly embarrassing, no two ways about it," Dad said, starting the engine. The dashboard lit up. The car in front of us and a section of the slope down to the river as well. "But what's he like as a teacher, this Vestby?"

"Pretty bad. He's got discipline problems. No one respects him. And he can't teach either."

"He got some of the top university grades ever recorded, did you know that?" Dad said.

"No, I didn't," I said.

He reversed a few meters, swung out onto the road, turned, and began to head out of town. The heater roared, the tire studs bit into the tarmac with a regular high-pitched whirr. He drove fast as usual. One hand on the wheel, one resting on the seat beside the gear stick. My stomach quivered, tiny flashes of happiness shot into my body for this had never happened before. He had never taken my side. He had never chosen to overlook anything reprehensible in my behavior. Handing over my report before the summer and Christmas holiday was always something I had anticipated with dread during the previous weeks. The slightest critical remark and his fury washed over me. The same with parents' evenings. The tiniest comment about my talking too much or a lack of care was followed by a venting of anger. Not to mention the few times I had been given a note to take home. That was Judgment Day. All hell broke loose.

Was it because I was becoming an adult that he treated me in this way? Were we becoming equals?

I felt an urge to look at him as he sat there with his eyes fixed on the road as we raced along. But I could not, I would have to say something then, and I had nothing to say.

Half an hour later we went up the last hill and entered the drive in front of our house. With the engine still running, Dad got out to open the garage door. I walked to the front door and unlocked it. Remembered our bags, went back as Dad switched off the engine and the red taillights died.

"Could you open the trunk?" I asked.

He nodded, inserted the key, and twisted. The lid rose like the tail of a whale, it seemed to me. Going into the house, I knew at once he had been cleaning. It smelled of green soap, the rooms were tidy, the floors shiny. And the dried-up cat shit on the sofa upstairs, that was gone.

Of course he had done it because my mother was coming home. But even though there was a specific reason and he had not done it simply because it had been so unbelievably filthy and disgusting there, it was a relief to me. Some order had been reestablished. Not that I had been worried or anything, it was more that I found it unsettling, especially as it had not been the only sign. Something about him had changed during the autumn. Presumably because of the way we lived, he and I together, barely that, it was palpable. He had never had any friends, never had people around at home, apart from the family. The only people he knew were colleagues and neighbors, when we were in Tromøya, I should add; here he didn't even know the neighbors. Although just a few weeks after Mom had moved to Bergen to study he had organized a gathering with a few work colleagues in the house at Sannes, they were going to have a little party, and he wondered whether I might perhaps spend that night in town? If I felt lonely I could always go up to my grandparents' if I wanted. But being alone was the last thing I feared, and he dropped by in the morning with a frozen pizza, Coke, and chips for me, which I ate in front of the television.

The next morning I caught the bus to Jan Vidar's, stayed a few hours, and then bussed back up to our house. The door was locked. I opened the garage to check whether he had just gone for a walk, or taken the car. It was empty. I walked back to the house and let myself in. On the table in the living room there were a few empty bottles of wine, the ashtrays were full, but considering no one had cleaned up it didn't look too bad, and I thought it must have been a small party. The stereo set was usually in the barn, but he had put it on a table beside the radiator, and I knelt down in front of the limited selection of records partly stacked against a chair leg and partly scattered across the floor. They were the ones he had played for as long as I could remember. Pink Floyd. Joe Dassin. Arja Saijonmaa. Johnny Cash. Elvis Presley. Bach. Vivaldi. He must have played the last two before the party started, or perhaps it was this morning. But the rest of the music wasn't very party-like either. I stood up and went into the kitchen, where there were a few unwashed plates and glasses in the sink, opened the fridge, which apart from a couple of bottles of white wine and some beers was as good as empty, and continued up the stairs to the first floor. The door to Dad's bedroom was open. I went over and looked inside. The bed from Mom's room had been moved in and was next to Dad's in the middle of the floor. So it had got late, and since they had been drinking and the house was so far off the beaten track that a taxi to town, or Vennesla, where Dad worked, would have been much too expensive, someone had slept over. My room was untouched, I grabbed what I needed, and although I had planned to sleep there I went back to town. Something unfamiliar had descended over all the things in the house.

Another time I had gone up there without warning, it was evening, I was too tired to go back to town after soccer practice, and Tom from the team had driven me. In the light from the kitchen I could see Dad sitting with his head supported on one hand and a bottle of wine in front of him. That was new too, he had never drunk before, at least not while I had been around, and certainly not alone. I saw it now and didn't want to know, but I couldn't go back, so I kicked the snow off my shoes as loudly and obviously as I could against the steps, jerked the door open, slammed it shut again, and so that he would be in no doubt as to where I was, I turned on both bath taps, sat on the toilet seat and waited for a few minutes. When I went into the kitchen no one was there. The glass was on the drainer, empty, the bottle in the cupboard under the sink, empty, Dad was in the flat beneath the hayloft. As if this were not mysterious enough I also saw him driving past the shop in Solsletta one early afternoon; I had skipped the last three classes and gone to Jan Vidar's before the evening training session in Kjevik sports hall. I was sitting on the bench outside the shop smoking when I saw Dad's snot-green Ascona, it was unmistakeable. I threw away the cigarette, but saw no reason to hide, and stared at the car as it passed, even raised my hand to wave. He didn't see me, he was talking to someone in the passenger seat. The next day he came by, I mentioned this to him, it had been a colleague, they were working together on a project and had spent a few hours after school at our house.

There was a great deal of contact with his colleagues during this period. One weekend he went to a seminar in Hovden with them, and he went to more parties than I can ever remember him going to before. No doubt because he was bored, or didn't like being on his own so much, and I was glad, at that time I had begun to see him with different eyes, no longer the eyes of a child, rather those of someone approaching adulthood, and from that point of view I preferred him to socialize with friends and colleagues, as other people did. At the same time I did not like the change, it made him unpredictable.

The fact that he had defended me at the parents' evening contributed to this view of him. Indeed, it was perhaps the most significant factor of them all.

I collected together the clothes in the room, replaced the cassettes one by one in the rack on the desk and stacked the schoolbooks in a neat pile. The house had been built in the mid-1800s, all the floors creaked, sounds permeated the walls, so I knew not only that Dad was in the living room below but also that he was sitting on the sofa. I had planned to finish *Dracula* but I didn't feel I could until the situation between us had been clarified. In other words, until he knew what I was planning to do and I knew what he was planning to do. Furthermore, I couldn't just go downstairs and say: "Hi, Dad, I'm upstairs reading." "Why are you telling me that?" he would ask, or at least think. But the imbalance had to be rectified, so I went downstairs, took a detour through the kitchen, something to do with food maybe, before taking the final steps into the living room, where he was sitting with one of my old comics in his hand.

"Are you eating this evening?" I asked.

He glanced up at me.

"You just help yourself," he said.

"Okay," I said. "I'll be up in my room afterward, alright?"

He didn't answer, kept reading *Agent X9* in the light from the sofa lamp. I cut off a large chunk of sausage and ate it while sitting at the desk. He probably hadn't bought me a birthday present, it occurred to me, Mom would be bringing one with her from Bergen. But wasn't it his job to order a cake? Had he thought about it?

When I returned home from school the next day, Mom was there. Dad had picked her up from the airport, they were sitting at the kitchen table, there was a roast in the oven, we ate with candles on the table, I was given a check for five hundred kroner and a shirt she had bought in Bergen. I didn't have the heart to say I would never wear it, after all she had gone around a string of shops in Bergen looking for something for me, found this, which she thought was great and I would like.

I put it on, we ate cake and drank coffee in the living room. Mom was happy, she said several times it was good to be home. Yngve rang to say happy birthday, he probably wouldn't be home until Christmas Eve, and I would get my present then. I left for soccer practice; when I returned at around nine they were up at the flat in the barn.

I would have liked to chat with Mom on my own, but it didn't look as if that was going to be possible, so after waiting up for a while I went to bed.

The next day I had a test at school, the last two weeks had been full of them, I walked out of every one early, frequented record shops or cafés in town, sometimes with Bassen, sometimes with some of the girls in the class, if it happened casually and couldn't be interpreted as my forcing myself on them. But with Bassen it was okay, we had begun to hang out together. One evening I had been at his place, all we did was play records in his room, even so I was flushed with happiness, I had found a new friend. Not a country boy, not a heavy metal fan, but someone who liked Talk Talk and U2, the Waterboys and Talking Heads. Bassen, or Reid, which was his real name, was dark and good-looking, immensely attractive to girls, although this didn't seem to have gone to his head, because there was nothing showy about him, nothing smug, he never occupied the position he could have, but he wasn't modest either, it was more that he had a ruminative, introverted side to him which held him back. He never gave everything. Whether that was because he didn't want to or he couldn't, I don't know, often of course they are two sides of the same coin. For me his most striking feature, though, was that he had his own opinions about things. Whereas I tended to think in boxes, for example in politics, where one standpoint automatically presupposed another, or in terms of taste, where liking one band meant liking similar bands, or in relationships, where I never managed to free myself from existing attitudes regarding others, he was an independent thinker, using his own more or less idiosyncratic judgments. Not even this did he boast about, on the contrary, you had to know him for quite a while before it became apparent. So this was not something he used, it was what he was. If I was proud to be able to call Bassen a friend it was not only because he had so many good qualities, or because of the friendship itself, but also, and not least, because his popularity might rub off on me as well. I was not conscious of this, but in retrospect, if nothing else, it is patently obvious; if you are on the outside you have to find someone who can let you in, at any rate when you are sixteen years old. In this case the exclusion was not metaphorical, but literal and real. I was surrounded by several hundred boys and girls of my age, but could not enter the milieu to which they all belonged. Every Monday I dreaded the question they would all ask, namely, "What did you do over the weekend?" You could say "Stayed at home watching TV" once, "Played records at a friend's house" once as well, but after that you had to come up with something better if you didn't want to be left out in the cold. This happened to some on day one, and that was how it stayed for the rest of their time at school, but I didn't want to end up like them at any price, I wanted to be one of those at the center of things, I wanted to be invited to their parties, go out with them in town, to live their lives.

The great test, the year's biggest party, was New Year's Eve. For the last few weeks people had been talking about nothing else. Bassen was going to be with someone he knew in Justvik, there was no chance of hanging onto his shirttails, so when school broke up for Christmas I had not been invited anywhere. After Christmas I sat down with Jan Vidar, who lived in Solsletta, about four kilometers down the hill from us, and that autumn had started to train as a pâtissier at the technical college, to discuss what possibilities were open to us. We wanted to go to a party and we wanted to get drunk. As far as the latter was concerned, that would not be much of a problem: I played soccer for the juniors, and the goalkeeper, Tom, was an all-round fixer and he wouldn't mind buying beer for us. A party, on the other hand . . . There were some ninth-class semicriminal, dropout types who apparently were getting together in a house nearby, but that was of no interest whatsoever, I would rather have stayed home. There was another crowd we knew well, but we were not part of it, they were based in Hamresanden and included people with whom we had either gone to school or played soccer, but we had not been invited and although we could probably have gate-crashed somehow they didn't have enough class in my eyes. They lived in Tveit, went to the technical college or had jobs, and those of them who had cars had fur-covered seats and Wunderbaum car fresheners dangling from the mirror. There were no alternatives. You had to be invited to New Year's parties. On the other hand, at twelve o'clock people came out, assembled in the square and at the intersection to fire off rockets and let the new year in amid screams and shouts. No invitation needed to participate in that. Lots of people at school were going to parties in the Søm area, I knew, so what about going there? It was then Jan Vidar remembered that the drummer in our group, whom we had accepted out of sheer desperation, an eighth-class kid from Hånes, had said he was going to Søm for New Year's Eve.

Two telephone calls later and everything had been arranged. Tom would buy beer for us and we would be with kids from the eighth and ninth classes, hang around in their cellar till midnight, then go to the intersection where everyone gathered, find some people I knew from school and hook up with them for the rest of the evening. It was a good plan. When I got home that afternoon, in a studied casual way, I told Mom and Dad I had been invited out on New Year's Eve, there was a party in Søm with some of my class, was it all right if I went? We had guests coming, my father's parents and brother, Gunnar, and his family, but neither Mom nor Dad had any objections to my going.

"How nice!" Mom said.

"That's alright," Dad said. "But you've got to be home by one."

"But it's New Year's Eve," I said. "Couldn't we make it two?"

"Okay. But two o'clock then, not half past. Is that understood?"

So, on the morning of the thirty-first we cycled to the shop in Ryensletta, where Tom was waiting, gave him the money, and were handed two bags, each containing ten bottles, in return. Jan Vidar hid the bags in the garden outside his house, and I cycled home. Mom and Dad were in full swing, cleaning and tidying in preparation for the party. The wind had picked up. I stood outside my bedroom window for a moment watching the snow whirl past, and the gray sky that seemed to have descended over the black trees in the forest. Then I put on a record, grabbed the book I was reading and lay down on the bed. After a while Mom knocked on the door.

"Jan Vidar on the phone," she said.

The telephone was downstairs in the room with the clothes cupboards. I went down, closed the door, and picked up the receiver.

"Hello?"

"Disaster," Jan Vidar said. "That bastatd Leif Reidar . . ."

Leif Reidar was his brother. He was twenty-something years old, drove a souped-up Opel Ascona, worked at the Boen parquet factory. His life was not oriented toward the southwest, toward the town, toward Kristiansand, like mine and most other people's, but toward the northeast, to Birkeland and Lillesand, and because of the age gap I never quite got a handle on him, on who he was, what he actually did. He had a moustache and often wore aviator sunglasses, but he was not the average poser, there was a correctness about his clothes and behavior that pointed in another direction.

"What's he done?" I asked.

"He found the bags of beer in the garden. Then he couldn't keep his damn mitts off, could he. The bastard. He's such a hypocritical jerk. He told me off, *him*, of all people. I was only sixteen and all that crap. Then he tried to make me tell him who had bought the beer. I refused of course. Doesn't have shit to do with him. But then he said he was going to tell my dad if I didn't spill the beans. The fucking hypocrite. The . . . Jesus Christ, I had to say. And do you know what he did? Do you know the little shit did?"

"No," I said.

In the gusts of wind, the snow projected like a veil from the barn roof. The light from the ground-floor windows shone softly, almost clandestinely, into the deepening dusk. I glimpsed a movement inside, it must have been Dad, I thought, and sure enough, the next second his face took shape behind the windowpane, he was looking straight at me. I lowered my eyes, half-turned my head.

"He forced me into the car and drove down to Tom's with the bags."

"You're kidding."

"What a prick he is. He enjoyed it. He seemed to be fucking reveling in it. Taking the moral high ground all of a sudden, the shit. *Him*. That really pissed me off."

"What happened?" I asked.

When I glanced over at the windows again the face had gone.

"What happened? What do you think? He gave Tom an earful. Then he told me to give the bags of beer to Tom. So I did. And then Tom had to give me the money. As though I were a little brat. As if he hadn't done the same when he was sixteen. Fuck him. He was lapping it up, he was, wallowing in it. The indignation, driving me there, giving Tom hell."

"What are we going to do now? Go there without the beer? We can't do that."

"No, we can't, but I winked at Tom as we left. He got the message. So I called him when I got home and said sorry. He still had the beers. So I told him to drive up to your place with them. He's picking me up on the way, so I can pay him."

"Are you coming *here*?"

"Yes, he'll be at my place in ten minutes. So we'll be with you in fifteen."

"I've got to think."

It was then I noticed that the cat was lying in the chair beside the telephone. It looked at me, started licking one paw. In the living room the vacuum cleaner roared into life. The cat turned its head in the direction of the sound. The next second it relaxed. I leaned over and stroked its chest.

"You can't drive all the way up. That's no good. But we can just leave the bags at the roadside somewhere. No one will find them up here anyway.

"Bottom of the hill maybe?"

"Below the house?"

"Yes."

"Bottom of the hill below the house in fifteen minutes?"

"Yes."

"All right. So remember to tell Tom not to turn around in our drive, and not by the mailboxes either. There's a shoulder a bit higher up the road. Can he use that?"

"Okay. See you."

I hung up and went into the living room to Mom. She switched off the vacuum cleaner when she saw me.

"I'm off to see Per," I said. "Just want to wish him a happy new year."

"Fine," Mom said. "Send our regards if you see his parents."

Per was a year younger than me and lived in the neighboring house a couple of hundred meters down the hill. He was the person I spent the most time with in the years we lived here. We played soccer as often as we could, after school, on Saturdays and Sundays, during vacations, and a lot of that was spent finding enough players for a decent game, but if we couldn't, we played two-a-side for hours, and if we couldn't do that, it was just Per and me. I booted the ball at him, he booted it at me, I crossed to him, he crossed it to me, or we played twosies, as we called it. We did this, day in, day out, even after I had started at the gymnas. Otherwise we went swimming, either under the waterfall, in the deep part of the pool and where you could dive from a rock, or down by the rapids where the torrent swept us along. When the weather was too bad to do anything outside, we watched a video in their cellar or just hung around chatting in the garage. I liked being there, his family was warm and generous, and even though his father could not stand me I was welcome all the same. Yet despite the fact that Per was the person I spent the most time with, I did not consider him a friend, I never mentioned him in any other context, both because he was younger than me, which was not good, and because he was a country boy. He wasn't interested in music, hadn't a clue about it, he wasn't interested in girls or drinking either, he was quite content to sit at home with his family on the weekends. Turning up for school in rubber boots didn't bother him, he was just as happy walking around in knitted sweaters and cords as jeans he'd outgrown and T-shirts emblazoned with Kristiansand Zoo. When I first moved here he had never been to Kristiansand on his own. He had hardly ever read a book, what he liked was comics, which for that matter I also read, but always alongside the endless list of MacLean, Bagley, Smith, Le Carré, and Follet books I devoured, and which I eventually got him interested in as well. We went to the library together some Saturdays, and to Start FC's home games every other Sunday, we trained with the soccer team twice a week, in the summer we played matches once a week, in addition to which we walked together to and from the school bus every day. But we didn't share the same seat, for the closer we got to school and the life there, the less of a friend Per became, until by the time we got to the playground we had no contact at all. Strangely enough, he never protested. He was always happy, always open, had a well-developed sense of humor and was, like the rest of his family, a warm person. Over the Christmas period I had been down to his place a couple of times, we had watched some videos and we had skied on the slopes behind our house. It had not occurred to me to invite him out on New Year's Eve, the idea didn't even exist as a possibility. Jan Vidar had a non-relationship with Per, they knew each other, of course, as everyone knew everyone else up here, but he was never alone with him and saw no reason to be either. When I moved here Jan Vidar hung out with Kjetil, a boy our age who lived in Kjevil, they were best friends and always in and out of each other's houses. Kjetil's father was in the service, and they had moved around a lot, from what I understood. When Jan Vidar started to spend time with me, mostly because of a common interest in music, Kjetil tried to win him back, kept calling and inviting him over, made inside jokes that only they understood when the three of us were together at school; if that didn't work he resorted to more devious methods and invited both of us. We cycled around the airport, hung out in the airport café, went to Hamresanden and visited one of the girls there, Rita. Both Kjetil and Jan Vidar were interested in her. Kjetil had a bar of chocolate which he shared on the hill with Jan Vidar, without offering me any, but that fell flat as well because all Jan Vidar did was break his piece in two and pass me half. Then Kjetil released his grip, directed his attention elsewhere, but for as long as we went to the same school he never found any friends who were as close as Jan Vidar had been. Kjetil was a person everyone liked, especially the girls, but no one wanted to be with him. Rita, who was generally cheeky and tough, and never spared anyone, had a soft spot for him, they were always laughing together and had their own special way of talking, but they were never more than friends. Rita always saved her most mordant sarcasm for me, and I was always on my guard when she was around, I never knew when or how the attack would be launched. She was small and delicate, her face thin, her mouth small, but her features were well-formed and her eyes, which were often so full of scorn, shone with a rare intensity; they almost sparkled. Rita was attractive, but still wasn't seen as such, and could be so unpleasant to others that perhaps she never would be.

One evening she called me.

"Hi, Karl Ove, this is Rita," she said.

"Rita?" I repeated.

"Yes, you cretin. Rita Lolita."

"Oh, yes," I said.

"I have a question for you," she said.

"Yes?"

"Would you like to date me?"

"I beg your pardon?"

"One more time. Would you like to date me? It's a simple question. You're supposed to say yes or no."

"I don't know . . ." I said.

"Oh, come on. If you don't want to, just say so."

"I don't think I do . . ." I said.

"Alright then," she said. "See you at school tomorrow. Bye."

And she hung up. The next day I behaved as if nothing had happened, and she behaved as if nothing had happened, though she was perhaps even keener to get a dig in whenever the opportunity arose. She never mentioned it, I never mentioned it, not even to Jan Vidar or Kjetil, I didn't want to be one up on them.

After I had said goodbye to Mom and she had switched the vacuum cleaner back on, I wrapped myself up warm in the hall and ventured out, my head ducked into the wind. Dad had opened one garage door and was dragging out the snowblower. The gravel inside was snow-free and dry, which aroused a faint unease in me, as always, because gravel belonged outdoors, and whatever was outdoors should be covered in snow, creating an imbalance between inside and outside. As soon as the door was closed I didn't think about it, it never crossed my mind, but when I saw it . . .

"I'm just off to see Per," I shouted.

Dad, who was having a tremendous battle with the snowblower, turned his head and nodded. I half-regretted having suggested meeting on the hill, it might be too close, my father tended to have a sixth sense when it came to deviations from the norm. On the other hand, it was quite a while now since he had taken any interest in me. On reaching the mailbox I heard the snowblower start. I looked up to check whether he could see me. He couldn't, so I walked down the hill, hugging the side to reduce the chance of being observed. At the bottom I stopped and gazed across the river while I waited. Three cars in succession drove past on the other side. The light from their headlights was like small stabs of yellow in the immense grayness. The snow on the flats had turned the color of the sky, whose light seemed to be enmeshed by the falling darkness. The water in the channel of the iced-up river was black and shiny. Then I heard a car charging down along the bend a few hundred meters away. The engine sounded tinny, it must have been an old car. Tom's probably. I peered up the road, raised a hand as it appeared around the bend. It braked and came to a halt beside me. Tom rolled down the window.

"Hi, Karl Ove," he said.

"Hi," I said.

He smiled.

"Did you get an earful?" I asked.

"What a stupid bastard, he is," said Jan Vidar, sitting in the seat beside him.

"No big deal," Tom said. "So, you boys are going out tonight?"

"Yes. And how about you?"

"May have a wander."

"Everything okay otherwise?"

"Yep, fine."

He looked at me with those good-natured eyes of his and smiled.

"Your stuff's in the trunk."

"Is it open?"

"Yep."

I went around and opened the trunk, took the two red-and-white bags lying among the clutter of tools, toolboxes, and those elastic thingies with hooks to secure stuff to the car roof.

"Got them," I said. "Thanks, Tom. We won't forget this."

He shrugged.

"See you then," I said to Jan Vidar.

He nodded, Tom wound up the window, cheerfully saluted with his fingers to his temple as always, put the car in gear and drove up the hill. I stepped over the bank of snow and went into the trees, followed the snow-covered stream perhaps twenty meters uphill, laid the bottles under an easily recognizable birch trunk and heard the car passing on its descent.

I stood at the edge of the forest waiting for a few minutes so that I wouldn't have been away for a suspiciously short time. Then I walked up the hill where Dad was busy clearing a broader path to the house. He was wearing neither gloves nor a hat as he walked behind the machine dressed in his old lambskin coat with a thick scarf loosely wrapped around his neck. The fountain of snow that was not carried off by the wind cascaded onto the ground a few meters away. I nodded to him as I passed, his eyes registered me fleetingly, but his face was impassive. When I went into the kitchen, after hanging my outdoor clothes in the hall, Mom was sitting there smoking. A candle flickered on the windowsill. The clock on the stove said half past three.

"Everything under control?" I asked.

"Yes," she said. "It's going to be nice. Do you want something to eat before you go?"

"I'll make a few sandwiches," I said.

On the counter was a large white packet of lutefisk. The sink was full of dark, unwashed potatoes. In the corner the coffee machine light was on. The pot was half full.

"I think I'll wait a bit though," I said. "Don't have to go before seven or so. When are they coming?"

"Dad's going to fetch your grandparents. Think he's off soon. Gunnar will be here at around seven."

"Then I'll just manage to catch them," I said, and went into the living room, stood in front of the window and gazed across the valley, went to the coffee table, took an orange, sat down on the sofa and began to peel. The

Christmas tree candles shone, the flames in the fire sparkled and the crystal glasses on the laid table at the far end glistened in the room lights. I thought of Yngve, wondered how he had coped with these things when he was at gymnas. Now at any rate he didn't have any problems; he was at a cabin in Aust-Agder with all his friends. He had come home at the latest possible moment, on Christmas Eve, and departed as soon as he could, on the twenty-seventh. He had never lived here. The summer we moved he was set to start the third and final year and did not want to leave his friends. That had made Dad furious. But Yngve had been uncompromising, he was not moving. He took out a study loan, because Dad refused to give him a single krone, and he rented digs not so far from our old house. Dad barely exchanged a word with him the few weekends he spent with us. The atmosphere between them was icy. The year after, Yngve did his national service, and I remember him coming home one weekend with his girlfriend, Alfhild. It was the first time he had done anything like this. Dad had of course stayed away, it had been just Yngve and Alfhild, Mom and me there. Not until the weekend was over and they were on their way downhill to catch the bus did Dad drive up. He stopped the car, rolled down the window, and gave them a friendly hello to Alfhild. The smile that accompanied it was something I had never seen on him before. It was radiant with happiness and fervor. He had certainly never looked at any of us in such a way. Then he shifted his gaze, put the car in first, and drove up the hill while we continued our descent to the bus.

Was that our father?

All Mom's kindness and thoughtfulness toward Alfhild and Yngve was completely overshadowed by Dad's four-second gaze. For that matter, this is how Mom had probably been on weekends as well, when Yngve was here alone and Dad stayed on the ground floor of the barn as much as possible, only turning up for meals, at which his refusal to ask Yngve a single question or grace him with even a minimum of attention is what lingered in the mind after the weekend, despite all Mom's efforts to make Yngve feel at home. It was Dad who set the tone at home; there was nothing anyone could do.

Outside, the roar of the snowblower suddenly stopped. I got up, grabbed the orange peel, went into the kitchen, where Mom was scrubbing potatoes, opened the cupboard beside her and dropped the peel in the wastebasket, watched Dad walk across the drive, running a hand through his hair in that characteristic way of his, after which I went upstairs to my room, closed the door behind me, put on a record and lay down on my bed again.

We had pondered for a while how we were going to get to Søm. Both Jan Vidar's father and my mother would certainly have offered to give us a ride, which in fact they did as soon as we told them of our plans. But the two bags of beer ruled out that possibility. The solution we arrived at was that Jan Vidar would tell his parents that my mother was taking us while I would say that it was Jan Vidar's father who was taking us. This was a bit of a risk because our parents did occasionally meet, but the odds on the driver question surfacing in conversation were so minute it was a chance we were prepared to take. Once that was resolved there was just the matter of getting there. Buses didn't come out here on New Year's Eve, but we found out that some passed the Timenes intersection about ten kilometers away. So we would have to hitch a ride – if we were lucky a car would take us the whole way, if not, we could catch the bus from there. To avoid questions and suspicion it would all have to happen after the guests had arrived. That is, after seven o'clock. The bus left at ten past eight, so with a bit of luck everything would work out fine.

Getting drunk required careful planning. Alcohol had to be procured safely in advance, a secure place for storage had to be found, transport there and back had to be arranged, and parents had to be avoided when you got home. After the first blissful occasion in Oslo I had therefore got drunk only twice. The second time threatened to go awry. Jan Vidar's sister Liv had just got engaged to Stig, a soldier she had met in Kjevik, where her and Jan Vidar's father worked. She wanted to get married young, have children, and be a housewife, a rather unusual dream for a girl of her age, so even though she was only a year older than us, she lived in quite a different world. One Saturday evening the two of them invited us to a little gathering with some of their friends. Since we didn't have any other plans, we accepted and a few days later were sitting on a sofa in a house somewhere drinking homemade wine and watching TV. It was meant to be a cozy evening at home, there were candles on the table and lasagne was served, and it probably would have been cozy had it not been for the wine, of which there was an immense quantity. I drank, and I became as euphoric as the first time, but on this occasion I had a blackout and remembered nothing between the fifth glass and the moment I woke up in a dark cellar wearing jogging bottoms and a sweatshirt I had never seen before and lying on top of a duvet covered with towels, my own clothes next to me bundled up and spattered with vomit. I could make out a washing machine by the wall, a basket of dirty laundry beside it, a chest freezer by the other wall with some waterproof trousers and jackets on the lid. There was also a pile of crab pots, a landing net, a fishing rod, and a shelf full of tools and junk. I took in these surroundings so new to me in one sweep of the eye, then woke up rested and with a clear head. A door a few strides from my head was ajar, I opened it and walked into the kitchen where Stig and Liv were sitting, hands interlaced and glowing with happiness.

"Hi," I said.

"Well, if it isn't Garfield," Stig said. "How are you?"

"Fine," I said. "What happened actually?"

"Don't you remember?"

I shook my head.

"Nothing?"

He laughed. At that moment Jan Vidar came in from the living room.

"Hi," he said.

"Hi," I said.

He smiled.

"Hi, Garfield," he said.

"What's with this Garfield?" I asked.

"Don't you remember?"

"No. I can't remember a thing. But I see that I must have thrown up."

"We were watching TV. A Garfield cartoon. Then you got up and beat your chest and shouted 'I'm Garfield.' Then you sat down again and chuckled.

Then you did it again. 'I'm Garfield! I'm Garfield!' Then you threw up. In the living room. On the carpet. And then you were out like a light. Bang. Thud. Sound asleep. In a pool of vomit. And it was absolutely impossible to communicate with you."

"Oh, shit," I said. "I'm sorry."

"Don't worry about it," Stig said. "The carpet's washable. Now we have to get you two home."

It was only then that fear gripped me.

"What's the time?" I asked.

"Almost one."

"No later? Oh, well, that's okay. I said I would be at home by one. I'll just be a few minutes late."

Stig didn't drink, and we followed him down to the car, got in, Jan Vidar in the front, me in the back.

"Do you really not remember anything?" Jan Vidar asked me as we drove off.

"No, I don't, nothing at all."

That made me proud. The whole story, what I had said and what I had done, even the vomiting, made me feel proud. It was close to the person I wanted to be. But when Stig stopped the car by the mailboxes and I walked up the dark driveway clad in someone else's clothes, with my own in a bag hanging from my wrist, I was scared.

Please let them be in bed. Please let them be in bed.

And it looked as if they were. The kitchen lights were off at any rate, and that was always the last thing they did before going to bed. But when I opened the door and tiptoed into the hall, I could hear their voices. They were upstairs on the sofa by the TV chatting. They never did that.

Were they waiting for me? Were they checking up on me? My father was the type to smell my breath. His parents had done that, they laughed about it now, but I bet he hadn't at the time.

It would have been impossible to sneak past them, the top of the stairs was right next to them. May as well face the music.

"Hello?" I said. "Anyone up there?"

"Hello, Karl Ove," Mom said.

I trudged up the stairs and stopped when I was in their field of vision.

They were sitting beside each other on the sofa, Dad with his arm resting on the side.

"Did you have a nice time?" Mom asked.

Couldn't she *see*?

I couldn't believe it.

"It was okay," I said, advancing a few steps. "We watched TV and had some lasagne."

"Nice," Mom said.

"But I'm pretty tired," I said. "Think I'll hit the hay."

"You do that," she said. "We'll be on our way soon."

I stood on the floor four meters from them, wearing someone else's jogging pants, someone else's sweatshirt, with my own soiled clothes in a plastic bag. And reeking of booze. But they didn't notice.

"Good night then," I said.

"Good night," they said.

And that was that. I didn't understand how I had managed it; I just accepted my good fortune. I hid the bag of clothes in a cupboard, and the next time I was alone in the house I rinsed them in the bath, hung them up to dry in the bedroom wardrobe, then put them in the laundry basket as usual.

Not a word from anyone.

Drinking was good for me; it set things in motion. And I was thrust into something, a feeling of . . . not infinity exactly, but of, well, something unlimited. Something I could go into, deeper and deeper. The feeling was so sharp and distinct.

No bounds. That was what it was, a feeling of boundlessness.

So I was full of anticipation. And even though it had passed off well enough previously I had taken a few precautionary measures this time. I would take a toothbrush and toothpaste with me, and I had bought eucalyptus pastilles, Freshmint, and chewing gum. And I would take an extra shirt.

In the living room below I could hear Dad's voice. I sat up, stretched my arms over my head, bent them backward, then stretched them out as far as they would go, first one way, then the other. My joints ached, and had all autumn. I was growing. In the ninth-class photograph, taken in late spring, my height was average. Now I was suddenly approaching six two. My great fear was that I would not stop there but just keep growing. There was a boy in the class above me at school who was close to six eight, and as thin as a rake. That I might follow in his shoes was something I imagined with horror several times a day. Now and then I prayed to God, in whom I did not believe, not to let this happen. I didn't believe in God, but I had prayed to him as a young boy, and doing it now was as if my childlike hope had returned. Dear God, please let me stop growing, I prayed. Let me stay six two, let me reach six two and a half or six three, but no more! I promise to be as good as gold if you do. Dear God, dear God, can you hear me?

Oh, I knew it was stupid, but I did it anyway, there was nothing stupid about my fear, it was just unbearable. Another even greater fear I had at that time was the one I had experienced on discovering that my dick was bent upright when I had an erection. I was deformed, it was misshapen, and ignorant as I was, I didn't know if there was anything you could do about it, have an operation or whatever options there had been then. At night I got out of bed, went to the bathroom and made myself erect to see if it had changed. But no, it never had. It was nearly touching my bloody stomach! And wasn't it crooked as well? It was as crooked and distorted as a fucking tree root in the forest. That meant I would never be able to go to bed with anyone. Since that was the only thing I really wanted, or dreamt about, my despair knew no bounds. It did enter my head of course that I could pull it down. And I did try, I pushed it down as far as it would go, until it ached. It was straighter. But it hurt. And you couldn't have sex with a girl with your hand on your dick like that, could you? What the hell should I do? Was there anything I could do? This preyed on my mind. Every time I had a hard-on, I was desperate. If I was making out with a girl on a sofa, and perhaps got my hand up her sweater, and my dick was as stiff as a ramrod against my trouser leg, I knew that was the closest I would get, and it would always be the closest I would get. It was worse than impotence because this not only rendered me incapable of action, but it was also grotesque. But could I pray to God for this to stop? Yes, in the end I could, and did, too. Dear God, I prayed. Dear God, let my sexual organ straighten when it fills with blood. I will only pray for this once. So please be kind and let my wish come true.

When I started at gymnas all the first-years were assembled one morning on the stage at Gimle Hall, I no longer remember the occasion, but one of the teachers, a notorious nudist from Kristiansand, who was said to have painted his house wearing no more than a tie, and was generally scruffy, dressed in a provincial bohemian manner, had curly, unkempt, white hair, anyway he read us a poem, walking along the rows on the stage proclaiming and, to general laughter, suddenly singing the praises of the upright erection.

I didn't laugh. I think my jaw fell when I heard that. With mouth agape and eyes vacant I sat there as the insight slowly sank in. All erect dicks are bent. Or, if not all, then at least enough of them to be eulogized in a poem.

Where did the grotesqueness come from? Only two years earlier, when we moved here, I had been a small thirteen-year-old with smooth skin, unable to articulate my "r"s and more than happy to swim, cycle, and play soccer in the new place where, so far at least, no one had it in for me. Quite the opposite, in fact, during the first few days at school everyone wanted to talk to me, a new pupil was a rare phenomenon there, everyone wondered of course who I was, what I could do. In the afternoons and on weekends girls sometimes cycled all the way from Hamresanden to meet me. I could be playing soccer with Per, Trygve, Tom, and William when, who was that cycling along the road, two girls, what did they want? Our house was the last; beyond it there was just forest, then two farms, then forest, forest and more forest. They jumped off their bikes on the hill, glanced across at us, disappeared behind the trees. Cycled down again, stopped, looked.

"What are they doing?" Trygve asked.

"They've come to see Karl Ove," Per said.

"You're kidding," Trygve said. "They can't have cycled all the way from Hamresanden for *that*. That's got to be ten kilometers!"

"What else would they come up here for? They certainly didn't come here to see you," Per said. "You've always been here, haven't you."

We stood watching them scramble through the bushes. One was wearing a pink jacket, the other light blue. Long hair.

"Come on," Trygve said. "Let's play."

And we continued to play on the tongue of land extending into the river where Per's and Tom's father had knocked together two goals. The girls stopped when they came to the swathe of rushes about a hundred meters away. I knew who they were, they were nothing special, so I ignored them, and after standing there in the reeds for ten minutes, like some strange birds, they walked back and cycled home. Another time, a few weeks later, three girls came up to us while we were working in the large warehouse at the parquet factory. We were stacking short planks onto pallets, each layer separated by stays, it was piecework, and once I had learned to throw an armful at a time, so that they fell into place, there was a bit of money in it. We could come and go as we pleased, we often popped in on the way home from school and did one stack, then went home and had a bite to eat, went back and stayed for the rest of the evening. We were so hungry for money we could have worked every evening and every weekend, but often there wasn't anything to do, either because we had filled the warehouse or because the factory workers had done the work during their normal hours. Per's father worked in the office, so it was either through Per or William, whose father was employed as a truck driver for the firm, that the eagerly awaited announcement came: there is work. It was on one such evening that the three girls came to see us in the warehouse. They lived in Hamresanden too. This time I had been warned, a rumor had been circulating that one of the girls in the seventh class was interested in me, and there she was, considerably bolder than the two wading birds in the rushes, for Line, that was her name, came straight over to me and rested her arms on the frame around the stack, stood there confidently chewing gum, watching what I was doing while her two friends kept in the background. On hearing that she was interested, I had thought that I should strike while the iron was hot, for even though she was only in the seventh class, her sister was a model, and even if she hadn't gotten that far herself yet, she was going to be good. That was what everyone said about her, she was going to be good, that was what everyone praised, her potential. She was slim and long-legged, had long, dark hair, was pale with high cheekbones and a disproportionately large mouth. This lanky, slightly gangly and calflike quality of hers made me skeptical. But her hips were nice. And her mouth and eyes too. Another factor to count against her was that she could not say her "r"s, and there was something a tad stupid or scatterbrained about her. She was known for it. At the same time she was popular in her class, the girls there all wanted to be with her.

"Hi," she said. "I've come to visit you. Does that make you happy?"

"There you go," I said. Turned aside, balanced a pile of planks on my forearm, hurled them into the frame where they clattered into place, pushed in the ones sticking out, grabbed another armful.

"How much do you earn an hour?" she asked.

"It's piecework," I said. "We get twenty kroner for a stack of doubles, forty for a stack of fours."

"I see," she said.

Per and Trygve, who were in the parallel class to hers, and had repeatedly expressed their disapproval of her and her crowd, were working a few meters away. It struck me that they looked like dwarfs. Short, bent forward, grim-faced, they stood in the middle of the enormous factory floor with pallets up to the roof on all sides, working.

"Do you like me?" she asked.

"Well, what's not to like?" I said. The moment I had seen her coming through the gates I had decided to go for it, but now, with her standing there and an open road ahead, I still couldn't do it, I still couldn't come up with the goods. In a way I didn't quite understand, yet sensed nonetheless, she was far more sophisticated than I was. Okay, she may have been a bit dim, but she was sophisticated. And it was this sophistication that I could not handle.

"I like you," she said. "But you already know that, don't you."

I leaned forward and adjusted one of the stays, flushing quite unexpectedly.

"No," I said.

Then she didn't say anything for a while, just lolled over the frame, chewing gum. Her girlfriends over by the pile of planks appeared impatient. In the end, she straightened up.

"Right," she said, turned and was gone.

Passing up the opportunity was not a huge problem for me; far more important was the way it had happened, not having the pluck to take the final steps, to cross that last bridge. And when the novelty interest in me had died down nothing was served on a plate anymore. On the contrary, the old judgments of me slowly trickled back. I could sense them close at hand, felt the reverberations, even though there was no contact between the two places I had lived. On the very first day at school I had spotted a particular girl, her name was Inger, she had beautiful narrow eyes, a dark complexion, a childish short nose which broke up otherwise long, rounded features, and she exuded distance, except when she smiled. She had a liberating, gentle smile that I admired and found endlessly appealing, both because it did not embrace me or others like me, it belonged to the very essence of her being, to which only she herself and her friends had recourse, and also because her top lip was slightly twisted. She was in the class below me, and in the course of the two years I spent at that school I never exchanged a single word with her. Instead, I got together with her cousin, Susanne. She was in the parallel class to mine, and lived in a house on the other side of the river. Her nose was pointed, her mouth small, and her front teeth a touch harelike, but her breasts were well-rounded and pert, her hips just the right width and her eyes provocative, as if they were always clear about what they wanted. She was always comparing herself with others. Whereas Inger in all her unattainability was full of mystery and secrets, and her appeal consisted almost entirely of things unknown, suspicions, and dreams, Susanne was more of an equal and more likeminded. With her I had less to lose, less to fear, but also less to gain. I was fourteen years old, she was fifteen and within a few days we drifted together, as can often happen at that age. Shortly afterward Jan Vidar got together with her friend, Margrethe. Our relationships were located somewhere between the world of the child and that of the adult and the boundaries between the two were fluid. We sat on the same seat on the school bus in the morning, sat beside each other when the whole school gathered for morning assembly on Fridays, cycled together to the confirmation classes held once a week in the church, and hung out together afterward, at an intersection or in the parking lot outside the shop, all situations where the differences between us were played down and Susanne and Margrethe were like pals. But on weekends it was different, then we might go to the cinema in town or sit in some cellar room eating pizza and drinking Coke while we watched TV or listened to music, entwined in each other's arms. It was getting closer, the thing we were all thinking about. What had been a huge step forward a few weeks ago, the kiss, had long been achieved: Jan Vidar and I had discussed the procedure, the practical details, such as which side to sit, what to say to initiate the process that would culminate in the kiss, or whether to act without saying anything at all. By now it was well on the way to becoming mechanical: after eating pizza or lasagne the girls sat on our laps and we started canoodling. Occasionally we stretched out on the sofa too, one couple at each end, if we felt sure no one would come. One Friday evening Susanne was alone at home. Jan Vidar cycled up to my place in the afternoon, we set off along the river, over the narrow footbridge and up to the house where she lived. They were waiting for us. Her parents had made a pizza, we ate it, Susanne sat on my lap, Margrethe on Jan Vidar's, Dire Straits was on the stereo, "Telegraph Road," and I was kissing Susanne, and Jan Vidar was fooling around with Margrethe, for what seemed like an eternity in the living room. *I love you, Karl Ove,* she whispered in my ear after a while. *Shall we go to my room?* I nodded, and we got up, holding hands.

"We're going to my room," she said to the two others. "So you can have a bit of peace here."

They looked up at us and nodded. Then they went back to it. Margrethe's long, black hair almost completely covered Jan Vidar's face. Their tongues went round and round in each other's mouths. He was stroking her back, up and down his fingers went, his body otherwise motionless. Susanne sent me a smile, squeezed my hand harder, and led me through the hall and into her bedroom. It was dark inside, and colder. I had been there before, and liked being in her house, even though her parents were always there, and in principle we only did what Jan Vidar and I normally did, that is, we sat chatting, moved into the living room and watched TV with her parents, had a bite to eat in the kitchen, went for long walks along the river, for this was not Jan Vidar's dark, sweaty room we were sitting in, with his amplifier and stereo equipment, his guitar and records, his guitar magazines and comics, no, this was Susanne's light, perfumed room, with its white flowery wallpaper, its embroidered bedspread, its white shelf full of ornaments and books, its white cupboard with her clothes nicely folded and hung up. When I saw a pair of her blue jeans there, or hanging over a chair, I gulped, because she would be pulling these very trousers over her thighs, hips, zipping up and buttoning. Her room was filled with such promise, which I could barely put it into words, it just sent surges of emotion through me. There were other reasons I liked being there. Her parents, for example; they were always friendly, and there was something in the family's manner that made it clear I meant something to them. I was a person in Susanne's life, someone she told her parents and younger sister about.

Now she went over to close the window. Outside it was misty, even the lights in the neighboring houses were almost invisible in the grayness. On the road below, a few cars drove past with their stereos throbbing. Then it went quiet again.

"Hmm," I said.

She smiled.

"Hmm," she said, sitting down on the edge of the bed. I had no expectations, other than that we would lie here rather than nestling against each other. Once I had put my hand inside her Puffa jacket and placed it on a breast, and she had said no, and I had removed it again. The "no" had not been sharp or reproachful, more a statement of fact, as if it invoked some law to which we were subject. We did some caressing, that was what we did, and even though I was always ready for it whenever we met, I soon became tired of it. After a while I felt almost nauseous because there was something futile and unresolved about this caressing, my whole being longed for a way out, which I knew existed, but it was not a route that could be taken. I wanted to move on, but was forced to remain where I was, in the vale of rotating tongues and hair perpetually falling over my face.

I sat down beside her. She smiled at me. I kissed her, she closed her eyes and leaned back onto the bed. I crawled up on top of her, felt her soft body beneath mine, she groaned a little, was I too heavy? I lay beside her instead, with my leg over hers. Caressed her shoulder and down, along her arm. When my hand reached her fingers she squeezed it hard. I lifted my head and opened my eyes. She was looking at me. Her face, white in the semi-darkness, was serious. I bent forward and kissed her neck. I had never done that before. Rested my head on her chest. She ran her hand through my hair. I could hear her heart beating. I stroked her hips. She tensed. I lifted her top and placed my hand on her stomach. Leaned forward and kissed it. She grabbed the hem of her top and slowly pulled it up. I couldn't believe my eyes. There, right in front of me, were her naked breasts. In the living room, "Telegraph Road" was played again. I did not hesitate and closed my mouth around them. First one, then the other. I rubbed my cheeks against them, licked them, sucked them, finally put my hands on them and kissed her, for a few seconds I had completely forgotten her. My dreams or imagination had never stretched beyond this point, and now I was there, but after ten minutes there was the same sense of satedness, all of a sudden it was not enough, not even this, however great it was, I wanted to move on wherever it led, and made an attempt, started fumbling with her trouser button. It came open, she said nothing, lay with her eyes closed as before and her sweater pulled up under her chin. I undid the zip. Her white panties came into view. I swallowed hard. I tugged her trousers around her hips and drew them down. She said nothing. Wriggled a bit so that it was easier to remove them. When they were down to her knees I put my hand on her panties. Felt the soft hair beneath. *Karl Ove*, she said. I lay on top of her again, we kissed, and while we kissed I pulled down her panties, not a lot, but enough to slip in a finger, it glided down through the hair, and the moment I felt her moistness against my fingertip, something in me seemed to crack. It was like a pain shooting through my abdomen, followed by a kind of spasm in my loins. The next second everything was alien to me. From one moment to the next, her naked breasts and her naked thighs lost all meaning. But I could see that she was not having the same experience as me, she was lying as before, with eyes closed, mouth half-open, breathing heavily, engrossed in what I had been engrossed, but was not any longer.

"What's the matter?" she asked.

"Nothing," I said. "But perhaps we should join the others?"

"No," she said. "Let's wait a bit."

"Okay," I said.

So we resumed. We embraced, but it did not arouse anything in me, I might just as well have been cutting a slice of bread, I kissed her breasts, that aroused nothing in me, everything was strangely neutral, her nipples were nipples, her skin was skin, her navel a navel, but then to my amazement and delight, everything about her suddenly changed back, and again there was nothing I would rather do than lie there kissing everything I touched.

That was when someone knocked on the door.

We sat up; she quickly wriggled her trousers into position and pulled down her top.

It was Jan Vidar.

"Are you coming out?" he asked.

"Yes," said Susanne. "We're on our way. Hang on."

"It's half past ten, you know," he said. "We'd better be off before your parents come back."

While Jan Vidar was collecting his records I met Susanne's eyes and smiled at her. When we were in the hall, ready to go, about to kiss them goodbye, she winked at me.

"See you tomorrow!" she said.

Outside, it was drizzling. The light from the streetlamps we walked under seemed to merge with every single water particle in large haloes.

"Well?" I said. "How did it go?"

"The usual," said Jan Vidar. "We made out. I'm not sure I want to be with her much longer."

"Oh yeah," I said. "You're not exactly in love then."

"Are you?"

I shrugged.

"Maybe not."

We arrived at the main road and set off up the valley. On one side there was a farm, the waterlogged ground that glistened in the light by the road disappeared in the darkness and did not reappear until the farmhouse, which was brightly illuminated. On the other side there were a couple of old houses with gardens reaching down to the river.

"How did it go with you?" Jan Vidar asked.

"Pretty well," I said. "She took off her top."

"What? Really?"

I nodded.

"You're lying, come on! She didn't."

"She did."

"Not Susanne surely?"

"She did."

"What did you do then?"

"Kissed her breasts. What else?"

"You lying toad. You didn't."

"I did."

I didn't have the heart to tell him she had also taken off her panties. If he had made any progress with Margrethe, I would have told him. But as he hadn't I didn't want to brag. Besides, he would never have believed me. Never.

I could hardly believe it myself.

"What were they like?" he asked.

"What were what like?"

"Her breasts of course."

"They were great. Just the right size and firm. Very firm. Stood up even though she was lying down."

"You bastard. It's not true."

"It is, for Christ's sake."

"Shit."

After that we didn't say anymore. Crossed the suspension bridge where the river, so shiny and black, silently swelled, went through the strawberry field, and onto the tarmac road which, after a sharp bend, climbed a steep pass with black spruce trees leaning over, and then after a couple of curves at the top passed our house. Everything was dark and heavy and wet, apart from my consciousness of what had happened, which overrode everything and rose to the light like bubbles. Jan Vidar had accepted my explanation, and I was burning to tell him that her breasts were not the whole story, there was more, but as soon as I saw his sullen look I let it go. And that was fine too, to keep it a secret between Susanne and me. Yet the spasm worried me. I had almost no pubes on my dick, just a couple of long, black hairs, otherwise it was mostly down, and one of the things I feared was that this would come to the ears of the girls, and in particular Susanne's. I knew I couldn't sleep with anyone until the hair was in situ, so I assumed the spasm was a kind of false orgasm, and that I had done more and gone further than what my dick was actually up to. And that was why it had hurt. That I had had a kind of "dry" ejaculation. For all I knew it might be dangerous. On the other hand, my underpants were wet. It might be pee, it might also be semen. Or blood even? The latter two I considered unlikely, after all I was not sexually mature, and I had not experienced pains in my loins until that moment. Whatever the reason, it had hurt, and I was concerned.

Jan Vidar had left his bike outside our garage, we stood there chatting, then he cycled home, and I went in. Yngve was at home that weekend, he was sitting with Mom in the kitchen. I could see them through the window. Dad must have been in the flat in the barn. After taking off my outdoor clothes, I went to the toilet, locked the door, dropped my trousers to my knees, lifted my underpants and pressed my forefinger against the damp patch. It was sticky. I raised my finger, rubbed it against my thumb. Shiny and sticky. Smelt of the sea.

Sea?

That must be semen then?

Of course it was semen.

I was sexually mature.

Exultant, I went into the kitchen.

"Do you want some pizza? We saved a few slices for you," Mom said.

"No thanks. We ate out there."

"Did you have a good time?"

"Of course," I said, unable to suppress a smile.

"His cheeks are all red," Yngve said. "Is that with happiness, I wonder?"

"You'll have to invite her here one day," Mom said.

"Yes, I will," I said and just went on smiling.

The relationship with Susanne came to an end two weeks later. Long ago I had made a deal with Lars, my best friend in Tromøya, to swap pictures of the most beautiful girls there with pictures of the most beautiful girls here. Don't ask me why. I had forgotten all about it until one afternoon when I received an envelope in the mail containing photographs. Passport photos of Lene, Beate, Ellen, Siv, Bente, Marianne, Anne Lisbet, or whatever they were all called. They were Tromøya's finest. Now I had to get my hands on pictures of Tveit's finest. I conferred regularly with Jan Vidar over the next days, we drew up a list and then all I had to do was get hold of the photos. I could ask some girls directly, such as Susann, the friend of Jan Vidar's sister, who was old enough for me to care about what she thought; I could get Jan Vidar to ask others for pictures of their girlfriends. As for myself, my hands were tied because asking for a photo was tantamount to showing an interest in them, and since I was going out with Susanne such an interest would be inappropriate enough for rumors to spread. But there were other methods. Per, for example, did he have any photos of Kristin in his class perhaps? He did, and in this way I eventually managed to scrape together six photos. That was more than enough, but the jewel in the crown, the most beautiful of them all, Inger, whom I very much wanted to show Lars, was missing. And Inger was Susanne's cousin . . .

So one afternoon I got my bike out of the garage and cycled to Susanne's. We hadn't made any arrangement and she seemed happy when she came downstairs to answer the door. I said hello to her parents, we went to her room and sat down for a while, discussed what we would do, without making any plans, chatted a bit about school and the teachers, before I presented my question as casually as I could. Did she have a photo of Inger I could borrow?

Sitting on the bed, she stiffened and stared at me with incredulity.

"Of Inger?" she queried, at length. "What do you want that for?"

It hadn't occurred to me that this might cause a problem. After all, I was going out with Susanne, and the fact that I was asking her, of all people, could only imply that my motives were pure.

"I can't tell you," I said.

And it was true. If I told her that I was going to send photos of the eight most attractive girls in Tveit to a pal in Tromøya she would expect to be among them. She was not, and I could not tell her that.

"You're not having a photo of Inger until you tell me what you're going to do with it," she said.

"But I can't," I said. "Can't you just give me a photo? It's not for me if that's what you're thinking."

"Who's it for then?"

"I can't say."

She got up. I could see she was furious. All her movements were truncated, clipped as it were, as if she no longer wanted to give me the pleasure of seeing them unfold freely and thereby let me share their fullness.

"You're in love with Inger, aren't you," she said.

I didn't answer.

"Karl Ove! Aren't you? I've heard lots of people say you are."

"Let's forget about the photo," I said. "Forget it."

"So you are?"

"No," I said. "Perhaps I was when I first moved here, right at the beginning, but I am not any longer."

"What do you want the photo for then?"

"I can't tell you."

She started to cry.

"You are,' she said. "You're in love with Inger. I know you are. I know."

If Susanne knew, it suddenly struck me, then Inger must know as well.

A sort of light flashed in my head. If she knew, then it might not be so difficult to get off with Inger. At a school party, for example, I could go over and ask her to dance and she would know what was what, would know she was not just one among many. She might even begin to show some interest in me. Sobbing, Susanne went to her desk at the other end of the room and pulled out a drawer.

"Here's your photo," she said. "Take it, and I never want to see you here again."

She held one hand in front of her face and handed me the photo of Inger with the other. Her shoulders were quivering.

"It's not for me," I said. "I promise. It's not me who wants it."

"You sack of shit," she said. "Get out of here!"

I took the photo.

"Is it over then?" I asked.

Two years had passed since that freezing cold, windblown New Year's Eve when I lay on my bed reading while waiting for the night's festivities to begin. Susanne had found someone else just a few months later. His name was Terje; he was small, plump, with a perm and an idiotic moustache. To me it was incredible that she could allow someone like him to take my place. All right, he was eighteen years old and, fair enough, he did have a car which they drove around in after school and on the weekends, but nevertheless: him instead of me? A short, fat dolt with a moustache? In that case, it definitely didn't matter about Susanne. That was what I had thought, and that was what I still thought, lying on the bed. However, now I was no longer a child, now I was sixteen years old, now I wasn't at Ve Middle School but Kristiansand Cathedral School.

From outside came the grating, unlubricated sound of the garage door being opened. The thud as it fell into position, the car being started straight afterward, its engine idling briefly. I went to the window and waited until the two red lights vanished around the bend. Then I went downstairs to the kitchen and boiled some water, took some of the Christmas fare, ham, brawn, lamb sausage, liver paté, cut a few slices of bread, fetched the newspaper from the living room, spread it out over the table and sat down to read it as I ate. It was pitch-black outside now. Inside it was nice and cozy with the red cloth on the table and the small candles flickering on the windowsill. When the water was boiling I warmed the teapot, dropped a couple of fingerfuls of tea leaves, and poured on the steaming hot water, calling: "Mom, do you want any tea?"

No answer.

I sat down and kept eating. After a while I picked up the teapot and poured. Dark brown, almost like wood, the tea rose inside the white cup. A few leaves swirled and floated up, the others lay like a black mat at the bottom. I added milk, three teaspoons of sugar, stirred, waited until the leaves had settled on the bottom, and drank.

Mmm.

Down on the road a snowplow raced past with lights flashing. Then the front door was opened. I heard the sound of shoes being kicked against the step and turned in time to see Mom, wearing Dad's capacious lambskin jacket, come in the door with an armful of wood.

Why was she wearing his clothes? That wasn't like her.

She went into the living room without a glance in my direction. She had snow in her hair and on her lapels. A loud thud in the wood basket.

"Would you like some tea?" I asked when she came back.

"Yes, please," she said. "I'll just get my things off first."

I stood up and found her a cup, placed it on the other side of the table and poured.

"Where have you been?" I asked as she sat down.

"Out fetching wood, that's all," she said.

"But before that? I've been sitting here for a while. It doesn't take twenty minutes to fetch wood, does it."

"Oh, I was changing a lightbulb on the Christmas tree. So now it works."

I turned and looked through the window in the other room. The spruce tree at the end of our plot glittered in the darkness.

"Is there anything I can do to help?" I asked.

"No, everything's ready now. I just need to iron a blouse. And then there's nothing to do until the food has to be cooked. But Dad'll do that."

"Could you iron my shirt while you're at it?" I asked.

She nodded.

"Just put it on the ironing table."

After eating I went up to my room, switched on the amplifier, plugged in the guitar, and sat down to play a little. I loved the smell the amplifier gave off when it got warm, I could play for that reason alone, almost. I also loved all the accessories guitar-playing involved, the fuzz box, the chorus pedal, the leads, the plugs, the plectrums, and the small packets of strings, the bottleneck, the capo, the lined guitar case and all its small compartments. I loved the brand names: Gibson, Fender, Hagstrøm, Rickenbacker, Marshall, Music Man, Vox, and Roland. I went into music shops with Jan Vidar and inspected the guitars with the air of a cognoscente. For my own guitar, a cheap Stratocaster imitation I had bought with my confirmation money, I had ordered new pick-ups, state of the art I was told, and a new pick guard from one of Jan Vidar's mail order catalogues. All that was great. The playing, on the other hand, was not so great. Even though I had been playing regularly and tenaciously for a year and a half, I had made very little progress. I knew all the chords and had practiced all the scales ad infinitum, but I never managed to free myself from them, never managed to *play*, there was no rapport between my mind and my fingers, my fingers didn't seem to belong to me, but to the scales, which they could play with ease, and what then emerged from the amplifier had nothing to do with music. I could spend a day or two learning a solo note by note, and then I could play it, but no more than that, it always stopped there. It was the same for Jan Vidar. But he was even more ambitious than me, he really practiced a lot, he did virtually nothing else at times, but his amplifier too produced nothing more than scales and copies of solos. He filed his nails so that they would be better for playing with, he let the nail of his right thumb grow so that he could use it as a pick, he bought a kind of training apparatus for his fingers which he was always flexing to strengthen them, he rebuilt his guitar, and with his father, who was an electrical engineer in Kjevik, he experimented with a kind of homemade guitar synthesizer. I often took my guitar to his place, the case dangling from one hand, while I steered my bike with the other, and even though what we played in his room didn't sound brilliant, it was still okay because I at least *felt* like a musician when I was carrying the case, it looked really cool, and if we were not yet where we would like to be, things might well change one day. We didn't know what the future might hold; no one could know how much practice was necessary for the situation to ease. A month? Six months? A year? In the meantime we kept playing. We also managed to get a sort of band up and running; one Jan Henrik in the seventh class could play a bit of guitar, and even though he wore yachting shoes and posh clothes and used hair cream we asked him if he wanted to play bass with us. He did, and I, being the worst guitarist, had to start playing drums. The summer we were about to begin the ninth class, Jan Vidar's father drove us up to Evje where we picked up a cheap drum kit we had pooled together to buy, and we were all set. We spoke to the headmaster, were given permission to use a classroom, and once a week we assembled the drums and amplifiers and away we went.

The year before, when I moved, I had been listening to groups like The Clash, The Police, The Specials, Teardrop Explodes, The Cure, Joy Division, New Order, Echo and the Bunnymen, The Chameleons, Simple Minds,

Utravox, The Aller Værste, Talking Heads, The B52s, PiL, David Bowie, The Psychedelic Furs, Iggy Pop, and Velvet Underground, all of them via Yngve, who not only spent all his money on music but also played guitar, with his very own sound and distinctive style, and wrote his own songs. In Tveit there was no one who had even heard of all these groups. Jan Vidar, for example, listened to people like Deep Purple, Rainbow, Gillan, Whitesnake, Black Sabbath, Ozzy Osbourne, Def Leppard, and Judas Priest. It was impossible for these worlds to meet, and since an interest in music was what we shared, one of us had to give way. Me. I never bought any records by these bands but I listened to them at Jan Vidar's and familiarized myself with them whereas I reserved my own bands, who at that time were extremely important to me, for when I was alone. And then there were a few "compromise bands," which both he and I liked, first and foremost Led Zeppelin, but also Dire Straits, for his part because of the guitar riffs. Our most frequent discussion concerned feeling versus technique. Jan Vidar would buy records by a group called Lava because they were such good musicians, and he wasn't averse to TOTO, who had their two hits at that time, while I despised technique with all my heart, it went against everything I had learned from reading my brother's music magazines, where musical competence was the foe, and the ideal was creativity, energy, and power. But no matter how much we talked about this or how many hours we spent in music shops or poring over mail order catalogues, we couldn't get our band to swing, we were useless at our instruments, and remained so, and we did not have the wit to compensate, by writing our own music for example, oh no, we played the most hackneyed, uninventive cover versions of them all: "Smoke on the Water" by Deep Purple, "Paranoid" by Black Sabbath, "Black Magic Woman" by Santana, as well as "So Lonely" by The Police, which had to be in our repertoire because Yngve had taught me the chords for it.

We were utterly hopeless, completely out of our depth, there was not a snowball's chance in hell of anything coming of this, we wouldn't even be good enough to perform at a school party, but although this was the reality we never experienced it as such. On the contrary, this was what gave our lives meaning. It wasn't my music we played, but Jan Vidar's, and it went against everything I believed in, yet this is what I trusted. The intro to "Smoke on the Water," the very incarnation of stupidity, the very antithesis of cool, was what I sat practicing at Ve School in 1983: first the guitar riff, then the cymbal, *chicka-chicka, chicka-chicka, chicka-chicka, chicka-chicka*, then the bass drum, *boom, boom, boom*, then the snare, *tick, tick, tick*, and then the stupid bass line kicked in, where we often looked at each other with a smile while nodding our heads and shaking our legs as the chorus, played completely out of sync, took off. We didn't have a vocalist. When Jan Vidar started at technical college he heard about a drummer from Hånes, admittedly he was only in the eighth class, but he would have to do, everything had to do, and he also had access to a practice room out there, with drums and PA, the whole thing, so there we were: me, first-year gymnas student dreaming about a life in indie music, but unmusical, on rhythm guitar; Jan Vidar, trainee pâtissier who practiced enough to be a Yngwie Malmsteen, an Eddie van Halen, or a Ritchie Blackmore, but who couldn't free himself from his finger exercises, on lead guitar; Jan Henrik whom we would have preferred to avoid outside the group, on bass, and Øyvind, a happy, thickset kid from Hånes without any ambitions at all, on drums. "Smoke on the Water," "Paranoid," "Black Magic Woman," "So Lonely" and, eventually, early Bowie's "Ziggy Stardust" and "Hang onto Yourself," for which Yngve had also taught me the chords. No singer, only the accompaniment. Every weekend. Guitar cases on the bus, long conversations on the beach about music and instruments, on the benches outside the shop, in Jan Vidar's room, in the airport café, in Kristiansand. Later on, we recorded our practice sessions, which we carefully analyzed in our futile, doomed attempt to raise the band to the level we were at in our heads.

Once I had taken a cassette recording of our sessions to school. I stood in the break with the headset on listening to our music while wondering whom I could play it to. Bassen had the same musical taste as I did, so that was no use, because this was quite different, and he would not understand it. Hanne maybe? She was a singer after all, and I liked her a lot. But that would be too big a risk to take. She knew I played in a band and that was good, it gave me a kind of elevated status, but my status might crumble if she heard us playing. Pål? Yes, he could listen to it. He played in a band himself, Vampire it was called, played fast, Metallica-inspired. Pål who was usually shy, sensitive, and delicate to the point of being almost effeminate, but who wore black leather, played bass, and howled onstage like the devil incarnate, he would understand what we were doing. So in the next break I went over to him, told him we had recorded a few songs the previous weekend, would he have a listen and say what he thought? Of course. He put on the headset and pressed play while I anxiously scrutinized his face. He smiled and stared at me quizzically. After a few minutes he started laughing and removed the headset.

"This is crap, Karl Ove," he said. "This is a joke. Why are you bothering me with this? Why should I listen to this stuff? Are you kidding me?"

"Crap? What do you mean crap?"

"You can't play. And you don't sing. There's nothing in it!"

He threw out his arms.

"I'm sure we can improve," I said.

"Give up," he said.

Do you think your band is so great then? I thought of saying, but I didn't.

"Okay, okay," I said instead. "Thanks, anyway."

He laughed again and sent me a look of astonishment. No one could fathom Pål because of his whole speed-metal thing, and the clueless side of him which made the class laugh, and which did not square with his shyness at all, which in turn did not square at all with the almost complete openness he could display making him unafraid of anything. Once, for example, he showed us a poem he had had published in a girls' magazine, *Det Nye*, which had also interviewed him. Outspoken, brazen, sensitive, shy, aggressive, rough. That was Pål. In a way it was good that it was Pål who heard our band because Pål's response didn't mean anything, whatever made him laugh didn't matter. So I calmly put the Walkman back in my pocket and went into class. He was probably right that we weren't very good. But since when was it important to be good? Hadn't he heard of punk? New Wave? None of those bands could play. But they had guts. Power. Soul. Presence.

Not long after this, in early autumn 1984, we got our first gig. Øyvind had set it up for us. Håne Shopping Center was celebrating its fifth anniversary; the occasion was to be marked with balloons, cakes, and music. The Bøksle Brothers, who had been famous all over the region for two decades with their interpretations of Sørland folk songs, were going to play. Then the center owner also wanted something local, preferably with some youth interest, and, since we practiced only a few hundred meters from the mall, we fitted the bill perfectly. We were to play for twenty minutes and would be paid five hundred kroner for the job. We hugged Øyvind when he told us. At long last it was our turn.

The two weeks before the gig, which was scheduled for eleven o'clock on a Saturday morning, passed quickly. We rehearsed several times, the whole band and Jan Vidar and I on our own, we discussed the order of our set list to and fro and back and forth, we bought new strings well in advance so that we could break them in, we decided what clothes we would wear, and when the day arrived we met early in the practice room to go through the set several times before the performance, for even though we were aware there was a risk we would peak too soon, we figured it was more important to feel at home with the songs.

How good I felt as I strolled across the parking lot of the shopping center, guitar case in hand. The equipment was already set up on one side of the passage leading to the square in the middle. Øyvind was adjusting the drum set, Jan Vidar was tuning his guitar with the new tuner he had bought for the occasion. Some kids were standing around watching. Soon they would be watching me too. I'd had my hair cut very short, I had a green military jacket on, black jeans, studded belt, blue-and-white baseball cleats. And of course the guitar case in my hand.

On the other side of the passage the Bøksle Brothers were already singing. A small crowd of people, maybe ten in all, was watching. There was a steady stream of passersby on their way to or from the shops. The wind was blowing, and something about it reminded me of The Beatles' concert on the roof of the Apple building in 1970.

"Everything alright?" I asked Jan Vidar, put down the guitar case, took out the guitar, found the strap and hung it over my shoulder.

"Yeah," he said. "Shall we plug in? What time is it, Øyvind?"

"Ten minutes past."

"Ten to go. Let's wait a bit. Five minutes, okay?"

He went over to the amplifier and took a swig of Coke. Around his forehead he had tied a rolled-up scarf. Otherwise he was wearing a white shirt with the tails hanging over a pair of black trousers.

The Bøksle Brothers were still singing.

I glanced at the set list stuck up behind the amplifier.

Smoke on the Water
Paranoid
Black Magic Woman
So Lonely

"Can I borrow the tuner?" I asked Jan Vidar. He passed it to me, and I plugged in the lead. The guitar was tuned, but I fiddled with the knobs anyway. Several cars drove into the parking area and slowly circled, looking for an empty spot. As soon as the doors were open the children on the rear seats crawled out, ran around a bit on the tarmac and grabbed their parents' hands on their way towards us. Everyone stared as they went by, no one stopped.

Jan Henrik plugged his bass into the amplifier and twanged a string hard. It resounded across the tarmac.

BOOM.

BOOM. BOOM. BOOM.

Both the Bøksle Brothers glared over at us while they were singing. Jan Henrik stepped over to the amp and fiddled with the volume button. Played a couple more notes.

BOOM. BOOM.

Øyvind tried a few thumps on the drums. Jan Vidar played a chord on the guitar. It was incredibly loud. Everyone in sight stared in our direction.

"Hey! Pack that in!" shouted one of the Bøksle Brothers.

Jan Vidar stared them out, then turned and took another swig of Coke. There was sound in the bass amp, there was sound in Jan Vidar's guitar amplifier. But what about mine? I lowered the volume on the guitar, struck a chord, raised it slowly until the amplifier seemed to leap at the sound and then raised it some more, all the time staring at the two guitar-strumming men on the other side of the passage, with legs akimbo and a smile on their faces, singing their droll ballads about seagulls, fishing boats, and sunsets. The moment they looked across at me, with glares it is difficult to describe as anything other than ferocious, I lowered the volume again. We had sound, everything was okay.

"What's the time now?" I asked Jan Vidar. His fingers were gliding up and down the neck of the guitar.

"Twenty past," he said.

"Retards," I said. "They should have finished by now."

The Bøksle Brothers represented everything I was against, the respectable, cozy, bourgeois world, and I looked forward to turning up the amplifier and blowing them off the block. So far my rebelliousness had consisted of expressing divergent opinions in class, resting my head on the desk and falling asleep and, once when I had thrown a used paper bag on the pavement and an elderly man had told me to pick it up, I told him to pick it up himself if it was so damn important to him. When I walked off, my heart was pounding so hard in my chest I could scarcely breathe. Otherwise, it was through listening to the music that I liked, uncompromising, anti-commercial, underground, bands that made me a rebel, someone who did not accept conventions, but fought for change. And the louder I played it, the closer I came to that ideal. I had bought an extra-long guitar lead so that I could stand in front of the hall mirror and play, with the amplifier upstairs in my room at full blast, and then things really started to happen, the sound became distorted, piercing, and almost regardless of what I did, it sounded good, the whole house was filled with the sound of my guitar, and a strange congruence evolved between my feelings and these sounds, as though *they* were me, as though *that* was the real me. I had written some lyrics about this, it had actually been meant as a song, but since no tune came to mind, I called it a poem when I later wrote it in my diary.

I distort my soul's feedback
I play my heart bare
I look at you and think:
We're at one in my loneliness
We're at one in my loneliness
You and me
You and me, my love

I wanted to be out, out in the great, wide world. And the only way I knew how, the only way I had, was through music. That was why I was standing outside this shopping center in Hånes on this day in early autumn, 1984, with my white-lacquered confirmation present, an imitation Stratocaster, hanging from my shoulder and my forefinger on the volume control, ready to flick it the moment the Bøksle Brothers' last chord faded.

The wind suddenly picked up across the square, leaves whirled past, rustling as they went, an ice cream ad spun round and round, flapping and clattering. I thought I felt a raindrop on my cheek, and peered up at the milky white sky.

"Is it starting to rain?" I asked.

Jan Vidar held out his palm. Shrugged his shoulders.

"Can't feel anything," he said. "But we'll play whatever. Even if it pisses down."

"Yes," I said. "You nervous?"

He resolutely shook his head.

Then the brothers were finished. The few people who were standing around clapped and the brothers gave a slight bow.

Jan Vidar turned to Øyvind.

"Ready?" he asked.

Øyvind nodded.

"Ready, Jan Henrik?"

"Karl Ove?"

I nodded.

"Two, three, four," said Jan Vidar, mostly to himself, and he played the first bars of the riff on his own.

The next second the sound of his guitar tore across the tarmac. People jumped with alarm. Everyone turned toward us. I counted in my head. Placed my fingers on the fret. My hand was shaking.

ONE TWO THREE – ONE TWO THREE FOUR – ONE TWO THREE – ONE TWO.

Then I was supposed to come in.

But there was no sound!

Jan Vidar stared up at me, his eyes frozen. I waited for the next round, cranked the volume up, came in. With two guitars it was deafening.

ONE TWO THREE – ONE TWO THREE FOUR – ONE TWO THREE – ONE TWO.

Then the hi-hat came in.

Chicka-chicka, chicka-chicka, chicka-chicka, chicka-chicka.

The bass drum. The snare.

And then the bass.

BOM-BOM-BOM bombombombombombombombombom-BOM

BOM-BOM-BOM-bombombombombombombombombom-BOM

It was only then I looked at Jan Vidar again. His face was contorted into a kind of grimace as he strained to say something without using his voice.

Too fast! Too fast!

And Øyvind slowed down. I tried to follow suit, but it was confusing because both the bass and Jan Vidar's guitar kept going at the same tempo, and when I changed my mind and followed them they suddenly slowed down, and I was the only one left playing at breakneck speed. Amidst this chaos I noticed the wind blowing through Jan Vidar's hair, and that some of the kids were standing in front of us with their hands over their ears. The next moment we had reached the first chorus and were more or less in synch. Then a man in tan slacks, a blue-and-white striped shirt and a yellow summer blazer came marching across the tarmac. It was the shopping center manager. He was heading straight for us. Twenty meters away he waved both arms as if trying to stop a ship. He kept waving. We continued to play, but as he stopped right in front of us, still gesticulating, there was no longer any doubt that he was addressing us, and we stopped.

"What the hell do you think you are doing!" he said.

"We were asked to play here," Jan Vidar answered.

"Are you out of your tiny minds! This is a shopping center. It's Saturday. People want to shop and have a good time. They don't want to listen to that goddawful racket."

"Shall we turn it down a bit?" Jan Vidar asked. "We can easily do that."

"Not just a bit," he said.

A crowd had gathered around us now. Maybe fifteen, sixteen people, including the kids. Not bad.

Jan Vidar craned around and lowered the volume on the amplifier. Played a chord and sent the shop owner an inquiring look.

"Is that okay?" he asked.

"Lower!" said the manager.

Jan Vidar lowered the volume a bit more, struck a chord.

"Is that alright then?" he asked. "We're not a dance band, you know," he added.

"Right," said the manager. "Try that, or even lower."

Jan Vidar made another adjustment. He seemed to be fiddling with the knob, but I saw he was only feigning.

"There we are," he said.

Jan Henrik and I also adjusted our volume.

"Let's start again," Jan Vidar said.

And we started again. I counted in my head.

ONE TWO THREE – ONE TWO THREE FOUR – ONE TWO THREE – ONE TWO.

The manager was walking back towards the main entrance to the shopping center. I watched him as we played. When we got to the part where we were interrupted he stopped and turned. Looked at us. Turned back, took a few steps toward the shops, turned again. Suddenly he came toward us, once again gesticulating furiously. Jan Vidar didn't see him, he had his eyes closed. Jan Henrik, however, did and raised an eyebrow.

"No, no, no," the manager yelled, stopping in front of us.

"It's no good," he said. "Sorry, you'll have to pack it in."

"What?" objected Jan Vidar. "Why? Twenty-five minutes you said."

"It's no good," he said, lowering his head and waving his hand in front of it.

"Sorry, guys."

"Why?" Jan Vidar repeated.

"I can't listen to that," he said. "You don't even sing! Come on. You'll get your money. Here you are."

He took an envelope from his inside pocket and held it out to Jan Vidar.

"Here you are," he said. "Thanks for pitching up. But that wasn't what I had in mind. No hard feelings, okay?"

Jan Vidar grabbed the envelope. He turned away from the manager, pulled the plug from the amplifier, switched it off, lifted the guitar over his head, went to his guitar case, opened it and replaced the guitar. People around us were smiling.

"Come on," Jan Vidar said. "We're going home."

After that the status of the band was shrouded in doubt; we practiced a few times but our hearts weren't in it, then Øyvind said he couldn't make the next session, and the time after that there was no drum set, and the time after that I had soccer practice . . . Meanwhile Jan Vidar and I saw less of each other since we went to different schools, and some weeks later he mumbled about having met someone in another class he jammed with, so when I played now it was mostly to pass the time.

I sang "Ground Control to Major Tom," strummed the two minor chords I liked so much and thought about the two bags of beer lying in the forest.

When Yngve had been home for Christmas he had brought a book of

Bowie songs. I had copied them into an exercise book which I now pulled out, complete with chords, lyrics and notes. Then I put "Hunky Dory" on the record player, track four, "Life on Mars?," and began to play along, softly so that I could hear the words and the other instruments. It sent a shiver down my spine. It was a fantastic song and as I followed the chord sequence on the guitar it was as if the song was opening itself up to me, as if I were inside it, and not outside, which was how it felt when I only listened. If I were to open a song and enter it unaided I would need several days because I couldn't hear which chords were being played, I had to grope my way painstakingly forward, and even if I found some chords which sounded similar I was never sure they were really the same ones. I put down my pen, listened with intense concentration, picked up the pen, strummed a chord. Hmmm. . . . Put down the pen, listened once again, played the same chord, was it *that* one? Or perhaps *this* one? Not to mention all the other guitar techniques that went on in the course of a song. It was hopeless. While Yngve, for example, only had to listen to a song once and then he could play it to perfection after a couple of stabs. I had known other people like him, they seemed to have the gift, music was not distinct from thinking, or it had nothing to do with thinking, it lived its own life inside them. When they played, they played, they didn't mechanically repeat some pattern they had taught themselves, and the freedom in that, which was what music was actually about, was beyond me. The same was true of drawing. Drawing conferred no status, but I liked it all the same and spent quite some time doing it when I was alone in my room. If I had a specific model, such as a cartoon character, I could make a tolerable attempt, but if I didn't copy and just sketched freehand the result was never any good. Here too I had seen people who had the gift, perhaps Tone in my class for one, who with minimal effort could draw whatever she wanted, the tree in the grounds outside the window, the car parked beyond it, the teacher standing in front of the board. When we had to choose optional subjects I wanted to take Form and Color, but since I knew how things stood, that the other students knew how to draw, had the gift, I decided against it. Instead I chose cinematography. The thought of this could sometimes weigh me down because I wanted so much to be someone. I wanted so much to be special.

I got up, placed the guitar on its stand, switched off the amplifier and went downstairs where Mom was ironing. The circles of light around the lamps above the door, and on the barn walls outside, were almost completely covered with snow.

"What weather!" I said.

"You can say that again," she said.

As I walked into the kitchen I remembered a snowplow had recently driven past. Perhaps it would be a good idea to clear the ridge of snow.

I turned to Mom.

"I think I'll go and shovel some snow before they come," I said.

"Fine," she said. "Can you light the torches while you're at it? They're in the garage, in a bag hanging on the the wall."

"Sure. Do you have a lighter?"

"In my handbag."

I put on my outdoor things and went out, opened the garage door, grabbed the shovel, knotted the scarf around my face, and went down to the intersection. Even with my back to the snow sweeping across the fields it stung my eyes and cheeks as I dug at the pile of new snow and the old clumps. After a few minutes I heard a bang, faraway and muffled, as if inside a room, and raised my head in time to see a flash of light from a tiny explosion in the depths of the windswept darkness. It must have been Tom and Per and their father testing the rockets they had bought. That may have excited them, but it drained me, for the only thing the tiny flash had done was intensify the feeling of uneventfulness that followed. There was not a car, not a soul around, just the murky forest, the driving snow, the motionless ribbon of light along the road. The darkness in the valley below. The scraping of the shovel's metal blade against the rock-hard lumps of compressed snow, my own breathing, somehow amplified by the scarf tightly trussed around my hat and ears.

When I had finished I went back up to the garage, replaced the shovel, found the four torches in the bag, lit them one by one in the dark, not without pleasure, for the flames were so gentle, and the blue in them rose and sank according to which way the current of air carried them. I considered for a moment what positions would be best and concluded that two should be placed on the front doorstep and two on top of the wall in front of the barn.

I had hardly put the torches out, the two on the wall with a small protective shield of snow behind them, and closed the garage door, when I heard a car coming around the bend below the house. I opened the garage door again and hurried into the house, I had to be *completely* ready before they came, with no visible signs of my recent activities. This little obsession grew so strong in me that I ran into the bathroom at full tilt, grabbed a towel, and dried my boots on it, so that the fresh snow would not be seen on them in the hall, after which I took off my outdoor clothes, that is, coat, hat, scarf, and mittens, in my room. Going downstairs, I saw the car idling outside, with the red taillights lit. My grandfather was waiting with his hand on the car door as my grandmother climbed out.

When I was at home on my own, every room had its own character, and though not directly hostile to me they were not exactly welcoming, either. It was more as if they did not want to subordinate themselves to me, but wanted to exist in their own right, with their own individual walls, floors, ceilings, skirting boards, yawning windows. I was aware of a deadness about the rooms, that was what made me uncomfortable, by which I mean not dead in the sense of life having ceased, but rather life being absent, the way that life is absent from a rock, a glass of water, a book. The presence of our cat, Mefisto, was not strong enough to dispel this, I just saw the cat in the yawning room; however, were a person to come in, even if it were only a small baby, the yawning room was gone. My father filled the rooms with disquiet, my mother filled them with gentleness, patience, melancholy, and on occasion, if she came home from work and was tired, also with a faint yet noticeable undercurrent of irritability. Per, who never ventured farther than the front hall, filled it with happiness, expectation, and submission. Jan Vidar, who was so far the only person outside my family to have been in my room, filled it with obstinacy, ambition, and friendliness. It was interesting when several people were present because there wasn't any space for the sway of more than one, at most two wills in a room, and it was not always the strongest that was the most obvious. Per's submissiveness, for example, the politeness he displayed to adults, was at times stronger than my father's lupine nature, such as when he came in, barely nodding to Per as he walked past. But it was rare there was anyone at home apart from us. The exception was visits by my father's parents and his brother Gunnar and family. They came every so often, perhaps seven or eight times a year, and I always looked forward to their arrival with pleasure. Partly because the person my grandmother had been for me while I was growing up had not changed to take account of the person I was now, and the radiance that emanated from her – which was not so much a result of the presents she always brought but stemmed from her genuine love of children – still shone in my image of her. But my pleasure was partly due to my father always perking up for such events. He became more friendly towards me, took me into his confidence, so to speak, and regarded me as someone to be considered, but this was not the most important thing, for this friendliness he showed to his son was merely one aspect of a greater magnanimity that infused him on such occasions: he became charming, witty, knowledgeable, and entertaining, which in a way justified the fact that I had such mixed emotions about him and was so preoccupied with them.

When they came into the porch, Mom opened the door to meet them.

"Hello, and lovely to see you!" she said.

"Hello, Sissel," said Grandad.

"What foul weather!" Grandma said. "Have you ever seen anything like it? But the torches were great, I must say."

"Let me take your coats," Mom said.

Grandma was wearing a dark, round fur hat, which she took off and slapped against her hand a few times to shake off the snow, and a dark fur coat, which she passed to Mom with the hat.

"Good thing you came to pick us up," she said, turning to Dad. "We certainly couldn't have driven in this weather."

"Oh, I don't know about that," Grandad said. "But it is quite a distance, and a windy road as well."

Grandma came into the hall, straightened her dress with her hands, and adjusted her hair.

"So there you are!" she said to me with a quick smile.

"Hello," I said.

Behind her came Granddad, carrying his gray coat. Mom took a stride past Grandma and grabbed it, hung it on the hall stand beside the mirror under the stairs. Outside, Dad came into view; he was kicking the snow off his shoes against the side of the doorstep.

"Hello there, you," Grandad said. "Your father says you're going to a New Year's Eve party."

"That's right," I said.

"How you children have grown," Grandma said. "Just imagine, a New Year's Eve party."

"Yes, seems like we're not good enough anymore," Dad said from the hall. He ran his hand through his hair, shook his head a couple of times.

"Shall we go into the living room?" Mom said.

I followed them in, sat in the wicker chair by the garden door as they took a seat on the sofa. Dad's heavy footsteps could be heard as he went upstairs, and then above the ceiling at the back of the living room, where his bedroom was.

"I'll go and put some coffee on," Mom said, getting up. The ensuing silence in the room after she had gone became my responsibility.

"Erling's in Trondheim, isn't he?" I said.

"I suppose he is, yes," Grandma said. "They should be at home relaxing this evening."

She was wearing a blue silk dress with a black pattern on her chest. White pearls in her ears, gold chain around her neck. Her hair was dark, it must have been dyed, but I wasn't sure, because if it was, why wasn't the gray lock over her forehead dyed? She wasn't fat, or even plump, yet somehow she still had a full figure. Her movements, always so lively, were in marked contrast to this. But what you noticed when you saw my grandmother, what struck you first about her, was her eyes. They were light blue and crystal clear, and whether it was because of their unusual color or because it contrasted with her otherwise dark appearance, they seemed almost artificial, as if they were made of stone. My father's eyes were exactly the same, and gave the same impression. Apart from her love for children, her other most prominent quality was her green thumb. When we visited her during the summer she was generally in the garden and when I thought about her it was often in a garden setting. Wearing gloves, her hair ruffled by the wind, walking across the lawn with an armful of dry twigs to be burnt, or kneeling in front of a little hole she had just dug, carefully loosening the bag around the roots to plant a tiny tree, or glancing over her shoulder to check that the sprinkler has started to rotate as she turns on the tap under the veranda and then standing with her hands on her hips enjoying the sight of the water being hurled into the air, sparkling in the sunlight. Or crouching on the slope behind the house to weed the beds that had been made in all the dips and hollows of the rocky mountainside, similar to the way that water forms pools on the sea-smoothed rocks in the archipelago, cut off from their original environment. I remember feeling sorry for these plants, positioned on their separate crags, lonely and exposed, how they must have yearned for the life they saw unfolding beneath them. Down where the plants merged into one another, continuously forming new combinations according to the time of day and year, like the old pear and plum trees she had once brought from her grandparents' country cottage, where the shadows flickered over the grass as the wind swept through the foliage on one of those lazy summer days while the sun was setting beyond the horizon at the mouth of the fjord and you could hear the distant sounds from the town rising and falling like the swell of waves in the air, mingling with the hum of wasps and bees at work among the rosebushes against the wall, where the pale petals shone white and calm in all the green. The garden already had the character of something old, a dignity and a fullness that only time can create and no doubt was the reason she had positioned a greenhouse at the bottom, half hidden behind a rock, where she could extend her handiwork and also cultivate rarer trees and plants without the rest of the garden being marred by the industrial and provisional nature of the construction. In the autumn and winter we caught glimpses of her down there, a faint silhouette of color behind the shiny walls, and, it was not without a touch of pride that she remarked, in a casual sort of way, that the tomatoes and cucumbers on the table didn't come from the shop but from her greenhouse in the garden.

Grandad was not interested in the garden at all, and when Grandma and Dad or Grandma and Gunnar, or Grandma and Grandad's brother Alf discussed various plants, flowers, or trees, our family had quite a passion for anything that grew, he preferred to take out a newspaper and flick through it, unless, of course, it was a pools coupon and the week's league tables he was consulting. I always thought it was so strange that a man whose job was about figures also spent his free time with figures and not, for example, doing gardening or carpentry or other hobbies that exercised the whole body. But no, it was figures at work, tables and figures in his leisure time. The only other thing I knew he liked was politics. If the conversation moved that way he always livened up, he had strong opinions, but his eagerness to debate was stronger, so if anyone contradicted him he appreciated that. At any rate, his eyes expressed nothing but kindness the few times Mom had presented her left-wing views, even though his voice grew louder and sharper. Grandma, for her part, always asked him to talk about something else, or calm down, on such occasions. She often made a sarcastic comment and could also be quite caustic, but he took it, and if we were present she would send us a wink so that we understood that it wasn't meant that seriously. She laughed easily and loved to recount all the amusing incidents she had experienced or had heard. All the funny remarks Yngve had made when he was little she remembered, those two were especially close, he had lived there for six months when he was a young boy, and had been there a lot later too. She also told us about the strange things Erling had experienced at his school in Trondheim, but her richest store was the stories from the 1930s when she had worked as a chauffeur for an elderly, presumably senile, capitalist's wife.

Now they were in their seventies, my grandma a few years older than my grandad, but both were hale and hearty, and they still traveled abroad in the winter, as they always had.

No one had spoken for some seconds. I strained to come up with something to say. Looked out of the window to make the silence less obtrusive.

"How's it going at the Cathedral School?" Grandad eventually asked. "Has Stray had anything sensible to say?"

Stray was our French teacher. He was a small, squat, bald, energetic man of around seventy who owned a house close to my grandfather's office. As far as I had gleaned they had been at loggerheads over something, perhaps a boundary issue; I didn't quite know whether it had gone to court, or even whether the matter had been settled, but at any rate they no longer greeted each other, and hadn't for many a year.

"Well," I said. "He just calls me 'the brat in the corner.'"

"Yes, I'm sure he does," Grandad says. "And old Nygaard?"

I shrugged.

"Fine, I suppose. Keeps doing the same old stuff. He's old-school, that one. How do you know him, by the way?"

"Through Alf," Grandad said.

"Oh of course," I said.

Grandad got up and walked over to the window, stood with his hands behind his back peering out. Apart from the sparse light that came through the windows, it was completely dark on this side of the house.

"Can you see anything, Father?" Grandma asked, with a wink at me.

"This place is very nicely situated," Grandad said.

At that moment Mom came into the living room carrying four cups. He turned to her.

"I was just telling Karl Ove that this house is very nicely situated!"

Mom stopped, as if unable to say anything while walking.

"Yes, we're very happy with the location," she said. Stood there with the cups in her hands, looking at Grandad with a tiny smile playing on her lips. There was something . . . yes, approaching a flush on her face. Not that she was blushing or she was embarrassed, it wasn't that. It was more that she wasn't hiding behind anything. She never did. Whenever she spoke it was always straight from the heart, never for the sake of speaking.

"The house is so old," she said. "These walls have years in them. That's both good and bad. But it's a nice place to live."

Grandad nodded and continued to stare out into the darkness. Mom went to the table to set the cups down.

"What has become of my host then?" Grandma asked.

"I'm here," Dad said.

Everyone turned. He was standing by the laid table in the dining room, stooping beneath the ceiling beams, with a bottle of wine, which he had obviously been studying, in his hands.

How had he got in there?

I hadn't heard a sound. And if there was one thing I was aware of in this house it was his movements.

"Will you get some more wood in before you go, Karl Ove?" he said.

"Okay," I answered, got up, and went into the hall, booted up, and opened the front door. The wind blasted my face. But at least it had stopped snowing. I crossed the yard and went into the woodshed under the barn. The light from the naked bulb hanging from the ceiling glared against the rough brick walls. The floor was almost completely covered with bark and wood chips. An ax was lodged in the chopping block. In one corner lay the orange-and-black chain saw my father had bought when we moved here. There had been a tree on the property he wanted to fell. When he was ready to set to work he couldn't get the saw to start. He eyed it for a long time, cursed it, and went to call the shop where he had bought it to complain. "What was wrong?" I asked on his return. "Nothing," he replied, "it was just something they had forgotten to tell me." It must have been a safety device of some kind, I inferred, to prevent children from using them. But now he had it started, and after felling the tree he spent the entire afternoon cutting it up. He liked the work, I could see that. Once it was done though, he had no further use for the saw, and since then it had been lying on the floor in here.

I loaded myself up with as many logs as I could carry, kicked open the door, and staggered back across the yard – the thought of how impressed they would be uppermost in my mind – levered off my boots and walked leaning backward slightly, almost collapsing under the weight, into the living room.

"Look at him!" said Grandma as I came in. "That's quite a load you've got there!"

I halted in front of the wood basket.

"Hang on a sec, I'll give you a hand," Dad said and came toward me, took the top logs, and put them in the basket. His lips were drawn, his eyes cold. I knelt down and let the rest tumble in.

"Now we've got enough wood until summer," he said.

I straightened up, picked some splinters of wood off my shirt, and sat in the chair while Dad crouched down, opened the stove door and pushed in a couple of logs. He was wearing a dark suit and a dark-red tie, black shoes, and a white shirt, which contrasted with his ice-blue eyes, black beard, and lightly tanned complexion. He spent the whole of the summer in the sun whenever he could, by August his skin was usually very dark, but this winter he must have gone to a tanning salon, it struck me now, unless he had eventually had so much sun that the tan had become permanent.

Around his eyes the skin had begun to crack, the way dry leather does, and form fine, closely set wrinkles.

He looked at his watch.

"Gunnar will have to get a move on if we're going to eat before midnight," he said.

"It's the weather," Grandma said. "He'll be driving carefully tonight."

Dad turned to me.

"Isn't it time you were on your way?"

"Yes," I said. "But I was going to say hello to Gunnar and Tove first."

Dad gave a snort.

"Off you go and enjoy yourself. You don't have to sit here with us, you know."

I got up.

"Your shirt's hanging over the cupboard in the other room," Mom said.

I took it up to my room with me and changed. Black cotton trousers, wide at the thigh, narrow at the calf, and with side pockets, white shirt, black suit jacket. I rolled up the studded belt I had planned to wear and put it in the bag, for though they might not actually forbid me to wear it, they would notice, and I didn't want to go through all that now. I added a pair of black Doc Martens, an extra shirt, two packs of Pall Mall mild, some chewing gum, and pastilles. When I was finished I stood in front of the mirror. It was five past seven. I should have been on my way, but had to wait for Gunnar for as long as possible because if he hadn't come there was a risk I would meet him on the road. With two bags of beer in my hands that was not a great idea.

Apart from the wind, and the trees at the forest edge, which you could just make out on the periphery of the light from the house, nothing stirred.

If they weren't here within five minutes, I would have to go anyway.

I put on my outdoor clothes, stood at the window for a moment straining to hear the drone of a car engine while staring down at the place where the headlights would come into view first, then turned, switched off the light, and went downstairs.

Dad was in the kitchen pouring water into a large pan. He looked up as I went in.

"Are you going?" he asked.

I nodded.

"Have a nice evening," he said.

At the bottom of the hill, where the morning's tracks had been covered over by the wind and snow, I stood stock-still and listened for a few seconds. When I was sure there were no cars coming I went up the slope and into the trees. The bags were where I had left them, covered with a thin layer of snow that slid down the smooth plastic when I picked them up. With one in each hand I walked back down, stopped behind a tree to listen, and when there was still nothing to be heard, I struggled over the bank of snow at the roadside and loped down to the bend. Not many people lived out here, and through-traffic used the road on the other side of the river, so if a car did come there was a good chance it would be Gunnar's. I walked up the hill, around the bend where William's family lived. Their house was set back a bit, right up against the forest that rose steeply behind it. The blue shimmer from the television flickered through the living room. The house was a seventies' build, the plot unworked, full of stones, uncovered rock, with a broken swing, a pile of wood under a tarpaulin, a wrecked car, and some tires. I didn't understand why they lived like that. Didn't they want to live like normal people? Or couldn't they? Didn't it matter to them? Or did they in fact think that they were living like normal people? The father was kind and gentle, the mother always angry, the three children always dressed in clothes that were either too big or too small.

One morning on my way to school I had seen the father and daughter clambering up a pile of rocks on the other side of the road, both bleeding from the forehead, the girl with a white scarf drenched with blood tied around her head. There had been something animal-like about them, I remember thinking, because they didn't say anything, didn't shout, just calmly climbed up the rocks. At the bottom, with its hood against a tree, was their truck. Beneath the trees flowed the dark, lustrous river. I had asked them if I could help, the father had told me they didn't need any help; they were fine, he had called from the slope, and even though the sight was so unexpected that it was almost impossible to drag yourself away, it also felt wrong to stand there watching, so I continued on my way to the bus stop. On turning, the one time I had allowed myself to do so, I saw them hobbling along the road, he was dressed in overalls as always, with his arm around his daughter's fragile eleven-year-old body.

We used to tease her and William, it was easy to make them lose their tempers and easy to put them in their place, words and ideas were not their strong suits, but I didn't realize this had any impact on them until one ordinary boring summer's day Per and I had rung William's doorbell to get him to come out and play soccer and their mother had come onto the veranda and given us an earful, especially me, because I thought I was superior to everyone else, and her son and daughter in particular. I answered her back, it turned out she was not very adept with words either, but her anger on the other hand was not to be quelled, so all I gained was Per's laughing admiration for my wit, which was forgotten a few hours later. But the people living on the bend did not forget. The father was too kind to intervene, but the mother . . . her eyes darkened every time she saw me. To me they were people I could lord it over, nothing more. If William came to school wearing trousers at half-mast he had made a monumental blunder; if he misused a word, there was no reason he shouldn't hear about it. That was only the truth, wasn't it? And it was up to him to stop our fun or find a way to overcome it. I was not exactly invulnerable, my weaknesses were there for all to see and exploit, and the fact that they didn't, because they didn't have enough insight to be able to see them, was surely not my problem. The conditions were the same for all. At school William hung out with a crowd who smoked in the wet weather shed, the ones who rode mopeds from the age of thirteen, who began to drop out of school when they were fourteen, who had fights and drank, and they too made fun of William, but in a way he could tolerate, because there was always something he could compare himself with, there were always ways of getting his own back. With us, that is, those who lived in the houses up here, it was different, here it was sarcasm, irony, and the killer remark that held sway, things which could drive him insane as it all was beyond his reach. But he needed us more than we needed him, and he kept coming back. For me this was a question of freedom. When I moved there, no one knew me, and although I was basically the same person as before it gave me the chance to do things I had never done. There was, for example, an old-fashioned village shop by the bus stop in which goods were bought and sold over the counter, and that was owned by two sisters aged around seventy. They were nice, and particularly slow off the mark. If you asked them for something on one of the top shelves they turned their backs to you for a minute or two, and this was your chance to stuff as much chocolate and as many sweets as you could in your jacket. Not to mention the opportunities if you asked them for something from the cellar. In Tromøya I would never have dreamed of doing such a thing, but here I didn't hesitate, here I was not only a person who stole chocolate and sweets from old ladies but also a person who enticed others into doing the same. They were a year younger than me and had hardly been out of the local area; compared to them I felt like a man of the world. They had all scrumped strawberries, for example, but I introduced a touch of refinement and got them to take plates, spoons, milk, and sugar into the strawberry field.

Down in the factory building we had to fill in lists of the work we had done and were paid accordingly, and apparently it had never even occurred to them that the system could be abused and it was possible to cheat. But that was where we came in. The most important change in my behavior, however, was linguistic; I had discovered the edge that words gave you to bully others. I taunted and harassed, manipulated and ridiculed, and never, not once, did it strike them that the basis of this power I had was so insecure that one single well-directed blow could have knocked it flying. I had a speech impediment, you see! I couldn't say my "r"s. After having been shown up by me it would have been enough for them to mimic me and I would have been crushed. But they never did.

Well, actually, Per's brother, who was three years younger than me, did do it once. Per and I were talking in their stable, which his father had just built onto the garage, to house the pony he had bought for his daughter, Per and Tom's little sister, Marit, we had been out all evening and ended up here, in the snug, warm room that smelled of horse and hay, when Tom, who didn't like me, presumably because I laid claim to the brother who previously had always been at his disposal, suddenly mimicked me.

"Fowd Siewa?" he said. "What's a Fowd Siewa when it's at home?"

"Now, now, Tom," Per reproved.

"A Fowd Siewa's a car," I said. "Never heard of one?"

"I haven't heard of any cars being called Fowds," he said. "And certainly not a Siewa."

"Tom!" Per shouted.

"Oh, you mean *Ford*!" Tom said.

"Yes of course," I answered.

"Why didn't you say so then?" he said. "Forrrrrd! Sierrrra!"

"Get lost, Tom," Per said. When Tom showed no signs of moving he punched him on the shoulder.

"Ow!" Tom howled. "Stoppit!"

"Scram, you brat!" Per said, and punched him again.

Tom left and we continued to chat as if nothing had happened.

It was remarkable that this was the only time any of the kids up there had made fun of my weaknesses, especially considering I pushed them around all the time. But they hadn't. Up there I was king, king of the young kids. But my power was limited. If anyone appeared who was as old as me, or who lived farther down the valley, it ceased to exist. So I kept a beady eye on those around me, then as now.

I put the bags down on the road for a second, opened my jacket and pulled out the scarf, and wound it around my face, grabbed the bags again, and kept on walking. The wind whistled round my ears, whisked up the snow on all sides, swept it into the air and swirled it around. It was four kilometers to Jan Vidar's place so I needed to hurry. I broke into a jog. The bags hung from my arms like lead weights. Farther along the road, on the far side of the bend, two headlights came into view. The beams sliced through the forest. The trees there seemed to flare up, one by one. I stopped, put one foot on the edge of the ditch and carefully rested the bags in the ditch below me. Then I walked on. I turned my head as the car passed. An old man I didn't recognize was in the driver's seat. I walked back the twenty meters and retrieved the bags from the ditch, carried on walking, rounded the bend, passed the house where the old man lived alone, emerged from the forest to see the factory lights, hazy in the snow-flurried darkness, walked past the small, dilapidated farm, in darkness tonight, and had almost reached the last house before the intersection with the main road when another car came along. I did the same as before, quickly hid the bottles in the ditch and carried on walking, empty-handed. It wasn't Gunnar this time either. After the car had passed I ran back, picked up the bags and set off even faster; it was already half past seven. I hurried along and was not far from the main road when three more cars appeared. I put down the bags again. Let it be Gunnar, I thought, because as soon as he had gone by I wouldn't need to keep stopping to hide the beer. Two of the cars drove across the bridge, the third turned off and passed me, but that wasn't Gunnar either. I collected the bags and made for the main road, followed it past the bus stop, the old-fashioned shop, the garage, the old houses, all of them bathed in light, all of them windblown, all deserted. Approaching the top of the long, gentle gradient I saw the headlights of another car coming over the brow. There was no ditch here, so I had to put the bottles in the banked up snow, and as they were visible, hurriedly put a few meters between them and me.

I peered into the car as it passed. This time it was Gunnar. He turned his head at that moment and, on recognizing me, braked. With a trail of swirling snow, reddish in the brake lights, the car gradually slowed down and when, twenty meters farther on, it finally came to a halt, he began to reverse. The engine was whining.

He opened the door when he was alongside me.

"Is that you out in this weather!" he cried.

"Brrr, yes," I answered.

"Where are you off to?"

"To a party."

"Jump in, and I'll drive you there," he said.

"No, don't bother," I said. "I'm almost there. I'm fine."

"No, no, no," Gunnar said. "Jump in."

I shook my head.

"You're late as well," I said. "It's almost eight."

"No problem at all," Gunnar said. "Hop in. After all, it's New Year's Eve and all that. We can't have you walking in the freezing cold, you know. We'll take you there. End of discussion."

I couldn't protest anymore without arousing suspicion.

"Okay then," I said. "That's very kind of you."

He snorted.

"Jump into the back," he said. "And tell me where to go."

I got in. It was nice and warm. Harald, their soon three-year-old son, was sitting in the child seat and silently watching me.

"Hi, Harald," I said to him with a smile.

Tove, who was sitting at the front, turned to me.

"Hi, Karl Ove," she said. "Good to see you."

"Hi," I said. "And Merry Christmas."

"Let's go then," Gunnar said. "I assume we have to turn around?"

I nodded.

We drove to the bus stop, turned, and drove back up. As we passed the place where I left the bags I resisted leaning forward to see if they were there. They were.

"Where are you going?" Gunnar asked.

"First to a pal's in Solsletta. Then we're going to Søm, to a party there."

"I can drive you all the way if you like," he said.

Tove sent him a look.

"No need," I said. "We're going to meet some others on the bus anyway."

Gunnar was ten years younger than my father and worked as an accountant in quite a large firm in town. He was the only one of the sons to follow in his father's footsteps; both the others were teachers. Dad at an upper secondary school in Vennesla, Erling at a middle school in Trondheim. Erling was the only one for whom we used the epithet "uncle," he was more laid-back and not so status conscious as the other two. We didn't see much of my father's brothers when we were growing up, but we liked them both, they were always fooling around, especially Erling, but also Gunnar, whom both Yngve and I liked best, perhaps because he was relatively close to us in age. He had long hair, played the guitar, and not least, he kept a boat with a twenty horse power Mercury engine at the cabin outside Mandal where he stayed for long stretches at a time in the summer when we were growing up. In my mind, the friends he talked about were wreathed in an almost mythical glow, partly because my father didn't have any, partly because we hardly ever saw them, they were just people he went out to meet in his boat, and I imagined their lives as an endless cruise between islets and skerries in racing boats during the daytime, with their long, blond hair fluttering in the wind and tanned, smiling faces; playing cards and strumming guitars in the evenings, when they were in the company of girls.

But now he was married and had children, and even though he still had the boat the aura of island romanticism had gone. The long hair too. Tove came from a police family somewhere in Trøndelag, and worked as a primary school teacher.

"Have you had a good Christmas?" she asked, turning to me.

"Yes, great," I said.

"Yngve was home, I heard?" Gunnar said.

I nodded. Yngve was his favorite, no doubt because he was the first-born and had been at my grandparents' for so long while Gunnar still lived there. But also presumably because Yngve had not been as fragile and weepy as I had been as a child. He had had great fun with Yngve. So when I saw them together I tried to counteract that, tried to be funny, to crack lots of jokes, to show them I was just as easygoing as they were, just as fun-loving, just as much of a Sørlander as they were.

"He went back a couple of days ago," I said. "Off to a cabin with some friends."

"Yes, he's turning into an Arendaler, you know," Gunnar said.

We passed the chapel, drove around the bend by the ravine where the sun never shone, crossed the tiny bridge. The windshield wipers beat a rhythm. The fan hummed. Beside me Harald sat blinking.

"Whose party is it?" Gunnar asked. "Someone in your class, I suppose?"

"Girl in the parallel class actually," I said.

"Yes, everything changes when you go to gymnas," he said.

"You went to the Cathedral School, didn't you? " I asked.

"I did," he said, twisting his head far enough to meet my eyes before returning his attention to the road. His face was long and narrow, like my father's, but the blue of his eyes was darker, more like Grandad's than Grandma's. The back of his head was big, like Grandad's and mine, while his lips, which were sensitive and almost revealed more information about his inner being than his eyes, were the same as Dad's and Yngve's.

We left the forest behind, and the light from the headlights which had for so long picked out trees and crags, sides of houses and escarpments, finally had some space around them.

"It's at the end of this stretch," I said. "You can pull up over by the shop there."

"Okay," said Gunnar. Slowed to a stop.

"Have a nice time," I said. "And Happy New Year!"

"Happy New Year to you too," Gunnar said.

I slammed the door and started to walk towards Jan Vidar's house while the car turned around and drove back the way we had come. When it was out of sight I began to run. Now we really were pressed for time. I jumped down the escarpment to their property, saw the light in his room was on, went over and banged on the window. His face appeared a second later, staring out into the dark through narrowed eyes. I pointed toward the door. When, at last, he saw me, he nodded, and I walked around to the other side of the house.

"Sorry," I said. "But the beers are up by Kragebo. We'll have to get a move on and fetch them."

"What are they doing there?" he asked. "Why didn't you bring them with you?"

"My uncle came along while I was walking here," I said. "I just managed to sling the bags in the ditch before he stopped. And then bugger me if he didn't insist on driving me here. I couldn't say no, he would have become suspicious, wouldn't he."

"Oh no," Jan Vidar said. "Shit. What a drag."

"I know," he said. "But come on. Let's get going."

A few minutes later we were clambering up the slope to the road. Jan Vidar had his hat down over his forehead, his scarf wrapped around his mouth, jacket collar up over his cheeks. The only part of his face that was visible was the eyes, and then only because the round John Lennon glasses he was wearing were misted up, which I noticed as he met my gaze.

"Let's go for it then," I said.

"I guess we'd better," he agreed.

At a steady pace, dragging our legs so as not to use up all our energy at once, we began to run along the road. We had the wind in our faces. The snow swept past. Tears trickled from my tightly pinched eyes. My feet began to go numb, they no longer did what I wanted them to do; they just lay inside my boots, stiff and loglike.

A car drove past, making our lack of speed painfully obvious as a moment later it rounded the curve at the end of the road and was gone.

"Shall we walk for a bit?" Jan Vidar asked.

I nodded.

"Let's just hope the bags are still there!" I said.

"What?" Jan Vidar shouted.

"The bags!" I said. "Hope no one's taken them!"

"There's no bugger around now!" Jan Vidar yelled.

We laughed. Came to the end of the flat and broke into a run again. Up the hill, where the gravel road led to the strange manorlike property by the river, over the little bridge, past the ravine, the ramshackle garage-cum-repair shop, the chapel and the small white 1950s houses on both sides of the road, until we finally arrived at the spot where I had left the two bags. We grabbed one each and began to walk back.

As we reached the chapel, we heard a car behind us.

"Shall we hitch a ride?" Jan Vidar suggested.

"Why not?" I said.

With our left hands clutching the bags and our right thumbs raised we stood with a smile on our faces until the car came. It didn't even dip its headlights. We jogged on.

"What are we going to do if we don't get a ride?" Jan Vidar asked after a while.

"We'll get one," I answered.

"Two cars go by every hour," he said.

"Have you got any better suggestions since you're asking the questions?" I said.

"None," he said. "But there are a few people at Richard's."

"No way," I said.

"And Stig and Liv are in Kjevik with some friends," he said. "That's a possibility too."

"We decided on Søm, didn't we," I said. "You can't start suggesting new places to go on New Year's Eve! This *is* New Year's Eve, you know."

"Yes, and we're standing at the roadside. How much fun is that?"

Headlights approached behind us.

"Look," I said. "Another car!"

It didn't stop.

By the time we got back to Jan Vidar's house, it was eight thirty. My feet were frozen, and for a brief instant I was at the point of suggesting we should give the beer a miss, go to his house and celebrate New Year's Eve with his parents. Lutefisk, soft drinks, ice cream, cakes, and fireworks. That was what we had always done. As our eyes met I knew the same thought had struck him. But we went on. Out of the residential area, past the road down to the church, around the bend up to the little cluster of houses where, among others, Kåre from our class lived.

"Do you think Kåre has gone out tonight?" I asked.

"Yes, he has," Jan Vidar said. "He's at Richard's."

"Yet another reason not to go there," I said.

There was nothing wrong with Kåre, but neither was there anything right. Kåre had large protruding ears, thick lips, thin, sandy hair, and angry eyes. He was invariably angry, and probably had good reason to be. The summer I began at the school he had been in the hospital with broken ribs and a broken wrist. He had been in town with his father to pick up some building materials, plasterboard, and they had put the sheets on the trailer behind the car, but failed to secure them properly so, as they were approaching Varodd Bridge, Kåre's father had asked him to get out and sit in the trailer to make sure the materials didn't move. He had been blown off along with the materials and knocked senseless. We laughed at that all autumn, and it was still one of the first things that came to mind whenever Kåre made an appearance.

Now he had got himself a moped and had started hanging around with the rest of the moped gang.

On the other side of the bend was Liv's house, Liv, for whom Jan Vidar had always had a soft spot. I could control myself. She had a nice body, but there was something boyish about her humor and manner that seemed to cancel out her breasts and hips. Besides, I had been sitting in front of her in the bus once when she waved her hands at some of the other girls, waved them about madly, and then said, "Yuck, they're so horrible! Those long hands of his! Have you seen them?" Surprised by the lack of reaction – the girls she was addressing were staring straight at me – she turned to me and blushed in a way I had never seen her blush, thereby removing any doubt that may have lingered about whose hands she found so disgusting.

Below was the community center, then came a short but steep hill down to the shop where the vast Ryen Plain began and finished at the airport.

"I think I'll have a smoke," I said, nodding in the direction of the bus stop on the other side of the community center. "Shall we stand there for a bit?"

"Go on, you have a smoke," Jan Vidar said. "It's New Year's Eve after all."

"How about a beer as well?" I suggested.

"Here? What's the point of that?"

"Are you in a bad mood or what?"

"Depends what you call bad."

"Oh come on now!" I said. I took off my rucksack, found the lighter and the packet of cigarettes, fished one out, shielded it against the wind with my hand, and lit up.

"Want one?" I asked, proffering the packet.

He shook his head.

I coughed and the smoke that seemed to get trapped in the upper part of my throat sent a feeling of nausea through my stomach.

"Agh, shit," I said.

"Is it good?" Jan Vidar asked.

"I don't usually cough," I said. "But the smoke went down the wrong way. It's not because I'm not used to it."

"No," Jan Vidar said. "Everyone who smokes takes it down the wrong way and coughs. It's a well-known phenomenon. My mother has been smoking for thirty years. Every time she smokes it goes down the wrong way and she coughs."

"Ha ha," I said.

Around the bend, out of the darkness, came a car. Jan Vidar took a step forward and stuck out his thumb. The car stopped! He rushed over and opened the door. Then he turned to me and waved. I threw away the cigarette, slung the rucksack onto my back, grabbed the bag, and walked over. Susanne stepped out of the car. She bent down, pulled a little lever, and slid the seat forward. Then she looked at me.

"Hi Karl Ove," she said.

"Hi Susanne," I said.

Jan Vidar was already on his way into the darkness of the car. The bottles clinked in the bag.

"Do you want to put the bag in the trunk?" Susanne suggested.

"No thanks," I said. "It's fine."

I got in, squeezed the bag down between my legs. Susanne got in. Terje, who was behind the wheel, turned around and looked at me.

"Are you hitchhiking on New Year's Eve?" he asked.

"We-ell . . . ," Jan Vidar hedged, as if he considered that this was not actually hitchhiking. "We've just been pretty unlucky this evening."

Terje put the car in gear, the wheels spun around until they caught up with the engine, and we rolled down the hill and onto the flat.

"Where are you going, boys?" he asked.

Boys.

What an idiot.

How could he go around with a perm and imagine it looked good? Did he think he looked tough with the moustache and the perm?

Grow up. Lose twenty kilos. Get rid of the stache. Get your hair cut. Then we can start talking.

What did Susanne see in him?

"We're going to Søm. To a party," I said. "How far are you going?"

"Well, we're just going to Hamre," he answered. "To Helge's party. But we can drop you at the Timenes intersection if you like."

"Great," Jan Vidar said. "Thanks. Very nice of you."

I looked at him. But he was staring out of the window and didn't catch my look.

"Who's going to Helge's then?" he asked.

"The usual suspects," Terje said. "Richard, Ekse, Molle, Jøgge, Hebbe, Tjådi. And Frode and Jomås and Bjørn."

"No girls?"

"Yes of course. Do you think we're stupid?"

"Who then?"

"Kristin, Randi, Kathrine, Hilde . . . Inger, Ellen, Anne Kathrine, Rita, Vibecke . . . Why? Would you like to join us?"

"No, we're going to another party," I said before Jan Vidar could say a word. "And we're pretty late already."

"Especially if you're going to hitch," he said.

Ahead of us, the airport lights came into view. On the other side of the river, which we crossed the very next second, the little slalom slope below the school was bathed in light. The snow had an orange tint.

"How's it going at commercial school, Susanne?" I asked.

"Fine," she said from her inviolable seat in front of me. "How's it going at Cathedral School?"

"It's fine," I said.

"You're in the same class as Molle, aren't you," Terje said, sending me a quick glance.

"That's right."

"Is that the class with twenty-six girls?"

"Yes."

He laughed.

"Quite a few class parties then?"

The camping site, snow-covered and forlorn, appeared on one side of the road; the little chapel, the supermarket, and the Esso garage on the other. The night sky above the rooftops of the houses huddled together on the hillside was riven with flares and flashes from fireworks. A crowd of children stood around a Roman candle in the parking lot, it was shooting up tiny balls of light that exploded in a myriad of sparks. A stream of cars crawled, bumper to bumper, along the road that ran parallel to ours for a stretch. On the other side was the beach. The bay was hidden beneath a white layer of ice that fissured and broke into a sea of blackness a hundred meters out.

"What time is it?" Jan Vidar asked.

"Half past nine," Terje said.

"Shit. That means we won't manage to get drunk before twelve," Jan Vidar said.

"Have you got to be home by twelve?"

"Ha ha," said Jan Vidar.

A few minutes later Terje pulled in by the bus stop at the Timenes intersection, and we climbed out and waited under the bus shelter with our bags.

"Wasn't the bus supposed to leave at ten past eight?" Jan Vidar asked.

"It was," I replied. "Could be late though?"

We laughed.

"Christ," I said. "Well, at least we can have a beer now!"

I couldn't open the bottles with the lighter, so I passed it to Jan Vidar. Without saying a word, he whipped the tops off both and handed me one.

"Oooh, that was good," I said, wiping my mouth with the back of my hand. "If we knock back two or three now we've got ourselves a base for later."

"My feet are fucking frozen," Jan Vidar said. "How about yours?"

"Same," I said.

I put the bottle to my mouth and drank for as long as I could. There was just a drop left after I lowered it. My stomach was full of froth and air. I tried to belch, but no air came up, just bubbles of froth that ran back into my mouth.

"Open another, will you," I said.

"Okay," Jan Vidar said. "But we can't stand here all night."

He flipped off another cap and passed me the bottle. I put it to my mouth and closed my eyes in concentration. I downed just over half. Another frothy belch followed.

"Oh *Christ*," I moaned. "Maybe not such a good idea drinking this fast."

The road we were standing by was the main thoroughfare between the towns in Sørland. It was normally packed with traffic. But in the ten minutes we had stood there only two cars had passed, both heading for Lillesand.

The air beneath the powerful streetlamps was full of swirling snow. The wind, made visible by the snow, rose and fell like waves, sometimes in long, slow surges, sometimes with sudden twists and twirls. Jan Vidar kicked his left foot against his right, the right against the left, the left against the right . . .

"Come on, drink" I said. I knocked back the rest, threw the empty into the forest behind the shelter.

"Another one," I demanded.

"You'll be chucking up soon," Jan Vidar said. "Take it easy."

"Come on," I said. "One more. Soon be damn near ten o'clock, won't it?"

He flipped the top off another bottle and passed it to me.

"What shall we do?" he asked. "It's too far to walk. The bus has gone. There are no cars to get a lift with. There isn't even a telephone box nearby so that we can ring someone to pick us up."

"We're going to die here," I said.

"Hey!" Jan Vidar shouted. "There's a bus. It's an Arendal bus."

"Are you kidding?" I said, staring up the hill. He wasn't, for there, around the bend at the top, came a wonderful, tall bus.

"Come on, sling the bottle," Jan Vidar said. "And smile nicely."

He stuck out his hand. The bus flashed, stopped, and the door opened.

"Two to Søm," Jan Vidar said, handing the driver a hundred-krone note. I looked down the aisle. It was dark and completely empty.

"You'll have to wait to drink that," the driver said, taking the change from his bag. "Okay?"

"Of course," Jan Vidar said.

We took a seat in the middle. Jan Vidar leaned back and placed his feet against the panel that shielded the door.

"Aahh, that's better," I said. "Nice and warm."

"Mm," Jan Vidar concurred.

I bent forward and started to unlace my boots.

"Have you got the address of where we're going?" I asked.

"Elgstien something or other," he said. "I know more or less where it is."

I removed my feet from the boots and rubbed them between my hands. When we came to the small unmanned service station, which had been there for as long as I could remember and had always been a sign that we were approaching Kristiansand and on our way to see my grandparents, I put my feet back, tied the laces, and was finished just as the bus pulled into the Varodd Bridge stop.

"Happy New Year," Jan Vidar shouted to the driver, before leaping into the darkness after me.

Even though I had driven past on numerous occasions I had never set foot here, except in my dreams. Varodd Bridge was one of the places I dreamt of most. Now and then I just stood at the foot and gazed at the towering mast, or I walked onto it. Then the railing usually disappeared and I had to sit down on the road and try to find something to hold onto, or the bridge suddenly disintegrated and I slid inexorably toward the edge. When I was smaller it was Tromøy Bridge that fulfilled this function in my dreams. Now it had become Varodd Bridge.

"My father was at the opening," I said, nodding toward the bridge as we crossed the road.

"Lucky him," Jan Vidar said.

We plodded in silence toward the built-up area. Normally there was a fantastic view from here, you could see Kjevik and the fjord that came into the land on one side and stretched far out to the sea on the other. But tonight everything was as black as the inside of a sack.

"Has the wind dropped a bit?" I asked at some point.

"Seems like it," Jan Vidar said, turning to me. "Have those beers had any effect, by the way?"

I shook my head.

"Nothing. What a waste."

As we walked, houses began to appear. Some were empty and dark, some were full of people dressed in party clothes. Here and there people were letting off rockets from verandas. In one place I saw a gaggle of children waving sparklers in the air. My feet were frozen again. I had curled up my fingers in the mitten not holding the bag of bottles, to little effect. Now we would soon be there, according to Jan Vidar, who then stopped in the middle of an intersection.

"Elgstien's up there," he pointed. "And up there. And down there, and down there too. Take your pick. Which one shall we take?"

"Are there four roads called Elgstien?"

"Apparently so. But which one should we take? Use your feminine intuition."

Feminine? Why did he say that? Did he think I was a woman?

"What do you mean by that?" I asked. "Why do you think I have feminine intuition?"

"Come on, Karl Ove," he said. "Which way?"

I pointed to the right. We started to walk that way. We were looking for number thirteen. The first house was twenty-three, the next twenty-one, so we were on the right track.

Some minutes later we were standing outside the house. It was a seventies build, and looked a bit run-down. The snow on the path to the front door had not been cleared, not for a long time, judging by the line of knee-deep tracks that wound toward the house.

"What was his name, the boy whose party this is?" I asked as we stood by the door.

"Jan Ronny," Jan Vidar said, and rang the bell.

"Jan Ronny?" I repeated.

"That's his name."

The door opened, it must have been the host standing in front of us. He had short, blond hair, pimples on his cheek and around the top of his nose, wore a gold chain around his neck, black jeans, a cotton lumberjack shirt, and white tennis socks. He smiled and pointed at Jan Vidar's stomach.

"Jan Vidar!" he said.

"Right first time," Jan Vidar said.

"And you are . . . ," he said, brandishing his finger at me. "Kai Olav!"

"Karl Ove," I said.

"What the fuck. Come on in! We've already started!"

We took off our outdoor clothes in the hall and followed him downstairs to a cellar room, where there were five people. Watching TV. The table in front of them was covered with beer bottles, bowls of chips, packs of cigarettes and tobacco pouches. Øyvind, who was sitting on the sofa with his arms around his girlfriend, Lene, only in the seventh class but still great and so forward you never thought about the age difference, smiled at us as we went in.

"Hi there!" Øyvind said. "Great you could make it!"

He introduced the others. Rune, Jens, and Ellen. Rune was in the ninth class, Jens and Ellen were in the eighth while Jan Ronny, who was Øyvind's cousin, was at technical school, a budding mechanic. None of them had dressed up. Not so much as a white shirt.

"What are you watching?" Jan Vidar asked, sitting on the sofa and taking out a beer. I leaned against the wall under the low cellar window, which was completely covered by snow on the outside.

"A Bruce Lee film," Øyvind replied. "It's almost over. But we've got *Bachelor Party* as well, and a Dirty Harry film. And Jan Ronny's got a few of his own. What would you like to see? We're easy."

Jan Vidar shrugged.

"I'm easy. What do you say, Karl Ove?"

I shrugged.

"Is there a bottle opener around?" I asked.

Øyvind bent forward and took a lighter from the table, tossed it over to me. But I couldn't open bottles with lighters. Nor could I ask Jan Vidar to open the bottle for me, that was too homo.

I took a bottle from the bag and put the top between my teeth, twisted it so the cap was right over a molar and bit. The cap came off with a hiss.

"Don't do that!" said Lene.

"It's fine," I said.

I downed the beer in one gulp. Apart from all the carbon dioxide filling my stomach with air, which meant I had to swallow the tiny belches that came up, I still didn't feel anything. And I couldn't manage another beer in one go.

My feet ached as the warmth began to return.

"Anyone got any liquor?" I asked.

They shook their heads.

"Just beer, I'm afraid," Øyvind said. "But you can have one if you want."

"Already got some, thanks," I said.

Øyvind raised his bottle.

"Clink'n'sink!" he said.

"Clink'n'sink!" the others said, touching bottles. They laughed.

I fished out the pack of cigarettes from the bag and lit up. Pall Mall mild, not exactly the coolest cigarette around and, standing there with the all-white cigarette in my hand – the filter was white too, I regretted not having bought Prince. But my mind had been focused on the party we were going to after twelve, the one that Irene from the class was throwing, and Pall Mall mild would not be too conspicuous there. It was, also, the brand that Yngve smoked. At least it had been the one time I had seen him smoking, one evening in the garden when Mom and Dad had been at Alf's, Dad's uncle's.

Time for another bottle. I didn't want to use my teeth again, something told me that sooner or later I would come up short, sooner or later the molar would give way and break. And now that I had shown that I could open bottles with my teeth, perhaps it wouldn't seem so homo to let Jan Vidar open it for me.

I went over to him, nabbed a few chips from the bowl on the table.

"Can you open this for me?"

He nodded, without taking his eyes off the film.

Over the last year he had been doing some kickboxing. I kept forgetting, was just as surprised every time he invited me to a session or some such thing. Of course I always refused. But this was Bruce Lee, the fighting was the whole point, and he had one foot in the door.

With a beer bottle in my hand I went back to my place by the wall. No one said anything. Øyvind looked at me.

"Take the weight off your feet, Karl Ove," he said.

"I'm fine standing," I said.

"Well, *skål*, anyway!" he said, raising his bottle to mine. I took two paces over to him, and we clinked.

"Down in one, John!" he said. His Adam's apple pumped up and down like a piston as he drained the bottle.

Øyvind was big for his age, and unusually powerful. He had the body of a grown man. He was also good-natured, and didn't take much notice of what was going on around him, or at least he was always relaxed about it. As if he were immune to the world. He played drums with us, yes, why not, might as well. He went out with Lene, yes, why not, might as well. He didn't talk much to her, dragged her around to see his friends mostly, but that was fine, she wanted to be with him more than anyone else. I had checked her out once, a couple of months ago, just to see how the land lay, but even though I was two years older than them she was not in the slightest bit interested. Oh, how stupid that was. Surrounded by girls at the gymnas and I tried it on with her. Girl from the seventh class. But her breasts looked great under her T-shirt. I still wanted to take it off. I still wanted to feel her breasts in my hands, whatever her age. And there was nothing about her body or manner that indicated she was only fourteen.

I put the bottle to my lips and downed the rest. I really wouldn't be able to keep this up, I thought as I placed it on the table and opened another with my teeth. My stomach was exploding with all the carbon dioxide. Any more and froth would be oozing out of my ears. Fortunately, it was nearly eleven now. At half past eleven we would leave and then be at the other party for the rest of the night. If not for that, I would have gone long ago.

A boy called Jens suddenly half-rose from the sofa, grabbed the lighter from the table and held it to his ass.

"Now!" he said.

He farted as he flicked the lighter, and a ball of flame flared out behind him. He laughed. The others laughed too.

"Stop that!" Lene said.

Jan Vidar smiled, and was careful not to meet my gaze. Bottle in hand, I wandered over to the far door in the room. Behind it there was a small kitchen. I leaned over the counter. The house was on a slope, and the window, well above ground level, faced the back of the garden. Two pine trees were swaying in the wind. There were more houses farther down. Through the window of one I saw three men and a woman standing, glass in hand, talking. The men wore black suits, the woman a black dress with bare arms. I went to the other door and opened it. A shower. On the wall was a wetsuit. Well, that's something at least, I thought, closed the door and went back to the living room. The others were sitting, as before.

"Can you feel anything?" Jan Vidar asked.

I shook my head.

"No. Not a thing. You?"

He smiled.

"A bit."

"We'll have to be off soon," I said.

"Where are you going?" Øyvind asked.

"Up to the intersection. Where everyone's going at twelve."

"But it's only eleven! And we're going there too. We can go together, for Christ's sake."

He looked at me.

"Why do you want to go there now?"

I shrugged.

"I've arranged to meet someone there."

"She'll wait for you, don't worry," Jan Vidar said.

It was half past eleven when we made a move to go. The quiet residential area where, apart from a few people on the odd veranda or drive, there had not been a soul half an hour earlier was now full of life and activity. Smartly dressed partygoers streamed out of the houses. Women with shawls over their shoulders, glasses in their hands and high-heeled evening shoes on their feet, men with coats over their suits, patent leather shoes, holding bags of fireworks, excited children running among them, many with fizzing sparklers, filled the air with shouts and laughter. Jan Vidar and I were carrying our white plastic bags of beer and walking alongside the pimply schoolkids dressed in everyday clothes with whom we had spent the evening. In actual fact, we were not alongside them. I kept a few steps ahead in case we should meet anyone I knew from school. Pretended to look with interest this way and that so it would be impossible for anyone who saw us to imagine we were together. Which of course we were not. I looked good, white shirt, sleeves rolled up the way Yngve had told me they should be that autumn. Over the suit jacket and my black suitlike trousers I was wearing a grey coat, on my feet Doc Martens, and leather straps around my wrists. My hair was long at the back and short, almost spiky, on top. The only thing that didn't belong was the bag of beer. Of that, however, I was painfully aware. It was what also linked me with the shabby crowd lurching along behind me, because they had plastic bags as well, each and every one of them.

At the intersection, which was on higher ground, and had been an assembly point because you could see the whole bay from there, there was total chaos. People stood shoulder to shoulder, most were drunk, and everyone was letting off fireworks. There were bangs and crackles on all sides, the smell of gunpowder tore at your nostrils, smoke drifted through the air and one after another multicolored rockets exploded beneath the cloudy sky. It shook with flashes of light looking as if it could rupture and burst at any moment.

We stood on the perimeter of the noise. Øyvind, who had brought along fireworks, took out a huge, dynamite-shaped stick and placed it in front of his feet. He seemed to be swaying to and fro as he did so. Jan Vidar was jabbering away, as he did when he was drunk, with a permanent smile on his lips. At the moment he was talking to Rune. They had found a common theme in kickboxing. His glasses were still misted up, but he could no longer be bothered to remove or wipe them. I was standing a few steps away and allowed my gaze to wander through the crowd. When the stick exploded for the first time and a red light was eructated right next to me I jumped out of my skin. Øyvind burst out laughing.

"Not bad!" he shouted. "Shall we try it again?" he said, putting down another firework and lighting it, without waiting for an answer. It immediately began to spew forth balls of light, and this, the steady succession of the explosions, excited him so much that he rummaged around in feverish haste for a third even before this one had died.

He couldn't contain his laughter.

Beside us, a man in a light-blue jacket, white shirt and red leather tie tumbled headlong into a snowdrift. A woman ran over to him in her high heels and pulled at his arm, not hard enough to lift him but enough to motivate him to stand up under his own steam. He brushed himself down while staring straight ahead as though he had not just been lying in the snow but had merely stopped to get a better overall view of the situation. Two boys were standing on the bus shelter roof, each holding a rocket at an angle; they lit them, and with their faces averted, gripped them in their hands as they hissed and fizzed until the rockets took off, flew a couple of meters and exploded with such intensity and power that all the bystanders looked round.

"Hey, Jan Vidar," I said. "Can you open this one as well?"

With a smile, he flipped the top off the bottle I passed him. At last I could feel something, but not pleasure nor a somberness, more a rapidly increasing blunting of the senses. I drank, lit a cigarette, looked at my watch. Ten to twelve.

"Ten minutes to go!" I said.

Jan Vidar nodded, went on chatting with Rune. I had decided not to look for Irene until after twelve. Those at the party would stick together until twelve, I was sure of that, then they would hug and wish one another a happy New Year, they already knew one another, they were friends, a clique, like everyone at my school they had their own, and I was too far outside this one to mingle. But after twelve, things would loosen up, they would stand around drinking, they would not return right away, and with the clique in this vaguely spontaneous, loose state, I would be able to make contact, chat and casually, or at least without revealing any obvious intentions, wheedle my way in and stay.

The problem was Jan Vidar. Would he want to come with me? They were all people he didn't know, people I had more in common with than he did. He seemed to be enjoying himself where he was, didn't he?

I would have to ask him. If he didn't want to come with me, that was up to him. But I would definitely never set foot in that damn cellar again, that was for certain.

And there she was.

Some distance away, perhaps thirty meters from us, surrounded by her party guests. I tried to count them, but outside the inner circle it was difficult to work out who belonged to her party and who belonged elsewhere. I was sure it was somewhere between ten and twelve people. I had seen almost all the faces before; she hung out with them during the breaks. She was not beautiful, I suppose, she had a bit of a double chin and chubby cheeks – although she was not in any way fat – blue eyes and blond hair. She was short and there was something duck like about her. But none of this mattered one bit in my judgment of her, for she had something else, which was more important: she was a focal point. No matter where she went or what she said, people paid attention. She was out every weekend, in Kristiansand or at private parties, unless she was staying in a chalet at a skiing center or in some other big town. Always with her clique. I hated these cliques, I really did, and when I stood listening to her going on about all the things she had done recently I hated her too.

Tonight she was wearing a dark-blue, knee-length coat. Underneath I glimpsed a light-blue dress and skin-colored tights. On her head she had . . . well, yes, it was a diadem, wasn't it? Like some little princess?

Around me the intensity had gradually increased. Now all you could hear was bangs and explosions and shouting on all sides. Then, as if from above, as though it was God himself making his pleasure known at the advent of the New Year, the sirens began to sound. The cheering around us rose in volume. I looked at my watch. Twelve.

Jan Vidar met my gaze.

"It's twelve o'clock!" he shouted. "Happy New Year!"

He started to trudge toward me.

No, shit, he wasn't going to hug me, was he?

No, no, no!

But over he came, put his arms around me and pressed his cheek against mine.

"Happy New Year, Karl Ove," he said. "And thanks for everything in the old one!"

"Happy New Year," I said. His stubble rubbed against my smooth cheek. He thumped me on the back twice, then took a step back.

"Øyvind!" he said, going toward him.

Why the hell did he have to hug me? What was the point? We never hugged. We weren't the sort of guys who would hug.

What a pile of shit this was.

"Happy New Year, Karl Ove!" said Lene. She smiled at me, and I leaned forward and gave her a hug.

"Happy New Year," I said. "You're so beautiful."

Her face, which seconds before had floated around and been part of everything else that was happening, froze.

"What did you say?" she asked.

"Nothing," I said. "Thank you for the old year."

She smiled.

"I heard what you said," she said. "Happy New Year too."

As she moved away, I had a stiffy.

Oh, not that as well.

I drank the rest of my beer. There were only three left in the bag. I ought to have saved them, but I needed something to occupy myself with, so I took one, opened it with my teeth and gulped it down. I lit a cigarette as well. They were my tools; with those in my hands I was equipped and ready to go. A cigarette in the left hand, a bottle of beer in the right. So I stood there lifting them to my mouth, first one, then the other. Cigarette, beer, cigarette, beer.

At ten past, I slapped Jan Vidar on the back and said I was going to join some friends, would be back soon, don't go away, he nodded, and I made my way through to Irene. At first she didn't notice me, she was standing with her back to me talking to some people.

"Hi, Irene!" I said.

As she didn't turn, presumably because my voice could not be heard over the ambient noise, I felt obliged to tap her on the shoulder. This was not good, this approach was too direct, tapping someone on the shoulder is not the same as bumping into them, but I would have to take a chance.

At any event, she did turn.

"Karl Ove," she said. "What are you doing here?"

"We're at a party nearby. Then I saw you up here and thought I would wish you a happy New Year. Happy New Year!'

"Happy New Year!" she said. "Are you enjoying yourself?"

"Certainly am!" I said. "And you?"

"Yes, having a great time."

There was a brief silence.

"You're throwing a party, aren't you?" I said.

"Yes."

"Anywhere near?"

"Yes, I live over there."

She pointed up the hill.

"In that house?" I said, nodding in the same direction.

"No, behind it. You can't see it from the road."

"I couldn't tag along, could I?" I said. "Then we could chat a bit more. That would be nice."

She shook her head and wrinkled her nose.

"Don't think so," she said. "It isn't a class party, you see."

"I know," I said. "But just for a little chat? Nothing more. I'm at a party quite close by."

"Go there then!" she said. "We can see each other at school in the New Year!"

She had completely out-maneuvered me. There was nothing else to say.

"Nice to see you," I said. "I've always liked you."

Then I about-faced and walked back. It had been hard to articulate the stuff about always liking her, because it was not true, but at least it would deflect her attention from the fact that I had tried to cadge an invitation to her party. Now she would think I asked because I was coming on to her. And I was coming on to her because I was drunk. Who doesn't do that on New Year's Eve?

Bitch. Fucking bitch.

Jan Vidar looked up at me when I got back.

"There won't be any party," I said. "We're not invited."

"Why not? Thought you said you knew them."

"Invited guests only. And we're not. Assholes."

Jan Vidar snorted.

"We'll just go back. It was great there, wasn't it."

I sent him a vacant stare and yawned, to let him know how great it was. But we had no choice. We couldn't call his father before two o'clock. We couldn't very well call at ten minutes past twelve on New Year's Eve. So once again it was the crowd of pimply schoolkids dressed in everyday clothes that I walked ahead of through the residential district of Søm on that windblown New Year's Eve of 1984/1985.

At twenty past two Jan Vidar's father pulled up outside the house. We were ready and waiting. I, who was less drunk, sat in the front while Jan Vidar, who only one hour earlier had been jumping around with a lampshade on his head, sat in the back, as we had planned. Fortunately, after he had thrown up and after drinking a few glasses of water and washing his face thoroughly under the tap, he was in a state to phone his father and tell him where we were. Not very convincingly. I stood beside him and heard him almost spewing up the first part of the word, then swallowing the last, but he did manage to spit out the address, and I don't suppose our parents imagined we were nowhere near alcohol on occasions such as these.

"Happy New Year, boys!" his father said as we got in. "Have you had a good time?"

"Yes," I said. "Lots of people out and about at twelve. Quite a scene. How was it in Tveit?"

"Fine," he said, stretching his arm along the back of my seat and craning his neck to reverse. "Whose house was it, actually?"

"Someone Øyvind knows. The one who plays drums in the band."

"Oh yes," the father said, changing gear and driving back the way he had just come. The snow in some of the gardens was stained with fireworks. A few couples were walking along the road. The occasional taxi passed. Otherwise all was quiet and peaceful. There was something I had always liked about gliding through the darkness with the dashboard illuminated beside a man who was confident and calm in his movements. Jan Vidar's father was a good man. He was friendly and interested, but also left us in peace when Jan Vidar indicated we had had enough. He took us on fishing trips, he repaired things for us – once when my bike had been punctured on the way there he had fixed the tire for me, without a word, it was all ready when I had to leave – and when they went on family holidays they invited me. He asked after my parents, as did Jan Vidar's mother, and whenever he drove me home, which was not so seldom, he always had a chat with Mom or Dad, if they were around, and he invited them over to his place. It wasn't his fault that they never went. But he also had a temper, I knew that, even though I had never seen any evidence of it, and hatred was also among the many feelings Jan Vidar had for him.

"So it's 1985," I said as we joined the E18 by Varodd Bridge.

"Indeed," Jan Vidar's father said. "Or what do you say in the back?"

Jan Vidar didn't say anything. And he hadn't when his father got there either. He had just stared straight ahead and got in. I twisted around in my seat and looked at him. He was sitting with his head transfixed and his eyes focused on a point in the neck rest.

"Lost your tongue?" his father asked, smiling at me.

Still total silence from the rear.

"Your parents," his father went on. "Did they stay at home tonight?"

I nodded.

"My grandparents and my uncle came over. Lutefisk and aquavit."

"Glad you weren't there?"

"Yes."

Onto the Kjevik road, past Hamresanden, along Ryensletta. Dark, peaceful, nice and warm. I could sit like this for the rest of my life, I thought. Past their house, into the bends up by Kragebo, down to the bridge on the other side, up the hill. It hadn't been cleared and was covered with five centimeters of fresh snow. Jan Vidar's father drove more slowly over the last stretch. Past the house where Susann and Elise lived, the two sisters who had moved here from Canada, and no one could quite figure out, past the bend where William lived, down the hill, and up the last bit.

"I'll drop you here," he said. "Then we won't wake them if they're asleep. Okay?"

"Okay," I said. "And thank you very much for the ride. See you, Jayvee!"

Jan Vidar blinked, then opened his eyes wide.

"See you, yes," he said.

"Are you going to sit in the front?" Jan Vidar's father asked.

"I don't," Jan Vidar said. I closed the door, raised my hand to wave goodbye and heard the car reversing behind me as I walked up the road to the house. "Jayvee"! Why had I said that? The nickname that signaled a friendship I didn't need to signal; I had never used it before since, in fact, we were friends.

The windows in the house were unlit. So they must have gone to bed. I was glad, not because I had anything to hide, but because I wanted to be left in peace. After hanging up my outdoor clothes in the hall I went into the living room. All traces of the party had been removed. In the kitchen the dishwasher was humming softly. I sat down on the sofa and peeled an orange. Although the fire had gone out you could still feel the heat from the wood burner. Mom was right, it was good living here. On the wicker chair the cat lazily raised its head. Meeting my gaze, it got up, padded across the floor and jumped onto my lap. I got rid of the orange peel, which the cat hated.

"You can lie here for a bit," I said, stroking it. "You can. But not all night, you know. I'm going to bed soon."

It began to purr as it curled up on me. Its head sank slowly, resting on one paw, and its eyes, which first had closed with pleasure, were closed in sleep within seconds.

"It's alright for some," I said.

The next morning I awoke to the radio in the kitchen, but stayed where I was, there was nothing to get up for anyway today, and I soon fell sleep again. The next time I awoke it was half past eleven. I got dressed and went downstairs. Mom was sitting at the kitchen table reading and looked up as I came in.

"Hi," she said. "Did you have a good time last night?"

"Yes," I said. "It was fun."

"When did you get home?"

"Half past two-ish. Jan Vidar's dad brought us back."

I sat down and spread some liver pâté on a slice of bread, succeeded after several attempts in spearing a pickle with a fork, put it on top, and lifted the teapot to feel if it was empty.

"Is there any left?" Mom asked. "I can boil some more water."

"Could probably squeeze a little cup out," I said. "But it might be cold."

Mom got up.

"Stay where you are," I said. "I can do it myself."

"It's fine," she said. "I'm sitting right by the stove."

She filled the saucepan and put it on the burner, which soon began to crackle.

"And what did you have to eat?" she asked.

"It was a cold buffet," I said. "I think the girl's mother made it. It was the usual . . . you know, shrimp and vegetables in jelly, transparent . . . ?"

"Shrimp in aspic?" Mom queried.

"Yes, shrimp in aspic. And ordinary shrimp. And crab. Two lobsters, there wasn't enough for everyone, but we all got to taste a bit. And then, oh yeah, some ham and other things."

"Sounds good," Mom said.

"Yes, it was," I said. "Then we went out at twelve, down to the intersection where everyone gathered and let off rockets. Well, we didn't, but lots of the others did."

"Did you meet anyone new?"

I hesitated. Took another slice of bread, scanned the table for something to put on it. Salami with mayonnaise, that looked good.

"Not exactly," I said. "Mostly I stuck with people I know."

I looked at her.

"Where's Dad?"

"In the barn. He's off to Grandma's today. Feel like going?"

"No, I'd rather not," I said. "There were so many people last night. I feel like being on my own now. Perhaps I'll wander down to Per's. But that's all. What are you going to do?"

"I'm not sure. Read a bit, maybe. And make a start on my packing. The plane leaves early tomorrow morning."

"That's right," I said. "When's Yngve off?"

"In a few days, I think. Then it'll be just you and Dad here."

"Yes," I said. I clapped my eyes on the brawn Grandma had made. Perhaps brawn wouldn't be a bad idea for the next slice? And then one with lamb sausage.

Half an hour later I was ringing the doorbell at Per's house. His father opened. He appeared to be on his way out: he was wearing a lined, green military jacket over a shiny blue tracksuit and had light-colored boots on; in his hand he had a lead. Their dog, an old Golden Retriever, was wagging its tail between its legs.

"Ah, it's you," he said. "Happy New Year."

"Happy New Year," I said.

"They're in the living room," he said. "Just go right in."

He walked past me, whistling, onto the forecourt and over to the open garage. I kicked off my shoes and went into the house. It was large and open, built not so many years ago, by Per's father, as far as I had understood, and you had a view of the river from almost all the rooms. From the hall there was first the kitchen, where Per's mother was working, she turned her head as I passed, smiled and said hello, then the living room, where Per was sitting with his brother Tom, sister Marit, and best friend Trygve.

"What are you watching?" I asked.

"*Guns of Navarone*," Per said.

"Been watching it long?"

"No. Half an hour. We can rewind it if you want."

"Rewind?" said Trygve. "Aw, we don't want to see the beginning again."

"But Karl Ove hasn't seen it," Per said. "It won't take long."

"It won't take long? It'll take half an hour," Trygve said.

Per went to the video player and knelt down.

"You can't decide that unilaterally," Tom said.

"Oh?" Per said.

He pressed STOP and then REWIND.

Marit got up and headed for the staircase.

"Call me when we're back to where we were," she said. Per nodded. The video machine click-clacked a few times while emitting some tiny hydraulic whines until it was ready to start, and the tape began to whir backwards with ever-increasing speed and volume until it came to a stop well before the end, whereafter the last part rotated extremely slowly, in a manner reminiscent of a plane which after flying at breakneck speed through the air approaches the ground at reduced speed and brakes on the runway, and then calmly and carefully taxis toward the terminal building.

"I suppose you were at home with Mommy and Daddy last night?" I said, looking at Trygve.

"Yes?" he said. "And I suppose you went out drinking?"

"Yes," I said. "I was having a drinky-winky, but I wish we'd stayed at home. We didn't have a party to go to, so we just trudged around in the storm each lugging a bag of beer bottles. We walked the whole way to Søm. But just wait. Soon it will be your turn to wander around aimlessly with plastic bags at night."

"Okay," Per said.

"Oh, this is fun," Trygve said as the first frames from the film appeared on the screen. Outside, everything was still, as only winter can be. And even though the sky was overcast and gray, the light over the countryside shimmered and was perfectly white. I remember thinking all I wanted to do was sit right there, in a newly built house, in a circle of light in the middle of the forest and be as stupid as I liked.

The next morning Dad drove Mom to the airport. When he returned, the buffer between us was gone, and we resumed the life we had lived all that autumn without further delay. He was back in the flat in the barn, I caught the bus down to Jan Vidar's house where we plugged into his amplifier and sat around playing for a while until we got sick of that and ambled over to the shop, where nothing happened, ambled back and watched some ski-jumping on TV, played a few records, and talked about girls. At around five I caught the bus back up, Dad met me at the door, asked if he could drive me to town. Great, I said. On the way he suggested dropping in on my grandparents, I was probably hungry, we could eat there.

Grandma stuck her head out of the window as Dad parked the car outside the garage.

"Oh, it's you!" she said.

A minute later she unlocked the front door.

"Nice to see you again!" she said. "It was lovely at your house."

She looked at me.

"And you had a good time too, I heard?"

"Yes, I did."

"Give me a hug then! You're a big boy now, but you can still give your grandmother a hug, can't you!"

I leaned forward and felt her dry, wrinkled cheek against mine. She smelled good, of the perfume she had always used.

"Have you eaten?" Dad asked.

"We've just had a bite, but I can heat something up for you, that's no problem. Are you hungry?"

"I think we are, aren't we?" Dad said, looking at me with a wry smile.

"I am at any rate," I said.

In my inner ear I heard how that must have sounded to them.

"At any wate."

We took our jackets off in the hall, I put my boots neatly at the bottom of the open wardrobe, hung my jacket on one of the ancient, chipped golden clothes hangers, Grandma stood by the stairs watching us with that impatience in her body she had always exhibited. One hand passed over her cheek. Her head twisted to one side. Her weight shifted from one foot to the other. Apparently unaffected by these minor adjustments she kept talking to Dad. Asked whether there was as much snow higher up. Whether Mom had left. When she would be back next. Mm, right, she said each time he said anything. Right.

"And what about you, Karl Ove," she said, focusing on me. "When do you start school again?"

"In two days."

"That'll be nice, won't it."

"Yes, it will."

Dad snatched a glance at himself in the mirror. His face was calm, but there was a visible shadow of displeasure in his eyes, they seemed cold and apathetic. He took a step toward Grandma, who turned to climb the stairs, lightly and nimbly. Dad followed, heavy-limbed, and I brought up the rear, eyes fixed on the thick, black hair at the back of his neck.

"Well, I'll be darned!" Grandad said as we entered the kitchen. He was sitting on a chair by the table, leaning back with legs apart, black suspenders over a white shirt buttoned up to the neck. Over his face hung a lock of hair that he pushed back into place with his hand. From his mouth hung an unlit cigarette.

"How were the roads?" he asked. "Icy?"

"They weren't so bad," Dad said. "Worse on New Year's Eve. And there was no traffic to speak of either."

"Sit yourselves down," Grandma said.

"No, then there's no room for you," Dad said.

"I'll stand," she said. "I have to heat your food up anyway. I sit all day, I do, you know. Come on, sit down!"

Grandad held a lighter to his cigarette and lit up. Puffed a few times, blew smoke into the room.

Grandma switched on the burners, drummed her fingers on the counter and whistled softly, as was her wont.

In a way Dad was too big to sit at the kitchen table, I thought. Not physically, there was plenty of room for him, it was more that he looked out of place. There was something about him, or whatever he radiated, that distanced itself from this table.

He took out a cigarette and lit it.

Would he have fit better in the living room? If we had been eating in there? Yes, he would. That would have been better.

"So it's 1985," I said to break the silence that had already lasted seconds.

"Yes, s'pose it is, my boy," Grandma said.

"What have you done with your brother?" Grandad said. "Is he back in Bergen?"

"No, he's still in Arendal," I said.

"Ah yes," Grandad said. "He's become a real Arendal boy, he has."

"Yes, he doesn't come by here so often any more," Grandma said. "We had such fun when he was small."

She looked at me.

"But you come though."

"What is it he's studying now?" Grandad asked.

"Isn't it political science?" Dad wondered, looking at me.

"No, he's just started media studies," I said.

"Don't you know what your own son's studying?" Grandad smiled.

"Yes, I do. I know very well," Dad said. He stubbed out his half-smoked cigarette in the ashtray and turned to Grandma. "I think it'll be ready now, Mother. It doesn't have to be scalding hot. It must be hot enough by now, don't you think?"

"Probably," Grandma said, and fetched two plates from a cupboard, placed them before us, took cutlery from a drawer and put it beside the plates.

"I'll do it this way today," she said, picking up Dad's plate and filling it with potatoes, creamed peas, rissoles, and gravy.

"That looks good," Dad said as she put his plate down in front of him and took mine.

The only two people I knew who ate as fast as me were Yngve and Dad. Our plates had hardly been put in front of us before they were picked clean. Dad leaned back and lit another cigarette, Grandma poured a cup of coffee and handed it to him, I got up and went into the living room, looked across the town with all its glittering lights, the gray, almost black, snow piled up against the walls of the warehouses along the quay. The harbor lights rippled across the shiny, pitch-black surface of the water.

For a moment I was filled with the sensation of white snow against black water. The way the whiteness erases all the detail around a lake or a river in the forest so that the difference between land and water is absolute, and the water lies there as a deeply alien entity, a black hole in the world.

I turned. The second living room was two steps higher than the one I was in and separated by a sliding door. The door was half-open and I went up, not for any particular reason, I was simply restless. This was the fancy room, they used it only for special occasions, we had never been allowed in there alone.

A piano stood adjacent to one wall, above it hung two paintings with Old Testament motifs. On the piano were three graduation photographs of the sons. Dad, Erling, and Gunnar. It was always strange to see Dad without a beard. He was smiling with the black graduation cap perched jauntily at the back of his head. His eyes shone with pleasure.

In the middle of the floor there were two sofas, one on either side of a table. In the corner at the very back of the room, which was dominated by two black leather sofas and an antique rose-painted corner cabinet, there was a white fireplace.

"Karl Ove?" Dad shouted from the kitchen.

I quickly took the four paces to the everyday living room and answered.

"Are we going?"

"Yes."

When I entered the kitchen he was already on his feet.

"Take care," I said. "Bye."

"You take care," Grandad said. As always, Grandma came down with us.

"Oh, I almost forgot," Dad said when we were in the hall putting on our coats and scarves. "I've got something for you."

He went out, opened and closed the car door, and then returned carrying a parcel which he passed to her.

"Many happy returns, Mother," he said.

"Oh, you shouldn't have!" Grandma said. "Goodness me. You shouldn't buy presents for me, dear!"

"Yes, I should," Dad said. "Come on. Open it!"

I didn't know where to look. There was something intimate about all this, which I had not witnessed before and had no idea existed.

Grandma stood with a tablecloth in her hand.

"My, how beautiful!" she exclaimed.

"I thought it would match the wallpaper upstairs," Dad said. "Can you see that?"

"Lovely," Grandma said.

"Well," Dad said in a tone that precluded any further embellishments, "we'll be off now."

We got into the car, Dad started the engine, and a cascade of light struck the garage door. Grandma waved goodbye from the steps as we reversed down the little slope. As always, she closed the door behind her when we were turning, and by the time we drove onto the main road she was gone.

In the next days I occasionally thought about the little episode in the hall, and my feeling was the same every time: I had seen something I shouldn't have seen. But it passed quickly; I wasn't exactly concerned with Dad and Grandma, so much else was happening during those weeks. In the first lesson of the new school year Siv handed out an invitation to everyone, she was going to have a class party the following Saturday, and this was good news, a class party was something I was entitled to attend, where no one could accuse me of trying to gate-crash, and where familiarity with the others could be extended into the wider world, which in class enabled me to come quite close to behaving in ways consistent with the person I really was. In short, I would be able to drink, dance, laugh, and perhaps pin someone against a wall somewhere. On the other hand, class parties had lower status precisely for that reason, it wasn't the kind of party you were invited to because of who you were but rather where you were, in this case class 1B. However, I didn't allow that to sour my pleasure. A party was not just a party, even if it was that too. The problem of acquiring alcohol was the same as before New Year's Eve, and I considered whether to call Tom again, but decided it was best to risk it myself. I may have been only sixteen but I looked older, and if I acted normally no one would even think of refusing me. If they did, it would be embarrassing, but that was all and I would still be able to ask Tom to organize it. So, on the Wednesday I went to the supermarket, put twelve lagers in my cart, with bread and tomatoes as alibis, queued up, put them on the conveyor belt, handed the checkout-girl the money, she took it without so much as a glance at me, and I hurried excitedly home with a clinking plastic bag in each hand.

When I came home from school on Friday afternoon, Dad had been in the flat. There was a message on the table.

Karl Ove,
I am at a seminar all this weekend. Coming home Sunday night. There are some fresh shrimp in the fridge and there's a loaf in the bread basket. Enjoy yourself!
Dad

On top there was a five-hundred-krone note.

Oh, this was just perfect!

Shrimp was what I loved most. I ate them in front of the television that evening, afterward I went for a walk through town, playing my Walkman, first "Lust for Life" by Iggy Pop and then one of the later Roxy Music albums, something to do with the distance between the inside and the outside worlds arose then, something that I liked so much; when I saw all the drunken faces of people who had gathered by the bars it was as if they existed in a different dimension from mine, the same applied to the cars driving by, to the drivers getting in and out of their cars at the gas stations, to the shop assistants standing behind counters with their weary smiles and mechanical movements, and to men out walking their dogs.

The next morning I dropped by my grandparents', ate fresh rolls with them, then went to town, bought three records and a big bag of sweets, a few music magazines and a paperback, Jean Genet, *Journal du Voleur*. Had two beers while watching a televised English soccer match, one more while showering and changing, another while smoking the last cigarette before going out.

I had arranged to meet Bassen at the Østerveien intersection at seven o'clock. He stood there smiling as I lumbered up with the bag of beer in my hand. He had all his in a backpack, and the second I saw that I felt like smacking my forehead. Of course! That was the way to do it.

We walked along Kuholmsveien, past my grandparents' place, up the hill and into the residential district around the stadium, where Siv's house was.

After searching for a few minutes we found the right number and rang the doorbell. Siv opened and let out a loud squeal.

Even before I awoke I knew that something good had happened. It was like a hand stretching down to me where I lay at the bottom of consciousness, watching one image after another rushing past me. A hand I grabbed and let lift me slowly, I came closer and closer to myself until I thrust open my eyes.

Where was I?

Oh, yes, the downstairs living room in the flat. I was lying on the sofa, fully clothed.

I sat up, supported my throbbing head in my hands.

My shirt smelled of perfume.

A heavy, exotic fragrance.

I had been making out with Monica. We had danced, we had drifted to the side, stood under a staircase, I had kissed her. She had kissed me.

But that's not what it was!

I got up and went into the kitchen, poured water into a glass and gulped it down.

No, it wasn't that.

Something fantastic had happened, a light had been lit, but it wasn't Monica. There was something else.

But what?

All the alcohol had created an imbalance in my body. But it knew what I needed to redress the balance. Hamburger, fries, hot dog. Lots of Coke. That's what I needed. And I needed it now.

I went into the hall, glanced at myself in the mirror while running a hand through my hair. I didn't look too bad, only slightly bloodshot eyes; I could definitely show my face like this.

I laced my boots, grabbed my jacket and put it on.

But what was it?

A button?

With *Smile* on it?

Yes, that was it!

That was the good thing!

We had been chatting for a long time. She had laughed and been so happy. She hadn't had anything to drink. But I had, so I could be where she was, in the lighthearted, happy zone. Then we danced.

Oh, we had danced to Frankie Goes to Hollywood. "The Power of Love."

The POWER of LO-OVE!

But Hanne, Hanne.

Feeling her so close to me. Standing nearly as close and talking. Her laughter. Her green eyes. Her small nose.

Just before we left, on the way out, she had pinned the button on me.

That was what had happened. It wasn't much, but the little there had been was fantastic.

I buttoned up my jacket and left. Low clouds hung over the town, a cold wind swept through the streets and onto the sea. Everything was gray and white, cold and inhospitable. But inside me the sun was shining. I heard *The POWER of LO-OVE!* again and again as I walked along the river towards the snack bar.

What had happened?

Hanne was Hanne, she hadn't changed, she was the same person she had been in the classroom all autumn and winter. I liked her but had not felt anything special for her. Till now! And then this!

It was as though I had been struck by lightning. At regular intervals happiness surged along my nerve channels. My heart trembled, my soul glowed. Suddenly I couldn't wait for Monday, I couldn't wait for school to begin.

Should I call?

Should I invite her out?

Without thinking, I ordered a cheeseburger with bacon and fries, and a large Coke. She was going out with someone, she had told me that, someone in the third class at Vågsbygd Gymnas. They had been together a long time. But the way she had looked at me, the closeness that had sprung up out of the blue, that could not be insignificant, could it? It had to mean something. There was an interest there, a desire in her for me. There had to be.

On Monday, on Monday, then I would see her again.

But what the hell was I to do until then?

That was almost *one whole* day!

She smiled when she saw me. I smiled too.

"You haven't taken off the button!" she said.

"No," I said. "I think about you whenever I see it."

She looked down. Fidgeted with a button on her jacket.

"You were pretty drunk," she said, peering up at me again.

"I suppose I was," I said. "I don't remember that much to be honest."

"You don't remember?"

"No, I do, I do! I remember Frankie Goes to Hollywood, for example . . ."

Down the corridor came Tønnesen, the young geography teacher with a beard and Mandal dialect, who was our class teacher.

"Well, you two, did you have a good weekend?" he asked, opening the door we were standing outside.

"We had a class party." Hanne smiled.

What a smile.

"Oh? And I wasn't invited?" he said, not expecting an answer to this remark because he didn't look at her, just strode through the room to the desk at the end where he deposited his small pile of books.

I was unable to concentrate on what was happening in the lesson. I was only thinking about Hanne, even though she was sitting in the same room I was. Or was it thinking? . . . It was more as if I were full to the brim with emotions which did not leave any space for thought. And so it remained for the whole of the winter and spring. I was in love, and it was not one of those trivial crushes, it was one of the *grands amours*, the ones you may experience only three, or perhaps four, times in a lifetime. This was the first, and since everything about it was new, perhaps the greatest. Everything in me was centered on Hanne. Every morning I awoke and looked forward to going to school, where she would be. If she wasn't there, if she was ill or out of town, all meaning immediately drained out of everything, the rest of the day was just a question of endurance. For what? What was I waiting for while I was waiting? Not hot embraces and deep kisses at any rate, for a relationship in that sense simply did not exist. No, what I was waiting and lived for was the hand that lightly caressed my shoulder, it was the smile that lit up her face whenever she saw me or I said something funny, it was the embrace when we met as friends after school. The few seconds there, when I put my arms around her and felt her cheek against mine, the scent of her, the shampoo she used, its faint apple fragrance. She was attracted to me, I knew that, but she had such strict limits around her and what she felt she could do that there was never a question of us becoming a couple. To be honest, I was not sure that she was actually attracted to me, it might simply have been that she was flattered by all the attention she was receiving, and found it entertaining. Nevertheless, I had hopes, when I got home to my flat I interpreted everything she said and did in the course of a school day, and that either sent me into the deepest vale of misery or up onto the highest peak of elation – there was nothing in between.

At school I started passing notes to her. Little remarks, little greetings, little messages I had often as not composed the night before. As soon as she sent an answer I read it and wrote a reply, which immediately returned and I carefully monitored her reactions as she read it. If she failed to continue a topic I had started, everything went black for me. If she responded, my insides quivered and jingled as though I were a bell. Later the slips of paper were replaced by a notebook that shuttled between us, not too frequently, I didn't want her to get sick of it, but it must have been two or three times a day. I often asked her if she wanted to go to the cinema or a café with me, to which she answered each time, *you know that I can't*.

We had discussions in the breaks, a bit of politics, mostly religion, she was a Christian, I was fervently anti-Christian, and she passed on my arguments to the young leader of her congregation, and returned with his answer the next time. Her boyfriend was a member of the same congregation, and if I did not threaten their relationship directly I was at least a contrast to her other life. In any event, the space for our brief meetings during breaks, which did not even take place every day, was cautiously and imperceptibly expanded to encompass life outside school. We were friends, schoolmates, wasn't it only natural that we should have a cup of coffee in a café after school now and then? Wasn't it only natural that we should walk together to the bus now and then?

I lived for this. The quick glances, the tiny smiles, the light touches. And oh, her laughter! When I made her laugh!

I lived for it. But I wanted more, much, much more. I wanted to see her all the time, be with her all the time, to be invited to her house, to meet her parents, go out with her friends, go on holiday with her, take her home . . .

You know that I can't.

The cinema, that had associations with relationships and love, but there were other arrangements that did not, and it was to one of them I invited Hanne to one day in early February; it was a meeting for young political activists somewhere in the town center. I had seen a notice at school, and one morning I wrote to her and asked whether she wanted to go. After reading the note she glanced over, without a smile. Wrote something. Sent the notebook, I opened and read it. *Yes!* it said.

Yes! I thought.

Yes! Yes! Yes!

I was sitting on the sofa waiting when she knocked on the door at around six.

"Hi!" I said. "Do you want to come in while I put my togs on?"

"Sure," she said.

Her cheeks were red from the cold. She was wearing a white wooly hat pulled down to her eyes and a large white scarf wrapped around her neck.

"So this is where you live!" she said.

"Yes," I answered, opening the door to the living room.

"That's the living room. Then the kitchen's over there. And there's a bedroom upstairs. That's actually my grandfather's office. There," I said, nodding to the door on the other side.

"Isn't it lonely living on your own here?"

"No," I said. "Not at all. I like being alone. And I'm up in Tveit a lot of the time."

I put on my jacket, still adorned with the *Smile* button, a scarf, and boots.

"Just have to go to the bathroom, and we'll be off," I said. Closed the bathroom door behind me. Heard her singing to herself in a low voice. The walls were thin in this house, perhaps she was trying to drown out what was going on here, perhaps she just wanted to sing.

I put the toilet lid up and tugged out the frankfurter.

All at once I realized it would be impossible to pee while she was outside. The walls were thin, the hall so small. She would even be able to hear that I hadn't done anything.

Oh hell.

I squeezed as hard as I could.

Not a drop.

She was singing and walking back and forth.

What must she be thinking?

After thirty seconds I gave up, turned on the tap, and let the water run for a few moments, so that at least something had happened in here, then turned it off, opened the door and went out, to meet her embarrassed, downcast eyes.

"Let's be off then," I said.

The streets were dark, and the wind was blowing, as it did so often in Kristiansand in winter. We didn't say much on the way. Talked a bit about school, the people who went there, Bassen, Molle, Siv, Tone, Anne. For some reason she started talking about her father, he was so fantastic. He wasn't a Christian, she said. That surprised me. Had she become one on her own initiative? She said I would have liked her father. Would have? I wondered. Mm, I mumbled. He sounds nice. Laconic. What does laconic mean? she asked, her green eyes looking at me. Every time she did that I almost fell apart. I could smash all the windows around us, knock all the pedestrians to the ground and jump up and down on them until all signs of life were extinguished, so much energy did her eyes fill me with. I could also grab her around the waist and waltz down the street, throw flowers at everyone we met and sing at the top of my voice. Laconic? I said. It's hard to describe. A bit dry and matter-of-fact, perhaps exaggeratedly matter-of-fact, I said. Sort of understated. But here it is, isn't it?

A venue in Dronningens gate, it had said. Yes, this was it, the posters were on the door.

We went in.

The meeting room was on the first floor, chairs, a speaker's platform at the top end, an overhead projector next to it. A handful of young people, maybe ten, maybe twelve.

Beneath the window there was a large thermos, beside it a small bowl of cookies and a tall stack of plastic cups.

"Would you like some coffee?" I asked.

She shook her head and smiled.

"A cookie maybe?"

I poured myself some coffee, took a couple of cookies, and went back to her. We sat down in one of the rows at the very rear.

Five or six more people drifted in, and the meeting started. It was under the auspices of the AUF, the Young Socialists, a kind of recruitment drive. Anyway, the AUF policies were presented, and then there was some discussion of youth politics in general, why it was important to be committed, how much you could actually achieve, and as a little bonus, what you yourself could get out of it.

Had Hanne not been sitting beside me, one leg crossed over the other, so close that inside I was ablaze, I would have got up and left. Beforehand, I had imagined a more traditional arrangement, a packed hall, cigarette smoke, witty speakers, gales of laughter sweeping through the room, a kind of a tub-thumping Agnar Mykle–type event, with the same Mykle-like significance, young men and women who were keen and eager, who burned inside for socialism, this magical fifties word, but not this, boring boys in boring sweaters and hideous trousers talking to a small collection of boys and girls like themselves about boring and uninspiring things.

Who cares about politics when there are flames licking at your insides?

Who cares about politics if you are burning with desire for life? With desire for the living?

Not me at any rate.

After the three talks there was to be be a short interval and then a workshop and group discussions, we were informed. When the interval came I asked Hanne if we should go, sure, she said, and so we were out in the cold, dark night again. Inside, she had hung her jacket on the back of her chair, and the sweater that was revealed, thick and woolen, bulged in a way that had made me gulp a few times, she was so close to me, there was so little that separated us.

I said what I thought about politics on the way back. She said I had an opinion about everything, how did I have the time to learn about it all? As for herself, she hardly knew what she thought about anything, she said. I said I hardly knew anything either. But you're an anarchist, aren't you! she said. Where did you get that idea from? I barely know what an anarchist is. But you're a Christian, I said. How did that come about? Your parents aren't Christians. And your sister isn't either. Just you. And you don't have any doubts. Yes, she said, you're right there. But you seem to do a lot of brooding. You should live more. I'm doing my best, I said.

We stopped outside the flat.

"Where do you catch the bus?" I asked.

"Up there," she said, nodding up the road.

"Shall I go with you?" I offered.

She shook her head.

"I'll go on my own. I've got my Walkman with me."

"Okay," I said.

"Thanks for this evening," she said.

"Nothing much to thank me for," I answered.

She smiled, stretched up on her toes and kissed me on the mouth. I pulled her to me, tightly, she returned the embrace, then tore herself away. We briefly looked into each other's eyes, and she went.

That night I couldn't sit still, I walked around the flat, to and fro in my room, up and down the stairs, in and out of the downstairs rooms. I felt as if I were bigger than the world, as if I had everything inside me, and that now there was nothing left to strive for. Humanity was small, history was small, the Earth was small, yes, even the universe, which they said was endless, was small. I was bigger than everything. It was a fantastic feeling, but it left me restless because the most important thing in it was the longing, for what was going to be, not for what I did or had done.

How to burn up all that was inside me now?

I forced myself to go to bed, forced myself to lie without moving, not to move a muscle, however long it took before sleep came. Strangely enough, it came after only a few minutes, it snuck up on me like a hunter stalking an unsuspecting prey, and I would not have felt the shot, had it not been for a sudden twitch in one foot, which alerted me to my thoughts, which were in another world, something about standing on the deck of a boat while an enormous whale dived into the depths close by, which I saw despite the impossible position. It was the beginning of a dream, I realized, the arm of the dream, which dragged my ego in, where it transformed into its surroundings, for that was what happened when I twitched, I was a dream, the dream was me.

I closed my eyes again.

Don't move, don't move, don't move . . .

The next day was Saturday and a morning training session with the senior team.

Many people could not understand why I was playing with them. I was no good, after all. There were at least six, perhaps even seven or eight players in the junior team who were better than me. Nevertheless, only I and one other player, Bjørn, had been promoted to the senior team that winter.

I understood why.

The senior team had a new coach, he wanted to see all the juniors, so we each had a week at their training sessions. That meant three opportunities to showcase your abilities. All that autumn I had run a lot and was in such good shape that I had been selected to represent the school in the 1500 meters even though I had never done any track or field events before. So when it was my turn to train with the seniors and I presented myself on the snow-covered shale field near Kjøyta, I knew I had to run. It was my only chance. I ran and ran. In every sprint up the field I came first. I gave everything I had every time. When we started to play it was the same, I ran and ran, ran for everything, all the time, I ran like someone possessed, and after three sessions of that I knew it had gone well, and when the announcement came that I was promoted I was not surprised. But the others in the junior team were. Whenever I failed to control the ball, whenever I made a bad pass, they let me know, what the hell are you doing with the seniors? Why did they pick you?

I knew why, it was because I ran.

You just had to run.

After practice, when the others laughed at my studded belt in the changing room as usual, I got Tom to drive me up to Sannes. He dropped me off at the mailboxes, did a U-turn, and went back down while I walked up to the house. The sun was low in the sky, it was clear and blue, the snow sparkled all around me.

I hadn't given prior notice that I was coming, I didn't even know if Dad was at home.

I tentatively pressed the door. It was open.

Music streamed out of the living room. He was playing it loud, the whole house was full of it. It was Arja Saijonmaa singing the Swedish version of "Gracias a la vida."

"Hello?" I said.

The music was so loud he probably couldn't hear me, I thought, and took off my shoes and coat.

I didn't want to burst in on him, so I shouted "Hello!" again in the corridor outside the living room. No answer.

I went into the living room.

He was sitting on the sofa with his eyes closed, his head moving back and forth in time with the music. His cheeks were wet with tears.

I noiselessly retraced my steps, into the hall, where I snatched my coat and shoes and hurried out before there was a break in the music.

I ran all the way to the bus stop with my bag on my back. Fortunately a bus arrived just a few minutes later. During the four or five minutes it took to go to Solsletta I debated with myself whether to jump off and see Jan Vidar or go all the way to town. But the answer was in fact self-evident, I didn't want to be alone, I wanted to be with someone, talk to someone, think about something else, and at Jan Vidar's, with all the kindness his parents always showed me, I would be able to do that.

He wasn't at home, he had gone to Kjevik with his father, but they would be back soon, his mother said, wouldn't I like to sit in the living room and wait?

Yes, I would. And that is where I was sitting, with the newspaper spread out in front of me and a cup of coffee and a sandwich on the table, when Jan Vidar and his father arrived an hour later.

As evening approached I went back to the house, he wasn't there, and I didn't want to be either. Not only was it dirty and messy, which somehow the sunlight must have masked since it hadn't struck me earlier in the day, but the waterpipes were frozen, I discovered. And must have been frozen for quite a while; at all events, there was already a system with buckets and snow in place. There were some buckets in the toilet with snow that had melted to slush which he must have used to flush the toilet. And there was a bucket of slush by the stove which I presumed he melted in saucepans and used for cooking.

No, I did not want to be there. To lie in bed in the empty room in the empty house in the forest, surrounded by clutter and without any water?

He would have to sort that out by himself.

Where was he, anyway?

I shrugged, even though I was all alone, put on my coat and walked to the bus, through a landscape that lay as if hypnotized beneath the moonlight.

After the kiss outside my flat, Hanne withdrew somewhat, she would not necessarily respond to my notes at once now, nor would we automatically sit together chatting during the breaks. However, there was no logic, no system; one day, out of the blue, she agreed to one of my suggestions, yes, she could go with me to the cinema that night, we were to meet at ten to seven in the foyer.

When she came in through the door, looking for me, I had a taste of what it would be like to be in a relationship with her. Then all the days would be like this one.

"Hi," she said. "Have you been waiting long?"

I shook my head. I knew the situation was finely poised and I would have to tone down anything that might suggest to her that what we were doing was the sort of activity only couples indulged in. At all costs she must not regret being here with me. Must not look around uneasily to check if anyone we knew was nearby. No arm around her shoulders, no hand in hers.

The film was French and being shown in the smallest auditorium. It was my idea. *Betty Blue* it was called, Yngve had seen it and was wildly enthusiastic, now it was running in town and obviously I had to see it, it wasn't often we had quality films here, normally everything was American.

We sat down, took off our jackets, leaned back. There was something a little strained about her, wasn't there? As if she didn't really want to be here.

My palms were sweaty. All the strength in my body seemed to dissolve, to disperse and vanish inside me, I no longer had any energy.

The film began.

A man and a woman were screwing.

Oh no. No, no, no.

I didn't dare to look at Hanne, but guessed she felt the same, didn't dare to look at me, I gripped the arms of the chairs tight, longing for the scene to end.

But it didn't. The couple was screwing on the screen without let-up.

Jesus Christ.

Shit, shit, shit.

I was thinking about that for the rest of the film, and the fact that Hanne was presumably also thinking about it. When the film was over I just wanted to go home.

It was also the natural thing to do. Hanne's bus went from the bus station; I had to go in the opposite direction.

"Did you like it?" I asked, stopping outside the cinema.

"Ye-es," Hanne said. "It was good."

"Yes, it was," I said. "French, anyway!"

We had both taken French as our optional subject.

"Did you understand any of what they were saying, without reading the subtitles, I mean?" I asked.

"A tiny bit," she said.

Silence.

"Well, I should be getting home, I think. Thank you for coming this evening!" I said.

"See you tomorrow," she replied. "Bye."

I turned around to look at her, to see if she had turned around, but she hadn't.

I loved her. There was nothing between us, she didn't want to be my girlfriend, but I loved her. I didn't think of anything else. Even when I was playing soccer, the only place where I was completely spared from invasive thoughts, where it was all about being physically present, even there she appeared. Hanne should have been here to see me, I thought, that would have surprised her. Whenever something good happened, whenever one of my comments hit the mark and made people laugh, I thought, Hanne should have seen that. She should have seen Mefisto, our cat. Our house, the atmosphere there. Mom, she should have sat down for a chat with her. The river by the house, she should have seen that. And my records! She should have heard them, every single one. But our relationship was not going in this direction, she wasn't the one who wanted to enter my world, I was the one who wanted to enter hers. Sometimes I thought it would never happen, sometimes I thought one blast of wind and everything would change. I saw her all the time, not in a scrutinizing or probing way, that wasn't how it was, no, it was a glimpse here, a glimpse there, that was enough. Hope lay in the next time I would see her.

In the midst of this spiritual storm spring arrived.

Few things are harder to visualize than that a cold, snow-bound landscape, so marrow chillingly quiet and lifeless, will, within mere months, be green and lush and warm, quivering with all manner of life, from birds warbling and flying through the trees to swarms of insects hanging in scattered clusters in the air. Nothing in the winter landscape presages the scent of sun-warmed heather and moss, trees bursting with sap and thawed lakes ready for spring and summer, nothing presages the feeling of freedom that can come over you when the only white that can be seen is the clouds gliding across the blue sky above the blue water of the rivers gently flowing down to the sea, the perfect, smooth, cool surface, broken now and then by rocks, rapids, and bathing bodies. It is not there, it does not exist, everything is white and still, and if the silence is broken it is by a cold wind or a lone crow caw-cawing. But it is coming . . . it is coming . . . One evening in March the snow turns to rain, and the piles of snow collapse. One morning in April there are buds on the trees, and there is a trace of green in the yellow grass. Daffodils appear, white and blue anemones too. Then the warm air stands like a pillar among the trees on the slopes. On sunny inclines buds have burst, here and there cherry trees are in blossom. If you are sixteen years old all of this makes an impression, all of this leaves its mark, for this is the first spring you know is spring, with all your senses you know this is spring, and it is the last, for all coming springs pale in comparison with your first. If, moreover, you are in love, well, then . . . then it is merely a question of holding on. Holding onto all the happiness, all the beauty, all the future that resides in everything. I walked home from school, I noticed a snowdrift that had melted over the tarmac, it was as if it had been stabbed in the heart. I saw boxes of fruit under an awning outside a shop, not far away a crow hops off, I turned my head to the sky, it was so beautiful. I walked through the residential area, a rain shower burst, tears filled my eyes. At the same time I was doing all the things I had always done, going to school, playing soccer, hanging out with Jan Vidar, reading books, listening to records, meeting Dad now and then, a couple of times by chance, such as when I met him in the supermarket and he seemed embarrassed to be seen there, or else it was the artificiality of the situation he reacted to, the fact that we were both pushing shopping carts and completely unaware of each other's presence, afterward we each went our separate ways, or the day I was on my way to the house and he came driving down with a colleague in the passenger seat, who I saw was completely gray though still young, but as a rule we had planned it, either he popped by the flat and we ate at my grandparents', or up at the house where, for whatever reason, he avoided me as much as possible. He had relinquished his grip on me, so it seemed, though not entirely, he could still bite my head off, such as on the day I had both ears pierced, when we ran into each other in the hall, he said I looked like an idiot, that he couldn't understand why I wanted to look like an idiot and that he was ashamed to be my father.

Early one afternoon in March I heard a car parking outside my flat. I went down and peered out the window, it was Dad, he had a bag in his hand. He seemed cheery. I hurried up to my room, didn't want to be a busybody with my face glued to the glass. I heard him clattering around in the kitchen downstairs, put on a Doors cassette, which Jan Vidar had lent me, I had wanted to listen to it after reading *Beatles* by Lars Saabye Christensen. Fetched the pile of newspaper cuttings about the Treholt spy case, which I had collected as I was sure it would come up in the exams, and was reading them when I heard his footsteps on the stairs.

I glanced up at the door as he entered. He was holding what looked like a shopping list in his hand.

"Could you nip down to the shop for me?" he said.

"Okay," I replied.

"What's that you're reading?" he asked.

"Nothing special," I said. "Just some newspaper cuttings for Norwegian."

I got up. The rays from the sun flooded the floor. The window was open, outside there was the sound of birdsong, birds were twittering on the branches of the old apple tree a few meters away. Dad handed me the shopping list.

"Mom and I have decided to separate," he said.

"What?" I said.

"Yes. But it won't affect you. You won't notice any difference. Besides, you're not a child anymore and in two years you'll be moving to a place of your own."

"Yes, that's true," I said.

"Okay?" Dad asked.

"Okay," I said.

"I forgot to write potatoes. And perhaps we should have a dessert? Oh, by the way, here's the money."

He handed me a five-hundred-krone note, I stuffed it in my pocket and went down to the street, along the river, and into the supermarket. I wandered between the shelves, filling the shopping basket. Nothing of what Dad had said managed to emerge above this. They were going to separate, fine, well, let them. It might have been different if I had been younger, eight or nine, I thought, then it would have meant something, but now it was of no significance, I had my own life.

I gave him the groceries, he made lunch, we ate without saying much.

Then he left.

I was pleased he did. Hanne was going to sing in a church that evening, and she had asked whether I wanted to go and watch, of course I did. Her boyfriend would be there, so I didn't make my presence known, but when I saw her standing there, so beautiful and so pure, she was mine, no one else's feelings could hold a candle to those I cherished. Outside, the tarmac was covered with grime, the remaining snow lay in dips and hollows and up shadowy slopes on both sides of the road. She sang, I was happy.

On the way home I jumped off at the bus station and walked the last part through town, although that did nothing to diminish my restlessness, my feelings were so varied and so intense that I couldn't really deal with them. After arriving home I lay on my bed and cried. There was no despair in the tears, no sorrow, no anger, only happiness.

The next day we were alone in the classroom, the others had left, we both lingered, she perhaps because she wanted to hear what I thought of the concert. I told her that her singing had been fantastic, she was fantastic. She lit up as she stood packing her satchel. Then Nils came in. I felt ill at ease, his presence cast a shadow over us. We were together in French class, and he was different from the other boys in the first class, he hung out with people who were a lot older than himself in the town's pubs, he was independent in his opinions and his life as a whole. He laughed a lot, made fun of everyone, me included. I always felt small when he did that, I didn't know where to look or what to say. Now he started talking to Hanne. It was as if he were circling her, he looked into her eyes, laughed, drew closer, was standing very close to her now. I would not have expected anything else of him, that was not what upset me, it was the way Hanne reacted. She didn't reject him, laugh off his advances. Even though I was there she opened herself to him. Laughed with him, met his gaze, even parted her knees at the desk where she was sitting, when he went right up to her. It was as if he had cast a spell over her. For a moment he stood there staring into her eyes, the moment was tense and full of disquiet, then he laughed his malicious laugh and backed away a few steps, fired a disarming remark, raised a hand in salute to me and was gone. Wild with jealousy, I looked at Hanne, she had gone back to packing her bag, though not as if nothing had happened, she was enclosed inside herself now, in quite a different way.

What had gone on? Hanne, blond, beautiful, playful, happy, always with a bemused, often also naïve, question on her lips, what had she changed into? What was it that I had witnessed? A dark, deep, perhaps also passionate side, was that her? She had responded, it was only a glimpse, but nonetheless. Then, at that moment, I was nobody. I was crushed. I, with all the notes I had sent her, all the discussions I'd had with her, all my simple hopes and childish desires, I was nothing, a shout on the playground, a rock in scree, the hooting of a car horn.

Could I do this to her? Could I have this effect on her?

Could I have this effect on *anyone*?

No.

For Hanne, I was a nobody and would remain so.

For me, she was everything.

I attempted to make light of what I had seen, also in my attitude to her, by continuing just as before, pretending that things were fine. But they were not, I knew that, I was never in any doubt. The only hope I had was that she shouldn't know. But what actually was this world I was living in? What actually were these dreams I believed in?

Two days later, when the Easter holiday started, Mom came home.

Dad had implied that the divorce was done and dusted. But when Mom came home, I could see that was not the way she saw things. She drove straight up to the house, where Dad was waiting for her, and they were there for two days while I wandered around town trying to kill time.

On Friday she parked her car outside my flat. I spotted her from the window. She had a large bruise around one eye. I opened the door.

"What happened?" I asked.

"I know what you're thinking," she said. "But that's not what happened. I fell. I fainted, I do that once in a while, you see, and this time I hit the edge of the table upstairs. The glass table."

"I don't believe you," I said.

"It's true," she said. "I fainted. There's no more to it than that."

I stepped back. She came into the hall.

"Are you divorced now?" I asked.

She put her suitcase down on the floor, hung her light-colored coat on the hook.

"Yes, we are," she said.

"Are you sorry?"

"Sorry?"

She looked at me with genuine surprise, as if the thought had never struck her as a possibility.

"I don't know," she said. "Sad maybe. And you? How will you be?"

"Fine," I said. "So long as I don't have to live with Dad."

"We talked about that too. But first I need a cup of coffee."

I followed her into the kitchen, watched while she put the water on to boil, sat on a chair, bag in hand, rummaged for her pack of cigarettes, she had started smoking Barclay in Bergen, evidently, took one out and lit up.

She looked at me.

"I'm moving up to the house. We two will live there. And then Dad can live here. I assume I'll have to buy him out, don't know quite how I'll manage that, but don't worry, I'll find a way."

"Mhm," I mumbled.

"And you?" she asked. "How are you? It's really good to see you, you know."

"Same here," I said. "I haven't seen you since Christmas. And so many things have happened."

"Have they?"

She got up to fetch an ashtray from the cupboard, took the packet of coffee, and placed it on the counter as the water began to hiss. It sounded a bit like the sea as you get close.

"Yes," I said.

"Good things by the look of it?" she smiled.

"Yes," I said. "I'm in love. Hook, line, and sinker."

"Lovely. Anyone I know?"

"Who would you know? No, someone from the class. That bit is perhaps not very smart, but that's how it is. It's not exactly something you can plan, is it."

"No," she agreed. "What's her name?"

"Hanne."

"Hanne," she said, looking at me with a faint smile. "When do I get to meet her?"

"That's the big question. We're not going out together. She has someone else."

"It's not so easy then."

"No."

She sighed.

"No, it isn't always easy. But you look good. You look happy."

"I've never been so happy. Never."

For some insane reason tears welled up in my eyes when I said that. It wasn't just that my eyes glazed over, which often happened when I said something that moved me, no, tears were coursing down my cheeks.

I smiled.

"They're really tears of happiness," I said. And then I let out a sob and had to turn away. Fortunately the water was boiling by then and I could take it off the stove, add coffee, press down on the lid, bang the pot on the burner a few times and pour two cups.

As I put them on the table I was fine again.

■ ■ ■

Six months later, one evening toward the end of July, I got off the last bus at the stop by the waterfall. Over my shoulder I was carrying a seaman's bag, I had been to Denmark for a soccer training camp, and after that, without going home first, to a class party in the skerries. I was happy. It was a few minutes past ten thirty, what darkness there was had fallen and lay like a grayish veil across the countryside. The waterfall roared beneath me. I walked uphill and along the road bordered with curbstones. Below, the meadow sloped toward a row of deciduous trees growing by the river bank. Above was the old farm with the tumbledown barn gaping open from the road. The lights were off in the main farmhouse. I walked around the bend to the next house, the guy who lived there was sitting in the living room with the TV on. A truck was rumbling along on the other side of the river. The sound reached me after a time lag; I didn't hear the change of gears as it sped up the small incline until it was at the top. Above the treetops, against the pale sky, I saw two bats, and I was reminded of the badger I often bumped into on my way home from the last bus. It used to come down the road beside the path of the stream as I was climbing. For safety's sake I always held a stone in each hand. Sometimes I encountered it on the road too, when it would stop and look at me before scuttling back with its distinctive jog-trot.

I stopped, threw down my bag, put one foot on the curb and lit a cigarette. I didn't want to go home right away, I wanted to drag the time out for a few moments. Mom, with whom I had been living all spring and half the summer, was in Sørbøvåg now. She still had not bought out my father and he had stuck to his rights and would be living there until school started again, together with his new girlfriend, Unni.

Over the forest came a large plane, it banked slowly, straightened up, and a second later passed overhead. The lights on the wingtips were flashing and the undercarriage was being lowered. I followed the plane until it was out of sight, and all that remained was the roar, though weaker and weaker, until it too was gone, just before it landed in Kjevik. I liked planes, always had. Even after living for three years under a flight path I still looked up with pleasure.

The river glinted in the summer darkness. The smoke from my cigarette did not rise, it drifted sideways and lay flat in the air. Not a breath of wind. And now the roar of the plane was gone, there was not a sound. Yes, there was, from the bats which soared and plummeted wherever their roaming took them.

I stuck out my tongue and stubbed out my cigarette on it, threw the butt down the slope, slung the bag over my shoulder, and continued on my way. The lights were on in the house where William lived. Above the approaching bend the tops of the deciduous trees were so close together that the sky was not visible. A few frogs or toads were croaking down in the marshlike area between the road and the river. Then I glimpsed movement at the bottom of the hill. It was the badger. It hadn't seen me and was trotting across the tarmac. I headed for the other side of the road to allow it a free passage, but it looked up and stopped. How elegant it was with its black-and-white striped chic snout. Its coat was gray, its eyes yellow and sly. I completed my maneuver, stepped over the curb and stood on the slope below. The badger hissed, but continued to look at me. It was clearly assessing the situation because the other times we had met it had turned at once and run back. Now it resumed its jog-trot and to my great delight disappeared up the hill. It was only then, as I stepped back onto the road, that I heard the faint sounds of music that must have been there the whole time.

Was it coming from our house?

I hurried down the last part of the hill and looked up the slope where the house stood, all lights ablaze. Yes, that was where the music was coming from. Presumably through the open living room door, I thought, and realized there was a party going on up there because a number of dark, mysterious figures were gliding around the lawn in the grayish light of the summer night. Usually I would have followed the stream to the west of the house, but with the party up there, and the place full of strangers, I didn't want to crash in from the forest, and accordingly followed the road all the way around.

There were cars all the way along the drive, parked half on the grass, and beside the barn and in the yard as well. I stopped at the top of the hill to collect my thoughts. A man in a white shirt walked across the yard without seeing me. There was a buzz of voices in the garden behind the house. At the kitchen table, which I could see through the window, were two women and a man, each with a glass of wine in front of them, they were laughing and drinking.

I took a deep breath and walked toward the front door. A long table had been set up in the garden close to the forest. It was covered with a white cloth that shimmered in the heavy darkness beneath the treetops. Six or seven people were sitting at the table, among them Dad. He looked straight at me. When I met his gaze he got up and waved. I unhitched the bag, put it beside the doorstep and went over to him. I had never seen him like this before. He was wearing a baggy white shirt with embroidery around the V-neck, blue jeans, and light-brown leather shoes. His face, tanned dark from the sun, had a radiant aura. His eyes shone.

"So, there you are, Karl Ove," he said, resting his hand on my shoulder.

"We thought you would have been here earlier. We're having a party, as you can see. But you can join us for a while, can't you? Sit yourself down!"

I did as he said and sat down at the table, with my back to the house. The only person I had seen before was Unni. She too was wearing a white shirt or blouse or whatever it was.

"Hi, Unni," I said.

She sent me a warm smile.

"So this is Karl Ove, my youngest son," Dad said, sitting down on the opposite side of the table, next to Unni. I nodded to the other five.

"And this, Karl Ove, is Bodil," he said, "my cousin."

I had never heard of any cousin called Bodil and studied her, probably in a rather quizzical way because she smiled at me and said:

"Your father and I were together a lot when we were children."

"And teenagers," Dad said. He lit a cigarette, inhaled, blew the smoke out with a contented expression on his face. "And then we have Reidar, Ellen, Martha, Erling, and Åge. Colleagues of mine, all of them."

"Hi," I said.

The table was covered with glasses, bottles, dishes, and plates. Two large bowls piled with shrimp shells left no doubt as to what they had been eating. The colleague my father had mentioned last, Åge, a man of around forty, with large, thinly framed glasses was observing me while sipping a glass of beer. Putting it down, he said:

"I gather you've been at a training camp?"

I nodded.

"In Denmark," I said.

"Where in Denmark?" he asked.

"Nykøbing," I said.

"Nykøbing, on Mors?" he queried.

"Yes," I said. "I think so. It was an island in the Limfjord."

He laughed and looked around.

"That's where Aksel Sandemose came from!" he declared. And then he looked straight at me again. "Do you know the name of the law he devised, inspired by the town you visited?"

What was this? Were we at school or what?

"Yes," I said, looking down. I didn't want to articulate the word; I didn't want to tell him.

"Which is?" he insisted.

As I raised my eyes to meet his, they were as defiant as they were embarrassed.

"Jante," I said.

"You got it!" he said.

"Did you have a good time there?" Dad asked.

"Yes, I did," I said. "Great fields. Great town."

Nykøbing: I had walked back to the school where we were lodged, after spending the whole evening and night out with a girl I had met, she had been crazy about me. The four others from the team who had been with me had gone back earlier, it was just me and her, and as I walked home, drunker than usual, I had stopped outside one of the houses in the town. All the detail was gone, I couldn't remember leaving her, couldn't remember going to the house, but once there, standing by this door, it was as if I came to myself again. I took the lit cigarette out of my mouth, opened the letter box, and dropped it on the hall floor inside. Then everything went fuzzy again, but somehow I must have found my way to the school, got in, and gone to bed, to be woken for breakfast and training three hours later. When we were sitting under one of the enormous trees around the training area chatting, I suddenly remembered the cigarette I had thrown in through the door. I got up, chilled deep into my soul, booted a ball up the field and began to give chase. What if it had started to burn? What if people had died in the fire? What did that make me?

I had succeeded in repressing it for several days, but now, sitting at the long table in the garden on my first evening home, fear reared up again.

"Which team do you play for, Karl Ove?" one of the others asked.

"Tveit," I said.

"Which division are you in?"

"I play for the juniors," I said. "But the seniors are in the fifth division."

"Not exactly IK Start then," he said. From his dialect I deduced that he came from Vennesla, so it was easy to come back with a retort.

"No, more like Vindbjart," I said. Vindbjart from Vennesla. Second Division, group three.

They laughed at that. I looked down. It felt as if I had already attracted too much attention. But when, immediately afterward, I let my gaze wander to Dad, he was smiling at me.

Yes, his eyes were shining.

"Wouldn't you like a beer, Karl Ove?" he said.

I nodded.

"Certainly would," I replied.

He scanned the table.

"Looks as if we've run out here," he said. "But there's a crate in the kitchen. You can take one from there."

I got up. As I made for the door two people came out. A man and a woman, entwined. She was wearing a white summer dress. Her bare arms and legs were tanned. Her breasts heavy, stomach and hips ample. Her eyes, in the somehow sated face, were gentle. He, wearing a light blue shirt and white trousers, had a slight paunch, but was otherwise slim. Even though he was smiling and his inebriated eyes seemed to be floating, it was the stiffness of his expression that I noticed. All the movement had gone, just the vestiges remained, like a dried-up riverbed.

"Hi!" she said. "Are you the son?"

"Yes," I said. "Hello."

"I work with your father," she said.

"Nice," I said, and luckily did not have to say anything more, for they were already on their way. As I went into the hall the bathroom door opened. A small, chubby, dark-haired woman with glasses stepped out. She barely glanced at me, cast her eyes down, and walked past me into the house. Discreetly I sniffed her perfume before following her. Fresh, floral. In the kitchen were the three people I had seen through the window when I arrived. The man, also around forty, was whispering something in the ear of the woman to his right. She smiled, but it was a polite smile. The other woman was rummaging through a bag she had on her lap. She looked up at me as she placed an unopened packet of cigarettes on the table.

"Hello," I said. "Just come for a beer."

There were two full crates stacked against the wall by the door. I grabbed a bottle from the top one.

"Anyone got an opener?" I asked.

The man straightened up, patted his thighs.

"I've got a lighter," he said. "Here."

He made to throw it underarm, at first slowly, so I could prepare myself to catch it, then, with a jerk, the lighter came flying through the air. It hit the door frame and clunked to the floor. But for that I would not have known how to resolve the situation because I didn't want any condescension because I let him open the bottle for me, but now he had taken the initiative and failed, so the situation was different.

"I can't open it with a lighter," I said. "Perhaps you could do it for me?"

I picked up the lighter and handed it to him with the bottle. He had round glasses, and the fact that half of his scalp was hairless, while the hair on the other half rose too high, like a wave at the edge of an endless beach on which it would never break, lent him a somewhat desperate appearance. That, at any rate, was the effect he had on me. The tips of his fingers, now tightening around the lighter, were hairy. From his wrist hung a watch on a silver chain.

The beer cap came off with a dull pop.

"There we are," he said, passing me the bottle. I thanked him and went into the living room, where four or five people were dancing, and out into the garden. A little gathering of people stood in front of the flagpole, each with glass in hand, looking across the river valley as they chatted.

The beer was fantastic. I had drunk every evening in Denmark, and all the previous evening and night, so it would take a lot for me to get drunk now. And I didn't want that either. If I got drunk I would slip into their world, in a sense, allow it to swallow me up whole and no longer be able to see the difference, I might even begin to get a taste for the women in it. That was the last thing I wanted.

I surveyed the landscape. Looked at the river flowing in a gentle curve around the grass-covered headland where the soccer goals were, and between the tall deciduous trees growing along the bank, which were now black against the dark-gray, shiny surface of the water. The hills that rose on the other side and then undulated down toward the sea were also black. The lights from the clusters of houses lying between the river and the ridge shone out strong and bright, while the stars in the sky – those close to the land grayish, those higher up a bluish hue – were barely visible.

The group by the flagpole were laughing at something. They were only a few meters from me, but their faces were still indistinct. The man with the slight paunch emerged from around the corner of the house, he appeared to glide. The confirmation photograph of me had been taken there, in front of the flagpole, between Mom and Dad. I took another swig and went toward the far end of the garden where no one else seemed to have found their way. I sat there with legs crossed, by the birch. The music was more distant, the voices and laughter too, and the movements from my vantage point even less distinct. Like apparitions, they floated in the darkness around the illuminated house. I thought of Hanne. It was as if she had a place inside me. As if she existed as a real location where I would always be. That I could go there whenever I wanted felt like an act of mercy. We had sat talking on a rock by the sea at a class party the previous night. Nothing happened, that was all there was. The rock, Hanne, the bay with the low islets, the sea. We had danced, played games, gone down the steps from the quay, and swum in the dark. It had been wonderful. And the wonder of it was indelible, it had stayed with me all of the next day, and it was in me now. I was immortal. I got up, aware of my own power in every cell of my body. I was wearing a gray T-shirt, calf-length military green trousers, and white Adidas basketball shoes, that was all, but it was enough. I was not strong, but I was slim, supple, and as handsome as a god.

Could I give her a call?

She had said she would be home this evening.

But it had to be close to twelve by now. And although she didn't mind being woken up, the rest of the family would probably take a different view.

What if the house had burned down? What if someone had been burned to death?

Oh, shit, shit, shit.

I started to walk across the lawn as I tried to push the thought to the back of my mind, ran my eyes along the hedge, over the house, the roof, to the big lilac bushes at the end of the lawn whose heavy pink blossoms you could smell right down by the road, took the last swig from the bottle as I walked, saw a couple of flushed women's faces, they were sitting on the steps by the door with their knees together and cigarettes between their fingertips, I recognized them from the table and gave a faint smile as I passed, on through the door into the living room, then the kitchen, which was empty now, took another bottle, went upstairs and into my room where I sat down in the chair under the window, leaned back, and closed my eyes.

Mm.

The speakers in the living room were directly beneath me, and sound traveled so easily in this house that I heard every note loud and clear.

What were they playing?

Agnetha Fältskog. The hit from last summer. What was it again?

There was something undignified about the clothes Dad was wearing tonight. The white shirt or blouse or whatever the hell it was. He had always, as far as I could remember, dressed simply, appropriately, a touch conservatively. His wardrobe consisted of shirts, suits, jackets, many in tweed, polyester trousers, corduroy, cotton, lambswool or wool sweaters. More a senior master of the old variety than a smock-clad schoolteacher of the new breed, but not old-fashioned, that wasn't where the difference lay. The dividing line was between soft and hard, between those who try to break down the distance and those who try to maintain it. It was a question of values. When he suddenly started wearing arty embroidered blouses, or shirts with frills, as I had seen him wearing earlier this summer, or shapeless leather shoes in which a Sami would have been happy, an enormous contradiction arose between the person he was, the person I knew him to be, and the person he presented himself as. For myself, I was on the side of the soft ones, I was against war and authority, hierarchies, and all forms of hardness, I didn't want to do any sucking up at school, I wanted my intellect to develop more organically; politically I was way out on the left, the unequal distribution of the world's resources enraged me, I wanted everyone to have a share of life's pleasures, and thus capitalism and plutocracy were the enemy. I thought all people were of equal value and that a person's inner qualities were always worth more than their outer appearance. I was, in other words, for depth and against superficiality, for good and against evil, for the soft and against the hard. So shouldn't I have been pleased then, that my father had joined the ranks of the soft? No, for I despised the way the soft expressed themselves, the round glasses, corduroy trousers, foot-formed shoes, knitted sweaters, that is, because along with my political ideals I had others, bound up with music, which in a very different way had to do with looking good, cool, which in turn was related to the times in which we were living, it was what had to be expressed, but not the top ten chart aspect, not the pastel colors and hair gel, for that was about commercialism, superficiality, and entertainment; no, the music that had to be expressed was the innovative but tradition-conscious, deeply felt but smart, intelligent but simple, showy but genuine kind that did not address itself to everyone, that did not sell well, yet expressed a generation's, my generation's, experiences. Oh, the new. I was on the side of the new. And Ian McCulloch of Echo & the Bunnymen, he was the ideal in this respect, him above all. Coats, military jackets, sneakers, dark sunglasses. It was miles away from my father's embroidered blouse and Sami shoes. On the other hand, this could not be what it was about because Dad belonged to a different generation, and the thought that this generation should start dressing like Ian McCulloch, start listening to British indie music, take any interest in what was happening on the American scene, discover REM's or Green on Red's debut album and perhaps eventually include a bootlace tie in their wardrobe was the stuff of a nightmare. What was more important was that the embroidered blouse and the Sami shoes were not him. And that he had slipped into this, entered this formless, uncertain, almost feminine world, as though he had lost a grip on himself. Even the hard tone in his voice had gone.

I opened my eyes and turned to look through the window at the table on the edge of the forest. Only four people were there now. Dad, Unni, the person she had called Bodil, and one more. At the back of the lilac bush, out of sight from them, but not from me, a man was peeing while staring across to the river.

Dad raised his head and directed his gaze up at the window. My heart beat faster, but I did not move, for if in fact he had seen me, which was not at all certain, it would be like admitting that I was spying. Instead I waited for a few moments, until I was sure that he had noticed that I had seen him watching, if he had seen that is, then withdrew and sat at my desk.

It was no good spying on Dad, he always noticed, he saw everything, had always seen everything.

I swigged some beer. A cigarette would have been good now. He had never seen me smoking, and perhaps it would become an issue if he did. On the other hand, had he not just told me to help myself to beer?

The desk, my property for as long as I could remember, orange like the bed and the cupboard doors, had been in my old room, was, apart from a rack of cassettes, completely clear. I had cleaned everything up at the end of the school year and had hardly been here, except to sleep. I put down the bottle and whirled the rack around a few times while reading the titles written in my own childish capitals on the spines. BOWIE – HUNKY DORY. LED ZEPPELIN – I. TALKING HEADS – 77. THE CHAMELEONS – SCRIPT OF THE BRIDGE. THE THE – SOUL MINING. THE STRANGLERS – RATTUS NORVEGICUS. THE POLICE – OUTLANDOS D'AMOUR. TALKING HEADS – REMAIN IN LIGHT. BOWIE –

SCARY MONSTERS (And super creeps). ENO BYRNE – MY LIFE IN THE BUSH OF GHOSTS. U2 – OCTOBER. THE BEATLES – RUBBER SOUL. SIMPLE MINDS – NEW GOLD DREAM.

I got to my feet, grabbed the guitar leaning against the small Roland Cube amplifier and strummed some chords, put it back, looked out over the garden again. They were still there, under the darkness of the treetops, which the two kerosene lamps did not dispel, but did soften, in that their faces took on the color of the light. Giving them dark, coppery complexions.

Bodil, she must be the daughter of Dad's father's second brother, whom I had never met. For some reason he had been banished from the family, long ago. I heard about him by chance for the first time a couple of years ago, there was a wedding in the family, and Mom mentioned that he was also there, and that he made a passionate speech. He was a lay preacher in the Pentecostal Church in town. A mechanic. Everything about him was different from his two brothers, even the name. When they, after consultation with their imposing mother, and upon entering the academic world and university, had decided to change their name from the standard Pedersen to the rather less standard Knausgaard, he had refused. Perhaps that is what caused the break?

I went out of the room and downstairs. As I came into the hall, Dad was in the room with the wardrobes, the light was off and he was staring at me.

"Is that where you are?" he said. "Wouldn't you like to join us?"

"Yes," I said. "Of course. I've just been having a look around."

"It's a great party," he said.

He twisted his neck and patted some hair into place. He had always had that mannerism, but there was something about his shirt and those trousers, which were so profoundly alien to him, that suddenly made it seem effeminate. As though this quirk had detected the conservative, reserved manner in which he had always dressed, and neutralized it.

"Everything alright with you, Karl Ove?" he asked.

"Yes," I said. "Fine. I'll come out and join you."

A gust of wind stirred the air as I emerged. The leaves on the forest edge trembled, almost reluctantly, as if waking from a deep sleep.

Or was it just that he was drunk, I thought. Because I wasn't used to that either. My father had never been a drinker. The first time I saw him in an inebriated state was one evening only two months before when I visited him and Unni in the flat in Elvegaten, and was served fondue, another thing which he would never have considered remotely possible in his own home on a Friday night. They had been drinking before I arrived, and although he was kindness itself, it was threatening nonetheless; not directly, of course, because, sitting there, I didn't fear him, but indirectly because I could no longer read him. It was as if all the knowledge I had acquired about him through my childhood, and which enabled me to prepare for any eventuality, was, in one fell swoop, invalid. So what was valid?

As I turned and walked toward the table I caught Unni's eye, she smiled and I returned the smile. Another gust of wind, stronger this time. The leaves on the tall bushes by the barn steps rustled. The lightest branches of the trees above the table swayed up and down.

"How are you doing?" Unni asked as I went over to them.

"Fine," I said. "But I'm a bit tired. Think I'll crash soon."

"Will you be able to sleep in this racket?"

"Oh, that won't bother me!"

"Your father spoke so warmly about you this evening," Bodil said, leaning across the table. I didn't know what to say, so I just gave a cautious smile.

"Isn't that right, Unni?"

Unni nodded. She had long, completely gray hair although she was only in her early thirties. Dad had been the supervisor during her teacher training. She was wearing flared green slacks and a similar smocklike affair to the one Dad had on. A necklace of wooden beads hung around her neck.

"We read one of your essays this spring," she said. "You didn't know perhaps? I hope you don't mind that I was allowed to see it. He was so proud of you."

Impossible. What the hell was she doing reading one of my essays?

But I was also flattered, that went without saying.

"You're like your grandfather, Karl Ove," Bodil said.

"My grandfather?"

"Yes. Same shape of head. Same mouth."

"And you're Dad's cousin, right?" I asked.

"Yes," she said. "You'll have to come and see us one day. We live in Kristiansand too, you know!"

I didn't know. Before tonight I didn't even know she existed. I should have said that. But I didn't. Instead I said that was nice, and asked what she did, and after a while if she had any children. That was what she was talking about when Dad returned. He sat down and looked at her, straining to tune into the topic of conversation, but then he leaned back, one foot resting on his knee, and lit a cigarette.

I got up.

"Are you going to leave now that I've come?" he asked.

"No. Just going to get something," I said. Opened my bag by the doorstep, took out the cigarettes, put one in my mouth on the way back, paused for a second to light up, so that I could already be smoking when I sat down. Dad said nothing. I could see that he had considered saying something, for a twinge of disapproval appeared around his mouth, but after a brief glare it was gone, as though he had told himself he was no longer like that.

That at least was what I thought.

"*Skål*," Dad said, raising his glass of red wine to us. Then he looked at Bodil, and added: "*Skål* to Helene."

"*Skål* to Helene," Bodil said.

They drank, looking into each other's eyes.

Who the hell was Helene?

"Haven't you got anything to toast with, Karl Ove?" Dad asked.

I shook my head.

"Take that glass," he said. "It's clean. Isn't it, Unni?"

She nodded. He passed me the bottle of white wine and poured. We said skål again.

"Who's Helene?" I asked, looking at them.

"Helene was my sister," Bodil said. "She's dead now."

"Helene was. . . well, we were very close when I was growing up. We were together all the time," Dad said. "Right up to our teenage years. Then she fell ill."

I took another sip. The couple from earlier appeared from behind the house, the buxom woman in the white dress and the man with the slight paunch. Two other men followed, one of whom I recognized as the man from the kitchen.

"So this is where you are," said the man with the paunch. "We were wondering. You're not taking very good care of your guests, I have to say." He patted my father's shoulder. "It's you we want to see, now that we've come all this way."

"That's my sister," Bodil whispered to me. "Elisabeth. And her husband, Frank. They live down in Ryen, you know, by the river. He's an estate agent."

Had these people my father knew always been around us?

They sat down at the table and things immediately livened up. And what, when I came, had been faces devoid of meaning or substance and which, consequently, I had only regarded in terms of age and type, more or less as if they had been animals, a bestiary of forty-year-olds, with all that that entailed, lifeless eyes, stiff lips, pendulous breasts and quivering paunches, wrinkles and folds, I now saw to be individuals, for I was related to them, the blood that was in their veins was in mine, and who they were suddenly became important.

"We were talking about Helene," Dad said.

"Helene, yes," the man called Frank said. "I never met her. But I've heard a lot about her. It was a great shame."

"I sat at her deathbed," Dad said.

I gaped. What was all this?

"I adored her."

"She was the most beautiful girl you could ever imagine," Bodil said to me, still in a whisper.

"And then she died," Dad said. "Ohh."

Was he crying?

Yes, he was crying. He was sitting there with his elbows on the table and his hands folded in front of his chest as the tears ran down his cheeks.

"And that was in the spring. It was spring when she died. Everything in flower. Ohh. Ohh."

Frank lowered his eyes and twirled the glass between his fingers. Unni placed her hand on Dad's arm. Bodil looked at them.

"You were so close to her," she said. "You were the most precious thing she had."

"Ohh. Ohh," my father cried, closing his eyes and covering his face with his hands.

A gust of wind blew across the yard. The overhanging flaps of the table cloth fluttered. A napkin went flying across the lawn. The foliage above us swished. I lifted my glass and drank, shuddered as the acidic taste hit my palate, and once again recognized that clear, pure sensation that arose with approaching intoxication, and the desire to pursue it that always followed.

Part 2

Having sat for some months in a basement room in Åkeshov, one of Stockholm's many satellite towns, writing what I hoped would be my second novel, with the Metro a few meters from the window, such that every afternoon after darkness fell I saw the train cars passing through the woods like a row of illuminated rooms, at the end of 2003 I finally found an office in the center of Stockholm. It was owned by one of Linda's friends, and it was perfect. In fact it was a studio, with a kitchenette, a small shower and a sofa bed in addition to a desk and bookshelves. I moved my things, that is, a pile of books and the computer between Christmas and the new year, and started work there on the first weekday of the new year. My novel was actually finished, a strange hundred-and-thirty-page affair, a short tale about a father and his two sons who were out fishing for crabs one summer's night, which led into a long essay about angels, which in turn led into a story about one of the sons, now an adult, and some days he spent on an island where he lived alone and wrote and self-harmed.

The publishing house had said they would publish it, and I was tempted, but also enormously unsure, not least after having had Erik Thure read it. He called me late one evening, both his mood and choice of words peculiar, as though he had had a few drinks so as to be able to say what he had to say, which was simple, it's no good, it isn't a novel. You have to tell a story, Karl Ove! he said several times. You have to tell a story! I knew he was right and that was what I started doing on this, my first day of work in 2004, as I sat at my new desk looking at the blank screen. After grafting for half an hour I leaned back and glanced at the poster behind the desk, it was from a Peter Greenaway exhibition I had been to in Barcelona with Tonje many years ago, some time in my former life. It showed four pictures: one of what I had long thought of as a cherub peeing, one of a bird's wing, one of a 1920s pilot, and one of a corpse's hand. Then I looked out the window. The sky above the hospital on the other side of the road was cloudless and blue. The low sun glistened on the panes, signs, railings, car hoods. The frozen breath rising from passersby on the pavement made them look as if they were on fire. All tightly wrapped up in warm clothes. Hats, scarves, mittens, thick jackets. Hurried movements, set faces. My eyes wandered across the flooring. It was parquet and relatively new, the reddish-brown tone at odds with the flat's otherwise fin-de-siècle style. I noticed that the knots and grain, perhaps two meters from the chair where I was sitting, formed an image of Christ wearing a crown of thorns.

This was not something I reacted to, I merely registered it, for images like this are found in all buildings, created by irregularities in the floors, walls, doors, and moldings – here a damp patch in a ceiling looks like a dog running, there a worn-through coat of paint on a doorstep looks like a snow-covered valley with a mountain range in the distance above which clouds appear to be gushing forth – but it must have set something going in me because when I got up ten minutes later and went over to the kettle and filled it with water I suddenly remembered something that had happened one evening a long time ago, deep in my childhood, when I had seen a similar image on the water in a news item about a missing fishing vessel. In the second it took to fill the pot, I saw our living room before me, the teak television cabinet, the shimmer of isolated snowflakes against the darkening hillside outside the window, the sea on the screen, the face that appeared in it. With the images came the atmosphere from that time, of spring, of the housing estate, of the seventies, of family life as it was then. And with the atmosphere, an almost uncontrollable longing.

At that moment the telephone rang. It startled me. Surely no one had my number here.

It rang five times before giving up. The hiss of the kettle boiling grew louder and I thought as so often before that it sounded as if something was approaching.

I unscrewed the lid of the coffee tin, put two spoonfuls in my cup, and poured in the water, which rose up the sides, black and steaming, then I got dressed. Before going out I stood in such a way that I could see the face in the wooden flooring. And it really was Christ. The face half-averted, as though in pain, eyes downcast, the crown of thorns on his head.

The remarkable thing was not that the face should be visible here, nor that I had once seen a face in the sea in the mid-seventies, the remarkable thing was that I had forgotten it and now remembered. Apart from one or two isolated events that Yngve and I had talked about so often they had almost assumed biblical proportions, I remembered hardly anything from my childhood. That is, I remembered hardly any of the events in it. But I did remember the rooms where they took place. I could remember all the places I had been, all the rooms I had been in. Just not what happened there.

I went into the street with the cup in my hand. A slight feeling of unease arose within me at seeing it out here, the cup belonged indoors, not outdoors; outdoors, there was something naked and exposed about it, and as I crossed the street I decided to buy a coffee at the 7-Eleven the following morning, and use their cup, made of cardboard, designed for outdoor use, from then on. There were a couple of benches outside the nearby hospital, and I walked up to them, ensconced myself on the ice-covered slats, lit a cigarette, and glanced down the street. The coffee was already lukewarm. The thermometer outside the kitchen window at home had shown minus twenty that morning, and even though the sun was shining it could not be much warmer now. Minus fifteen, perhaps.

I took the mobile phone from my pocket to see if anyone had called. Well, not anyone: we were expecting a child in a week's time, so I was prepared for Linda to call at any moment and say things were on the move.

At the intersection by the top of the gentle incline the traffic lights began to tick. Soon after, the street below was free of cars. Two middle-aged women came out of the entrance below me and lit up. Wearing white hospital coats, they squeezed their arms against their sides and took small, stabbing steps to keep warm. To me they looked like some strange kind of duck. Then the ticking stopped, and the next moment cars shot out of the hilltop shadow like a pack of baying hounds into the sunlit street below. The studded tires lashed the tarmac. I put the mobile back in my pocket, wrapped my hands around the cup. The steam from the coffee rose slowly and mingled with the breath from my mouth. On the school playground that lay squashed between two blocks of flats twenty meters up from my office the shouts of children suddenly fell quiet, it was only now that I noticed. The bell had rung. The sounds here were new and unfamiliar to me, the same was true of the rhythm in which they surfaced, but I would soon get used to them, to such an extent that they would fade into the background again. You know too little and it doesn't exist. You know too much and it doesn't exist. Writing is drawing the essence of what we know out of the shadows. That is what writing is about. Not what happens there, not what actions are played out there, but the *there* itself. There, that is writing's location and aim. But how to get there?

This was the question I asked myself, sitting in a suburb of Stockholm drinking coffee, my muscles contracting with the cold and the cigarette smoke dissolving into the vast mass of air above me.

The shouts from the school playground came at specific intervals and were one of the many rhythms that traversed the district everyday, from the time the traffic began to get heavy in the morning until, as if emerging on the other side, it began to lighten in late afternoon. The workmen gathering in cafés and bakeries for breakfast at half past six, with their protective boots and strong, grimy hands, their folding rulers tucked into trouser pockets and their constantly ringing mobile phones. The less easily identifiable men and women who filled the streets in the following hour, whose soft well-dressed exteriors said no more about them than that they spent their days in some office, and could equally well have been lawyers as TV journalists or architects, could equally well have been advertising copy writers as clerks in an insurance company. The nurses and orderlies the buses disgorged in front of the hospital, mostly middle-aged, mostly women, with the occasional young man, in groups that increased in size as eight o'clock approached, then decreased until in the end there was only a pensioner with a wheelie bag alighting onto the pavement during the quiet mornings when mothers and fathers began to appear with their strollers and the street traffic was dominated by vans, trucks, pickups, buses, and taxis.

At this time, with the sun flashing on the windows on the opposite side of the street from the office, and with footsteps no longer, or at least seldom, echoing down the stairwell outside, groups of nursery children barely taller than sheep walked past, all wearing identical high visibility jackets, often serious-faced, as if spellbound by the adventurous nature of the enterprise, while the seriousness of the nannies, who towered like shepherds above them, felt instead to be verging on boredom. It was also during this period that the noise of all the work going on in the vicinity had enough space around it to come to the fore in one's consciousness, whether it be a Stockholm Parks and Gardens employee blasting leaves from the lawns or pruning a tree, the Highways Department scraping a layer of tarmac from the street or a landlord totally renovating a block of flats nearby. Then a wave of white-collar workers and business people surged into the streets and filled all the restaurants to the rafters: it was lunchtime. When the wave, equally suddenly, retreated, it left a void which resembled that of the morning, yet had a character of its own, because though the pattern was repeated it was in reverse order: the scattered schoolchildren who passed my window now were on their way home and there was something unrestrained and boisterous about them, whereas when they had walked past on their way to school in the morning they still bore the silent imprint of sleep and the innate wariness we feel toward things that have not yet begun. The sun was shining now on the wall just inside the window, in the corridor the first clomping footsteps could be heard from the stairwell outside, and at the bus stop by the main hospital entrance the crowd of waiting passengers was bigger every time I looked out. More cars were in the street now, the number of pedestrians along the pavement leading to the high-rises was growing. This mounting activity culminated at about five o'clock, after that the area was quiet until the nightlife started at about ten, with crowds of raucous young men and shrill young women, and again at about three when it was over. At around six the buses started operating again, the traffic picked up, people streamed from gateways and stairways, a new day had begun.

So strictly regulated and demarcated was life here that it could be understood both geometrically and biologically. It was hard to believe that this could be related to the teeming, wild, and chaotic conditions of other species, such as the excessive agglomerations of tadpoles or fish spawn or insect eggs where life seemed to swarm up from an inexhaustible well. But it was. Chaos and unpredictability represent both the conditions of life and its decline, one impossible without the other, and even though almost all our efforts are directed toward keeping decline at bay, it does not take more than one brief moment of resignation to be thrust into its light, and not, as now, in shadow. Chaos is a kind of gravity, and the rhythm you can sense in history, of the rise and fall of civilizations, is perhaps caused by this. It is remarkable that the extremes resemble each other, in one sense at any rate, for in both immense chaos and a strictly regulated, demarcated world the individual is nothing, life is everything. In the same way that the heart does not care which life it beats for, the city does not care who fulfills its various functions. When everyone who moves around the city today is dead, in a hundred and fifty years, say, the sound of people's comings and goings, following the same old patterns, will still ring out. The only new thing will be the faces of those who perform these functions, although not that new because they will resemble us.

I threw the cigarette end on the ground and drank the last drop of the coffee, already cold.

I saw life; I thought about death.

I got up, rubbed my hands on my thighs a few times, and walked down to the intersection. The passing cars left tails of swirling snow behind them. A huge articulated truck came down the hill with its chains clanking, it braked and just managed to shudder to a halt before the crosswalk as the lights changed to red. I always had a bad conscience whenever vehicles had to stop because of me, a kind of imbalance arose, I felt as though I owed them something. The bigger the vehicle, the worse the guilt. I tried to catch the driver's eye as I crossed so that I could nod to restore the balance. But his eyes were following his hand, which he had raised to take something down from inside the cab, perhaps a map because the truck was Polish. He didn't see me, but that didn't matter, in which case braking couldn't have bothered him to any great extent.

I stopped at the front entrance, tapped in the code and opened the door, found my key while taking the few steps up to the first floor where my office was situated. The elevator droned and I unlocked the door as quickly as I could, darted in, and closed it behind me.

The sudden heat made the skin on my hands and face tingle. Outside, one of the numerous ambulances drove past with siren wailing. I put on some water for another cup of coffee and while I was waiting for it to boil, I skimmed through what I had written so far. The dust hovering in the broad, angled shafts of light anxiously followed every tiny current in the air. The neighbor in the adjacent flat had begun to play piano. The kettle hissed. What I had written was not good. It wasn't bad but it wasn't good either. I went to the cupboard, unscrewed the lid of the coffee tin, put two spoonfuls of coffee in the cup, and poured the water, which rose up the sides, black and steaming.

The telephone rang.

I put the cup down on the desk and let the phone ring twice before I answered.

"Hello?" I said.

"Hi, it's me."

"Hi."

"I was just wondering how things were going. Are you managing okay down there?"

She sounded happy.

"I don't know. I've only been here a few hours," I said.

Silence.

"Are you coming home soon?"

"You don't need to hassle me," I said. "I'll come when I come."

She didn't answer.

"Shall I buy something on the way?" I asked at length.

"No, I've done the shopping."

"Okay. See you then."

"Good. Bye. Hold on. Cocoa."

"Cocoa," I said. "Anything else?"

"No, that's all."

"Okay. Bye."

"Bye."

After putting down the receiver I remained in the chair for a long while, sunk in something that was not thoughts, or feelings, more a kind of atmosphere, the way an empty room can have an atmosphere. When I absentmindedly raised the cup to my lips I drank a mouthful, the coffee was lukewarm. I nudged the mouse to remove the screen saver and check the time. Six minutes to three. Then I read the text I'd written again, cut and pasted it into my jottings file. I'd been working on a novel for five years, and so whatever I wrote could not be lackluster. And this was not radiant enough. Yet the solution lay in the existing text, I knew that, there was something in it I was after. It felt as if everything I wanted was there, but in a form that was too compressed. The germ of an idea that had set the text in motion was particularly important, namely that the action took place in the 1880s while all the characters and tangibles were from the 1980s. For several years I had tried to write about my father, but had gotten nowhere, probably because the subject was too close to my life, and thus not so easy to force into another form, which of course is a prerequisite for literature. That is its sole law: everything has to submit to form. If any of literature's other elements are stronger than form, such as style, plot, theme, if any of these overtake form, the result suffers. That is why writers with a strong style often write bad books. That is also why writers with strong themes so often write bad books. Strong themes and styles have to be broken down before literature can come into being. It is this breaking down that is called "writing." Writing is more about destroying than creating. No one knew that better than Rimbaud. The remarkable thing about him was not that he arrived at this insight at such a disturbingly young age but that he applied it to life as well. For Rimbaud everything was about freedom, in writing as in life, and it was because freedom was paramount that he could put writing behind him, or perhaps even had to put writing behind him, because it too became a curb on him that had to be destroyed. Freedom is destruction plus movement. Another writer to realize this was Aksel Sandemose. His tragedy was that he was only able to perform the latter part in literature, not in life. He destroyed, and never moved on from what he had destroyed. Rimbaud went to Africa.

A sudden subconscious impulse made me look up, and I met the gaze of a woman. She was sitting in a bus opposite the window. Night had begun to fall and the sole source of light in the room was the desk lamp, which must have attracted attention from outside as it would a moth. When she realized that I had seen her she averted her gaze. I got up and went over to the window, loosened the blinds, and lowered them as the bus moved off. It was time to go home. I had said "soon" and that was an hour ago.

She had been in such a cheery mood when she rang.

A pang of unhappiness went through me. How could I possibly have met her anxiety and hope with annoyance?

I stood stock-still in the middle of the floor, as if the pain radiating from my body might disappear of its own accord. But it didn't. It had to be removed with action. I would have to make amends. The very thought was a help, not just through its promise of reconciliation, but also through the practical follow-up it demanded, for how could I make amends? I switched off the computer, slid it into my bag, rinsed the cup and placed it in the sink, pulled out the loose electrical cable, turned off the light, and donned hat and coat in the moonlight filtering through the cracks in the blinds, all the time picturing her in my mind's eye in the large flat.

The cold stung my face as I stepped into the street. I pulled the hood of my parka over my hat, bent my head to shield my eyes from the tiny snow particles whirling through the air, and started to walk. On good days I would take Tegnérgatan down to Drottninggatan which I followed to the Hötorg area, from where I walked up the steep hill to St. Johannes' Church and down again to Regeringsgatan, where our flat was. This route was full of shops, shopping malls, cafés, restaurants, and cinemas and was always packed. The streets there teemed with people of all types. In the brightly lit shop windows there was the most varied assortment of goods; inside, escalators circled like wheels inside enormous, mysterious machinery, elevators glided up and down, TV screens showed beautiful people moving like apparitions, in front of hundreds of tills, lines formed, dwindled and reformed, dwindled and reformed in patterns as unpredictable as the clouds in the sky above the city's rooftops. On good days I loved this, the stream of people, with their more or less attractive faces, whose eyes expressed a certain state of mind, could wash through me as I watched them. On less good days, however, the same scenario had the opposite effect, and if possible I would choose a different route, one more off the beaten track. As a rule it was along Rådmansgatan, then down Holländergatan to Tegnérgatan where I crossed Sveavägen and followed Döbelnsgatan up to St. Johannes' Church. This route was dominated by private houses, most people you met were types who hurried through the streets alone, and the few shops and restaurants that existed were not especially select. Driving schools with windows veiled in exhaust fumes, secondhand shops with boxes of comics and LPs outside, laundries, a hairdresser's, a Chinese restaurant, a couple of seedy pubs.

This was such a day. With head bent to avoid the gusting snow I walked through the streets, which between the towering walls and snow-covered roofs of apartment buildings, resembled narrow valleys, occasionally I peered in through the windows I passed: the deserted reception area of a small hotel, the yellow fish swimming around against the green background of the fish tank; large advertisements for a firm that produced signs, brochures, stickers, cardboard stands; the three black hairdressers tending to their three black customers in the African hair salon, one of whom craned around to see two kids sitting on the stairs at the back of the shop and laughing, and then jerked his head back with barely concealed impatience.

On the other side of the street was a park called Observatorielunden. The trees appeared to grow from the top of a steep mound there, and since a dim light spread from the row of buildings beneath, it looked as though it were the crowns of the trees that bestowed the darkness. So dense was the canopy that the lights at the top of the observatory, built some time in the 1700s, in the city's heyday, were not visible. A café was there now, and the first time I went it struck me how much closer to our times the eighteenth century seemed here in Sweden than in Norway, perhaps especially in the countryside where a Norwegian farmhouse from, let's say 1720, is really ancient while all the splendid buildings in Stockholm from the same period give the impression of being almost contemporary. I recalled my maternal grandmother's sister Borghild – who lived in a little house above the very farm from which the family originated – sitting on the veranda and telling us that houses had been there from the sixteenth century right through to the 1960s, when they had been demolished to make way for more modern constructions. This sensational revelation contrasted with the everyday experience of coming across a building from that era here. Perhaps this was all about closeness to the family, and hence to me? That the past in Jølster was relevant to me in quite a different way from Stockholm's past? That must be it, I thought, and closed my eyes briefly to rid myself of the feeling that I was an idiot, which this train of thought had produced, since it was so obviously based on an illusion. I had no history, and so I made myself one, much as a Nazi party might in a satellite suburb.

I continued down the street, rounded the corner and came into Holländergatan. With its deserted sidewalks and two lifeless rows of snowed-in cars, squeezed between two of the city's most important streets, Sveavägen and Drottninggatan, it had to be the backstreet to end all backstreets. I shifted the bag into my left hand while grabbing my hat with my right and shaking off the snow that had accumulated on it, ducking at the same time to avoid hitting my head on the scaffolding that had been erected over the sidewalk. High above, tarpaulins thrashed in the wind. As I emerged from the tunnel-like structure a man stepped in front of me. He did this in such a way that I was forced to stop.

"Cross over to the other sidewalk," he said. "There's a fire here. For all I know, there may be something explosive inside."

He put a mobile phone to his ear, then lowered it.

"I'm serious," he said. "Cross over to the other side."

"Where's the fire?" I asked.

"There," he said, pointing to a window ten meters away. The top part was open and smoke was seeping out. I crossed into the street so that I could see better while at least to some degree heeding his strong appeal for me to keep my distance. The room inside was illuminated by two floodlights and full of equipment and cables. Paint buckets, toolboxes, drills, rolls of insulation, two stepladders. Amid all this the smoke curled slowly, groping its way.

"Have you called the fire department?" I asked.

He nodded.

"They're coming."

Again he raised his mobile to his ear, only to lower it again the next moment.

I could see the smoke forming new patterns inside and gradually filling the room while the man paced frenetically to and fro on the other side of the street.

"I can't see any flames," I said. "Can you?"

"It's a smoldering fire," he said.

I stood there for a few minutes but as I was cold and nothing appeared to be happening I continued homeward. By the traffic lights in Sveavägen I heard the sirens of the first fire engines which then came into view at the top of the hill. All around me heads turned. The sirens' promise of speed stood in strange contrast to the way the large vehicles slowly crept down the hill. At that moment the lights went green and I crossed over to the supermarket.

That night I couldn't sleep. Usually I fell asleep within minutes, regardless of how tumultuous the day had been, or how unsettling the prospects of the new day, and apart from a period of sleepwalking, I always slept soundly till morning. But that night I already knew as I laid my head on the pillow and closed my eyes that sleep was not going to come. Wide awake, I lay listening to the sounds of the city rising and falling in sync with the human activity outside, and to those emanating from the flats above and below us, which died away bit by bit until only the gurgling of the air-conditioning remained, as my mind darted back and forth. Linda was asleep beside me. I knew that the child she bore inside also influenced her dreams, which were worryingly often about water: enormous waves crashing down on distant beaches she was walking along; the flat flooding with water sometimes completely filling it, either trickling down walls or rising from sinks and toilets; lakes in new places in town, such as under the railway station where her child might be in a left-luggage locker she couldn't reach, or simply disappeared from her side while she had her hands full of bags. She also had dreams in which the child she gave birth to had an adult face, or it turned out there wasn't a child at all and all that flowed from her during the birth was water.

My dreams, what were they like?

Not once had I dreamed about the baby! Now and then that would give me a bad conscience since, if you regarded the currents in those parts of your conscious mind without volition as more indicative of the truth than those controlled by volition, which I suppose I did, it became so obvious that the significance of expecting a baby was nothing special for me. On the other hand, nothing was. After the age of twenty I had hardly ever dreamed about anything that had a bearing on my life. It was as though in dreams I had not grown up, I was still a child surrounded by the same people and places I had been surrounded by in childhood. And even though the events that occurred there were new every night, the feeling they left me with was always the same. The constant feeling of humiliation. Often it could take several hours after waking before that feeling had left my body. Moreover, when conscious, I hardly remembered anything from my childhood, and the little I did remember no longer stirred anything in me, which of course created a kind of symmetry between past and present, in a strange system whereby night and dreams were connected with memory, day and consciousness with oblivion.

Only a few years ago it had been different. Until I moved to Stockholm I had felt there was a continuity to my life, as if it stretched unbroken from childhood up to the present, held together by new connections, in a complex and ingenious pattern in which every phenomenon I saw was capable of evoking a memory which unleashed small landslides of feeling in me, some with a known source, others without. The people I encountered came from towns I had been to, they knew other people I had met, it was a network, and it was a tight mesh. But when I moved to Stockholm this flaring up of memories became rarer and rarer, and one day it ceased altogether. That is, I could still remember; what happened was that the memories no longer stirred anything in me. No longing, no wish to return, nothing. Just the memory, and a barely perceptible hint of an aversion to anything that was connected with it.

This thought made me open my eyes. I lay quite still looking at the rice lamp hanging like a miniature moon from the ceiling in the darkness above the bedstead. This really was not anything to regret. For nostalgia is not only shameless, it is also treacherous. What does anyone in their twenties really get out of a longing for their childhood years? For their own youth? It's like an illness.

I turned and looked at Linda. She was lying on her side, facing me. Her belly was so big it was becoming hard to associate it with the rest of her body even though it too had swollen. Only yesterday she had been standing in front of the mirror laughing at the thickness of her thighs.

The baby was lying with its head resting in the pelvis, and would lie like that through to the birth. In the maternity unit they had said it was quite normal for a baby not to move for long periods. Its heart was beating, and soon, when it felt the time was ripe it would, in cooperation with the body that it had outgrown, start the birth itself.

I got up carefully and went into the kitchen for a glass of water. Outside the entrance to Nalen concert hall there were several groups of older people standing around and chatting. Once a month dance nights were arranged for them, and they came in droves, men and women between the ages of sixty and eighty, all in their finest clothes, and when I saw them lining up, excited and happy, it made my soul ache. One person in particular had made quite an impression on me. Wearing a pale yellow suit, white tennis shoes, and a straw hat, he first appeared, a bit unsteady on his feet, at the intersection by David Bagares gate one evening in September, but it wasn't so much the clothes that made him stand out from the others, it was more the presence he radiated, for while I perceived the others to be part of a collective, older men out to have a good time with their wives, so alike that the individual left your mind the second your gaze shifted, he was alone here, even when he was outside chatting with others. But the most conspicuous thing about him was the willpower he demonstrated, which in this company was unique. When he strode into the crowded foyer it struck me that he was searching for something, and that he would not find it there, or anywhere else. Time had passed him by, and with it, the world.

Outside, a taxi pulled onto the curb. The nearest group closed their umbrellas and good-humoredly shook the snow off them before getting in. Farther down the street a police car drove up. The blue light was on, but not the siren, and the silence lent the scene a sense of the ominous. After that, another followed. They both slowed as they passed and when I heard them stop outside I put the glass of water down on the kitchen counter and went to the window in the bedroom. The police cars were parked one behind the other by US VIDEO. The first was a standard police car, the second a van. The rear door was being opened as I arrived. Six police officers ran to the shop front and disappeared into the building, two remained in front of the patrol car waiting. A man in his fifties walking past did not so much as cast a glance at the police. I sensed that he had been planning to go in, but had gotten cold feet when he saw the police outside. All day long a regular stream of men went in and out of the door to US VIDEO, and having lived here for close to a year, in nine cases out of ten I could pick out who was about to go in and who would walk by. They invariably had the same body language. They walked along as they normally did, and when they opened the door it was with a movement intended to appear as a natural extension of their last. So intent were they on not looking around that this was what you noticed. Their attempts to appear normal radiated from them. Not only when they entered but also when they reemerged. The door opened and without pausing they seemed to glide out onto the pavement and into this gait that was supposed to give the impression that they were merely continuing a walk started a couple of blocks away. They were men of all ages, from sixteen to seventy or so, and they came from all layers of society. Some seemed to go there as if this was their sole errand, others on their way home from work or early in the morning after a night out. I had not been there myself, but I knew very well what it was like: the long staircase down, the deep, murky basement room with the counter where you paid, the row of black booths with TV monitors, the multitude of films to choose from, all according to your sexual preferences, the black, synthetic leather chairs, the rolls of toilet paper on the adjacent bench.

August Strindberg once claimed in his profound, deranged seriousness that the stars in the sky were peepholes in a wall. Occasionally I was reminded of that when observing the endless stream of souls descending the stairs to masturbate in the darkness of the cellar booths as they watched the illuminated screens. The world around them was closed off, and one of the few ways they could look out was through these boxes. They never told anyone what they saw, it belonged to the unmentionable; it was incompatible with everything a normal life entailed, and most of those who went there were normal men. But it was not the case that the unmentionable was reserved for the world above, it also applied down below, at any rate if one were to judge from their behavior, where no one spoke, no one looked at the others, the solipsistic paths they all trod, from the stairs, to shelves of films, to counter, to booth, and back to the stairs. The fact that there was something essentially laughable about this, this row of men sitting with their pants round their knees, each in his own booth, grunting and groaning and pulling at their penises while watching films of women having intercourse with horses or dogs, or men with lots of other men, could not have escaped their attention, but neither could they acknowledge it, since true laughter and true desire are incompatible, and it was desire that had driven them here. But why here? All the films you could see in US VIDEO were also available on the net, and could therefore be viewed in absolute isolation without the risk of being seen by others. So there must have been something in the unmentionable situation itself that they sought. Either the lowness, the vileness, or the squalidness of it, or the closed-off-ness. I had no idea, this was foreign territory for me, but I couldn't help thinking about it, for every time I gazed in that direction someone was going down to the cellar.

It was not unusual for the police to show up, but they generally appeared as a result of the demonstrations that were regularly staged outside. They left the place itself alone, to the enormous disgruntlement of the demonstrators. All they could do was stand there with their banners, shout slogans, and boo every time someone went in or came out, under the watchful eye of the police who stood shoulder to shoulder with shields, helmets and batons, keeping them under surveillance.

"What's that?" Linda asked from behind me.

I turned and looked at her.

"Are you awake?"

"More or less," she said.

"I can't get to sleep," I said. "And there are police cars outside. Go back to sleep."

She closed her eyes. Down on the street, the door opened. Two policemen came into view. Behind them were two more. They were holding a man between them, so tight that his feet were off the ground. It looked brutal, but presumably it was necessary because the man's trousers were around his knees. When they came out they let go of him and he fell onto all fours. Two more officers came out. The man got to his feet and pulled up his trousers. One of the officers cuffed his hands behind his back, another escorted him into the car. As the other policemen began to get in, two of the shop employees came onto the street. They stood with their hands in their pockets watching the vehicles starting up, driving down the street, and disappearing from view as their hair slowly went white with the falling snow.

I padded into the living room. The light from the streetlamps hanging from cables above the street shone dimly against the walls and floor. I watched TV for a while. I kept thinking it might worry Linda if she woke up and came in. Any irregularities or any suggestion of excess could remind her of the manic periods her father went through when she was growing up. I switched it off, took one of the art books from the shelf above the sofa instead, and sat flicking through it. It was a book about Constable I had just bought. Mostly oil sketches, studies of clouds, countryside, sea.

I didn't need to do any more than let my eyes skim over them before I was moved to tears. So great was the impression some of the pictures made on me. Others left me cold. That was my only parameter with art, the feelings it aroused. The feeling of inexhaustibility. The feeling of beauty. The feeling of presence. All compressed into such acute moments that sometimes they could be difficult to endure. And quite inexplicable. For if I studied the picture that made the greatest impression, an oil sketch of a cloud formation from September 6, 1822, there was nothing there that could explain the strength of my feelings. At the top, a patch of blue sky. Beneath, whitish mist. Then the rolling clouds. White where the sunlight struck them, pale-green in the least shadowy parts, deep-green and almost black where they were at their densest and the sun was farthest away. Blue, white, turquoise, greenish-black. That was all. The text describing the picture said Constable had painted it in Hampstead at noon, and that a certain Mr. Wilcox had doubted the accuracy of the date as there was another sketch made on the same day between twelve o'clock and one that showed quite a different, more rain-laden sky, an argument which was rendered invalid by London weather reports for this day, as they could easily have described the cloud cover in both pictures.

I had studied history of art and was used to describing and analyzing art. But what I never wrote about, and this is all that matters, was the experience of it. Not just because I couldn't, but also because the feelings the pictures evoked in me went against everything I had learned about what art was and what it was for. So I kept it to myself. I wandered around the Nationalgalleri in Stockholm or the Nasjonalgalleri in Oslo or the National Gallery in London and looked. There was a kind of freedom about this. I didn't need to justify my feelings, there was no one to whom I had to answer and no case to answer. Freedom, but not peace, for even though the pictures were supposed to be idylls, such as Claude's archaic landscapes, I was always unsettled when I left them because what they possessed, the core of their being, was inexhaustibility and what that wrought in me was a kind of desire. I can't explain it any better than that. A desire to be inside the inexhaustibility. That is how I felt this night as well. I sat leafing through the Constable book for almost an hour. I kept flicking back to the picture of the greenish clouds, every time it called forth the same emotions in me. It was as if two different forms of reflection rose and fell in my consciousness, one with its thoughts and reasoning, the other with its feelings and impressions, which, even though they were juxtaposed, excluded each other's insights. It was a fantastic picture, it filled me with all the feelings that fantastic pictures do, but when I had to explain why, what constituted the "fantastic," I was at a loss to do so. The picture made my insides tremble, but for what? The picture filled me with longing, but for what? There were plenty of clouds around. There were plenty of colors around. There were enough particular historical moments. There were also plenty of combinations of all three. Contemporary art, in other words, the art which in principle ought to be of relevance to me, did not consider the feelings a work of art generated as valuable. Feelings were of inferior value, or perhaps even an undesirable by-product, a kind of waste product, or at best, malleable material, open to manipulation. Naturalistic depictions of reality had no value either, but were viewed as naïve and a stage of development that had been superseded long ago. There was not much meaning left in that. But the moment I focused my gaze on the painting again all my reasoning vanished in the surge of energy and beauty that arose in me. *Yes, yes, yes*, I heard. *That's where it is. That's where I have to go.* But what was it I had said yes to? Where was it I had to go?

It was four o'clock. So it was still night. I couldn't go to my office at night. But at half past four, surely that was morning?

I got up and went into the kitchen, put a plate of meatballs and spaghetti in the microwave, because I hadn't eaten since lunch the day before, went into the bathroom and showered, mostly to pass the minutes it took for the food to heat, dressed, found myself a knife and fork, poured a glass of water, fetched the plate, sat down to eat.

In the streets outside everything was still. The hour before five was the only time of day this city slept. In my earlier life, during the twelve years I had lived in Bergen I used to stay up at night as often as I could. I never reflected on this, it was just something I liked and did. It had started as a student ideal, grounded in a notion that in some way night was associated with freedom. Not in itself but as a response to the nine-to-four reality which I, and a couple of others, regarded as middle-class and conformist. We wanted to be free, we stayed up at night. Continuing with this had less to do with freedom than a growing need to be alone. This, I understood now, I shared with my father. In the house where we lived he had a whole studio apartment to himself and he spent more or less every evening there. The night was his.

I rinsed the plate under the tap, put it in the dishwasher and went into the bedroom. Linda opened her eyes when I stopped by the bed.

"You're such a light sleeper," I said.

"What time is it?" she asked.

"Half past four."

"Have you been up all night?"

I nodded.

"I think I'll head for the office. Is that all right?"

She pulled herself half up.

"*Now?*"

"I can't sleep anyway," I said. "I might just as well spend the time working."

"Love . . ." she said. "Come and lie down."

"Don't you hear what I'm saying?" I said.

"But I don't want to be alone here," she said. "Can't you go to the office in the early morning?"

"It's early morning now," I said.

"It's not, it's the middle of the night," she said. "And, in fact, I could give birth at any moment. It could happen in an hour, you know that."

"Bye," I said, closing the door after me. In the hall I put on my coat and hat, grabbed the bag with my computer and left. Cold air rose from the snow-covered pavement. At the end of the street a snowplow was on its way. The weighty metal blade thundered over the tarmac. She always wanted to hold me back. Why was it so important for me to be there when she was asleep and didn't notice my presence anyway?

The sky hung over the rooftops, black and heavy. But it had stopped snowing. I began to walk. The snowplow passed me with engine roaring, chains clattering, blade scraping. A mini-inferno of noise. I turned to go up David Bagares gate, deserted and still, toward Malmskillnadsgatan, where your eyes were drawn to the restaurant initials KGB. Outside the entrance to the old people's home, I stopped. It was true what she had said. The birth could start at any moment. And she didn't like being alone. So what was I doing here? What was I going to do in the office at half past four in the morning? Write? Do today what I had not succeeded in doing for the last five years?

What an idiot I was. It was our child she was expecting, my child, she shouldn't have to go through that alone.

I headed back. Putting down my bag and removing my coat, I heard her voice from the bedroom.

"Is that you, Karl Ove?"

"Yes," I said and went in to see her. She gave me a quizzical look.

"You're right," I said. "I wasn't thinking. Sorry I just took off that way."

"It's me who should apologize," she said. "Of course you have to go to work!"

"I'll do it later," I said.

"But I don't want to hold you back," she said. "I'll be fine here. I promise. Just go. I'll call you if there is anything."

"No," I said, lying down beside her.

"But Karl Ove . . ." She smiled.

I liked her saying my name, I always had.

"Now you're saying what I said while I'm saying what you said. But I know you *really* mean the opposite."

"This is getting too complicated for me," I said. "Hadn't we better just go to sleep? Then we'll have breakfast together before I go."

"Okay," she said, snuggling up to me. She was as hot as an oven. I ran my hand through her hair and kissed her lightly on the mouth. She closed her eyes and leaned her head back.

"What did you say?" I asked.

She didn't answer, just took my hand and placed it on her stomach.

"There," she said. "Did you feel it?"

The skin suddenly bulged beneath my palm.

"Oooh," I said, lifting it up to see. Whatever was pressing up against the stomach, making it bulge, whether a knee, a foot, an elbow or a hand, was now shifting. It was like watching something move under the surface of otherwise tranquil water. Then it was gone again.

"She's impatient," Linda said. "I can feel it."

"Was that a foot?"

"Mm."

"It's as if she was testing to see if she could get out that way," I said.

Linda smiled.

"Did it hurt?"

She shook her head.

"I can feel it, but it doesn't hurt. It's just weird."

"I can believe that."

I snuggled up to her and placed my hand on her stomach again. The mailbox in the hall banged. A truck drove past outside, it must have been big, the windows vibrated. I closed my eyes. As all the thoughts and images of consciousness began to move in directions over which I had no control, and I seemed to be lying there watching them, like a kind of lazy sheepdog of the mind, I knew sleep was around the corner. It was just a question of lowering myself into its dark vaults.

I was woken by Linda clattering about in the kitchen. The clock on the mantelpiece said five to eleven. Shit. The workday was gone.

I dressed and went into the kitchen. Steam was hissing from the little coffeepot on the stove. The table was set with food and juice. Two slices of toast lay on a plate. Two more jumped up in the toaster beside them.

"Did you sleep well?" Linda asked.

"Like a log," I said and sat down. I spread butter over the toast, it melted at once and filled the tiny pores on the surface. Linda took the pot and switched off the burner. Her bulging stomach made it look as if she were constantly leaning back, and if she did something with her hands she seemed to be doing it on the other side of an invisible wall.

The sky outside was gray. But there must have still been some snow on the roofs because the room was lighter than usual.

She poured coffee into the two cups she had set out and placed one in front of me. Her face was swollen.

"Are you feeling worse?"

She nodded.

"I'm all blocked up. And I've got a bit of a temperature."

She sat down heavily, poured milk into her coffee.

"Typical," she said. "I have to get sick now of all times. When I need my energy most."

"The birth may hold off," I said. "Your body won't make a move until it's completely ready."

She glared at me. I swallowed the last morsel and poured juice in my glass. If there was one thing I had learned over recent months it was that everything you heard about pregnant women's fluctuating and unpredictable moods was true.

"Don't you understand that this is a disaster?" she said.

I met her gaze. Took a swig of juice.

"Yes, yes, of course," I said. "But it'll be alright. Everything will be alright."

"Of course it will," she said. "But that's not what this is about. This is about my not wanting to be sick and feeble when I have to give birth."

"I understand that," I said. "But you won't be. We're still a few days away."

We ate in silence.

Then she looked at me again. She had fantastic eyes. They were grayish-green, and occasionally, most often when she was tired, she squinted. The photograph in the poetry collection she had published showed her squinting, and the vulnerability it revealed that the self-confidence in her facial expression countered, but did not override, had once utterly hypnotized me.

"Sorry," she said. "I'm just nervous."

"You don't need to be," I said. "You're as well prepared as it's possible to be."

And she really was. She had devoted herself fully to the task at hand; she had read piles of books, bought a kind of meditation cassette she listened to every night, on which a voice mesmerically repeated that pain was not dangerous, that pain was good, that pain was not dangerous, that pain was good, and we had gone to a class together and been shown around the maternity ward where the birth was scheduled to take place. She had prepared herself for every session with the midwife by writing down questions in advance, and she noted down with the same conscientiousness all the curves and measurements she got from her in a diary. She had, furthermore, sent a sheet of her preferences to the maternity ward, as requested, on which she said she was nervous and needed a lot of encouragement, but at the same time she was strong and wanted to give birth without any anesthetics.

This cut me to the quick. I had of course been to the maternity ward, and even though they had tried to create a homey atmosphere, with sofas, carpets, pictures on the walls and CD players in the room where the birth would take place, as well as a TV room and a kitchen where you could cook your own food, and where you had your own room with an en suite after the birth, there was no denying another woman had given birth in the same room shortly before, and even though it had been washed immediately afterward, the bed linen changed and fresh towels put out, this had happened so infinitely many times that a faint metallic smell of blood and intestines hung in the air nonetheless. In the nice, cool room that was to be ours for twenty-four hours after the birth another couple with a newborn had been lying in the same bed. What for us was new and life-changing, was an endless cycle for those employed at the hospital. The midwives always had responsibility for several births happening at the same time, they were forever going in and out of a number of rooms where a variety of women were howling and screaming, yelling and groaning, all according to whichever phase of the birth they were in, and this went on continually, day and night, year in, year out, so if there was one thing they could not do, it was take care of someone with the intensity of expectations that Linda's letter expressed.

She looked out the window, and I followed her gaze. On the roof of the opposite building, perhaps ten meters from us, was a man with a rope around his waist shoveling snow.

"They're crazy in this country," I said.

"Don't you do that in Norway?"

"No, are you out of your mind?"

The year before I arrived here a boy had been killed by a lump of ice falling from a roof. Since then all roofs were cleared of snow from almost the moment it fell, with dire consequences; when mild weather came virtually all pavements were cordoned off with red-and-white tape for a week. Chaos everywhere.

"But all the fear keeps employment levels high," I said, before devouring the slice of bread, getting up and drinking the last gulp of coffee. "I'm off now."

"Okay," Linda said. "Feel like renting some films on the way back?"

I put the cup down and wiped my mouth with the back of my hand.

"Of course. Anything?"

"Yes, you choose."

I brushed my teeth. As I went into the hall to get ready, Linda followed me.

"What are you going to do today?" I asked, taking the coat from the cupboard with one hand while winding the scarf round my neck with the other.

"Don't know," she said. "Go for a walk in the park maybe. Have a bath."

"You okay?" I said.

"Yes, I'm fine."

I stooped to tie my shoes as she, with one arm supporting her back, towered above me.

"Okay," I said, pulling my hat on and grabbing the computer bag. "I'm off."

"Okay," she said.

"Call me if there is anything."

"I will."

We kissed, and I closed the door behind me. The elevator was on its way up, and I caught a brief glimpse of the neighbor from the floor above as she glided past with her face lowered in front of the mirror. She was a lawyer, usually wore black trousers or black, knee-length skirts, gave a curt greeting, always with a pinched mouth and radiating hostility, at least to me. Periodically her brother stayed with her, a lean, dark-eyed, restless and rough-looking but attractive man whom one of Linda's friends had noticed and with whom she had fallen in love, they were having a relationship of sorts which appeared to be based on him despising her as much as she worshipped him. The fact that he lived in the same house as her friend seemed to bother him, he had a hunted look in his eyes when we stopped and exchanged a few words, but even though I assumed that had something to do with my knowing more about him than he knew about me, there may have been other reasons – that he was a typical drug addict, for example. I knew nothing about that, I had no knowledge of such worlds, in this respect I really was as credulous as Geir – my only real friend in Stockholm – always claimed when he compared me to the deceived figure in Caravaggio's *Card Players*.

Downstairs in the hall, I decided to smoke a cigarette before proceeding on my way, walked along the corridor past the laundry room and out into the backyard where I put my computer down, leaned against the wall, and peered up at the sky. There was a ventilation duct directly above me, which filled the air close to the house with the smell of warm, freshly washed clothes. From the laundry room you could hear the faint whine of a spin cycle, so strangely angry compared with the slow, gray clouds drifting through the air far above. Here and there the blue sky behind them was visible, as if the day was a surface they scudded across.

I walked to the fence separating the innermost part of the yard from the nursery at the rear, now deserted, as the children were indoors eating at this time of day, rested my elbows on it and smoked while looking up at the two towers rising from Kungsgatan. Built in a kind of new baroque style, and testimony to the 1920s, they filled me with longing, as so often before. At night the towers were floodlit, and while in the daylight you could clearly distinguish the various details and see how different the materials in the wall were from the materials in the windows and the gilt statues and the verdigris copper surfaces, the artificial light bound them together. Perhaps it was the light itself that did this, or perhaps it was a result of the combination of the light and the surroundings; whatever the cause, it was as if the statues "talked" at night. Not that they came to life, they were as lifeless as before, it was more that the lifeless expression was changed, and in a way intensified. During the day there was nothing; at night this nothing found expression.

Or else it was because the day was filled with so much else to dissipate the concentration. The traffic in the streets, people on the sidewalks and on steps and in windows, helicopters flying across the sky like dragonflies, children who could come running out at any moment and crawl in the mud or snow, ride tricycles, shoot down the gigantic slide in the middle of the playground, climb the bridge of the fully equipped "ship" beside it, play in the sandpit, play in the small "house," throw balls or just scamper around, screaming and shouting, filling the yard with a cacophony like a cliff of nesting birds from morning to early afternoon, only interrupted, as now, by the peace of mealtimes. Then it was nearly impossible to be outdoors, not because of the noise, which I seldom noticed, but because the children had a tendency to flock around me. The few times I had tried that autumn they had started climbing up the low fence that divided the yard into two, and hung off it, four or five of them, and asked me about all sorts of things, or else they would amuse themselves by crossing the forbidden line and rushing past me laughing their heads off. The boy who was the pushiest was also the one who was usually picked up last. Whenever I walked home that way it was not unusual for me to see him messing around in the sandpit on his own, or with some other unfortunate, if he wasn't hanging off the fence by the exit, that is. Then I usually greeted him. If no one else was around with two fingers to my brow, I may even have raised my "hat." Not so much for his sake, because he sent me a fierce look every time, but for my own.

Sometimes I mused that if all soft feelings could be scraped off like cartilage around the sinews of an injured athlete's knee, what a liberation that would be. No more sentimentality, sympathy, empathy . . .

A scream rent the air.

AAAAAAAAAAAAAAAAAAAAAhhhh.

It startled me. Even though this scream was heard often, I never got used to it. The flats in the building it came from, on the opposite side of the nursery, were part of an old people's home. I visualized someone lying in their bed, not moving, completely out of touch with the outside world, for the screams could be heard late at night, early in the morning, or during the day. Another man smoked on a balcony with death-rattle coughing fits that could last several minutes. Apart from that, the old people's home was self-enclosed. Walking to my office, sometimes I happened to see caregivers in the windows on the other side of the building, they had a kind of recreation room there, and occasionally I saw some residents in the street, sometimes with police officers accompanying them home, a couple of times wandering around alone. Generally, though, I didn't give the place a thought.

What a piercing scream.

All the curtains were drawn, including those behind the balcony door, which was ajar and from where the sound came. I watched for a while. Then

I turned and headed for the door. Through the laundry room windows I saw the neighbor who lived in the flat below me folding a white sheet. I took my computer bag and went down the narrow grotto-like corridor, where the garbage cans stood, unlocked the metal gate, and came out onto the street, hurried off in the direction of KGB and the steps down to Tunnelgatan.

Twenty minutes later I was in my office. I hung my coat and scarf on the hook, put my shoes on the mat, made a cup of coffee, connected my computer and sat drinking coffee and looking at the title page until the screen saver kicked in and filled the screen with a myriad of bright dots.

The America of the Soul. That was the title. And virtually everything in the room pointed to it, or to what it aroused in me. The reproduction of William Blake's famous, underwater-like Newton picture hanging on the wall behind me, the two framed drawings from Churchill's eighteenth-century expedition next to it, purchased in London at some point, one of a dead whale, the other of a dissected beetle, both drawings showing several stages. A night mood by Peder Balke on the end wall, the green and the black in it. The Greenaway poster. The map of Mars I had found in an old *National Geographic* magazine. Beside it the two black-and-white photographs taken by Thomas Wågström; one of a gleaming child's dress, the other of a black lake beneath the surface of which you can discern the eyes of an otter. The little green metal dolphin and the little green metal helmet I had bought on Crete and which now stood on the desk. And the books: Paracelsus, Basileios, Lucretius, Thomas Browne, Olof Rudbeck, Augustin, Thomas Aquinas, Albertus Seba, Werner Heisenberg, Raymond Russell, and the Bible, of course, and works about national romanticism and about curiosity cabinets, Atlantis, Albrecht Dürer and Max Ernst, the Baroque and Gothic periods, nuclear physics and weapons of mass destruction, about forests and science in the sixteenth and seventeenth centuries. This wasn't about knowledge but about the aura knowledge exuded, the places it came from, which were almost all outside the world we lived in now, yet were still within the ambivalent space where all historical objects and ideas reside.

In recent years the feeling that the world was small and that I grasped everything in it had grown stronger and stronger in me, despite my common sense telling me that actually the reverse was true: the world was boundless and unfathomable, the number of events infinite, the present time an open door that stood flapping in the wind of history. But that is not how it felt. It felt as if the world were known, fully explored and charted, that it could no longer move in unpredicted directions, that nothing new or surprising could happen. I understood myself, I understood my surroundings, I understood society around me, and if any phenomenon should appear mysterious I knew how to deal with it.

Understanding must not be confused with knowledge for I knew next to nothing – but should there be, for example, skirmishes in the borderlands of an ex-Soviet republic somewhere in Asia, whose towns I had never heard of, with inhabitants alien in everything from dress and language to everyday life and religion, and it turned out that this conflict had deep historical roots that went back to events that took place a thousand years ago, my total ignorance and lack of knowledge would not prevent me from understanding what happened, for the mind has the capacity to deal with the most alien of thoughts. This applied to everything. If I saw an insect I hadn't come across, I knew that someone must have seen it before and categorized it. If I saw a shiny object in the sky I knew that it was either a rare meteorological phenomenon or a plane of some kind, perhaps a weather balloon, and if it was important it would be in the newspaper the following day. If I had forgotten something that happened in my childhood it was probably due to repression; if I became really furious about something it was probably due to projection, and the fact that I always tried to please people I met had something to do with my father and my relationship with him. There is no one who does not understand their own world. Someone who understands very little, a child, for example, simply moves in a more restricted world than someone who understands a lot. However, an insight into the limits of understanding has always been part of understanding a lot: the recognition that the world outside, all those things we don't understand, not only exists but is also always greater than the world inside. From time to time I thought that what had happened, at least to me, was that the children's world, where everything was known, and where with regard to the things that were not known, you leaned on others, those who had knowledge and ability, that this children's world had never actually ceased to exist, it had just expanded over all these years. When I, as a nineteen-year-old, was confronted with the contention that the world is linguistically structured I rejected it with what I called sound common sense, for it was obviously meaningless, the pen I held, was that supposed to be language? The window gleaming in the sun? The yard beneath me with students crossing it dressed in their autumn clothes? The lecturer's ears, his hands? The faint smell of earth and leaves on the clothes of the woman who had just come in the door and was now sitting next to me? The sound of pneumatic drills used by the road workers who had set up their tent on the other side of St. Johannes' Church, the regular drone of the transformer? The rumble from the town below – was that supposed to be a linguistic rumble? My cough, is it a linguistic cough? No, that was a ridiculous idea. The world was the world, which I touched and leaned on, breathed and spat in, ate and drank, bled, and vomited. It was only many years later that I began to view this differently. In a book I read about art and anatomy Nietzsche was quoted as saying that "physics too is an interpretation of the world and an arrangement of the world, and not an explanation of the world," and that "we have measured the value of the world with categories *that refer to a purely fabricated world.*"

A fabricated world?

Yes, the world as a superstructure, the world as a spirit, weightless and abstract, of the same material with which thoughts are woven, and through which therefore they can move unhindered. A world that after three hundred years of natural science is left without mysteries. Everything is explained, everything is understood, everything lies within humanity's horizons of comprehension, from the biggest, the universe, whose oldest observable light, the farthest boundary of the cosmos, dates from its birth fifteen billion years ago, to the smallest, the protons and neutrons and mesons of the atom.

Even the phenomena that kill us we know about and understand, such as the bacteria and viruses that invade our bodies, attack our cells, and cause them to grow or die. For a long time it was only nature and its laws that were made abstract and transparent in this way, but now, in our iconoclastic times, this not only applies to nature's laws but also to its places and people. The whole of the physical world has been elevated to this sphere, everything has been incorporated into the immense imaginary realm from South American rain forests and the islands of the Pacific Ocean to the North African deserts and Eastern Europe's tired, gray towns. Our minds are flooded with images of places we have never been, yet still know, people we have never met, yet still know and in accordance with which we, to a considerable extent, live our lives. The feeling this gives that the world is small, tightly enclosed around itself, without openings to anywhere else, is almost incestuous, and although I knew this to be deeply untrue, since actually we know nothing about anything, still I could not escape it. The longing I always felt, which some days was so great it could hardly be controlled, had its source here. It was partly to relieve this feeling that I wrote, I wanted to open the world by writing, for myself, at the same time this is also what made me fail. The feeling that the future does not exist, that it is only more of the same, means that all utopias are meaningless. Literature has always been related to utopia, so when the utopia loses meaning, so does literature. What I was trying to do, and perhaps what all writers try to do – what on earth do I know? – was to combat fiction with fiction. What I ought to do was affirm what existed, affirm the state of things as they are, in other words, revel in the world outside instead of searching for a way out, for in that way I would undoubtedly have a better life, but I couldn't do it, I couldn't, something had congealed inside me, a conviction was rooted inside me, and although it was essentialist, that is, outmoded and, furthermore, romantic, I could not get past it, for the simple reason that it had not only been thought but also experienced, in these sudden states of clearsightedness that everyone must know, where for a few seconds you catch sight of another world from the one you were in only a moment earlier, where the world seems to step forward and show itself for a brief glimpse before reverting and leaving everything as before . . .

The last time I experienced this was on the commuter train between Stockholm and Gnesta a few months earlier. The scene outside the window was a sea of white, the sky was gray and damp, we were going through an industrial area, empty railway cars, gas tanks, factories, everything was white and gray, and the sun was setting in the west, the red rays fading into the mist, and the train in which I was traveling was not one of the rickety, old, run-down units that usually serviced this route, but brand-new, polished and shiny, the seat was new, it smelled new, the doors in front of me opened and closed without friction, and I wasn't thinking about anything in particular, just staring at the burning red ball in the sky and the pleasure that suffused me was so sharp and came with such intensity that it was indistinguishable from pain. What I experienced seemed to me to be of enormous significance. Enormous significance. When the moment had passed the feeling of significance did not diminish, but all of a sudden it became hard to place: exactly *what* was significant? And why? A train, an industrial area, sun, mist?

I recognized the feeling, it was akin to the one some works of art evoke in me. Rembrandt's portrait of himself as an old man in London's National Gallery was such a picture, Turner's picture of the sunset over the sea off a port of antiquity at the same museum, Caravaggio's picture of Christ in Gethsemane. Vermeer evoked the same, a few of Claude's paintings, some of Ruisdael's and the other Dutch landscape painters, some of J.C. Dahl's, almost all of Hertervig's . . . But none of Rubens's paintings, none of Manet's, none of the English or French eighteenth-century painters, with the exception of Chardin, not Whistler, nor Michelangelo, and only one by Leonardo da Vinci. The experience did not favor any particular epoch, nor any particular painter, since it could apply to a single work by a painter and leave everything else the painter did to one side. Nor did it have anything to do with what is usually termed quality; I could stand unmoved in front of fifteen paintings by Monet, and feel the warmth spread through my body in front of a Finnish impressionist of whom few outside Finland had heard.

I didn't know what it was about these pictures that made such a great impression on me. However, it was striking that they were all painted before the 1900s, within the artistic paradigm that always retained some reference to visible reality. Thus, there was always a certain objectivity to them, by which I mean a distance between reality and the portrayal of reality, and it was doubtless in this interlying space where it "happened," where it appeared, whatever it was I saw, when the world seemed to step forward from the world. When you didn't just see the incomprehensible in it but came very close to it. Something that didn't speak, and that no words could grasp, consequently forever out of our reach, yet within it, for not only did it surround us, we were ourselves part of it, we were ourselves of it.

The fact that things other and mysterious were relevant to us had led my thoughts to angels, those mystical creatures who not only were linked to the divine but also to humanness, and therefore expressed the duality of the nature of otherness better than any other figure. At the same time there was something deeply dissatisfying about both the paintings and angels, since they both belonged to the past in such a fundamental way, that part of the past we have put behind us, that is, which no longer fit in, into this world we had created where the great, the divine, the solemn, the holy, the beautiful, and the true were no longer valid entities but quite the contrary, dubious or even laughable. This meant that the great beyond, which until the Age of Enlightenment had been the Divine, brought to us through the Revelation, and which in Romanticism was nature, where the concept of Revelation was expressed as the sublime, no longer found expression. In art, that which was beyond was synonymous with society, or the human masses, which fully encompassed its concepts of validity. As far as Norwegian art is concerned, the break came with Munch; it was in his paintings that, for the first time, man took up all the space. Whereas man was subordinate to the Divine through to the Age of Enlightenment, and to the landscape he was depicted in during Romanticism – the mountains are vast and intense, the sea is vast and intense, even the trees are vast and intense while humans, without exception, are small – the situation is reversed with Munch. It is as if humans swallow up everything, make everything theirs. The mountains, the sea, the trees, and the forests, everything is colored by humanness. Not human actions and external life, but human feelings and inner life. And once man had taken over, there seemed not to be a way back, as indeed there was no way back for Christianity as it began to spread like wildfire across Europe in the first centuries of our era. Man is gestalted by Munch, his inner life is given an outer form, the world is shaken up, and what was left after the door had been opened was the world as a gestalt: with painters after Munch it is the colors themselves, the forms themselves, not what they represent, that carry the emotion. Here we are in a world of images where the expression itself is everything, which of course means that there is no longer any dynamism between the outer and the inner, just a division. In the modernist era the division between art and the world was close to absolute, or put another way, art was a world of its own. What was taken up in this world was of course a question of individual taste, and soon this taste became the very core of art, which thus could and, to a certain degree in order to survive, had to admit objects from the real world. The situation we have arrived at now whereby the props of art no longer have any significance, all the emphasis is placed on what the art expresses, in other words, not what it is but what it thinks, what ideas it carries, such that the last remnants of objectivity, the final remnants of something outside the human world have been abandoned. Art has come to be an unmade bed, a couple of photocopiers in a room, a motorbike in an attic. And art has come to be a spectator of itself, the way it reacts, what newspapers write about it; the artist is a performer. That is how it is. Art does not know a beyond, science does not know a beyond, religion does not know a beyond, not anymore. Our world is enclosed around itself, enclosed around us, and there is no way out of it. Those in this situation who call for more intellectual depth, more spirituality, have understood nothing, for the problem is that the intellect has taken over everything. *Everything* has become intellect, even our bodies, they aren't bodies anymore, but ideas of bodies, something that is situated in our own heaven of images and conceptions within us and above us, where an increasingly large part of our lives is lived. The limits of that which cannot speak to us – the unfathomable –

no longer exist. We understand everything, and we do so because we have turned everything into ourselves. Nowadays, as one might expect, all those who have occupied themselves with the neutral, the negative, the nonhuman in art, have turned to language, that is where the incomprehensible and the otherness have been sought, as if they were to be found on the margins of human expression, on the fringes of what we understand, and of course, actually, that is logical: where else would it be found in a world that no longer acknowledges that there is a beyond?

It is in this light we have to see the strangely ambiguous role death has assumed. On the one hand, it is all around us, we are inundated by news of deaths, pictures of dead people; for death, in that respect, there are no limits, it is massive, ubiquitous, inexhaustible. But this is death as an idea, death without a body, death as thought and image, death as an intellectual concept. This death is the same as the word "death," the bodiless entity referred to when a dead person's name is used. For while the person is alive the name refers to the body, to where it resides, to what it does; the name becomes detached from the body when it dies and remains with the living, who, when they use the name, always mean the person he was, never the person he is now, a body which lies rotting somewhere. This aspect of death, that which belongs to the body and is concrete, physical and material, this death is hidden with such great care that it borders on a frenzy, and it works, just listen to how people who have been involuntary witnesses to fatal accidents or murders tend to express themselves. They always say the same, *it was absolutely unreal*, even though what they mean is the opposite. It was so real. But we no longer live in that reality. For us everything has been turned on its head, for us the real is unreal, the unreal real. And death, death is the last great beyond. That is why it has to be kept hidden. Because death might be beyond the term and beyond life, but it is not beyond the world.

I was almost thirty years old when I saw a dead body for the first time. It was the summer of 1998, a July afternoon, in a chapel in Kristiansand. My father had died. He was laid out on a table in the middle of the room, the sky was overcast, the light in the room dull, outside the window a lawn mower was slowly circling around a lawn. I was there with my brother. The funeral director had left the room so that we could be alone with the deceased, at whom we were staring from a distance of some meters. The eyes and mouth were closed, the upper body dressed in a white shirt, the lower half in black trousers. The idea that I could scrutinize this face unhindered for the first time was almost unbearable. It felt like an act of violation. At the same time I sensed a hunger, an insatiability that demanded I keep looking at him, at this dead body that a few days earlier had been my father. I was familiar with the facial features, I had grown up with this face, and although I hadn't seen it as often over recent years hardly a night had passed without my dreaming about it. I was familiar with the features, but not the expression they had assumed. The dark, yellowy complexion, along with the lost elasticity of the skin, made his face seem as if it had been carved out of wood. The woodenness forbade any feelings of intimacy. I was no longer looking at a person but something that resembled a person. He had been taken from us, and what he had been still existed in me, it lay like a veil of life over death.

Yngve walked slowly to the other side of the table. I didn't look at him, just registered the movement as I raised my head and looked outside. The gardener who was riding the lawn mower kept turning in his seat to check if he was following the line of the previous cut. The short blades of grass the bag didn't catch whirled through the air above him. Some must have gotten stuck to the underside of the machine because it regularly left behind damp clumps of compressed grass, darker than the lawn from which they came. On the gravel path behind him there was a small cortège of three persons, all with bowed heads, one in a red cloak, resplendent against the green grass and gray sky. Behind them cars streamed past toward the town center.

Then the roar of the lawn-mower engine reverberated against the chapel wall. The expectation the sudden noise created, that it would make Dad open his eyes, was so strong that I involuntarily recoiled.

Yngve glanced across at me with a little smile on his lips. Did I believe the dead could wake? Did I believe wood could become human again?

It was a terrible moment. But when it was over and he, despite all the noise and commotion, remained inert, I understood that he did not exist. The feeling of freedom that rose in my breast then was as difficult to control as the earlier waves of grief, and it found the same outlet, a sob that, quite against my will, escaped the very next moment.

I met Yngve's glance and smiled. He came over and stood next to me. His presence totally reassured me. I was so glad he was there, and I had to fight not to destroy everything by losing control again. I had to think about something else, I had to let my attention find neutral ground.

Someone was cleaning up next door. The sounds were low and disrupted the atmosphere in our room, they were alien, in the same way that sounds of reality that break into the dreams of someone asleep are alien.

I looked down at Dad. The fingers, which had been interlaced and placed over his stomach, the yellow patch of nicotine along his forefinger, a discoloring, the way a carpet is discolored. The disproportionately deep wrinkles in the skin over the knuckles, which now looked carved, not created. Then the face. It was not at rest, for even though it was peaceful and calm, it was not vacant, there were still traces of what I could only describe as determination. It struck me that I had always tried to interpret the expression on his face, that I had never been able to look at it without trying to read it at the same time.

But now it was closed.

I turned to Yngve.

"Shall we go?" he said.

I nodded.

The funeral director was waiting for us in the anteroom. I left the door open behind me. Even though I knew it was irrational, I didn't want Dad lying there on his own.

After shaking hands with the funeral director and exchanging a few words about what was going to happen in the days before the funeral, we went out to the parking lot and lit up, Yngve leaning against the car, me sitting on the edge of a wall. There was rain in the air. The trees in the copse behind the cemetery bowed under the pressure of the gathering wind. For a moment the rustling of leaves drowned the traffic noise at the other end of the lowland. Then they were quiet again.

"Well, that was strange," Yngve said.

"Yes," I said. "But I'm glad we did it."

"Me too. I had to see it to believe it."

"Do you believe it now?"

He smiled. "Don't you?"

Instead of returning the smile, which I had intended to do, I began to cry again. Pressed my hand against my face, bowed my head. Sob after sob shook through me. Once it had abated, I glanced up at him and laughed.

"This is like when we were small," I said. "I cry and you watch."

"Are you sure . . . ?" he asked, searching my eyes. "Are you sure you can manage the rest on your own?"

"Of course," I said. "It's not a problem."

"I can call and say I'm staying."

"No, go home. We'll do what we arranged."

"Okay. I'll be off now."

He threw down his cigarette and took the car key from his pocket. I got to my feet and went closer, but not so close that any handshaking or hugging could take place. He unlocked the door, got in, looked up at me as he twisted the ignition key and the engine started.

"So I'll see you soon," he said.

"Bye. Drive carefully. Say hello to everyone!"

He closed the door, backed out, stopped, buckled his seat belt, put the car in gear, and drove slowly toward the main road. I started to follow. Then his taillights lit up, and he reversed.

"Maybe you should take this," he said, passing a hand through the rolled-down window. It was the brown envelope the funeral director had given us.

"No point in me taking it all the way to Stavanger," he said. "Would make more sense for it to be here. Okay?"

"Okay," I answered.

"See you," he said. The window slid up, and the music, which had been blaring across the parking lot seconds ago, now seemed to be coming from under water. I didn't move until his car had turned onto the main road and was lost from view. It was a childhood instinct; disaster would strike if I moved. Then I put the envelope in my inside jacket pocket and set off for town.

Three days earlier, at around two in the afternoon, Yngve had called me. At once I could hear from his voice that something had happened, and my first thought had been that my father was dead.

"Hi," he said. "It's me. Something has happened. Yes . . ."

"Yes?" I prompted. I was in the hall, standing with one hand against the wall, the other holding the receiver.

"Dad's died."

"Oh," I said.

"Gunnar just called. Grandma found him in a chair this morning."

"What did he die of?"

"I don't know. Probably heart."

There were no windows in the hall, and the main lamp was switched off, so what dim light there was came from the kitchen at one end and the open bedroom door at the other. The face in the mirror that met me was dark and watching me from somewhere faraway.

"What do we do now? I mean, from a practical point of view?"

"Gunnar's expecting us to organize everything. So we have to get ourselves down there. As fast as possible, basically."

"Alright," I said. "I was on my way to Borghild's funeral, was just about to leave in fact. So my suitcase is packed. I can leave now. Shall we meet there?"

"Fine," Yngve said. "I'll drive down tomorrow."

"Tomorrow," I said. "Let me just think for a second."

"Why don't you fly over so we can go together?"

"Good idea. I'll do that. I'll give you a call when I know which plane I'll be on, okay?"

"Okay, see you."

After hanging up I went to the kitchen and filled the kettle, took a tea bag from the cupboard, put it in a clean cup, leaned over the counter and looked up the cul-de-sac outside the house, visible only as patches of gray between the green shrubs that formed a dense clump from the end of the small garden to the road. On the other side were some enormous, towering deciduous trees, beneath which a little dark alley led to the main road on which Haukeland Hospital was situated. All I could think was that I couldn't think about what I should be thinking about. That I didn't feel what I should be feeling. Dad's dead, I thought, this is a big, big event, it should overwhelm me, but it isn't doing that, for here I am, staring at the kettle, feeling annoyed that it hasn't boiled yet. Here I am, looking out and thinking how lucky we were to get this flat, which I do every time I see the garden, because our elderly landlady looks after it, and not that Dad's dead, even though that is the only thing that actually has any meaning. I must be in shock, I thought, pouring water into the cup although it hadn't boiled yet. The kettle, a shiny deluxe model we had been given by Yngve as a wedding present. The cup, a yellow Höganes model, I couldn't remember who had given it to us, only that it had been at the top of Tonje's wedding list. I tugged at the tea bag string a few times, threw it in the sink, where it landed with a smack, and went into the dining room carrying the cup. Thank goodness no one else was at home!

I paced up and down for minutes, trying to invest the fact that Dad was dead with some meaning, but failed. There was no meaning. I understood it, I accepted it, and it was not meaningless in the sense that a life had been snatched away that might well not have been snatched away, but it was in the sense that it was one fact among many, and it did not occupy the position in my consciousness that it should have.

I wandered around the room, cup of tea in hand, the weather outside was gray and mild, the gently sloping countryside was full of rooftops and abundant green hedges. We had only lived there for a few weeks, we came from Volda where Tonje had been studying radio journalism and I had written a novel that was due to come out in two months. It was the first real home we had had; the flat in Volda didn't count, it was temporary, but this was permanent, or represented something permanent, our home. The walls still smelled of paint. Oxblood red in the dining room, on advice from Tonje's mother, who was an artist but who spent most of her time doing interior design and cooking, both at a high level – her house looked the way houses did in interior decor magazines, and the food she served was always meticulously prepared and exquisite – and eggshell white in the living room, as well as in the other rooms. But this was nothing like an interior decor magazine here, too much furniture, and too many posters and bookshelves, were a testimony to the student existence we had just left behind. We lived on student loans while I wrote the novel, for officially I was studying literary science as my main subject up to Christmas when my money ran out, and I had to ask for an advance from the publishing house, which had lasted me until just recently. Dad's death came therefore as manna from heaven, because he had money, surely he must have had money. The three brothers had sold the house on Elvegata and shared the proceeds between them less than two years ago. Surely he couldn't have squandered it in that short time.

My father is dead, and I am thinking about the money that will bring me.

So what?

I think what I think, I can't help thinking what I think, can I?

I put the cup down on the table, opened the slender door, and went onto the balcony, supporting myself stiffly on the balustrade and gazing around as I drew the warm summer air, so full of the smells of plants and cars and town, into my lungs. A moment later I was back in the living room casting my eyes around. Should I eat something? Drink? Go out and do some shopping?

I drifted into the hall, peeped into the bedroom, at the broad unmade bed, behind it the bathroom door. I could do that, I thought, have a shower, good idea, after all soon I would have to set off.

Clothes off, water on, steaming hot, over my head, down my body.

Should I beat off?

No, for Christ's sake, Dad's dead.

Dead, dead, Dad was dead.

Dead, dead, Dad was dead.

Having a shower did nothing for me either, so I turned it off and dried myself with a large towel, rubbed a bit of deodorant under my armpits, dressed and went into the kitchen to see what time it was, drying my hair with a smaller towel.

Half past two.

Tonje would be home in an hour.

I couldn't bear the thought of unloading all this onto her as she came in the door, so I went into the corridor, threw the towel through the open bedroom door, picked up the telephone receiver and keyed in her number. She answered at once.

"Tonje?"

"Hi, Tonje, it's me," I said. "Everything all right?"

"Yes, actually I'm editing at the moment, just popped into the office to get something. I'll be home when I've finished."

"Great," I said.

"What are you up to?" she asked.

"Well, nothing," I said. "But Yngve called. Dad died."

"What? He's died?"

"Yes."

"Oh, you poor thing! Oh, Karl Ove . . ."

"I'm fine," I said. "It wasn't exactly unexpected. But I'll be going there this evening anyway. First to Yngve's place, and then we'll drive to Kristiansand together early tomorrow."

"Do you want me to come with you? I can do that."

"No, no, no. You have to work! You stay here, and then come to the funeral."

"Oh, you poor thing," she repeated. "I can get someone else to do the editing. Then I can come right away. When are you leaving?"

"There's no hurry," I said. "I'll be leaving in a few hours. And being alone for a while is not such a bad thing."

"Sure?"

"Yeah. I'm sure. In fact, I don't feel anything. But we've been through this plenty of times already. If he keeps this up, he'll be dead soon. So, I've been prepared for it."

"Okay," Tonje said. "I'll finish what I'm doing and hurry home. Take care of yourself. I love you."

"I love you too," I said.

After putting down the phone I thought about Mom. She would have to be informed of course. I lifted the receiver again and dialed Yngve's number. He had already called her.

I was dressed and waiting in the living room when I heard Tonje at the door. She skipped into the room like a fresh summer breeze. I got up. Her movements were flustered, her eyes compassionate, and she hugged me, said she wanted to be with me, but I was right, it was best that she stayed here, and then I called for a taxi and stood on the step outside the front door waiting the five minutes it took to come. We're a married couple, I thought, we are husband and wife, my wife is standing outside the house, waving me off, I thought, and smiled. So where did this image's unreal surface come from? Were we playing husband and wife, weren't we really a couple?

"What are you smiling at?"

"Nothing," I said. "A stray thought."

I squeezed her hand.

"Here it is," she said.

I looked down the row of houses. Black and beetle-like, the taxi was crawling up the slope; beetle-like, it stopped and hesitated at the intersection before gingerly scrabbling to the right where the street had the same name as ours.

"Shall I run after it?" Tonje asked.

"No, why? I can do that just as well as you."

I took the suitcase and climbed the steps to the road. Tonje followed.

"I'm going to walk to the intersection," I said. "I'll catch it there. But I'll call this evening. Okay?"

We kissed, and as I looked back from the intersection, with the taxi reversing down the hill, she waved.

"Knausgaard?" the driver inquired as I opened the door and looked in.

"That's right," I said. "Flesland airport."

"Hop in, and I'll take your suitcase."

I clambered onto the rear seat and leaned back. Taxis, I loved taxis. Not the ones I came home drunk in, but the ones I caught to airports or railway stations. Was there anything better than sitting in the rear seat of a taxi and being driven through towns and suburbs before a long journey?

"Tricky street, this one," the driver said, getting in. "It forks. I've heard about it, but this is my first time here. After twenty years. Strange."

"Mm," I said.

"I think I've been everywhere now. I think this must be the last street."

He smiled at me in the mirror.

"Are you going on holiday?"

"No," I said. "Not exactly. My father died today. I have to sort out the funeral. In Kristiansand."

That put an end to the small talk. I sat motionless, staring at the houses along the way, not thinking of anything in particular, just staring. Minde, Fantoft, Hop. Gas stations, car showrooms, supermarkets, detached houses, forest, lake, housing project. Approaching the final stretch of road I could see the control tower, and I took my bank card from an inside pocket and leaned forward to see the taximeter. Three hundred and twenty kroner. It had not been such a great idea to catch a taxi, the airport bus was a tenth of the price, and if there was one thing I didn't have enough of right now, it was money.

"Could I have a receipt for three hundred and fifty?" I said, handing him my bank card.

"Course you can," he said, grabbing it from my hand. Swiped it and the machine chuntered out a receipt. He placed it on a pad with a pen and passed it back, I signed, he tore off another receipt, and gave it to me.

"Thank you very much," he said.

"Thank you," I said. "I'll take the case."

Even though the suitcase was heavy I carried it by the handle as I walked into the departure hall. I detested the tiny wheels, first of all because they were feminine, thus not worthy of a man, a man should carry, not roll, secondly because they suggested easy options, shortcuts, savings, rationality, which I despised and opposed wherever I could, even where it was of the most trivial significance. Why should you live in a world without feeling its weight? Were we just images? And what were we actually saving energy for with these energy-saving devices?

I put my case down on the floor of the small concourse and looked up at the departures board. There was a plane to Stavanger at five o'clock, which I could easily make. But there was also one at six. Since I loved sitting in airports, perhaps even more than I loved sitting in taxis, I opted for the latter.

I turned around and scanned the check-in desks. Apart from the three farthest ones – where the lines seemed chaotic and stretched back a long distance, and I could see from the passengers' apparel, which without exception was light, and the amount of luggage, which was immense, and the mood, which was as cheery as it can be after a few glasses, that they were taking a charter flight to southern Europe – there was not a lot happening. I bought a ticket, checked in, and ambled over to the phones on the other side to ring Yngve. He picked up at once.

"Hi, Karl Ove here," I said. "Plane goes at a quarter past six. So I'll be in Sola by a quarter to seven. Are you going to come and get me or what?"

"I can do that, no problem."

"Have you heard any more?"

"No . . . I rang Gunnar and told him we were coming. He didn't know any more. I thought we could set off early and drop by the undertaker's before it closes. It's Saturday tomorrow."

"Okay," I said. "Sounds good. See you then."

"Yeah, see you."

I hung up and went upstairs to the café, bought a cup of coffee and a newspaper, located a table with a view of the concourse, hung my jacket over the back of the chair while surveying the room to see if there was anyone I knew, and sat down.

Thoughts of my father surfaced at regular intervals, as they had ever since

Yngve called, but unconnected with emotions, always as a stark statement. That was probably because I had been prepared. Ever since the spring when he had left my mother, his life had been going in only one direction. We didn't realize that then, but at some point he had crossed a line and from then on we knew anything could befall him, even the worst. Or the best, according to how you viewed things. I had long wished him dead, but from the very second I realized his life could soon be over I began to hope for it. When there was news on TV of fatal accidents in the district where he lived, whether they were fires or car accidents, corpses found in the forest or at sea, my immediate feeling was one of hope: perhaps it is Dad. However, it was never him, he coped, he survived.

Until now, I thought, observing the crowds circulating in the concourse below. In twenty-five years a third of them would be dead, in fifty years two-thirds, in a hundred all of them. And what would they leave behind, what had their lives been worth? Gaping jaws, empty eye sockets, somewhere beneath the earth.

Perhaps the Day of Judgment really would come? All these bones and skulls that had been buried for the thousands of years that man had lived on earth would gather themselves up with a rattle, and stand grinning into the sun, and God, the almighty, the all-powerful, would, with a wall of angels above and below Him, judge them from his heavenly throne. Above the earth, so green and so beautiful, trumpets would sound, and from all the fields and valleys, all the beaches and plains, all the seas and lakes, the dead would rise and go to the Lord their God, be raised to His level, judged and cast into the flames of hell, judged and elevated into the divine light. Also those walking around here, with their roller suitcases and tax-free bags, their wallets and bank cards, their perfumed armpits and their dark glasses, their dyed hair and their walking frames, would be awakened, impossible to discern any difference between them and those who died in the Middle Ages or in the Stone Age, they were the dead, and the dead are the dead, and the dead would be judged on the Last Day.

From the back of the concourse, where the luggage carousels were, came a group of perhaps twenty Japanese. I placed my smoldering cigarette in the ashtray and took a sip of coffee as I watched their progress. The foreignness of them, which resided not in their clothes or appearance but their behavior, was compelling, and to live in Japan, surrounded by all this foreignness, all the things one saw but did not understand, whose meaning one might intuit without ever being sure, was a dream I had long held. To sit in a Japanese house, furnished in simple, Spartan fashion, with sliding doors and paper partitions, created for a neatness that was alien to me and my northern European impetuosness, would be fantastic. To sit there and write a novel and see how the surroundings slowly and imperceptibly shaped the writing, for the way we think is of course as closely associated with the specific surroundings of which we form part as the people with whom we speak and the books we read. Japan, but also Argentina, where familiar European features were lent quite a different hue, shifted to quite a different place, and the USA, one of the small towns in Maine, for example, with landscape so like Norway's southern coast, what might have sprung off the page there?

I put down my cup and resumed smoking, swiveled in my chair, and looked over at the gate where there were already quite a number of passengers, even though it was only a few minutes to five.

But now it was Bergen's turn.

A chill wind blew through me.

Dad is dead.

For the first time since Yngve had called I could see him in my mind's eye. Not the man he had been in recent years, but the man he was when I was growing up, when, in winter, we went fishing with him, off the island of Tromøya, with the wind howling round our ears and the spray high in the air from the huge, gray breakers that smashed against the rocks below us, and he stood there, rod in hand, reeling in, laughing in our direction. Thick black hair, a black beard, slightly asymmetrical face, covered with small drops of water. Blue oilskins, green rubber boots.

That was the image.

Typical that I would conjure up one of the times when he was good. That my subconscious would select a situation where I had warm feelings for him. It was an attempt at manipulation, obviously intended to smooth the path for irrational sentimentality, which, once the floodgates were open, would brim up without constraint and take possession of me. That was how the subconscious worked, it clearly saw itself as a kind of corrective force on thoughts and desires, and undermined everything that might be considered antagonistic to the prevailing common sense. But Dad had got what was coming to him, it was good that he was dead, anything in me that said otherwise was lying. And that went not only for the man he had been when I was growing up, but also the man he became when in midlife he broke off all the old connections and started afresh. Because he had changed, also in his attitude to me, but it didn't help, I didn't want to know anything about what he became either. In the spring when he left he had started drinking and that went on right through the summer, that was what they did, Unni and Dad, they sat in the sun drinking, wonderful long drunken days, and when school started the drinking continued, but just in the afternoons and evenings, and on weekends. They moved to northern Norway and both worked in a school there, and that was where we got the first inkling of the state he was in, because we flew there once to visit him, Yngve, his girlfriend, and I. Dad picked us up, he was pale and his hands were shaking, he hardly said a word, and when we got to his flat he knocked back three beers in quick succession in the kitchen, then seemed to come to life, stopped shaking, became aware of us, started talking, and went on drinking. Over these few days, it was a winter holiday, he drank nonstop, kept emphasizing that he was on holiday, you can allow yourself one then, especially up here, where it was so dark all winter. Unni was pregnant at the time, so now he drank alone. In the spring he worked as an external examiner at a school in the Kristiansand district and had invited Yngve, his girlfriend, and me to lunch at the Hotel Caledonien, but when we arrived at the reception where we were supposed to meet, he wasn't there, we waited for half an hour, then asked the receptionist, he was in his room, we went upstairs, knocked on the door, no one answered, he must have been asleep, we knocked harder and called his name, but no reaction, and we left none the wiser. Two days later the Hotel Caledonien burned to the ground, twelve people died, I drove down with Bassen in the lunch break, I was in the second class at gymnas then, and watched the firemen extinguishing the fire. If my father had been there, he would have been one of the victims, no question given the state he was in, I said to Bassen, but still neither I nor Yngve understood what was happening to him, we had no experience with alcoholics, there were none in the family, and even though we understood he was drinking, for soon we had experienced a lot of boozy nights culminating in tears, arguments, and jealousy, with every scrap of dignity cast to the four winds, but not for long, the next morning it was back in place, he always did his job properly, and he was proud of that, didn't we understand that he couldn't stop, and maybe he didn't want to. This was his life now, this was what he did, even though he had just had a child. He took a hair of the dog some mornings when he had to work, but was never drunk at school, a few beers during the course of the day had no effect, look at the Danes, they drink at lunch, and they're managing pretty well in Denmark, aren't they?

In the winter they went south and complained to the travel guides, I saw this in a letter I happened to find when I was staying with them once, there had been a legal case, Dad had collapsed and been taken to the hospital by ambulance, he had had violent chest pains and had sued the travel company because he claimed his medical treatment had brought on the heart attack, to which the company responded rather drily that it had not been a heart attack, but a collapse caused by alcohol and pills.

Eventually they left northern Norway and moved back to Sørland where Dad, now fat and bloated, with an enormous gut, drank nonstop. Staying sober enough for a few hours to be able to pick us up by car was now out of the question. They split up, Dad moved to a town in Østland where he had a new job, which he lost some months later, and then there was nothing left – no marriage, no job, and barely a child, because although Unni wanted them to spend time together, and in fact allowed him to do so, which did not work out very well, visiting rights were eventually withdrawn, not that that affected him much. Nevertheless he was furious, presumably because it was his right, and he held firm to his rights at every opportunity now. Terrible things happened, and all Dad had left was his flat in Østland, where he hung out drinking, when he wasn't in the pubs in town, hanging out there drinking. He was as fat as a barrel, and even though his skin was still tanned, it had a kind of matte tone, there was a matte membrane covering him, and with all the hair on his face and head and his messy clothes he looked like some kind of wild man as he charged around in search of a drink. Once he went missing for several weeks, and it was as if he had vanished into the bowels of the earth. Gunnar called Yngve and said he'd reported Dad missing to the police. He reappeared in a hospital somewhere in Østland, bedridden, unable to walk. The paralysis, however, was not permanent, he struggled to his feet again, and after a few weeks spent in a detox clinic he carried on where he had left off.

During this phase I had no contact with him. But he visited his mother more and more often, and stayed longer and longer each time. In the end, he moved in with her and erected a barricade. He stowed what belongings he had in the garage, got rid of the home-help Gunnar had organized for Grandma, who was no longer capable of looking after herself, and locked the door. He remained inside with her until the day he died. Gunnar had called Yngve on one occasion and told him how the land lay. Told him, among other things, how he had once gone over and found Dad lying on the living room floor. He had broken his leg, but instead of asking Grandma to phone for an ambulance to take him to the hospital, he had instructed her not to say a word to anyone, not even Gunnar, so she didn't, and he lay there surrounded by plates of leftovers, bottles of beer and spirits that she had brought him from his abundant stockpile. Gunnar didn't know how long he had been lying there, perhaps a day, perhaps two. The sole interpretation of his telephone call to Yngve was that he felt we should intervene and remove our father from the house, because he would die there, and we did discuss this, but decided not to do anything, he would have to plow his own furrow, live his own life, die his own death.

Now he had.

I got up and went to the counter for some more coffee. A man wearing a dark, elegant suit, with a silk scarf around his neck and dandruff on his shoulders, was pouring coffee as I arrived. He set the white cup, full to the brim with black coffee, on the red tray, and looked at me quizzically as he lifted the pot.

"I'll help myself, thank you," I said.

"As you wish," he said, replacing the pot on one of the two hotplates. I guessed he was an academic of some kind. The waitress, a substantial woman in her fifties, a Bergensian for certain, I had seen that face all over town in the years I had lived there, on buses and in the streets, behind bars and in shops, with that same short dyed hair and the square glasses that only women of that age can admire, stretched out her hand as I raised my cup.

"Top off?"

"Five kroner," she said in a broad Bergen accent. I placed a five-krone coin in her hand and went back to my table. My mouth was dry and my heart was beating fast, as if I were excited, but I was not, on the contrary, I felt calm and sluggish as I sat staring at the small plane hanging from the enormous glass roof beneath which the light shimmered as if from a reflection, and glanced at the departures board where the clock showed a quarter past five, and then down at the people lined up, walking across the concourse floor, sitting and reading newspapers, standing and chatting. It was summer, clothes were vibrant, bodies tanned, the mood light, as always wherever people gather to travel. Sitting like this, as I sometimes did, I could experience colors as bright, lines as sharp, and faces as incredibly distinct. They were laden with meaning. Without that meaning, which is what I was experiencing now, they were distant and somehow hazy, impossible to grasp, like shadows without the darkness of shadows.

I twisted around and glanced toward the gate. A crowd of passengers, who must have just arrived, were making their way along the tunnel-like jet bridge from the plane. The departure lounge door opened, and with jackets folded over their arms, and bags of all descriptions hanging against their thighs, the passengers came in, looked up for the baggage claim sign, turned right and disappeared from sight.

Two boys walked past me carrying paper cups of Coke. One had some fluff over his top lip and on his chin, and must have been about fifteen. The other was smaller, and his face was hairless, although that did not necessarily mean he was younger. The taller of the two had big lips which stayed open, and, in combination with the vacant eyes, made him look stupid. The smaller boy had more alert eyes but the way a twelve-year-old is alert. He said something, both laughed, and as they came to the table he must have repeated it, for the others sitting there laughed too.

I was surprised by how small they were, and it was impossible to imagine that I had been that small when I was fourteen or fifteen. But I must have been.

I pushed away my coffee cup, got up, folded my jacket over my arm, grabbed my suitcase, and walked to the gate, sat down by the counter, where a uniformed woman and man each stood working at a computer screen. I leaned back and closed my eyes for a few seconds. Dad's face appeared again. It was as though it had been lying in wait. A garden in the mist, the grass slightly muddy and trampled, a ladder up a tree, Dad's face turns to me. He is holding the ladder with both hands, he is wearing high boots and a thick knitted sweater. Two white tubs beside him in the field, a bucket hanging from a hook on the top rung.

I opened my eyes. I couldn't remember ever experiencing this, it was not a memory, but if it was not a memory, what was it?

Oh, no, he was dead.

I took a deep breath and got up. A short line had developed by the counter, here passengers interpreted everything the staff did, as soon as there was any evidence to suggest that departure was imminent, they were there, physically.

Dead.

I took my place behind the last person in the queue, a broad-shouldered man half a head shorter than me. There was hair growing on the nape of his neck and in his ears. He smelled of aftershave. A woman joined the line behind me. I craned my neck to catch a glimpse, and saw her face, which with its neatly applied lipstick, rouge, eyeliner, and powder, looked more like a mask than a human physiognomy. But she did smell good.

The cleaning staff scurried up the bridge from the plane. The uniformed woman talked into a telephone. After putting it down she picked up a small microphone and announced that the plane was ready for boarding. I opened the outside pocket of my bag and took out the ticket. My heart beat faster again, as though it was on a trip of its own. It was unbearable standing there. But I had to. I shifted my weight from one foot to the other, bent my head forward to see the runway through the window. One of the small vehicles towing the baggage carts drove past. A man in overalls with ear protectors walked across, he was holding those things like ping-pong rackets used to direct planes into position. The line began to inch forward. My heart was beating rapidly. My palms were sweaty. I yearned for a seat, yearned to be high in the air and looking down. The squat fellow in front of me was handed the stub from his ticket. I passed mine to the uniformed woman. For some reason she looked me straight in the eye as she took it. She was attractive in a severe way with regular features, nose perhaps a bit pointed, mouth narrow. Her eyes were bright and blue, the dark circle around the iris unusually distinct. I returned the gaze for a brief moment, then lowered it. She smiled.

"Have a good flight," she said.

"Thank you," I replied and followed the others down the tunnel-like gangway into the plane, where a middle-aged stewardess nodded a welcome to the new arrivals, moved down the aisle, as far as the last row of seats. Up went my bag and coat into the overhead compartment, down I flopped into the cramped seat, on with the belt, out with my feet, back I leaned.

That's the way.

Meta-thoughts, that I was sitting on the plane on my way to bury my father while thinking that I was sitting on the plane on my way to bury my father, increased. Everything I saw, faces, bodies ambling through the cabin, stowing their baggage here, sitting down, stowing their baggage there, sitting down, was followed by a reflective shadow that could not desist from telling me that I was seeing this now while aware that I was seeing this, and so on ad absurdum, and the presence of this thought-shadow, or perhaps better, thought-mirror, also implied a criticism, that I did not feel more than I did.

Dad was dead, I thought – and an image of him flashed up before me, as though I needed an illustration of the word "Dad" – and I, sitting in a plane on my way to bury him, am reacting coldly to it, I think, as I watch two ten-year-old girls taking a seat in one row and what must have been their mother and father taking a seat on the other side of the aisle to them, I think that I think that I think. Events were racing through me at great speed, nothing that made any sense. I started to feel nauseous. A woman put her case in the overhead compartment above me, took off her coat and put it in, met my gaze, smiled automatically, and sat down beside me. She was around forty, had a gentle face, warm eyes, black hair, was short, a bit chubby, but not fat. She was wearing a kind of suit, that is, pants and jacket of the same color and design, what did women call them? An outfit? And a white blouse. I faced the front, but my attention was not on what I saw there, it was on what I saw through the corner of my eye, that was where "I" was, I thought, looking at her. She must have been holding a pair of glasses which I hadn't noticed because now she perched them on the tip of her nose and opened a book.

There seemed to be something of the bank teller about her. Not the gentleness, though, nor the whiteness. Her thighs, which seemed to spread outward in the fabric when pressed down against the seat, how white would they be in the dark late one night in a hotel room somewhere?

I tried to swallow, but my mouth was so dry that the little saliva I could muster was not enough to cover the distance to my throat. Another passenger stopped by our row, a middle-aged man, sallow, stern and thin, dressed in a gray suit, he occupied the aisle seat without a sideways glance at either her or me. *Boarding completed*, a voice said in the intercom. I leaned forward to look at the sky above the airport. To the west the bank of cloud had split open, and a strip of low forest was lit up by the sun, a shiny, almost glistening green. The engines were started. The window vibrated faintly. The woman beside me had marked her page with a finger and was staring ahead.

Dad had always had a fear of flying. They were the only times in my childhood that I could recall him drinking. As a rule, he avoided flying, we traveled by car if we were going anywhere, regardless of how far it was, but sometimes he had to, and then it was a case of knocking back whatever alcoholic drinks were available at the airport café. There were several other things he avoided as well, but which I had never considered, had never seen, because what a person does always overshadows what he does not do, and what Dad didn't do was not so conspicuous, also because there was nothing at all neurotic about him. But he never went to the barber's; he always cut his own hair. He never traveled by bus. He hardly ever did his shopping at the local shop, but always at the large supermarkets outside town. All these were scenarios where he might have come into contact with people, or have been seen by them, and even though he was a teacher by profession and so stood in front of a class every day, occasionally summoned parents to meetings, and also spoke to his colleagues in the staff room every day, he still consistently avoided these social situations. What was it they had in common? That he might be assimilated into a community with no more than chance as its basis? That he might be seen in a way over which he had no control? That he felt vulnerable sitting on the bus, in the barber's chair, by the supermarket till? That was all quite possible. But when I was there I didn't notice. It was only many, many years later that it struck me I had never seen Dad on a bus. And that he had never taken part in any of the social events that sprang up around Yngve's and my activities. Once he attended an end-of-term show, sat close to the wall to see the play we had rehearsed, in which I performed the main role, but unfortunately I had not studied it hard enough, after the previous year's success I was suffering from child hubris, I didn't need to learn all the lines, everything would be fine, I had thought, but standing there, affected I suppose by my father's presence, I could barely remember a line, and our teacher prompted me all the way through a long play about a town of which I was supposed to be the mayor. In the car on the way home he said he had never been so embarrassed in his life and he would never attend any of my end-of-term shows again. That was a promise he kept. Nor did he go to any of the countless soccer matches I played in as I was growing up, he was never one of the parents who drove to away games, never one of the parents who watched home matches, and I didn't react to that either, I didn't even consider it unusual, for that was the way he was, my father, and many other fathers like him, this was the end of the seventies and the beginning of the eighties, when being a father had a different and, at least on a practical level, a less comprehensive significance than today.

No, that's not true, he did watch me once.

It was during the winter, when I was in the ninth class. He drove me to the shale pitch in Kjevik, he was going onto Kristiansand, we had a practice match against some team from up country. We sat in the car, as silent as ever, him with one hand on the steering wheel, the other resting on the door, I with both mine in my lap. Then I had a sudden inspiration and asked him if he wanted to see the match. No, he couldn't, he had to get to Kristiansand, didn't he. Well, I hadn't expected him to say yes, I said. There was no disappointment in my comment, no sense that I really wanted him to see this match, which was of no importance anyway, it was merely a statement, I really hadn't believed he would want to. When the second half was nearing the end I spotted his car by the sideline, behind the tall piles of snow. Could vaguely make out his dark figure behind the windshield. With only a few minutes left of the match I received a perfectly weighted pass from Harald on the wing, all I had to do was stick out my foot, which I did, but it was my left foot, I didn't have much feel with that one, the ball skidded off, and the shot missed. In the car on the way home he commented on it. You didn't jump on your chance, he said. You had a great chance there. I didn't think you'd mess that up. Oh well, I said. But we won anyway. What was the score? 2–1, I said, glancing at him, because I wanted him to ask who had scored the two goals. Which, mercifully, he did. Did you score? he asked. Yes, I said. Both of them.

With my forehead resting against the window, the plane stationary at the end of the runway, revving its engines in earnest now, I began to cry. The tears came from nowhere, I knew that as they ran down, this is idiotic, I thought, it's sentimental, it's stupid. But it didn't help, I found myself caught in soft, vague, boundless emotions, and couldn't extricate myself until a few minutes later when the plane took off and, with a roar, started to climb. Then, my mind clear again at last, I lowered my head to my T-shirt and wiped my eyes with a corner I held between thumb and index finger, and sat for a long time peering out, until I could no longer feel my neighbor's eyes on me. I leaned back in my seat and closed my eyes. But it was not over. I sensed that it had only just begun.

No sooner had the plane straightened after the ascent than it lowered its nose and started the approach. The stewardesses raced up and down the aisle with their trolleys, trying to serve everyone tea and coffee. The scenery beneath, first just isolated tableaux visible through rare openings in the cloud cover, was rugged and beautiful with its green islands and blue sea, its steep rock faces and snowy white plains, but gradually it was erased or toned down, as the clouds vanished, until the flat Rogaland terrain was all you could see. My insides were in turmoil. Memories I didn't know I had flowed through me, whirling and chaotic, as I tried to extricate myself, because I didn't want to sit there crying, constantly analyzing everything, with little actual success though. I saw him in my mind's eye, when we went skiing together once, in Hove, gliding in and out of the trees, and in every clearing we could see the sea, gray and heavy and vast, and smell it too, the aroma of salt and seaweed that seemed to lie pressed up against the aroma of snow and spruce, Dad ten meters in front of me, perhaps twenty, because despite the fact that his equipment was new, from the Rottefella bindings to the Splitkein skis to the blue anorak, he couldn't ski, he staggered forward almost like a senile old man, with no balance, no flow, no pace, and if there was one thing I did not want it was to be associated with that figure, which was why I always hung back, with my head full of notions about myself and my style, which, what did I know, would perhaps take me far one day. I was embarrassed by him. At that time I had no idea that he had bought all this skiing equipment and driven us to the far side of Tromøya in an attempt to get close to me, but now, sitting there with closed eyes and pretending to sleep while the announcement to fasten seat belts and straighten seat backs was broadcast over the speakers, the thought of it threatened to send me into another bout of crying, and when yet again I leaned forward and propped my head against the side of the aircraft to hide, it was half-hearted, since my fellow passengers must already have known from takeoff that they had ended up next to a young man in tears. My throat ached, and I had no control, everything flowed through me, I was wide open, but not to the outside world, I could hardly see it anymore, but to the inside world, where emotions had taken over. The only thing I could do to salvage the last scraps of dignity was to stop myself from making noise. Not a sob, not a sigh, not a moan, not a groan. Just tears in full flow, and a face distorted into a grimace every time the thought that Dad was dead reached a new climax.

Aah.

Aah.

Then, all of a sudden, everything cleared, it was as though all the emotion and the haze that had filled me for the last fifteen minutes had retreated, like the tide, and the immense distance I gained as a result caused me to burst into laughter.

Ha ha ha, I heard myself chuckle.

I held up my forearm and rubbed my eyes with it. The thought that the woman beside me had seen me sitting there with my face distorted in constant lachrymose grimaces, and was now listening to me in gales of laughter, brought on another fit.

Ha ha ha. Ha ha ha.

I looked at her. She didn't look away; her gaze was fixed on the page of the book in front of her. Directly behind us two of the stewardesses sat down on the fold-up seats and buckled their seat belts around their waists. Outside the window, it was sunny and green. The shadow following us on the field came closer and closer, like a fish being reeled in, until it was under the fuselage the moment the wheels hit the tarmac and it stayed there attached during the braking and taxiing.

Around me people were starting to get up. I took a deep breath. The sense that I had cleared my mind was strong. I wasn't happy, but I was relieved, as always when a heavy burden was unexpectedly removed. The woman beside me, who had closed her book and now allowed me a chance to see what she was reading, got up with it in her hand and stood on tiptoe to reach the overhead compartment. *The Woman and the Ape* by Peter Høeg was what was engaging her. I had read it once. Good idea, poor execution. Would I, under normal circumstances, have initiated a conversation with her about the book? When it would be so easy to do, as now? No, I wouldn't, but I would have sat thinking I ought to. Had I ever initiated a conversation with a stranger?

No, never.

And there was no evidence to suggest I ever would.

I leaned forward to look out the window, down onto the dusty tarmac, which I had once done twenty years ago with the bizarre but clear intention of remembering what I saw, forever. On board an airplane like now, in Sola airport like now, but on my way to Bergen then, and from there to my grandparents in Sørbøvåg. Every time I traveled by plane I recalled this memory I had imposed upon myself. For a long time it opened the novel I had just finished writing, which now lay in the case in the hold beneath me, in the form of a six-hundred-page manuscript I had to proofread within a week.

That at least was one good thing.

I was also looking forward to meeting Yngve. After he had moved from Bergen, first to Balestrand, where he met Kari Anne, with whom he had a child, and then to Stavanger, where another child was born, our relationship had changed, he was no longer someone I could go and see when I had nothing to do, go to a café or a concert with, but someone I visited now and then for days at a stretch, with all that implied for family life. I liked it though, I had always liked staying the night with other families, having your own room with a freshly made bed, full of unfamiliar objects, with a towel and washcloth nicely laid out, and from there straight into the heart of family life, despite there always being, no matter whom I visited, an uncomfortable side, because even though people always try to keep any existing tensions in the background whenever guests are present, the tensions are still noticeable, and you can never know if it is your presence that has caused them or whether they are just there and indeed your presence is helping to suppress them. A third possibility is, of course, that all these tensions were just tensions that lived their own lives in my head.

The aisle was less crowded now, and I stood up, retrieved my bag and jacket, and made my way forward, from the cabin into the corridor to the arrivals hall, which was small but self-contained with its jumble of gates, kiosks, and cafés, travelers rushing to and fro, standing, sitting, eating, reading. I would immediately recognize Yngve in any crowd, and I didn't need his face to identify him, the back of his head or a shoulder was enough, perhaps not even that, you have a kind of receptivity to those with whom you have grown up and to whom you have been close during the period when your personality is being shaped or asserting itself, you receive them directly, without thought as a filter. Almost everything you know about your brother you know from intuition. I never knew what Yngve was thinking, seldom had an inkling as to why he did the things he did, didn't seem to share so many of his opinions, but I could make a reasonable guess, in these respects he was as unknown as everyone else. But I knew his body language, I knew his gestures, I knew his aroma, I was aware of all the nuances of his voice, and, not least, I knew where he came from. I could put none of this into words, and it was seldom articulated in thought, but it meant everything. So I didn't need to scan the tables in the pizzeria, didn't need to search the faces of those sitting by the gates or those crossing the hall, for as soon as I stepped into the concourse I knew where he was. My eyes were drawn there, to the front of the mock-old, mock-Irish pub where indeed he was, arms crossed, wearing greenish, but not military, pants, a white T-shirt with a picture of Sonic Youth's *Goo*, a light-blue denim jacket and a pair of dark-brown Puma shoes. He hadn't seen me yet. I looked at his face, which I knew better than anything. The high cheekbones he had inherited from Dad, and the slightly awry mouth, but the shape of his face was different, and around his eyes he was more like Mom and me.

He turned his head and met my gaze. I was about to smile, but at that moment my lips twisted, and with a pressure it was impossible to resist, the emotions from earlier rose again. They released in a sob, and I began to cry.

Half-raised my arm to my face, took it back down, a new wave came, my face puckered once again. I will never forget the look on Yngve's face. He watched me in disbelief. There was no judgment in it, it was more like him watching something he could not understand, and had not expected, and for which therefore he was completely unprepared.

"Hi," I said through tears.

"Hi," he said. "I've got the car below. Shall we go?"

I nodded and followed him down the stairs, through the entrance hall, and into the parking lot. Whether it was the special sharpness of Vestland air, which is always present irrespective of the temperature, and which was particularly noticeable as we first walked into the shade proffered by a large roof, that cleared my head or the immense feeling of space the surrounding landscape opened, I cannot say, but at any rate I was out of it again by the time we reached his car, and Yngve, now wearing sunglasses, bent forward and inserted the key in the lock on the driver's side.

"Is this all the luggage you've got?" he said, motioning toward my bag.

"Oh shit," I said. "Wait here. I'll run over and get it."

Yngve and Kari Anne lived in Storhaug, a suburb slightly outside Stavanger town center, in an end-of-terrace house with a road on the other side and a forest behind that stretched down to the fjord a few hundred meters away. There was also a collection of allotments close by, and behind that lived, in another estate, Asbjørn, an old friend of Yngve's with whom he had just started up a graphic design business. Their office was in the loft, it was already fitted out with the equipment they had bought, which they were currently learning to use. Neither of them had had any training in this branch, apart from Media Studies at Bergen University, nor did they have any contacts of any significance in the industry. But now they sat there, each behind powerful Macs, working on the few commissions they had. A poster for the Hundvåg Festival, a few folders and leaflets, that was all for the time being. They had put all their eggs in one basket, and for Yngve's part I could understand it; after finishing his studies he had worked as a cultural consultant on

Balestrand District Council for a few years, and the world was not exactly his oyster. But it was a risk, all they had to offer was their taste, which, however, was well-grounded, and had become quite sophisticated, developed as it had been through twenty years of dealing with a variety of pop cultures, from films and record sleeves through to clothes, music, magazines and photo albums, from the obscure to the most commercial, always ready to distinguish between what was good from what was not, whether past or present. Once we went to Asbjørn's, I remember, we had been drinking for three days, when Yngve played the Pixies to us, a then-new, unknown American band, and Asbjørn lay on the sofa convulsed with laughter because what we were listening to was so good. That's so good! he shouted over the loud music. Ha ha ha! That's so good! When I went to Bergen as a nineteen-year-old, he and Yngve were in my studio on one of the first days, and neither my John Lennon picture, which I had hung above the desk, nor the poster of a cornfield with the small patch of grass glowing with such miraculous intensity in the foreground, nor the poster of *The Mission* starring Jeremy Irons found any favor in their eyes. No chance. The Lennon picture was a reminder of my last year at gymnas, when with three others I had discussed literature and politics, listened to music, watched films and drunk wine, extolled the inner life and distanced myself from all things external, and that was why the apostle of impassioned sincerity, Lennon, was hanging on my wall, even though I had always, right from childhood, preferred McCartney's saccharine sweetness. But here the Beatles were *not* an icon, not under *any* circumstances, and it was not long before the Lennon picture came down. But their sureness of taste did not apply only to pop culture; it was Asbjørn who first recommended Thomas Bernhard, he had read *Concrete* in Gyldendal's Vita series, which appeared ten years before all the literati in Norway began to allude to him, while I, I remember, was unable to understand Asbjørn's fascination with this Austrian, and it was only ten years later, together with the rest of literary Norway, that I discovered his greatness. Asbjørn had a nose, that was his great talent, I had never met anyone with such sureness of taste as him, but what use was it, apart from being the hub student life revolved around?

The essence of a nose is judgment, to judge you have to stand outside, and that is not where creativity takes place. Yngve was much more inside, he played guitar in a band, wrote his own songs, and listened to music from there; moreover, he also had an analytical, academic side that Asbjørn did not have, or use, to such an extent. Graphic design was in many ways perfect for them.

My novel had been accepted at more or less the same time that they had started their business, and there was never going to be any other option than their designing the cover and getting a foot in the doorway to the world of publishing. Naturally, the publishing house didn't see things like that. The editor, Geir Gulliksen, said that he would get in touch with a design agency and asked if I had any thoughts about the cover. I said I would like my brother to do it.

"Your brother? Is he a graphic designer?"

"Well, he's just started. He's set up a business with an old friend in Stavanger. They're good. I can vouch for them."

"This is how we'll do it," Geir Gulliksen said. "They make a proposal and we'll look at it. If it's good, okay, then there's no problem."

And that was what happened. I went down to see them in June, I had a book about space travel from the 1950s, it had belonged to Dad, and was full of drawings in the optimistic, futuristic style of the fifties. I also had an idea about a creamy color I had seen on the cover of Stefan Zweig's *The World of Yesterday*. Furthermore, Yngve had managed to lay his hands on a couple of pictures of zeppelins which I believed would suit the book. Then they sat in their new office chairs in the loft, with the sun baking down, putting together a proposal while I sat in the armchair behind, watching. In the evenings we drank beer and watched the World Cup. I was happy and optimistic; the feeling that one era had finished and a new one was starting was strong in me. Tonje had completed her studies and had a job at the Norwegian Broadcasting Corporation in Hordaland, I was making my debut as a novelist, we had just moved into our first real flat, in Bergen, the town where we had first met. Yngve and Asbjørn, on whose coattails I had hung throughout my student days, had set up on their own, and their first real job was my book cover. Everything was brimming with possibilities, everything pointed forward, and it must have been the first time in my life I had experienced that.

The yield from these days was good, we had six or seven wonderful covers, I was satisfied, but they wanted to try something else, and Asbjørn brought over a bag of American photographic magazines, which we scoured. He showed me some pictures by Jock Sturges, they were quite exceptional, I had never seen anything like them, and we selected one, of a long-limbed girl, twelve years old perhaps, or thirteen, standing naked with her back to us and looking across a lake. It was beautiful but also charged, pure but also threatening, and possessed an almost iconic quality. In another magazine there was an advertisement where the writing was white in two blue strips, or boxes; they decided to snatch the idea, but do it in red, and half an hour later Yngve had the cover ready. The publishers were given five different proposals, but were in little doubt, the Sturges one was the best, and the book due to come out in a few months' time bore the young girl on the cover. It was asking for trouble, Sturges was a controversial photographer, his house had been turned upside down by FBI agents, I had read, and searching for his name on the net I found some of the links always led to child pornography sites. Yet I had not seen any photographer reproduce the rich world of childhood in such an impressive way, Sally Mann included. So I was happy about that. Also that it was Yngve and Asbjørn who had done it.

In the car on the way from Sola on this strange Friday evening we did not say much. Chatted a little about the practical details of what awaited us, the funeral itself, of which neither Yngve nor I had had any previous experience. The low sun made the passing rooftops glow. The sky was high here, the countryside flat and green, and all the space gave me a sense of wasteland that not even the largest gathering of people would succeed in filling. Small by comparison were the people I saw, standing outside a shelter and waiting for the bus to town, cycling along the road, heads bowed over the handlebars, sitting on a tractor and driving across a field, leaving the gas station shop with a hot dog in one hand and a bottle of Coke in the other. The town was deserted as well, the streets were empty, the day was over and the evening had not yet begun.

Yngve played Björk on the car stereo. Outside the windows, the number of shops and office blocks dwindled, apartment buildings increased. Small gardens, hedges, fruit trees, children on bikes, children skipping.

"I don't know why I started crying back there," I said. "But something touched me when I saw you. I suddenly understood that he was dead."

"Yes . . . ," Yngve said. "I'm not sure it's sunk in for me yet."

He shifted down as we rounded the bend and ascended the last hill. There was a play area to the right; two girls were sitting on a bench with what looked like cards in their hands. A bit farther up, on the other side of the road, I saw the garden in front of Yngve's house. No one was there, but the sliding door to the living room was open.

"Here we are," Yngve said, driving slowly into the open garage.

"I'll leave the suitcase here," I said. "We're off tomorrow anyway."

The front door opened, and Kari Anne came out with Torje in her arms. Ylva stood beside her, holding her leg, watching me as I closed the car door and walked over to them. Kari Anne offered her cheek and put an arm around me, I gave her a hug, ruffled Ylva's hair.

"Sorry to hear about your father," she said. "My condolences."

"Thank you," I said. "But it didn't exactly come as a surprise."

Yngve slammed the trunk and walked over with a shopping bag in each hand. He must have done some shopping on the way to the airport.

"Shall we go in?" Kari Anne said.

I nodded and followed her into the living room.

"Mmm, that smells good," I said.

"It's what I always make," she said. "Spaghetti with ham and broccoli."

With Torje still hanging from one arm, she moved a cooking pot to the side of the stove with her other hand, switched it off, bent down and took a colander from the cupboard as Yngve came in, placed the bags on the floor and began to put things away. Ylva, who apart from a diaper was quite naked, stood motionless in the middle of the room, looking back and forth between us. Then she ran off to a doll's bed beside a bookshelf, lifted up a doll, and came over to me holding it at arm's length.

"What a nice doll you've got," I said, kneeling in front of her. "Can I see her?"

She held the doll to her chest with a determined expression on her face, and half-turned.

"Show Karl Ove your doll now," Kari Anne said.

I straightened up.

"I'm going out for a smoke, if that's okay," I said.

"I'll join you," Yngve said. "Just have to finish this first."

I went through the veranda door, closed it, and sat down on one of the three white plastic chairs on the flagstones. There were toys scattered across the whole lawn. At the far end, by the hedge, there was a round plastic pool filled with water and littered with grass and insects. Two golf clubs leaned against the leeward wall, next to a couple of badminton rackets and a soccer ball. I took my cigarettes from my inside pocket and lit one, leaned back. The sun had disappeared behind a cloud, and the bright green, gleaming grass and leaves were suddenly grayish and matte, drained of life. The uninterrupted sounds of a manual lawn mower being trundled back and forth reached me from the neighbor's garden. The clatter of plates and cutlery from inside the kitchen.

I loved being here.

At home in our flat everything was us, there was no distance; if I was troubled, the flat was also troubled. But here there was distance, here the surroundings had nothing to do with me and mine, and they could shield me from whatever was troublesome.

The door opened behind me. It was Yngve. He was holding a cup of coffee in one hand.

"Tonje sends her love," I said.

"Thanks," he said. "How is she?"

"Fine," I said. "She started work on Monday. She had an item on the news on Wednesday. Fatal accident."

"You said," he said, sitting down.

What was that? Was he grumpy?

We sat for a while without speaking. In the sky above the blocks of flats to the left of us, a helicopter flew past. The distant whump of the rotor blades was muffled. The two girls from the play area came walking up the road. Someone from one of the gardens farther away shouted a name. *Bjørnar*, it sounded like.

Yngve took out a cigarette and lit up.

"Have you taken up golf?" I said.

He nodded.

"You should give it a try. You're bound to be good. You're tall and you've played soccer and you've got that killer instinct. Feel like having a few whacks? I've got some practice balls lying around somewhere."

"Now? I don't think so."

"It was a joke, Karl Ove," he said.

"Me playing golf or trying it now?"

"Trying it now."

The neighbor, who was standing just behind the hedge separating the two gardens, stopped, straightened up and ran his hand across his bare, sweaty skull. On the veranda sat a woman dressed in a white T-shirt and shorts, reading a magazine.

"Do you know how Grandma is?" I said.

"No, I don't," he said. "But she was the one who found him. So you can imagine she probably isn't feeling too good."

"In the living room, right?"

"Yes," he said, stubbing out his cigarette in the ashtray and getting up.

"Well, shall we go in and have a bite to eat?"

The next morning I was woken by Ylva standing at the bottom of the stairs in the hall and howling. I half-propped myself up in bed and raised the blinds so that I could see what time it was. Half past five. I sighed and sank back down. My room was full of packing cases, clothes, and various other things that had not yet found their place in the house. An ironing board stood by one wall, piled with neatly stacked clothes, next to it an Asian-looking screen, folded and leaning against the wall. Beyond the door I could hear Yngve's and Kari Anne's voices, soon afterward their footfalls on the old wooden staircase. The radio being switched on downstairs. We had decided to set off at around seven, then we would be in Kristiansand at about eleven, but there was nothing to stop us going earlier, I supposed, swung my feet onto the floor, put on my trousers and T-shirt, leaned forward and ran a hand through my hair while inspecting myself in the wall mirror. No traces of yesterday's emotional outbursts visible; I just looked tired. So, back to where I was. Because yesterday had not left any traces internally either. Feelings are like water, they always adapt to their surroundings. Not even the worst grief leaves traces; when it feels so overwhelming and lasts for such a long time, it is not because the feelings have set, they can't do that, they stand still, the way water in a forest mere stands still.

Fuck, I thought. This was one of my mental tics. Fuck, ferk, fuckeroo was another. They flashed into my consciousness at odd intervals, they were impossible to stop, but why should I stop them, they didn't do anyone any harm. You couldn't see from my face that I was thinking them. Shit a brick, I thought, and opened the door. I saw straight into their bedroom, and looked down, things existed that I did not want to know, pulled the little wooden gate aside and went downstairs into the kitchen. Ylva was sitting on her Tripp Trapp chair with a slice of bread in her hand and a glass of milk in front of her, Yngve was standing by the stove and frying eggs while Kari Anne shuttled back and forth between the table and cupboards, setting the table. The coffee machine light was on. The last drops from the filter were on their way into the pot. The extractor hood hummed, the eggs bubbled and spat in the pan, the radio blared out the traffic news jingle.

"Good morning," I said.

"Good morning," said Kari Anne.

"Hello," said Yngve.

"Karl Ove," said Ylva, pointing to the chair opposite her.

"Shall I sit there?" I asked.

She nodded, sweeping head movements, and I pulled the chair out and sat down. Of her parents, she looked more like Yngve, she had his nose and eyes, and oddly many of his expressions also appeared in them. Her body had not yet outgrown the baby fat stage, there was something soft and rounded about all her limbs and parts, so that when she frowned and her eyes assumed Yngve's knowing air, it was hard not to smile. It didn't make her older but him younger: suddenly you saw that one of his typical expressions was not associated with experience, maturity, or worldly wisdom, but must have lived its life unchanged and independent of his face right from the time it was forming at the beginning of the 1960s.

Yngve slipped the spatula under the eggs and transferred them, one by one, onto a broad dish, put it on the table, beside the bread basket, fetched the pot of coffee, and filled the three cups. I generally drank tea at breakfast and had since I was fourteen, but I didn't have the heart to point this out, instead I took a slice of bread and flipped an egg on top with the spatula Yngve had rested against the dish.

I scoured the table for salt. But there was none to be found.

"Any salt?" I asked.

"Here," Kari Anne said, handing it to me across the table.

"Thank you," I said, flipping open the little plastic cap and watching the tiny grains sink into the yellow yolk, barely puncturing the surface, as the butter melted and seeped into the bread.

"Where's Torje?" I said.

"He's upstairs asleep," said Kari Anne.

I bit a chunk off the bread. The fried egg-white was crispy underneath, large brownish-black pieces crunched between palate and tongue as I chewed.

"Does he still sleep a lot?" I said.

"Well . . . sixteen hours a day possibly? I don't know. What would you say?" She turned to Yngve.

"No idea," he said.

I bit into the yolk and it ran, yellow and lukewarm, into my mouth. Took a swig of coffee.

"He was so frightened when Norway scored," I said.

Kari Anne smiled. We had seen the second of Norway's World Cup games here, and Torje had been sleeping in a cradle at the other end of the room. Whence a high-pitched howl arose, after our cheering to celebrate the goal had subsided.

"Shame about the Italy game by the way," Yngve said. "Have we actually talked about it?"

"No," I said. "But they knew what they were doing. You just had to give Norway the ball and everything broke down."

"They must have been on their knees after the Brazil game," Yngve said.

"I was too," I said. "Penalties are just too painful. I could hardly watch."

I had seen the match in Molde, with Tonje's father. As soon as it was over I called Yngve. We were both close to tears. Behind our choked voices lay an entire childhood supporting a national soccer team that had not had a sniff of success. Afterward I had gone down to the town center with Tonje, it had been full of cars honking their horns and people waving flags. Strangers were hugging, the sounds of shouting and singing came from all corners, people were running around with flushed faces, Norway had beaten Brazil in a decisive World Cup match, and no one knew how far this team could go. The whole way maybe?

Ylva slid down from her chair and held my hand.

"Come on," she said.

"Karl Ove has to eat first," Yngve said. "Afterward, Ylva!"

"No, don't worry," I said, joining her. She dragged me over to the sofa, took a book from the table and sat down. Her short legs didn't even reach to the edge.

"Shall I read?" I said.

She nodded. I sat beside her and opened the book. It was about a caterpillar that ate everything in sight. After I had finished reading she crawled forward and grabbed another book from the table. This one was about a mouse called Fredrik who, unlike other mice, didn't gather food in the summer but preferred to sit around dreaming. They said he was lazy, but when winter came and everything was cold and white, he was the one who gave their lives color and light. That was what he had been gathering, and that was what they needed now, color and light.

Ylva sat next to me perfectly still, looking at the pages with intense concentration, occasionally pointing to things and asking what they were called. It was wonderful sitting with her, but also a bit boring. I wanted to be out on the veranda, alone with a cigarette and a cup of coffee.

On the last page Fredrik was a blushing hero and savior.

"That was uplifting. Wonderful!" I said to Yngve and Kari Anne after finishing the book.

"We had it when we were boys," Yngve said. "Don't you remember?"

"Vaguely," I lied. "Is it actually the same book?"

"No, Mom's got it."

Ylva was on her way to the pile of books again. I got up and fetched my cup of coffee from the kitchen table.

"Have you had enough?" Kari Anne said, on her way to the dishwasher with her plate.

"Yes, thanks," I said. "A nice breakfast."

I looked at Yngve.

"When shall we make tracks?"

"I'll have to shower first," he said. "And do some packing. Half an hour maybe?"

"Okay," I said. Ylva had accepted that Book Hour was over for today and had gone into the hall, where she sat putting on my shoes. I opened the sliding door to the veranda and went out. The weather was mild and overcast. The seats were covered with fine droplets of dew which I wiped away with my hand before sitting down. Normally I would not have been up so early, my mornings tended to start at around eleven, twelve or one, and everything that my senses were breathing in now reminded me of summer mornings in my childhood when I used to cycle to a gardening job at half past six. The sky was mostly hazy, the road I took empty and gray, the air rushing toward me chilly, and it was almost inconceivable that the heat in the field where later we would be squatting would be baking, or that we would shoot off on bikes to Lake Gjerstad during the lunch break for a dip before work resumed.

I sipped the coffee and lit a cigarette. I can't say that I enjoyed the taste of the coffee or the feeling of smoke descending into my lungs, I could barely distinguish the two, the point was to do it, it was a routine, and as with all routines, protocol was everything.

How I had hated the smell of smoke when I was a child! Journeys at the back of a boiling car with two parents puffing away at the front. The smoke that filtered from the kitchen through the crack in my bedroom door in the morning, before I had gotten used to it, when it filled my sleeping nostrils and I twitched, the unpleasantness of it, as it had been every day until I started to smoke myself and became immune to the odor.

The exception was the period when Dad had smoked a pipe.

When would that have been?

All the bother of knocking out all the old black tobacco, cleaning the pipe with the flexible white cleaners, tamping in fresh tobacco and sitting there puffing it into life, matchstick in the bowl, puff, another matchstick, puff, puff, and then lean back, cross one leg over the other and smoke. Oddly enough, I associated this with his outdoor phase. Knitted sweaters, anorak, boots, beard, pipe. Long walks inland to pick berries for the winter, sporadic trips to the mountains looking for cloudberries, the berry of all berries, but more often than not into the forest off the roads, with the car left at the edge, everyone with a berry picker in one hand, bucket in the other, combing the countryside for blueberries or lingonberries. Rests in lay-bys beside rivers or on clifftops with a view. Sometimes by a rock face along a river, sometimes on a log inside a pine forest. Slamming on the brakes when there were raspberry bushes by the roadside. Out with the buckets, for this was Norway in the 1970s, families stood on the roadside picking raspberries on weekends, with large, square, plastic cooler bags containing provisions in the trunk. It was also around this time that he used to go fishing, to the far side of the island on his own after school, or with us on the weekend, fishing for the big cod in the waters around here in the winter: 1974 to 1975. Even though neither of my parents had anything to do with the sixty-eighters, after all they had had children when they were twenty and since then had worked, and even though the ideology was alien to my father, he was not untouched by the spirit of the time, it was alive in him as well, and when you saw him sitting there with pipe in hand, bearded and if not long-haired, at least thick-haired, in a knitted sweater and a pair of flared jeans, his bright eyes smiling at you, you could have taken him for one of the softie fathers beginning to emerge and assert themselves at that time, those who were not averse to pushing strollers, changing diapers, sitting on the floor and playing with children. However, nothing could be farther from the truth. The only thing he had in common with them was the pipe.

Oh, Dad, have you died on me now?

From the open window on the floor above came the sound of crying. I craned my neck. Kari Anne was in the kitchen, emptying the dishwasher, two glasses on the table, she ran across the floor to the staircase. Ylva, who was pushing a little cart with a doll inside, trundled in the same direction. Seconds later I heard Kari Anne's consoling voice through the window, and the crying abated. I got up, opened the door, and went in. Ylva was standing by the gate in front of the stairs looking up. The plumbing in the wall gurgled.

"Do you want to sit on my shoulders?" I asked.

"Yes," she said.

I squatted down and lifted her onto my shoulders, held her small legs tight with my hands and ran back and forth between the living room and the kitchen a few times, whinnying like a horse. She laughed, and whenever I stopped and bent forward as if I were going to throw her off she screamed. After a couple of minutes I'd had enough, but continued for another two as a matter of form, before crouching down and unsaddling her.

"More!" she said.

"Another time," I said, looking out of the window, down to the road where a bus pulled in and stopped to let on a meager group of commuters from the flats.

"Now," she said.

I looked at her and smiled.

"Okay. One more time then," I said. Up she went again, back and forth again, halt and pretend to throw her off, whinny. Fortunately, Yngve came down just afterward, so stopping seemed natural enough.

"Are you ready?" he said.

His hair was wet, and his cheeks smooth after a shave. In his hand he was holding the old blue-and-red Adidas bag he had had at school.

"Yup," I said.

"Is Kari Anne upstairs?"

"Yes, Torje woke up."

"I'll just have a smoke and then we can go," Yngve said. "Will you keep an eye on Ylva?"

I nodded. By a stroke of good fortune she seemed to have found something to occupy herself with, so I was able to collapse on the sofa and flick through one of the music magazines there. But I wasn't up to absorbing record reviews and interviews with bands, so I put it down and instead took his guitar from the stand by the sofa, in front of the amplifier and boxes of LPs. It was a black Fender Telecaster, relatively new, while the tube amplifier was an old Music Man. In addition, he had a Hagström guitar, but that was in his office. I strummed a few chords without thinking, it was the opening of Bowie's "Space Oddity" and I started to sing to myself quietly. I no longer had a guitar, after all these years I hadn't managed much more than the very basic skills it would take a somewhat talented fourteen-year-old a month to master. But the drum set, which I had paid a pretty krone for five years ago, that at least was in the loft, and now we were back in Bergen perhaps it could be used again.

In this house you really ought to be able to play Pippi Longstocking, I thought.

I put the guitar back and grabbed the pop magazine again as Kari Anne came downstairs with Torje in her arms. He was hanging there and grinning from ear to ear. I got up and went over to them, leaned forward and said *booh* to him, an unusual and unnatural action for me, I immediately felt stupid, but that clearly didn't bother Torje, who hiccupped with laughter, and looked at me expectantly when he stopped laughing, he wanted me to do it again.

"Booh!" I said.

"Eeha eeha eeha!" he said.

Not all rituals involve ceremonies, not all rituals are rigidly demarcated, there are those that take shape in the midst of everyday life, and are recognizable by the weight and charge they give the otherwise normal event. As I stepped out of the house that morning and followed Yngve to the car, for a moment it was as if I was entering a larger story than my own. The sons leaving home to bury their father, this was the story I suddenly found myself in, as I stopped by the passenger door while Yngve unlocked the trunk and stowed his bag, and Kari Anne, Ylva, and Torje stood watching us from the front door. The sky was grayish-white and mild, the estate quiet. The slam of the trunk lid, which reverberated against the house wall on the other side, sounded almost obtrusively clear and sharp. Yngve opened the door and got in, leaned across and unlocked my side. I waved to Kari Anne and the children before squeezing into the seat and closing the door. They waved back. Yngve started the engine, hung his arm across the back of my seat and reversed, up to the right. Then he too waved, and we set off down the road. I leaned back.

"Are you tired?" Yngve asked. "Just sleep if you want."

"Sure?"

"Of ourse. So long as I can play some music."

I nodded and closed my eyes. Heard him press the CD player button, hunt for a CD on the narrow shelf under the dashboard. The low hum of the car. Then the disc being slipped in, and straight afterward, a folksy mandolin intro.

"What is it?" I asked.

"Sixteen Horsepower," he said. "Do you like it?"

"Sounds good," I said, closing my eyes again. The sensation of the great story had gone. We were not two sons, we were Yngve and Karl Ove; we were not going home but to Kristiansand; this was not a father we were burying, it was Dad.

I wasn't tired, and didn't manage to fall asleep, but it was pleasant sitting with my eyes closed, mostly because it was undemanding. When we were growing up, I chatted all the time with Yngve and we never had any secrets, but at some juncture, perhaps as early as when I was at upper secondary, this changed: from then on I was immensely conscious of who he was and who I was when we were talking, all spontaneity vanished, every statement I made was either planned in advance or analyzed retrospectively, mostly both, apart from when I was drinking, then I regained the old freedom. With the exception of Tonje and my mother, that was how I behaved with everyone, I couldn't sit and chat with people anymore, my awareness of the situation was too acute, and that put me outside it. Whether it was the same for Yngve I didn't know, but I didn't think so, it didn't seem so when I saw him with others. Whether he knew that was how I felt, I didn't know, but something told me he did. Often it felt to me as if I were false, or deceitful, since I never played with an open deck, I was always calculating and evaluating. This didn't bother me any more, it had become my life, but right now, at the outset of a long car journey, now that Dad was dead, I experienced a yearning to escape from myself or at least the part that guarded me so assiduously.

Shit a brick.

I straightened up and flicked through his CDs. Massive Attack, Portishead, Blur, Leftfield, Bowie, Supergrass, Mercury Rev, Queen.

Queen?

He had liked them ever since he was small, had always stayed true to them, and was ready to defend them at the drop of a hat. I remembered him sitting in his room copying one of Brian May's solos note for note on his new guitar, a black imitation Les Paul, bought with his confirmation money, and the Queen fan club magazine he got through the mail. He was still waiting for the world to come to its senses and accord to Queen what Queen was rightfully due.

I smiled.

When Freddie Mercury died, the revelation that shocked was not the fact that he was gay but that he was an Indian.

Who could have imagined that?

Buildings were few and far between now. The traffic in the oncoming roadway had increased for a while, as rush hour approached, but was beginning to die down as we emerged into the unpopulated area between towns.

We passed huge, yellow cornfields, vast expanses of strawberries, patches of green pastureland, newly plowed fields of dark brown, almost black soil. Occasional copses, villages, some river or other, some lake or other. Then the terrain totally changed character and became almost mountainous with green, treeless, uncultivated upland. Yngve drove into a gas station, filled up, poked his head in and asked if I wanted anything, I shook my head, but on his return he passed me a bottle of Coke and a Bounty bar.

"Feel like a smoke?" he said.

I nodded and clambered out. We walked to a bench at the end of the parking lot. Behind it flowed a little stream, with a bridge farther on. A motorbike roared by, then a juggernaut, then one more.

"What did Mom actually say?" I said.

"Not much," Yngve said. "She needs time to think things through. But she was sad. Probably thinking about us mostly, I would imagine."

"Borghild's being buried today," I said.

"Yes," he said.

A juggernaut drove into the gas station from the west, parked with a sigh at the other end, a middle-aged man jumped down from the cab and held his windblown, flapping hair in place as he walked to the entrance.

"Last time I saw Dad he talked about setting up as a truck driver," I said with a smile.

"Oh," Yngve said. "When was that?"

"Winter, um, year and a half ago. When I was in Kristiansand, writing."

I unscrewed the bottle top and took a swig.

"When did you last see him?" I said, wiping my mouth with the back of my hand.

Yngve stared across the flatland on the other side of the road and took a couple of drags from the dying cigarette.

"Must have been at Egil's confirmation. May last year. But you were there too, weren't you?"

"Shit, I was," I said. "That was the last time. Or was it?" Now I wasn't so sure.

Yngve lowered his foot from the bench seat, replaced the top on the bottle and set off for the car as the truck driver came out of the door with a newspaper under his arm and a hot dog in his hand. I chucked the smoking cigarette onto the tarmac and followed. By the time I reached the car the engine was already running.

"Right," Yngve said. "Two hours to go, give or take. We can eat when we get there, can't we?"

"Okay," I said.

"Anything you'd like to hear?"

He halted at the junction, glanced a few times back and forth, then we were on the main road again, and he accelerated.

"No," I said. "You decide."

He chose Supergrass. The music I had bought in Barcelona, where I had accompanied Tonje while she went to some European local radio seminar. We had seen them live there, and since then I had played them nonstop, along with a couple of other CDs, while writing the novel. The mood of that year suddenly overwhelmed me. So it had already become a memory, I marveled. So it had already become "the time in Volda when I wrote around the clock while Tonje was left to twiddle her thumbs."

Never again, she had said afterward, the first evening we sat in the new flat in Bergen, the next day we were going to Turkey on holiday. I'll leave you.

"In fact I did see him once after that," Yngve said. "Last summer when I was in Kristiansand with Bendik and Atle. He was sitting on the bench outside the kiosk by Rundingen, as we drove past. He looked like a bit of a rascal, Bendik said when he saw him. And of course he was right."

"Poor Dad," I said.

Yngve looked at me.

"If there is anyone you shouldn't feel sorry for, it's him," he said.

"I know. But you know what I mean."

He didn't answer. The silence which in the first few seconds was charged, drifted into mere silence. I surveyed the scenery, which was sparse and windblown here so close to the sea. A red barn or two, a white farmhouse or two, a tractor or two with a forage harvester in a field. An old car without wheels in a yard, a yellow plastic ball blown under a hedge, some sheep grazing on a slope, a train slowly trundling past on the raised railway track a few hundred meters beyond the road.

I had always suspected we had different relationships with Dad. The differences were not enormous, but perhaps significant. What did I know? For a while Dad had tried to get closer to me, I remembered that well, it was the year Mom had done a continuing education course in Oslo and had her practical in Modum, and we lived at home with him. It was as though he had given up on Yngve, who was fourteen, but still nourished a hope that he could reach me. At any rate, I had to sit in the kitchen every afternoon and keep him company while he made the meal. I sat on the chair, he stood by the stove frying something or other while asking me all sorts of questions. What the teacher had had to say, what we had learned in the English lesson, what I was going to do after the meal, whether I knew which teams were on the pools coupon for this weekend. I gave terse answers and writhed in the chair. It was also the winter he took me skiing. Yngve could do what he liked, so long as he said where he was going and was back by half past nine, and I envied him for that. The period stretched beyond the year Mom was away, however, because the autumn afterward Dad took me fishing in the morning before school, we used to get up at six, it was as dark outside as at the bottom of a well, and cold, particularly on the sea. I was frozen and wanted to go home, but I was with Dad, there was no point in whining, there was no point in saying anything, you had to tough it out. Two hours later we were back, just in time for me to catch the school bus. I hated this, I was always cold, the sea was freezing of course, and it was my job to grab the trawl floats and pull up the first lengths of net while he maneuvred the boat, and if I missed the floats he gave me an earful, more often than not I ended up trying to grab the damn things with tears in my eyes, as he powered back and forth, glaring at me with those wild eyes of his in the autumn darkness off Tromøya. But I know he did this for my sake, and he had never done it for Yngve.

On the other hand, I also know that the first four years of Yngve's life – when they were living in Thereses gate in Oslo, and Dad was studying at the university and working as a night watchman, and Mom was doing a nursing degree while Yngve was in kindergarten – were good, perhaps even happy. I know that Dad was happy, and loved Yngve. When I was born we moved to Tromøya, at first into an old, former military, house in Hove, in the forest by the sea, then to the house on the estate in Tybakken, and the only thing I was told about that time was that I fell down the stairs and hyperventilated so much that I fainted, and Mom ran with me in her arms to the neighbor's house to call the hospital, as my face was going bluer and bluer, and I had screamed so much that in the end my father had dumped me in the bathtub and showered me with ice cold water to make me stop. Mom, who told me about the incident, had shielded us, and had given him an ultimatum: one more time and she would leave him. It didn't happen again, and she stayed.

Dad's attempts at closeness did not mean that he didn't hit me or yell at me in a rage or concoct the most ingenious ways of punishing me, but it did mean that my image of him was not clear-cut, which perhaps it was to a greater degree for Yngve. He hated Dad with a greater intensity, and that was simpler. I had no idea what relationship Yngve had with him above and beyond that. The notion of having children one day was not without its complications for me, and when Yngve told me that Kari Anne was pregnant it had been impossible to imagine what kind of father Yngve would make, whether what Dad had handed down to us was in our bone marrow or whether it would be possible to break free, maybe even without a problem. Yngve became a kind of test case for me: if all went well it would also go well for me. And it did go well, there was nothing of Dad in Yngve regarding his attitude to children, everything was very different and seemed to be integrated into the rest of his life. He never rejected them, he always had time for them whenever they went to him or he was needed, and he never tried to get close to them, by which I mean he didn't make them compensate for something in himself, or in his life. He handled such incidents as Ylva's kicking, wriggling, howling, and not wanting to get dressed with ease. He had been at home with her for six months, and the closeness they shared was still apparent. Yngve and Dad were the only models I had.

The countryside around us changed again. Now we were driving through forest. Sørland forests with mountain crags here and there among the trees, hills covered with spruce and oaks, aspen and birch, sporadic dark moorland, sudden meadows, flatland with densely growing pine trees. When I was a boy I used to imagine the sea rising and filling the forests so that the hilltops became islets you could sail between and on which you could bathe. Of all my childhood fantasies this was the one that captivated me most; the thought that everything was covered by water had me spellbound, the thought that you could *swim* where now you were walking, *swim* over bus shelters and roofs, perhaps dive down and glide through a door, up a staircase, into a living room. Or just through a forest, with its slopes, cliffs, cairns, and ancient trees. At a certain point in childhood my most exciting game was building dams in streams, watching the water swell and cover the marsh, the roots, the grass, the rocks, the beaten earth path beside the stream. It was hypnotic. Not to mention the cellar we found in an unfinished house filled with shiny, black water we sailed on in two styrofoam boxes, when we were around five years old. Hypnotic. The same applied to winter when we skated along frozen streams in which grass, sticks, twigs, and small plants stood upright in the translucent ice beneath us.

What had been the great attraction? And what had happened to it?

Another fantasy I had at that time was that there were two enormous saw blades sticking out from the side of the car, chopping off everything as we drove past. Trees and streetlamps, houses and outhouses, but also people and animals. If someone was waiting for a bus they would be sliced through the middle, their top half falling like a felled tree, leaving feet and waist standing and the wound bleeding.

I could still identify with that feeling.

"Down there is Søgne," Yngve said. "A place I've often heard about but have never been. Have you?"

I shook my head.

"Some of the girls at school came from there. But I've never been."

It wasn't far to go now.

Soon the countryside began to merge into shapes I vaguely recognized, it became more and more familiar until what I saw through the window coalesced with the images I had in my mind's eye. It felt as if we were driving into a memory. As if what we were moving through was just a kind of backdrop for my youth. Entering the suburbs, Vågsbygd, where Hanne had lived, the Hennig Olsen factory, Falconbridge Nikel Works, dark and grimy, surrounded by the dead mountains, and then to the right, Kristiansand harbor, the bus station, the ferry terminal, Hotel Caledonien, the silos on the island of Odderøya. To the left, the part of town where Dad's uncle had lived until recently, before dementia had taken him to an old folks' home somewhere.

"Shall we eat first?" Yngve said. "Or go straight to the undertaker's?"

"May as well jump right in," I said. "Do you know where it is?"

"Elvegata. Don't remember the number."

"Then we'll have to find the road from the top. Do you know where it starts?"

"No. But just drive. It'll turn up."

We stopped at the traffic lights, Yngve bent over the wheel looking in all directions. The lights changed to green, he put the car into gear and slowly followed a small truck with a filthy, gray tarpaulin over the back, still peering to the sides, the truck picked up speed, and when he noticed the gap opening he straightened and accelerated.

"It was down there," he said, nodding to the right. "We'll have to go through the tunnel now."

"That doesn't matter," I said. "We just come in from the other side."

But it did matter. When we emerged from the tunnel and were on the bridge, the studio where I lived was on my right, I saw it from the road, and only a few meters beyond, on the other side of the river, hidden from us, was Grandma's house where Dad had died the day before.

He was still here in this town, in some cellar somewhere, being handled by strangers, as we sat there in a car on our way to the undertaker's. He had grown up in the streets we saw around us, and had been walking them until a few days ago. At the same time my memories of the streets were aroused, for over there was the gymnas, there was the neighborhood I walked through every morning and afternoon, so in love it hurt, there was the house where I had been so often alone.

I cried, but it was nothing serious, just a few tears down my cheeks. Yngve didn't notice until he looked at me. I dismissed them with a wave and was pleased my voice carried as I said: "Take a left there."

We drove down to Torridalsveien, past the two shale soccer fields where I had trained so hard with the seniors the winter I turned sixteen, past Kjøita and up to the intersection by Østerveien, which we followed over the bridge, then again we bore right, onto Elvegata.

"What number was it?" I said.

Yngve scanned the house numbers as we drove slowly past.

"There it is," he said. "Now we'll have to find somewhere to park."

A black sign with gold lettering hung from the wooden façade on the left. Gunnar had given Yngve the undertaker's name. It was the company they had used when Grandad died, and for all I knew, it was the one the family had always used. I had been in Africa at the time, on a two-month visit to Tonje's mother, and hadn't been told about Grandad until after his funeral. Dad had assumed responsibility for informing me. He never did. But at the funeral he said he had spoken to me and that I had told him I couldn't come. I would have liked to attend that funeral, and even though it would have been difficult from a practical point of view it would not necessarily have been impossible, and even if it had turned out to be impossible, I would have liked to have been informed of his death when it happened and not three weeks later, when he was already in the ground. I was furious. But what could I do?

Yngve drove down a little side street and pulled up to the curb. We unbuckled our seat belts at precisely the same moment and opened the door at precisely the same moment, and looked at each other with a smile. The air outside was mild but more sultry than in Stavanger, the sky a touch darker. Yngve went to the parking meter, and I lit a cigarette. I hadn't been to my maternal grandmother's funeral either. I had been in Florence with Yngve at the time. We had caught the train down and stayed at some random *pensione*, and since this was before mobile phones were the norm it had been impossible to locate us. It was Asbjørn who told us what had happened, on the evening we arrived home, he sat with us drinking the alcohol we had brought back. So, the only funeral I had attended was my maternal grandfather's. I had helped to carry the coffin, it was a fine funeral, the cemetery was on a hill overlooking the fjord, the sun was shining, I cried when my mother spoke in the church and, after it was all over and he was in the ground, and when she tarried by the open grave. She stood there alone, head bowed, the grass was green, the fjord far below blue and glassy smooth, the mountain opposite massive, towering and dark, and the earth in the grave shiny black and glistening.

Afterward we had meat broth. Fifty people, guzzling and slurping, there is nothing better for sentimentality than salted meat, or hot soup, for emotional outbursts. Magne, Jon Olav's father, spoke, but cried so much it was hard to understand what he was saying. Jon Olav made an attempt at a speech in church, but had to give up, he had been so close to his grandfather, and was unable to say a single word.

I took a few steps with stiff legs, looked up the street, which was almost deserted, apart from at the end, where it met the town's shopping street and from this distance seemed almost black with people. The smoke stung my lungs, as it always did when I hadn't smoked for a while. A car stopped about fifty meters farther up, and a man alighted. He bent forward and waved to those who had dropped him off. He had dark, curly hair and a bald patch, was probably around the fifty mark, wore light-brown velvet pants and a smart black jacket, narrow, square glasses. I turned away so he couldn't see my face as he approached, because I had recognized him, it was my Norwegian teacher from the first class at upper secondary, what was his name again? Fjell? Berg? Who cares, I thought, and turned around after he had passed. He had been enthusiastic and warm, but there had also been a sharpness about him, it didn't surface often, but when it did I had considered it evil. He raised the bag he was holding to check his wristwatch, sped up, and shot round the corner.

“I’ve got to have one, too,” Yngve said, joining me.

“The man who just went past, that was my old teacher,” I said.

“Oh yeah?” Yngve said, lighting a cigarette. “Didn’t he recognize you, or what?”

“I don’t know. I hid my face.”

I flicked the butt away and ransacked my pocket for some chewing gum. Seemed to remember there was some lying loose there. And there was.

“Only got the one,” I said. “Would have given you some otherwise.”

“Sure you would’ve,” he said.

Tears were close, I could feel, and I took a few deep breaths while opening my eyes wide as if to clear them. On a doorstep opposite sat an alcoholic I hadn’t noticed. His head was resting against the wall and he appeared to be asleep. The skin on his face was dark and leathery and covered with cuts. His hair so greasy it had taken on a rasta style. Thick winter jacket, even though the temperature was at least twenty degrees, and a bag of junk next to him. Three gulls stood on the ridge of the roof above him. As I focused on them, one lifted its head back and screamed.

“Well,” Yngve said. “Shall we take the plunge then?”

I nodded.

He flicked his cigarette end away, and we set off.

“Have we got an appointment by the way?” I said.

“No, that’s what we haven’t got,” he said. “But there can’t be such a rush, can there?”

“I’m sure we’ll be fine,” I said.

Between some trees I saw a fleeting glimpse of the river, and as we rounded the corner, all the signs, shop windows and cars in Dronningens gate. Gray tarmac, gray buildings, gray sky.

Yngve opened the door to the undertaker’s and went in. I followed, closed the door behind me, and was met with a kind of waiting room, a sofa, a few chairs and a table along one wall, a counter along the other. The counter was unmanned, and Yngve went over to peer into the room behind, knocked softly on the glass with a knuckle while I remained in the middle of the room.

A door in the side wall was ajar, I saw a figure in a black suit passing in the room behind. He looked young, younger than me.

A woman with blond hair and wide hips, closer to fifty, came out and sat behind the counter. Yngve said something to her, I didn't hear what, just the sound of his voice.

He turned.

"Someone will be here soon," he said. "We've got to wait five minutes."

"It feels like going to the dentist," I said as we took a seat and looked around the room.

"If it were, he'd be drilling into our souls," Yngve said.

I smiled. Remembered the chewing gum, which I took out of my mouth and hid in my hand while hunting for somewhere to dispose of it. Nowhere. I tore off a corner from the newspaper on the table, wrapped it around the gum, and put the package in my pocket.

Yngve drummed his fingers on the armrest.

Well, in fact, I had been to another funeral. How could I have forgotten? It had been for a young boy, the mood in the church was hysterical, there was crying, there was howling, there was shouting and moaning and sobbing, but also laughter and giggles, and it went in waves, one shout had been enough to trigger an avalanche of further emotional outbursts, there had been a storm in there, and it had all been unleashed by the white coffin at the altar in which Kjetil lay. He had died in a car, fallen asleep at the wheel early one morning, driven off the road and into a fence, an iron pole had impaled his head. He was eighteen years old, the kind of boy everyone liked, a boy who was always in a good mood and did not represent a threat to anyone. When we left school at sixteen he opted for the same branch as Jan Vidar and that was why he had been up so early, his job at the bakery started at four in the morning. Listening to news of the accident on the radio, I thought it had been Jan Vidar and was relieved when I discovered it wasn't, but I was also sorry, if not quite as sorry as the girls in our old class, they let their feelings go completely, and I know that because together with Jan Vidar I visited everyone in the days after the death to collect names and money for a class wreath. I was not entirely at ease with this role, it felt as if I were drawing on a relationship with Kjetil to which I had no right, so I kept a low profile, occupied as little space as I could, walking around the village with Jan Vidar, who radiated grief, anger, and bad conscience.

I remember Kjetil well, I can picture him at will, hear his voice in my inner ear, although only one specific incident from the four years I knew him has stayed with me, and that is an extremely insignificant one: someone was playing Madness's "Our House" on the stereo in the school bus, and Kjetil, who was next to me, was laughing at how fast the vocalist sang. I have forgotten everything else. But in the cellar I still have a book I borrowed from him, *The A–Z of the Driving Test*. His name is on the title page written in the childish style almost everyone of our generation has. I should have returned it, but to whom? The book would have been the last thing his parents would have wanted to see.

The school he and Jan Vidar attended was only a block away from where I was waiting with Yngve now. Apart from several weeks two years before, I had hardly been to Kristiansand since that time. One year in northern Norway, six months in Iceland, close to six months in England, one year in Volda, nine years in Bergen. And except for Bassen, whom I still met sporadically, I no longer had any contact with anyone from my time here. My oldest friend was Espen Stueland whom I had met in the literary science department at Bergen University ten years before. It had not been a conscious choice, it was just the way it had come about. For me Kristiansand had vanished off the face of the earth. Intellectually, I was aware that almost everyone I knew from that era still lived and had their lives here, but not emotionally, as the time in Kristiansand had stopped for me that summer I left school and headed off for good.

The fly that had been buzzing around in the window ever since we came in suddenly set a course for the center of the room. I watched it circle around a few times under the ceiling, settle on the yellow wall, take off again and glide in a small arc around us to land on the armrest where Yngve was now drumming his fingers. Its front legs went back and forth, crossed, as if brushing something off, then it moved forward and did a little jump through the air, its wings whirring, and down onto Yngve's hand, he, of course, lifted it at once, causing the fly to set off again and it flew back and forth before us, almost in irritation. Eventually, it settled back on the window, where it wandered up and down, confused.

"Actually we haven't talked about what sort of funeral he should have," Yngve said. "Have you given it any thought?"

"You mean whether it should be in a church or not?"

"For example."

"No, I haven't given it any thought. Do we have to decide that now?"

"We don't. But soon we'll have to."

I caught a glimpse of the young man in the suit as he passed by the half-open door again. It struck me that bodies might be stored here. Perhaps this was where they received them for preparation. Where else would they do it?

As though someone inside had sensed the direction of my thoughts, the door was closed. And as though the door movements were coordinated as part of some secret system, the one opposite us opened at the same moment. A portly man, who might have been in his mid-sixties, stepped out, impeccably dressed in a dark suit and white shirt, and looked at us.

"Knausgaard?" he queried.

We nodded and rose to our feet. He said his name and shook our hands in turn.

"Come with me," he said.

We followed him to a relatively large office with windows looking onto the street. He ushered us to two chairs in front of a desk. The chairs were of dark wood with black, leather upholstered seats. The desk he sat behind was deep, and it too was dark. A letter tray, the kind with several tiers, was on his left, beside it a telephone, otherwise the desk was empty.

Well, not quite, for on our side, right on the edge was a box of Kleenex. Practical of course, but how cynical it seemed! Seeing it, you visualized all the bereaved relatives who had come here and wept in the course of the day and you realized that your grief was not unique, not even exceptional, and ultimately not particularly precious. The box of Kleenex was a sign that here weeping and death had undergone inflation.

He looked at us.

"How can I help you?" he said.

The suntanned dewlap beneath his chin hung over his white shirt collar. His hair was gray and neatly combed. A dark shadow hovered above his cheeks and chin. The black tie did not hang, it lay, along the curve of his bloated stomach. He was fat, but also erect, there was nothing flabby about him, punctilious was probably the word, and thus also confident and safe. I liked him.

"Our father died yesterday," Yngve said. "We were wondering, well, if you might take care of the practical details. The funeral and so on."

"Yes," the funeral director said. "Then I'll start by filling in a form."

He pulled out a drawer from the desk and took out a document.

"We used you when our grandfather died. And have had only good experiences," Yngve said.

"I remember that," the director said. "He was an accountant, wasn't he? I knew him well."

He reached for a pen lying beside the telephone, raised his head and looked at us.

"But now I need some information from you," he said. "What's your father's name?"

I said his name. It felt strange. Not because he was dead, but because I hadn't said it for so many years.

Yngve glanced at me.

"Well . . . ," he said cautiously. "He did change his name a few years ago."

"Ah, I'd forgotten that," I said. "Of course."

The idiotic name he had chosen.

What an idiot he had been.

I looked down and blinked a few times.

"Have you got his National Insurance number?" the director said.

"No, not all of it," Yngve said. "Sorry. But he was born on April 17, 1944. We can find out the other numbers later if we have to."

"That's fine. Address?"

Yngve gave Grandma's address. Then glanced at me.

"Mm, I'm not sure that's his official address. He died at his mother's house. That's where he was living."

"We'll sort that out. And then I need your names as well. And a telephone number where I can reach you."

"Karl Ove Knausgaard," I said.

"And Yngve Knausgaard," Yngve said, and gave him his mobile number. After noting that, he put down the pen and looked at us again.

"Have you had an opportunity to think about the funeral? When it would be appropriate to hold it and what form you would like it to take?"

"No," Yngve said. "We haven't. But I suppose it's normal to hold the funeral a week after the death?"

"That is the norm, yes. So would next Friday be a suitable date?"

"Ye-es," Yngve said. "What do you think?"

"Friday's fine," I said.

"Well, let's say that for the time being. As far as the practical details are concerned, we can meet again, can't we? And in that case, if the funeral is to be on Friday, we would have to meet early next week. Perhaps no later than Monday. Does that work for you?"

"Yes," Yngve said. "Could it be early?"

"Certainly. Shall we say nine o'clock?"

"Nine's good."

The funeral director jotted this in his book. Once he had finished he stood up.

"We'll make the arrangements now. If you have any worries, do by all means give me a call. Any time at all. I go to my cabin in the afternoons and stay there all weekend, but I take my mobile phone with me, so all you need to do is call. Don't be shy. We'll meet again on Monday."

He proffered his hand and we both shook it before leaving the room, and he closed the door behind us with a brief nod and a smile.

Back out on the street, as we walked toward our car, something had changed. What I saw, what we were surrounded by, was no longer in focus, it had been pushed into the background, as though a zone had been installed around me from which all meaning had been drained. The world had vanished, that was the feeling I had, but I didn't care because Dad was dead. While in my mind the undertaker's office in all its detail was very vivid and clear, the town around it was fuzzy and gray, I walked through it because I had no choice. I wasn't thinking differently, inside my mind I was unchanged, the only difference was that now I demanded more room and hence I was excluding external reality. I couldn't explain it in any other way.

Yngve unlocked the car door. I noticed a white band wrapped around the roof rack, it was glossy and resembled the sort of ribbon you tie around presents, but surely it couldn't be?

He opened the door for me, and I got inside.

"That went well, didn't it," I said.

"Yes," he said. "Shall we drive to Grandma's then?"

"Let's," I said.

He indicated and moved into the traffic, took the first left, then another left, onto Dronningens gate, and soon we saw our grandparents' house from the bridge, yellow and imposing above the small marina and harbor basin. Up Kuholmsveien and into the alley that was so narrow you had to drive downhill a little way, then reverse into the footpath before you could drive up to and park by the front steps. I had seen my father perform the operation perhaps a hundred times in my childhood, and the fact that Yngve was doing exactly the same now moved my tears to the very edge of my consciousness, only a mental wrench prevented them from falling again.

Two large seagulls took off from the steps as we drove up the gentle slope. The space in front of the garage door was covered with sacks and garbage bags, that was what had been entertaining the gulls. They had pulled out all sorts of discarded plastic and strewn it around in their search for food.

Yngve switched off the engine but did not move. I too remained where I was. The garden was completely overgrown. The grass was knee-high, like a meadow, grayish-yellow in color, flattened in some places by the rain. It had spread everywhere, covering all the beds, I wouldn't have been able to see the flowers had I not known where they were, now only scattered glimpses of color allowed you to guess. A rusty wheelbarrow lay on its side by the hedge, looking as if it had grown into the wilderness. The ground under the trees was brown with rotten pears and plums. Dandelions abounded and in some places stripling trees had sprung up. It was as if we had parked by a clearing in the forest and not in front of a detached house in the middle of Kristiansand.

I leaned forward and looked up at the house. The bargeboards were rotten and the paint was peeling in various places, but the decay was not as obvious there.

Some drops of rain struck the windshield. A few more drummed lightly on the roof and hood.

"Gunnar isn't here anyway," Yngve said, undoing his seat belt. "But I suppose he'll be down eventually."

"He must be at work," I said.

"Figures for rainfall might go up in the holiday month, but that doesn't attract accountants back to work," Yngve commented drily. He withdrew the car key, put the bunch in his jacket pocket, opened the door, and got out.

I would have preferred to stay put, but of course that was not possible, so I followed suit, closed the door, and looked up at the kitchen window on the second floor where Grandma's gaze had always met us whenever we came.

No one home today.

"Hope it's open now that we're here," Yngve said, climbing the six steps that once had been painted dark red but were now just gray. The two gulls had settled on the roof of the neighbor's house and were carefully monitoring our movements.

Yngve pressed down the handle and pushed in the door.

"Oh Christ," he said.

I clambered up the stairs, and as I followed him through the doorway into the vestibule I had to turn away. The smell inside was unbearable. It stank of mold and piss.

Yngve stood in the hall surveying the scene. The blue wall-to-wall carpet was covered with dark stains. The open built-in wardrobe was full of loose bottles and bags of them. Clothes had been tossed all over the place. More bottles, clothes hangers, shoes, unopened letters, advertising brochures, and plastic bags were strewn across the floor.

But the worst was the stench.

What the hell could reek like that?

"He's destroyed everything," Yngve said, slowly shaking his head.

"What is that godawful stench?" I said. "Is something rotting?"

"Come on," he said, moving towards the stairs. "Grandma's waiting for us."

Empty bottles were strewn halfway up the staircase, five, six, maybe, but the closer we got to the second floor landing the more there were. Even the landing outside the door was almost totally covered with bottles and bags of bottles and every step of the staircase that continued up to the third floor, where my grandparents' bedroom had been, was full, apart from a few centimeters in the middle to put your feet. Most were plastic 1.5 liter bottles and vodka bottles, but there were a few wine bottles as well.

Yngve opened the door and we went into the living room. There were bottles on top of the piano and bags full of them below. The kitchen door was open. That was always where she sat, as indeed she was doing today, by the table, eyes downcast and a smoking cigarette in her hand.

"Hello," Yngve said.

She looked up. At first there was no sign of recognition in her eyes, but then they lit up.

"So it *was* you boys! I thought I heard someone coming through the door."

I swallowed. Her eyes seemed to have sunk into the cavities; her nose protruded and looked like a beak in the lean face. Her skin was white, shrunken, and wrinkled.

"We came as soon as we heard what had happened," Yngve said.

"Oh, yes, it was terrible," Grandma said. "But now you're here. That's good at least."

The dress she was wearing was discolored with stains and hung off her scrawny body. The top part of her bosom the dress was supposed to cover revealed ribs shining through her skin. Her shoulder blades and hips stuck out. Her arms were no more than skin and bone. Blood vessels ran across the backs of her hands like thin, dark blue cables.

She stank of urine.

"Would you like some coffee?" she asked.

"Yes, please," Yngve said. "That wouldn't be a bad idea. But we can put it on. Where's the coffeepot?"

"Damned if I know," Grandma said, casting around.

"It's there," I said, pointing to the table. There was a note beside it, I craned my head to read what it said.

BOYS COMING AT TWELVE. I'LL BE DOWN AROUND ONE. GUNNAR.

Yngve took the coffeepot and went to empty the grains in the sink, where there were piles of filthy plates and glasses. The whole length of the counter was covered with plastic trays, mostly from microwave meals, many still containing leftovers. Between them bottles, mostly the same 1.5 liter ones, some with dregs at the bottom, some half-full, some unopened, but bottles of spirits too, the cheapest Vinmonopolet vodka, a couple of half-liter bottles of Upper Ten whisky. Everywhere there were dried coffee dregs, crumbs, shriveled food remains. Yngve pushed one of the piles of packaging away, lifted some of the plates out of the sink, and put them on the counter before cleaning the coffeepot and filling it with fresh water.

Grandma was sitting as she had when we entered, eyes fixed on the table, the cigarette, now extinguished, in her hand.

"Where do you keep the coffee?" Yngve said. "In the cupboard?"

She looked up.

"What?" she said.

"Where do you keep the coffee?" Yngve repeated.

"I don't know where he put it," she said.

He? Was that Dad?

I turned and went into the living room. For as long as I could remember, it had only been used on church holidays and special occasions. Now Dad's huge TV was in the middle of the floor and two of the large leather chairs had been dragged in front of it. A little table swimming with bottles, glasses, pouches of tobacco, and overflowing ashtrays stood between them. I walked past and examined the rest of the room.

In front of the three-piece suite by the wall lay some articles of clothing. I could see two pairs of trousers and a jacket, some underpants and socks. The smell was awful. There were also overturned bottles, tobacco pouches, dry bread rolls, and other rubbish. I slouched past. There was excrement on the sofa, smeared and in lumps. I bent down over the clothes. They were also covered with excrement. The varnish on the floor had been eaten away, leaving large, irregular stains.

By urine?

I felt an urge to smash something. Lift the table and sling it at the window. Tear down the shelf. But I felt so weak I could barely get there. I rested my forehead against the window and looked down into the garden. The paint had almost peeled completely off the overturned garden furniture, which seemed to be growing out of the soil.

"Karl Ove?" Yngve said from the doorway.

I turned and went back.

"It's fucking disgusting in there," I said in a low voice so that she couldn't hear.

He nodded.

"Let's sit with her for a bit," he said.

"Okay."

I went in, pulled out the chair on the opposite side of the table from her, and sat down. A ticking sound filled the kitchen, coming from a thermostat-style device that was intended to switch off the burners on the stove automatically. Yngve sat at the end and took his cigarettes from his jacket, which for some reason he had not taken off. I had my jacket on as well, I discovered.

I didn't want to smoke, it felt dirty, yet I needed to and rummaged for my cigarettes. The fact that we had joined Grandma seemed to give her a boost. Her eyes lit up once again.

"Did you drive all the way from Bergen today?" she said.

"From Stavanger," Yngve said. "That's where I live now."

"But I live in Bergen," I said.

Behind us the coffeepot crackled on the stove.

"Oh?" she said.

Silence.

"Would you like some coffee, boys?" she asked suddenly.

I met Yngve's glance.

"I've put some on," Yngve said. "It'll be ready soon."

"Oh yes, so you have," Grandma said. She looked down at her hand, and with a start, as if it were only now she had discovered she was holding a cigarette, she grabbed a lighter and lit up.

"Did you drive here all the way from Bergen today then?" she said, puffing on her cigarette a few times before looking at us.

"From Stavanger," Yngve said. "It only took four hours."

"Yes, they're good roads now," she said.

Then she sighed.

"Oh dear. Life's a pitch, as the old woman said. She couldn't pronounce her *b*'s."

She chuckled. Yngve smiled.

"It would be nice to have something with the coffee," he said. "We've got some chocolate in the car. I'll get it."

I felt like telling him not to go, but of course I couldn't. When he had gone I got up, left the barely smoked cigarette on the edge of the ashtray and went to the stove, pressed the pot down harder so that it would boil quicker.

Grandma had sunk into herself again, stared down at the table. She sat bowed in the chair, shoulders slumped, rocking back and forth.

What could she be thinking?

Nothing. There was nothing in her mind. Couldn't be. It was just cold and dark inside.

I let go of the coffeepot and looked around for the coffee tin. Not on the counter beside the fridge, not on the opposite counter either, beside the sink. In a cupboard perhaps? Or not. Yngve had found it, hadn't he? Where did he put it?

There, for Christ's sake. He had put it on the stove's hood where the old spice jars were. I took it down, and pushed the coffeepot aside even though the water hadn't boiled yet, opened the lid and sprinkled in a few spoonfuls of coffee. It was dry and seemed stale.

Glancing up, I saw that Grandma was watching me.

"Where's Yngve?" she asked. "He hasn't left, has he?"

"No," I said. "He just went down to the car."

"Oh," she said.

I took a fork from the drawer and stirred the mixture in the coffeepot, banged it on the burner a few times.

"It'll brew for a bit and then it's done," I said.

"He was sitting in the chair when I got up in the morning," Grandma said. "He was sitting quite still. I tried to wake him. But I couldn't. His face was white."

I felt nauseous.

I heard Yngve's footsteps on the stairs, and I opened the cupboard to look for glasses, but there weren't any. I couldn't bring myself to think about using the ones in the sink, so I leaned forward and was drinking from the tap when Yngve arrived.

He had taken off his jacket. He was holding two Bounty bars and a packet of Camel cigarettes. Sat down and tore the paper off one bar.

"Would you like a piece?" he asked Grandma.

She scrutinized the chocolate.

"No, thank you," she said. "You eat it."

"I don't feel like it," I said. "But the coffee's ready anyway."

I put the pot on the table, opened the cupboard door again and took out three cups. I knew that Grandma took sugar lumps, and opened the long cupboard on the other wall where the food was. Two half loaves of bread, blue with mold, three spaghetti TV dinners that should have been in the freezer, bottles of spirits, the same cheap brand.

Never mind, I thought, and sat down again, lifted the pot of coffee, and poured. It hadn't brewed properly, from the spout came a light-brown stream, full of tiny coffee grains. I removed the lid and poured it back.

"It's good you're here," Grandma said.

I started to cry. I took a deep breath, carefully though, and laid my head in my hands, rubbed from side to side, as though I were tired, not as though I were crying. But Grandma didn't notice anything anyway; again she seemed to have disappeared inside herself. This time it lasted perhaps five minutes. Yngve and I said nothing, drank coffee, staring into space.

"Oh dear," she said then. "Life's a pitch, as the old woman said. She couldn't pronounce her *b*'s."

She grabbed the red rolling machine, opened the pouch of tobacco, Petterøe's Menthol, pressed the tobacco into the gap, inserted an empty casing into the small tube at the end, clicked the lid into place, and pushed it through hard.

"Think we ought to get the bags," Yngve said, and looked at Grandma. "Where can we sleep?"

"The big bedroom downstairs is empty," she said. "You can sleep there."

We got up.

"We'll just go down to the car then," Yngve said.

"Will you?" she said.

I stopped by the door and turned to him.

"Have you seen inside?" I said.

He nodded.

On the way downstairs a huge surge of tears overcame me. This time there was no question of trying to hide it. My whole chest trembled and shook, I couldn't draw breath, deep sobs rolled through me, and my face contorted, I was completely out of control.

"Oooooooh," I said. "Oooooooh."

I sensed Yngve behind me and forced myself to continue down the stairs, through the hall, out to the car, and into the narrow lawn between the house and the neighbor's fence. I raised my head and gazed up at the sky, tried to take deep, regular breaths, and after a few attempts the trembling eased.

When I returned Yngve was standing behind the open car trunk. My suitcase was on the ground beside him. I grabbed the handle and carried it up the steps, deposited it in the hall and turned to Yngve, who was right behind me with a backpack on and a bag in his hand. After being in the fresh air the stench indoors seemed stronger. I breathed through my mouth.

"Are we supposed to sleep in there?" I said, motioning to the door of the bedroom my grandparents had used for the last few decades.

"We'd better check it out," Yngve said.

I opened the door and peeped in. The room was ravaged, clothes, shoes, belts, bags, hairbrushes, curlers, and cosmetics were everywhere, on the bed, on the floor, on the dressing tables and covered with dust and dust balls, but it had not been defiled in the way the upstairs living room was.

"What do you think?" I said.

"I don't know," he said. "Where do you think he slept?"

He opened the adjacent door, to what once had been Erling's room, and went in. I followed.

The floor was littered with garbage and clothes. There was a table that looked as if it had been smashed to pieces lying under the window. Papers and unopened letters stacked in heaps. Something that might have been vomit had dried as an uneven yellowish-red patch on the floor, just under the bed. The clothes were stained with feces and dark patches that must have been old blood. One of the garments was black with excrement on the inside. Everything stank of pee.

Yngve stepped over to the window and opened it.

"Looks as if drug addicts have been living here," I said. "Place looks like a damn junkie's."

"It does," Yngve said.

Strangely enough, the dressing table by the wall between the bed and the door had not been touched. There were photographs of Dad and Erling wearing black graduation caps. Without his beard Dad bore a striking resemblance to Yngve. Same mouth, same setting round the eyes.

"What the hell shall we do?" I said.

Yngve didn't answer, just studied the room.

"We'd better clean it up," he said.

I nodded and left the room. Opened the door to the laundry room, which was in a wing parallel to the staircase, next to the garage. Inhaling the air inside, I began to cough. In the middle of the floor was a pile of clothes as tall as I was, it almost reached the ceiling. That was where the rotting smell must have come from. I switched on the light. Towels, sheets, tablecloths, trousers, sweaters, dresses, underwear, they had thrown it all in here. The lowest layers were not only mildewed, they were decomposing. I squatted down and prodded with my finger. It was soft and sticky.

"Yngve!" I called.

He came and stood in the doorway.

"Look at this," I said. "This is where the stench is coming from."

Footsteps sounded on the stairs. I stood up.

"We'd better go out," I said. "So she doesn't think we're prying."

When she came down we were standing in front of the bags in the middle of the floor.

"Is it alright for you in there?" she said, opening the door and peering in. "We'll have to clear up a bit and it'll be fine."

"We were thinking about the room in the loft," Yngve said. "What would you say to that?"

"I suppose it's a possibility," she said. "But I haven't been up there for a long time."

"We'll go up and have a look," Yngve said.

The loft room, which had been my grandparents' bedroom once upon a time but which for as long as we could remember had been reserved for guests, was the only one in the house he hadn't touched. Everything in it was as before. There was dust on the floor, and the duvets had a slightly stale odor, but it was no worse than what you find in a mountain cabin you haven't entered since the previous summer, and after the nightmare downstairs this was a relief. We unloaded our bags on the floor, I hung my suit on a cupboard door and Yngve stood with his arms propped against the window frame, looking out at the town.

"We can start by getting rid of all the bottles, can't we," he said. "To a supermarket for the deposit. That way we can get out a little."

"Right," I said.

After going down to the kitchen we heard the sound of a car in the drive. It was Gunnar. We stood waiting for him to come up.

"There you are!" he said with a smile. "Long time, no see, eh!"

His face was suntanned, hair blond, body sinewy and strong. He wore well.

"It's good to have the boys here, I imagine," he said to Grandma. Then he turned to us again.

"It's terrible, what happened here," he said.

"Yes," I said.

"I suppose you've had a look around? So you've seen what he got up to . . ."

"Yes," Yngve said.

Gunnar shook his head, jaws clenched.

"I don't know what to say," he said. "But he was your father. I'm sorry that things went as they did for him. But you probably knew which way the wind was blowing."

"We're going to clean the whole house," I said. "We'll deal with everything from now on."

"That's good. I got rid of the worst in the kitchen early this morning and threw out some trash, but there's quite a bit left, of course."

There was a flicker of a smile.

"I've got a trailer outside," he continued. "Could you move your car, Yngve? Then we can put it on the lawn beside the garage. We can't have the furniture here, can we? And all the clothes and everything. We'll drive it over to the dump. Isn't that the best idea?"

"Yep," I said.

"The boys and Tove are at the cabin. I just dropped by to say hello. And to leave the trailer. But I'll be back tomorrow morning. Then we can take it from there. It's terrible. But that's life. You two will manage."

"Course we will," Yngve said. "You parked behind me, didn't you? So you'll have to pull out first."

Grandma had watched us for the first few seconds when Gunnar arrived, and smiled at him, but then she went back inside her shell, and sat staring ahead as if she were all alone.

Yngve started down the stairs. I was thinking I ought to stay with her.

"You'll have to come with us as well, Karl Ove," Gunnar said. "We have to push it up the slope and it's pretty heavy."

I followed him down.

"Has she said anything?" he asked.

"Grandma?" I said.

"Yes. About what happened?"

"Hardly anything. Just that she found him in the chair."

"With her it was always your father," he said. "She's in shock now."

"What can we do?" I asked.

"What is there to do? Time will help. But as soon as the funeral is over she should go into a home. You can see for yourselves the state she's in. She needs professional care. As soon as the funeral's over she has to go."

He turned and placed his foot on the step, squinted up at the bright sky. Yngve was already in the car.

Gunnar addressed me again.

"We'd arranged some home-help for her, you know, they turned up every day and took care of her. Then your father came and sent them packing. Closed the door and locked himself in with her. Even I wasn't allowed in. But Mother called once, he had broken his leg and was lying on the living-room floor. He'd crapped his pants. Can you imagine? He'd been lying on the floor drinking. And she had served him. 'This is no good,' I told him before the ambulance arrived. 'This is beneath your dignity. Now you pull yourself together.' And do you know what your father said? 'Are you going to push me even deeper into the shit, Gunnar? Is that why you've come, to push me even deeper into the shit?"

Gunnar shook his head.

"That's my mother, you know, sitting up there now. Whom we've been trying to help all these years. He destroyed everything. This house, her, himself. Everything. Everything."

He quickly laid his hand on my shoulder.

"But I know you're good kids."

I cried, and he looked away.

"Well, now we'd better get the trailer in position," he said and went down to the car, slowly reversed downhill to the left, hooted his horn when the way was clear, and Yngve reversed. Then Gunnar drove forward, got out of the car, and unhooked the trailer. I joined them, grabbed the bar, and began to pull it up the hill while Yngve and Gunnar pushed.

"It'll be fine here," Gunnar said, after we had maneuvred it a fair way into the garden, and I dropped the end on the ground.

Grandma was watching us from the first-floor window.

While we collected the bottles, put them in plastic bags, and carried them down to the car, she sat in the kitchen. She watched as I poured beer and spirits from the half-full bottles down the sink, but said nothing. Perhaps she was relieved they were going, perhaps she wasn't really assimilating anything. The car was full, and Yngve went upstairs to tell her we were going to the shop. She got to her feet and joined us in the hall, we assumed she wanted to see us off, but when she came out, she walked straight down the steps to the car, put her fingers on the door handle, opened the door, and was about to get in.

"Grandma?" Yngve said.

She stopped.

"We were thinking of going alone. Someone has to be here to keep an eye on the house. It's best if you stay, I think."

"Do you think so?" she said, stepping back.

"Yes," Yngve said.

"Alright then," she said. "I'll stay here."

Yngve reversed down the drive, and Grandma went back indoors.

"What a nightmare," I said.

Yngve stared past me, then signaled left and slowly nosed out.

"She's clearly in shock," I said. "I wonder whether I should phone Tonje's father and sound him out. I'm sure he could prescribe something to sedate her."

"She's already taking medicine," Yngve said. "There's a whole trayful on the kitchen shelf."

He stared past me once again, this time up Kuholmsveien as three cars came down. Then he looked at me.

"But you can tell Tonje's father anyway. Then he can decide."

"I'll call when we get back," I said.

The last car, one of those ugly new bubbles, drove past. Raindrops landed on the windshield, and I remembered the previous rain which had started, then had second thoughts and left it at that.

This time it continued. When Yngve signaled to pull out and drove down the slope, he had the windshield wipers on.

Summer rain.

Oh, the raindrops that fall on the dry, hot tarmac, and then evaporate, or are absorbed by the dust, yet still perform their part of the job, for when the next drops fall the tarmac is cooler, the dust damper, and so dark patches spread, and join, and the tarmac is wet and black. Oh, the hot summer air that is suddenly cooled, making the rain that falls on your face warmer than your face itself, and you lean back to enjoy the feeling it gives you. The leaves on the trees that quiver at the light touch, the faint, almost imperceptible drumming of the rain falling at all levels: on the scarred rock face by the road and the blades of grass in the ditch below, the roof tiles on the other side and the saddle of the bike locked to the fence, the hammock in the garden beyond and the road signs, the curbside gutter and the hoods and roofs of the parked cars.

We stopped at the lights, the rain had just gotten heavier, the drops that were falling now were large, heavy, and profuse. The whole area around the Rundingen intersection had been changed in the course of seconds. The dark sky made all the lights clearer while the rain that fell, and which was even bouncing off the tarmac, blurred them. Cars had their windshield wipers on, pedestrians ran for cover with newspapers spread above their heads or hoods flipped up, unless they had an umbrella with them and could continue as though nothing had happened.

The lights changed, and we headed down towards the bridge, past the old music shop, which had been shut for ages, where Jan Vidar and I had gone on our fixed route every Saturday morning, visiting all the music shops in town, and across Lund Bridge. That was where my first childhood memory originated. I had been walking over the bridge with Grandma, and there I had seen a very old man with a white beard and white hair, he walked with a stick and his back was bowed. I stopped to watch him, Grandma dragged me on. In my father's office there had been a poster up on the wall, and once when I was there with Dad and a neighbor, Ola Jan, who taught at the same school as Dad, Roligheden School, he taught Norwegian too, I pointed to the poster and said I had seen the man in the picture. For it was the selfsame gray-haired, gray-bearded and bowed man. I didn't find it at all surprising that he was on a poster in my father's office, I was four years old and nothing in the world was incomprehensible, everything was connected with everything else. But Dad and Ola Jan laughed. They laughed, and said it was impossible. That's Ibsen, they said. He died nearly a hundred years ago. But I was sure it was the same man, and I said so. They shook their heads, and now Dad was not laughing when I pointed to Ibsen and said I had seen him, he shooed me out.

The water under the bridge was gray and full of rings from the rain lashing the surface. There was also a tinge of green in it though, as always where the water from the Otra met the sea. How often had I stood there watching the currents? Sometimes it flooded forth like a river, eddying round and forming small whirlpools. Sometimes it formed white froth around the pillars.

Now, however, it is calm. Two fishing boats, both with tarpaulin covers open, chugged toward the mouth of the fjord. Two rusty hulks were moored to the quay on the other side, and behind them there was a gleaming white yacht.

Yngve stopped at the lights, which immediately changed to green, and we bore left by the small shopping center with the rooftop parking lot. Up the ramplike, traffic light–regulated concrete driveway, and onto the roof, where fortunately, for this was a national holiday Saturday, there was a space free at the back.

We got out, I leaned my head back and allowed the warm rain to wash my face. Yngve opened the trunk, and we grabbed as many bags as we could carry and took the elevator down to the supermarket on the ground floor. We had decided there was no point trying to get a deposit on the spirits bottles, we would drop them off at the dump, so our load consisted mainly of plastic bottles, and they were not heavy, just awkward.

"You start while I go and get more," Yngve said when we reached the bottle machine.

I nodded. Put bottle after bottle on the conveyor belt, crumpled the bags as they became empty, and placed them in the garbage bin located there for that purpose. I didn't care if anyone saw me and was taken aback by the large number of beer bottles. I was indifferent to everything. The zone that had come into existence when we first left the undertaker's, and that seemed to make everything around me dead, or meaningless, had grown in size and strength. I barely noticed the shop, bathed in its own strong light, with all its glittering, colorful products. I might just as well have been in a swamp somewhere. As a rule I was always aware of how I looked, of how others might think of what they saw, sometimes I was elated and proud, at others downcast and full of self-hatred, but never indifferent, it had never happened that the eyes that saw me meant nothing at all, or that the surroundings I was in were as if expunged. But such was my state now, I was numb, and the numbness prevailed over everything else. The world lay like a shadow around me.

Yngve returned with more bags.

"Shall I take over for a bit?" he said.

"No, I'm fine," I said. "But you could go and do some shopping. Whatever happens we need detergent, rubber gloves, and garbage bags. And at least something to eat."

"There's another load in the car. I'll get that first," he said.

"Okay," I said.

When the last bottle had been delivered and I had been given a receipt, I joined Yngve, who was standing in front of the household detergents section. We took Jif for the bathroom, Jif for the kitchen, Ajax all-purpose cleaner, Ajax window cleaner, Klorin disinfectant, Mr. Muscle for extra difficult stains, an oven cleaner, a special chemical product for sofas, steel wool, sponges, kitchen cloths, floor rags, two buckets and a broom from this aisle, some fresh rissoles from the meat counter, potatoes, and a cauliflower from the vegetable section. Apart from that, things to put on bread, milk, coffee, fruit, a tray of yogurts, and a few packets of biscuits. While we were walking around I was already dying to fill the kitchen with all these new, fresh, shiny, untouched goods.

When we emerged onto the roof it had stopped raining. A pool had formed around the rear wheels of the car, by a slight dip in the concrete. Up here, the air was fresh, it smelled of sea and sky, not of town.

"What do you think happened?" I said when we were on our way down through the dark parking lot. "She says she found him in the chair. Did he just fall asleep?"

"Probably," Yngve said.

"His heart stopped?"

"Yes."

"Mm, perhaps not so surprising the way he must have been living."

"No."

Nothing was said for the rest of the journey to the house. We hauled the shopping bags up to the kitchen, and Grandma, who had been watching us from the window as we arrived, asked where we had been.

"Shopping," Yngve said. "And now we need a bite to eat!"

He started unpacking the groceries. I took a pair of yellow gloves and a roll of trash bags, and went down to the ground floor. The first thing to go would be the mountain of moldy clothes in the washroom. I blew into the gloves, eased them on, and started stuffing clothes into the bags, while breathing through my mouth. Gradually as the bags filled I dragged them out and piled them in front of the two green drums by the garage door. I had almost cleared the whole lot – only the sheets stuck together at the bottom were left – when Yngve shouted that the food was ready.

He had cleared the mass from the counter, and on the table, also cleared, there was a dish of fried rissoles, a bowl of potatoes, one of cauliflower, and a little jug of gravy. The table had been set with Grandma's ancient Sunday best service, which must have spent the last few years in the dining room cupboard, unused.

Grandma didn't want anything. Yngve put half a rissole, a potato, and a small floret of cauliflower on her plate, nevertheless, and managed to persuade her to try some. I was as hungry as a wolf and ate four rissoles.

"Did you put any cream in the gravy?" I said.

"Uh-huh. And some brown goat's cheese."

"That's good," I said. "That's exactly what I needed right now."

After eating, Yngve and I went onto the veranda and had a smoke and a cup of coffee. He reminded me to call Tonje's father, which I had completely forgotten. Or perhaps repressed, this was not a call I was looking forward to making. But I had to, so I went up to the bedroom, fetched my address book from my case and dialed his number from the telephone in the dining room while Yngve cleared the kitchen table.

"Hello, this is Karl Ove," I said when he answered. "I was wondering if you could help me with a medical matter. I don't know if Tonje mentioned it, but my father died yesterday . . ."

"Yes, she did, she called me," he said. "I was sorry to hear that, Karl Ove."

"Mm," I said. "Well, anyway, I'm down in Kristiansand at the moment. In fact, it was my grandmother who found him. She's over eighty, and she seems to be in shock. She hardly speaks, all she does is sit. And I was wondering if there were any sedatives or anything that could help. In fact, she's taking some medication already that probably includes some kind of sedative, but I was thinking . . . Yes, that's it. She's in a bad way."

"Do you know what the medication is?"

"I'm afraid not," I said. "But I can try to find out. Just a moment."

I put the receiver down on the table and went into the kitchen, to the shelf where her medication tray was. Beneath it, I seemed to remember having seen some yellow and some white bits of paper, presumably prescriptions.

Yes, here, but only one.

"Have you seen the packaging?" I asked Yngve. "The boxes? I'm on the phone with Tonje's father."

"There are some in the cupboard next to you," Yngve said.

"What are you looking for?" Grandma asked from her chair.

I didn't want to patronize her, and I had been aware of her eyes on my back while I was rummaging, but at the same time I couldn't take any notice of that.

"I'm talking to a doctor on the telephone," I said to her, as though that was supposed to explain everything. Strangely enough, it seemed to calm her, and I left with the prescription and the packets semiconcealed in my hands.

"Hello?" I said.

"I'm still here," he said.

"I've just found some of the boxes," I said and read out the names on them.

"Aha," he said. "She's already taking a sedative, but I can prescribe one more for you, that won't be a problem. As soon as we hang up I'll phone it through. Is there a pharmacy nearby?"

"Yes, there's one in Lund. It's a suburb."

"I'll care of it. Thanks a lot."

I cradled the phone and went back to the veranda, looked across to the mouth of the fjord where the sky was still overcast but the clouds had a quite different, lighter hue. Tonje's father was a good person and a lovely man. He would never do anything offensive or go too far in any direction, he was respectable and decent, though not stiff or formal, on the contrary, he was often fired up with enthusiasm, a kind of boyishness, and if he didn't go too far it was not because he didn't want to or couldn't, it was because it wasn't in his repertoire, it was simply impossible for him, I had reflected, and I liked him for that, there was something in it, in decent behavior, that I had always sought, and whenever I found it I always liked being close to it, although at the same time I also realized that I liked it and him so much because he reminded me of my father. When I got married at the age of twenty-five it was because I wanted a middle-class, stable, settled existence. That side of me, of course, was counteracted by the fact that we didn't live that kind of life, the middle-class, stable, routine-anchored lifestyle, quite the opposite, and the fact that no one married so young anymore, and therefore it was, if not radical, then at least original.

This being my thinking, and also because I loved her, I had fallen on bended knee one evening, alone on the terrace outside Maputo in Mozambique, beneath a coal-black sky, with the air full of the sound of chirruping grasshoppers and distant drums from one of the villages a few kilometers away, and asked her if she would marry me. She said something I didn't understand. It certainly wasn't yes. What did you say? I queried. Are you asking me to marry you? she said. Are you really? Is that what you're asking? Yes, I said. Yes, she said. I want to marry you. We embraced, both of us with tears in our eyes, and right at that moment the sky rumbled, a deep, powerful clap of thunder, it rippled and Tonje shivered, and then the torrents fell. We laughed, Tonje ran inside for her camera, and when she came out she put one arm around me and took a photo with the other hand outstretched.

We were two children.

Through the window I saw Yngve going into the living room. He walked towards the two chairs, stared at them, moved on and was lost from view.

Even outside there were bottles lying around, some had been blown against the picket fence, others had got stuck under the two faded, rusty garden seats that must have been there since the spring, at the very least.

Yngve reappeared, I couldn't see his facial expression, just his shadow as it passed through the living room and disappeared into the kitchen.

I went down the steps into the garden. There were no houses below, the hillside was too steep, but at the bottom lay the marina, and outside it the relatively small harbor basin. On the eastern side, however, the garden bordered another property. It was as well-tended as this one had once been, and the neatness and control that manifested itself in the trimmed hedges, the manicured grass, and the gaily colored flower beds, made the garden here seem sickly. I stood there for some minutes in tears, then walked around to the front of the house and continued my work in the cellar. When the last item of clothing had been carried out, I sprinkled the Klorin over the floor, using half of the bottle, and then I scrubbed it with the broom before hosing it all down the drain. Then I emptied the rest of the green soap all over it, and scrubbed it again, this time with a cloth. After hosing it down again I supposed that would have to do and went back up to the kitchen. Yngve was washing the inside of a cupboard. The dishwasher was running. The counter was cleared and scrubbed.

"I'm having a break," I said. "Want to join me?"

"Yes, I'll finish this first," Yngve said. "Perhaps you could put some coffee on?"

I did so. Then I suddenly remembered Grandma's prescription. That could not wait.

"I'll just run down to the pharmacy," I said. "Is there anything you want, maybe from the newsstand?"

"No," he said. "Actually, yes, a Coke."

I buttoned up my jacket as I emerged onto the steps. The pile of garbage bags in front of the beautiful wooden 1950s garage door glistened black in the gray summer light. The dark-brown trailer stood with the bar resting on the ground, as if humbled, I thought, a servant who bowed as I appeared. I stuffed my hands in my pockets and walked down the drive, along the pavement to the main road, where the rain had now completely dried up. On the overhanging cliff opposite, however, its many surfaces were still wet and the tufts of grass growing there shone with an intense green against all the dark colors, so very different from when it was dry and dusty, when there were fewer contrasts between colors and everything under the sky seemed indifferent, resistant, open, vast and empty. How many such open, empty days had there been when I used to walk around here? Seeing the black windows in houses, seeing the wind whistling through the countryside, the sun that lit it up, all the blindness and deadness in it? Oh, and this was the time you adored in the town, this was the time you regarded as the best, when the town really came alive. Blue sky, boiling hot sun, dusty streets. A car with a blaring stereo and an open roof, two young men at the front dressed only in trunks, with sunglasses, they are heading for the beach . . . An old woman with a dog, clothed from head to toe, her sunglasses are large, the dog strains at the leash, wanting to sniff a fence. A plane with a long banner behind, there is a match at the stadium the following day. Everything is open, everything is empty, the world is dead, and in the evening restaurants are filled with suntanned, happy men and women wearing brightly colored clothes.

I hated this town.

After a hundred meters down Kuholmsveien I reached the intersection, the pharmacy was a hundred meters away, in the middle of the small suburban center. Behind it was a grass slope, on top of which stood some fifties or sixties blocks of flats. On the other side of the road, quite a way up the slope, were the Elevine Assembly Rooms. Perhaps we should use them for the gathering after the funeral?

The thought that he was not only dead for me, but also for his mother and his brothers, his uncles and aunts, made me weep again. I wasn't concerned about this happening on a sidewalk with people walking past all the time, I hardly saw them; however, I wiped away the tears anyway, mostly for practical reasons, to be able to see where I was going, as a thought suddenly struck me: we shouldn't hold the wake in the Elevine Rooms but in my grandparents' house, which he had ruined.

The thought excited me.

We should clean every damned centimeter of every damned room, throw out everything he had ruined, recover everything that had been left and use it, restore the entire house, and then gather everyone there. He might have ruined everything, but we would restore it. We were decent people. Yngve would say it wasn't possible, and there was no point, but I could insist. I had as much right as he to decide what the funeral would be like. Of course it was possible. All we had to was clean. Clean, clean, clean.

There wasn't a line at the pharmacy, and after I had shown my ID, the white-clad assistant went between the shelves and found the tablets, printed out a label and stuck it on, slipped them in a bag, and referred me to the cash register on the other side to pay.

A vague feeling of some good here, maybe only caused by the slightly cooler air against my skin, made me pause on the steps outside.

Gray, gray sky; gray, gray town.

Glistening car bodies. Bright windows. Wires running from lamp post to lamp post.

No. There was nothing here.

Slowly I began to walk toward the newsstand.

Dad had talked about suicide several times, but always as a generality, as a conversation topic. He thought suicide statistics lied, and that many, perhaps nearly all, car accidents with a single occupant were camouflaged suicides. He mentioned it more than once, that it was common for people to drive a car into the side of a mountain or an oncoming truck to avoid the disgrace of a blatant suicide. It was at this time he and Unni had moved to Sørland after having lived in northern Norway for such a long time, and they were still together. Dad's skin was close to black from all the sun he had absorbed, and he was as fat as a barrel. He lay on a sunbed in the garden behind the house and drank, he sat on the veranda in front of the house and drank, and in the evenings he would be drunk and drifting, he stood in the kitchen in no more than his shorts, frying chops, that was all I ever saw him eat, no potatoes, no vegetables, just blackened chops. During one such evening he said that Jens Bjørneboe, the Kristiansand author, had hung himself by the feet, that was how he had committed suicide, hanging upside down from the rafters. The impossibility of this procedure – for how could he have managed that on his own in the house in Veierland? – never struck either him or me. The most considerate method would be, he said, to go to a hotel, write a letter to the hospital saying where you could be found, and then drink spirits and take pills, lie down on the bed, and go to sleep. It was incredible that I had never interpreted this topic of conversation as anything except conversation, I thought now, as I approached the newsstand behind the bus stop, but that was how it had been. He had imprinted his image of himself in me so firmly that I never saw anything else, even when the person he became diverged so widely from the person he had been, both in terms of physiognomy and character, that any similarities were barely visible any longer, it was always the person he had been with whom I engaged.

I climbed the wooden steps and opened the door to the newsstand, which was empty except for the assistant, took a newspaper from the stand by the till, slid open the glass door of the freezer compartment, took out a Coke, and placed both on the counter.

"*Dagbladet* and a Coke," the assistant said, lifting them for the bar code scanner. "Was there anything else?"

He didn't make eye contact when he said that, he must have seen me crying as I came in.

"No," I said. "That's all."

I pulled a creased note from my pocket and examined it. Fifty kroner. I smoothed it before passing it to him.

"Thank you," he said. He had thick, blond hair on his arms, wore a white Adidas T-shirt, blue jogging pants, probably Adidas as well, and did not look like someone who worked in a newsstand, more like a friend who had taken over for a few minutes. I grabbed my things and turned to leave as two ten-year-old boys came in with their money poised in their hands. Their bikes were thrown carelessly against the steps outside. A stretch of cars in both lanes began to move. I had to call Mom this evening. And Tonje. I walked along the sidewalk, crossed at the narrow pedestrian crossing down from the newsstand and was back in Kuholmsveien. Of course the funeral should be held there. In . . . six days. By then everything ought to be ready. By that time we should have put an advertisement in the newspaper, planned the funeral, invited guests, restored the house, come to terms with the worst aspects of the garden and organized the catering. If we got up early and went to bed late, and did nothing else, it should be feasible. It was just a question of getting Yngve on board. And Gunnar, of course. He might not have much of a say in the funeral, but he did as far as the house was concerned. But, hell, it should be fine. He would understand the reasons.

When I went into the kitchen Yngve was cleaning the stove with steel wool. Grandma was sitting in the chair. There was a splash of what would have to be pee on the floor below it.

"Here's your Coke," I said. "I'll put it on the table."

"Fine," he said.

"What have you got in that bag?" Grandma said, eyeing the paper bag from the pharmacy.

"It's for you," I said. "My father-in-law's a doctor and when I described what had happened here he prescribed you some sedatives. I don't think it's a bad idea. After all you've been through."

I took the square cardboard box from the bag, opened it, and removed the plastic container.

"What does it say?" Grandma said.

"One tablet to be taken once morning and night," I said. "Do you want one now?"

"Yes, if the doctor said so," Grandma said. I passed her the container, and she opened it and shook out a tablet. She looked around the table.

"I'll get you some water," I said.

"No need," she said, placing the tablet on her tongue, raising the cup of cold coffee to her mouth, jerking back and swallowing.

"Ugh," she said.

I put the newspaper on the table and glanced at Yngve, who had resumed scouring.

"It's good you're here, boys," Grandma said. "But don't you want to take a break, Yngve? You don't have to kill yourself working."

"That might not be such a bad idea," Yngve said, and removed the gloves, hung them over the oven handle, wiped his fingers over his T-shirt a few times, and sat down.

"I wonder if I should start on the downstairs bathroom," I said.

"It might be better to stick to the same floor," Yngve said. "Then we'll have some company along the way."

I inferred he didn't want to be alone with Grandma, and nodded.

"I'll take the living room then," I said.

"What hard workers you are," Grandma said. "It's not necessary, you know."

Why did she say that? Was she ashamed of the way the house looked and the fact that she had not managed to keep it in order? Or was it that she didn't want us to leave her alone?

"A bit of cleaning doesn't do any harm," I said.

"No, I suppose it doesn't," she said. Then she glanced at Yngve.

"Have you contacted the undertaker's yet?"

A chill went down my spine.

Had she been so clear-headed the whole time?

Yngve nodded.

"We dropped by this morning. Everything's in hand."

"That's good." She sat quite still, immersed in herself, for a moment, then continued.

"I didn't know if he was dead or not when I saw him. I was on my way to bed, I said good night, and he didn't answer. He was sitting in the chair in there, as he always did. And then he was dead. His face was white."

I met Yngve's eyes.

"You were going to *bed*?" he said.

"Yes, we'd been watching TV all evening," she said. "And he didn't move when I got up to go downstairs."

"Was it dark outside? Do you remember?" Yngve asked.

"Yes, I think so," she said.

I was close to retching.

"But when you called Gunnar," Yngve said, "that was in the morning, wasn't it? Can you remember?"

"It might have been in the morning," she said. "Now that you say so. Yes, it was. I went upstairs and there he was, in the chair. In there."

She got to her feet and left the kitchen. We followed. She stopped halfway into the living room and pointed to the chair in front of the television.

"That's where he was sitting," she said. "That's where he died."

She covered her face with her hands for an instant. Then she walked quickly back to the kitchen.

Nothing could bridge this. It was impossible to deal with. I could fill the bucket with water and start washing, and I could clean the whole damned house, but it would not help an iota, of course it wouldn't, nor would the idea that we should reclaim the house and hold the funeral here, there was nothing I could do that would help, there was nowhere I could escape to, nothing that could protect me from this.

"We need to talk," Yngve said. "Shall we go onto the veranda?" I nodded and followed him down into the second living room and onto the veranda. There was not a breath of air. The sky was as gray as before but a touch lighter above the town. The sound of a car in a low gear rose from the narrow alley below the house. Yngve stood with both hands around the railing staring out to the fjord. I sat down on the faded sun-lounger, got up the next moment, collected some bottles and put them by the wall, cast around for a bag but couldn't see one.

"Are you thinking what I'm thinking?" Yngve asked at length and straightened up.

"I think so," I said.

"Grandma is the only person to have seen him," he said. "She's the only witness. Gunnar didn't see him. She called him in the morning, and he called an ambulance. But he didn't see him."

"No," I said.

"For all we know he might have been alive. How would Grandma know? She finds him on the sofa, he doesn't answer when she speaks to him, she calls Gunnar, and then the ambulance arrives, the house is full of doctors and medical staff, they carry him out on a stretcher and are gone, and that's that. But suppose he wasn't dead? Suppose he was only dead drunk? Or was in some kind of coma?"

"Yes," I said. "When we turned up she said she'd found him in the morning. Now she said she found him in the evening. And that's it."

"And she's going senile. She keeps asking the same questions. How much did she understand when the place was full of paramedics?

"And then there's the medication she's taking," I said.

"Right."

"We have to know," I said. "I mean for certain."

"Oh, shit, what if he was alive," Yngve said.

I was filled with a horror I hadn't felt since I was small. I paced to and fro alongside the railing, stopped and glanced through the window to see if Grandma was there, turned to Yngve, who once again was staring into the horizon, his hands clasped around the railing. Oh, fuck. The logic was as clear as crystal. The only person to see Dad was Grandma, her testimony was the only one we had, and with her being in that confused, devastated state, there was no reason to believe it was accurate. By the time Gunnar appeared it was all over, the ambulance had taken him away, and after that no one spoke to the hospital or the staff who had been here. And they didn't know anything at the undertaker's. Just over twenty-four hours had passed since she found him. He could have been in a hospital during that time.

"Shall we call Gunnar?" I said.

Yngve turned to me.

"He doesn't know any more than we do."

"We'll have to talk to Grandma again," I said. "And then perhaps give the funeral director a call. I suppose he must be able to find out."

"I was thinking the same," Yngve said.

"Will you call?"

"Yes, I'll do that."

We went in. A sudden gust of wind blew the curtains hanging in front of the door into the living room. I closed the door and followed Yngve up into the dining room and kitchen. Down below, the front door slammed. I met Yngve's look. What was going on?

"Who could that be?" Grandma asked.

Was it Dad?

Was he returning?

I was as frightened as I had ever been.

Footfalls sounded on the stairs.

It was Dad, I knew it.

Oh, shit, shit, shit, here he is.

I turned and went into the living room, to the veranda door, ready to step out, run across the lawn and flee the town, never to return.

I forced myself to stand still. Heard the sound of footsteps twisting as they reached the bend in the stairs. Up the last steps, into the living room.

He would be incandescent with fury. What the hell were we doing, messing around with his things like this, coming here and bursting into his life?

I stepped back and watched Gunnar walk past into the kitchen.

Gunnar, of course.

"You two have done quite a bit, I can see," he said from the kitchen.

I joined them. I didn't feel stupid, more relieved, for if Gunnar was here when Dad came it would be easier for us.

They were sitting around the table.

"I thought I could take a load to the dump this afternoon," Gunnar said. "It's on the way to the cabin. Then I'll come back with the trailer tomorrow morning and give you a hand. I think what's in front of the garage will probably be close to a full load."

"So do I," Yngve said.

"We can fill a couple more bags," Gunnar said. "With clothes from his room and whatever else."

He got up.

"Let's get cracking then. Won't take long."

In the living room he stopped and looked around.

"We can take these clothes while we're at it, can't we? That'll save you having to look at this while you're here . . . disgusting . . ."

"I can take them," I said. "Better use gloves, I suppose."

I put on the yellow gloves as I went in and dropped everything on the sofa into a black garbage bag. Closed my eyes as my hands held the dried shit.

"Take the cushions as well," Gunnar said. "And the rug. It doesn't look too good."

I did as he said, carried the load downstairs to the front of the house where I hurled it into the trailer. Yngve brought up the rear, and we threw in the bags that had been left there. Gunnar's car was parked on the other side, that was why we hadn't heard the engine. As soon as the trailer was full, he and Gunnar repeated the shunting forwards and backwards until Gunnar's car was backed up and all we had to do was attach the trailer to the tow bar. After he had driven off and Yngve was parked by the garage again, I sat down on the doorstep. Yngve leaned against the door frame. His brow was shiny with sweat.

"I was sure that was Dad coming up the stairs," he said after a while.

"Me too," I said.

A magpie flew down from the roof on the other side of the garden and glided toward us. It flapped its wings a couple of times and the sound, somehow leatherlike, was unreal.

"He's probably dead," Yngve said. "He is. But we have to be sure. I'll call."

"Damned if I know what to think," I said. "We have only Grandma's word for it. And with all the booze and mess there's been in the house he might well have been no more than dead drunk. In fact, that could easily have been the case. That would be typical, wouldn't it. He comes back while we're nosing through his things. And what she said about . . . how come she didn't find him until the morning? What about the evening? How is it possible to be mixed up about this?"

Yngve looked at me.

"Perhaps he died in the evening. But she thought he was just sleeping. Then she found him in the morning. That's a possibility. This might be tormenting her so much she can't admit it. So she made up the business about him dying in the morning."

"Yes," I said. "That's possible."

"But it doesn't change the main point," Yngve said. "I'll go upstairs and call."

"I'll come with you," I said, and followed him upstairs. While he searched his wallet for the funeral director's business card, I closed the door to the kitchen, where Grandma was sitting, as quietly as possible, and went back down to the second living room. Yngve dialed. I barely had the strength to listen to the conversation, but couldn't resist, either.

"Hello, this is Yngve Knausgaard speaking. We came to see you earlier today, if you remember . . . yes, exactly. Mm, we were wondering . . . well, if you knew where he was. The circumstances have been a bit hazy, you see . . . The only person present when he was taken away was our grandmother. And she's very old and not always compos mentis. So we simply don't know for certain what happened. Would you be able to make a few inquiries for us? . . . Yes . . . Yes . . . Yes. Very good. Thank you . . . Thank you very much. Yes . . . Goodbye."

Yngve looked down at me as he replaced the receiver.

"He was at his cabin. But he's going to make a few calls, and he'll find out. He'll call back later."

"Good," I said.

I went into the kitchen and filled a bucket with hot water, poured in some green soap, found a cloth, went into the living room and stood for a while not quite knowing where to begin. There was no point starting on the floor until we had thrown out the furniture that had to be thrown out, and then in the days to come there would still be some to-ing and fro-ing. Cleaning the window and door frames, doors, sills, bookshelves, chairs and tables was too little and too fiddly, I wanted something that would make a difference. The bathroom and toilet downstairs were best, where every centimeter had to be scrubbed. It was also the logical next step as I had already done the laundry room in the cellar and it was opposite the bathroom. And I could be alone there.

A movement to my left caused me to turn my head. An enormous seagull was standing outside the window and staring in. It banged its beak against the glass, twice. Waited.

"Seen this?" I called to Yngve in the kitchen. "There's a huge seagull here knocking on the glass with its beak."

I heard Grandma getting up.

"We'll have to find it some food," she said.

I went to the doorway. Yngve was emptying the wall cupboards; he had piled up the glasses and plates on the counter beneath. Grandma was standing beside him.

"Have you two seen the seagull?" I said.

"Film or play?" Yngve said.

He smiled.

"He usually comes here," Grandma said. "He wants some food. There. He can have that."

She put the rissole on a small dish, stood over it, bowed and lean, a lock of black hair hanging over her eyes, and quickly cut up the meat that was half-covered with dried gravy.

I followed her into the living room.

"Does it usually come here?" I said.

"Yes," she said. "Almost every day. And has been doing for more than a year now. I always give him something, you know. He's understood that. So he comes here."

"Are you sure it's the same one?"

"Of course I am. I recognize him. And he recognizes me."

When she opened the veranda door the gull hopped onto the floor and went to the dish she put out, completely fearless. I stood in the doorway and watched it grab the bits with its beak and throw its head back when it had a good hold. Grandma stood close by, looking across the town.

"Told you," she said.

The telephone rang. I stepped back to make sure it was Yngve who answered. The conversation was brief. As he hung up Grandma walked past and the seagull hopped onto the railing where it waited a few seconds before spreading its large wings and launching itself. A couple of flaps and it was high above the lawn. I watched it glide down to the harbor. Yngve stopped behind me. I closed the door and faced him.

"He's dead, no question," he said. "He's in the hospital cellar. We can see him on Monday afternoon if we wish. And I've got the telephone number of the doctor who was here."

"Seeing is believing," I said.

"Well, we will now," he said.

Ten minutes later I put a bucket of steaming water, a bottle of Klorin and a bottle of Jif down on the floor by the bath. I shook the garbage bag open, then started clearing everything from the bathroom. First of all, the stuff on the floor: dried-up bits of old soap, sticky shampoo bottles, empty toilet paper rolls, the brown-stained toilet brush, medical packaging – silver paper and plastic, a few loose pills, a sock or two, the odd hair curler. After finishing this, I emptied everything from the wall cupboard, apart from two expensive-looking bottles of perfume. Blades, safety razors, hairpins, several bars of soap, old, desiccated creams and ointments, a hair net, aftershave, deodorants, eyeliners, lipstick, some small cracked powder puffs, not sure what they were used for, but it must have been something to do with make-up, and hair, both short, curly ones and longer, straighter ones, nail scissors, Band-Aids, dental floss, and combs. Once the cupboard was empty, a yellow-brown, thickish residue was left on the shelf that I decided to wash last of all. The wall tiles beside the toilet seat, on which the toilet paper holder was fixed, were covered with light brown stains and the floor beneath was sticky, and these seemed to me to be most in need of attention, so I squirted a line of Jif over the tiles and began to scrub them, methodically, from the ceiling right down to the floor. First, the right-hand wall, then the mirror wall, then the bathtub wall and then finally around the door. I rubbed every single tile clean; it must have taken me an hour and a half. Every so often it went through my mind that this was where my grandfather had collapsed, one autumn night six years ago, and he had called Grandma, who had called for an ambulance and sat here holding his hand until it came. It was the first time it had struck me that everything had been as it always was, right up until that moment. He had been suffering massive internal bleeding over a long period, it transpired when he was in the hospital. Only a few more days and he would have died, there was almost no blood left in him. He must have known something was wrong, but had been reluctant to go to the doctor with it. Then he collapsed on the bathroom floor, close to death, and although they caught him in time at the hospital, and initially he was saved, he was so weakened that he gradually wasted away and, eventually, died.

When I was a boy I had been afraid of this downstairs bathroom. The cistern, which must have been from the 1950s, the type with a metal lever and a small black ball on the side, always got stuck and kept flushing long after anyone had used it, and the noise, issuing from the darkness of the floor no one used, empty, with its clean, blue wall-to-wall carpeting, its wardrobe with neatly hung coats and jackets, its shelf for my grandparents' hats and another for their shoes, which in my imagination represented beings, everything did then, and its yawning staircase to the floor above, always frightened me to such a degree that I had to use all my powers of persuasion to defy my fears and enter the bathroom. I knew no one was there, I knew the flushing water was only flushing water, that the coats were only coats, shoes only shoes, stairs only stairs, but I suppose the certainty only magnified the terror, because I didn't want to be alone with all of it, that was what frightened me, a feeling which the dead non-beings intensified. I could still recognize that way of perceiving the world. The toilet seat looked like a being, and the sink, and the bath, and the garbage bag, that greedy, black stomach on the floor.

This particular evening, however, my unease with it rose again because my grandfather had collapsed here and because Dad had died upstairs in the living room yesterday, so the deadness of these non-beings combined with the deadness of the two of them, of my father and his father.

So how could I keep this feeling at arm's length?

Oh, all I had to do was clean. Scour and scrub and rub and wipe. See how each tile became clean and shiny. Imagine that all that had been destroyed here would be restored. All. Everything. And that I would never, never ever ever, end up where he had ended up.

After I had washed the walls and floor, I poured the water down the toilet, pulled off the yellow gloves and turned them inside out and hung them over the rim of the empty red bucket while making a mental note that I had to buy a toilet brush as soon as possible. Unless there was one in the other bathroom, that is. I looked. Yes, there was. I would have to use that for now, whatever its state, and then buy another one on Monday. On my way across the floor to the stairs I stopped. The door to Grandma's room was ajar, and for some reason I went over, opened it, and peeped in.

Oh no.

There were no sheets on her bed, she slept directly on the hard, piss-permeated mattress. There was a kind of commode beside her bed with a bucket underneath. Clothes were strewn everywhere. A row of withered plants in the window. The stench of ammonia stung my nostrils.

What a pile of shit this was. Shit, shit, shit, fuck, cunt.

I left the door as I had found it, and trudged slowly up the stairs to the first floor. In places the banister was almost black with dirt. I put my hand on it and could feel it was sticky. On the landing I heard the sounds of the TV. When I entered the living room, Grandma was watching it from the chair in the middle. The TV2 news was on. So the time must have been somewhere between half past six and seven.

How could she sit there next to the chair in which he had died?

My stomach contracted, the tears that flowed seemed to have erupted and my grimaces, which I was unable to control, were light years from any vomiting reflex, and this sensation of disequilibrium and asymmetry overwhelmed me and created panic, it was as if I were being torn apart. If I had been able to, I would have fallen to my knees, clasped my hands and cried to God, shouted, but I couldn't, there was no mercy in this, the worst had already happened, it was over.

When I went into the kitchen it was empty. All the cupboards were washed, and although there was a lot left to do – the walls, the floor, the drawers, the table, and the chairs – the kitchen seemed airier. On the counter there was a 1.5 liter plastic bottle of beer. Tiny droplets of condensation covered the label. Beside it was a slab of brown cheese with a slicer on top, a yellow cheese and a packet of margarine with a butter knife angled into it, the shaft resting against the edge. The chopping board had been pulled out, on it there was a whole grain loaf, half out of its red-and-white paper bag. In front, a bread knife, a crust, crumbs.

I took a plastic bag from the lowest drawer, emptied the two ashtrays on the table into it, tied it up, and dropped it into the half-full, black garbage bag in the corner, found a cloth, cleaned the tobacco and crumbs off the table, placed the tobacco pouches and her roller machine on the box of cigarette tubes at one end of the table, under the windowsill, opened the window and put it on the latch. Then I went to look for Yngve. He was sitting on the veranda, as I had thought. He had a glass of beer in one hand, a cigarette in the other.

"Want some?" he said as I went out. "There's a bottle in the kitchen."

"No, thanks," I said. "Not after what's happened here. I'll never drink beer from plastic bottles again."

He looked at me and smiled.

"You're so sensitive," he said. "The bottle was unopened. It was in the fridge. It isn't as if he'd been drinking from it."

I lit a cigarette and leaned back against the railings.

"What shall we do about the garden?" I asked.

Yngve shrugged.

"We can't sort out everything here."

"I want to," I said.

"Really?"

"Yes."

Now was the moment to tell him about my idea. But I couldn't bring myself to do it. I knew that Yngve would come up with counterarguments and in the disagreement that would ensue there were things I did not want to see or experience. Oh, they were trivial, but had my life ever consisted of anything else? When we were children I admired Yngve, the way that younger brothers admire their older brothers, there was no one I would rather receive acknowledgment from, and although he was a bit too old for our paths to cross when we were out, we stuck together when we were at home. Not on an equal footing, of course, it was generally his wishes that held sway, but still we were close. Also because we faced a common foe, Dad, that is.

I couldn't remember that many specific incidents from our childhood, but the few that stood out were eloquent. I recalled laughing until our sides split at little things, such as the time we went camping in England in 1976, an unusually hot summer, and one evening we were walking up a hill near the campsite, and a car passed us, and Yngve said that the two people in it were kissing, which I heard as "pissing," and we were doubled up with laughter for several minutes, laughter which would reignite at the slightest cause for the rest of the evening.

If there is anything I miss from my childhood it has to be that, laughing uncontrollably with my brother over some tiny stupidity. The time we played soccer for an entire evening on the field by the tent on that same trip, with two English boys, Yngve with his Leeds cap, me with my Liverpool cap, the sun going down over the countryside, the darkness growing around us, the low voices from the tents nearby, me unable to understand a word they said, Yngve proud to be able to translate. The swimming pool we went to one morning before setting off, where I, a nonswimmer, still managed to paddle to the deep end by holding onto a plastic ball, which suddenly slipped from my grasp, me sinking in a pool with no one else around, Yngve calling for help, a young man running over and dragging me to the surface, my first thought, after regurgitating a little chlorinated water, was that Mom and Dad must not find out about what had happened. The days from which these incidents are drawn were countless, the bonds they created between us indestructible. The fact that he could be more malicious to me than anyone else changed nothing, it was part and parcel of it, and in the context we lived, the hatred I felt for him was no more than a brook is to an ocean, a lamp to the night. He knew exactly what to say to make me so furious that I completely lost control. He sat there, utterly calm with that teasing smile of his, poking fun at me until anger had me in its grip and I could no longer see clearly, I literally saw red and no longer knew what I was doing. I could throw the cup I was holding at him, with all my strength, or a slice of bread, if that was in my hand, or an orange, if I didn't attack him with fists flying, blinded by tears and red-eyed fury while he stayed in control and held my wrists and said *there, there, little baby, are you angry now, poor little* . . . He also knew about all the things that frightened me, so when Mom was on night duty and Dad was at a council meeting and there was a repeat showing of *Stowaway*, a sci-fi film, which was usually on late at night so that people like me wouldn't be watching, it was the easiest thing in the world for him to switch off all the lights in the house, lock the front door, turn to me and say *I am not Yngve. I am a stowaway* while I screamed with terror and begged him to say he was Yngve, *say it, say it, you are Yngve, I know you are, Yngve, Yngve, you're not a stowaway, you're Yngve* . . . He also knew I was frightened of the sound the pipes made when you turned on the hot water, a shrill screech that quickly changed to knocking, impossible for me to cope with, I had to take to my heels, so we had a deal whereby he wouldn't pull the plug after washing in the morning but leave the water in the sink for me. Accordingly, every morning for perhaps six months I washed my face and hands in Yngve's dirty water.

When he was seventeen and left home our relationship changed, of course. Without our daily contact, my image of him, and his life, grew, especially the one he had in Bergen, where eventually he went to study. I wanted to live the way he did.

During my first autumn at gymnas I visited him at the Alrek Hall of Residence, where he had a room. Getting off the airport bus in the city center, I headed straight for a kiosk and bought a packet of Prince cigarettes and a lighter. I had never smoked before, but had long planned that I would, and alone in Bergen I had imagined an opportunity would present itself. So there I was, beneath the green spire of St. Johannes' Church, with Bergen's main square in front of me, Torgallmenningen, packed with people, cars, and gleaming glass. The sky was blue, my backpack was beside me on the tarmac, a cigarette in the corner of my mouth, and as I lit it with the yellow lighter cupped in my hand against the wind, I had a strong, almost overwhelming, sense of freedom. I was alone, I could do what I wanted, all of life lay open at my feet. I spluttered, of course the smoke burned my throat, but I managed tolerably well, the feeling of freedom did not diminish, and after finishing the cigarette I put the red-and-white packet in my jacket pocket, slung the backpack on my back, and went to meet Yngve. At the Cathedral School in Kristiansand nothing was mine, but Yngve was mine, what was his was mine too, so I was not only happy but also proud when, a few hours later, I was on my knees in his room, where the sunlight fell through the pollution-matt windows, flicking through the record collection in the three wine cases by the wall. We went out that night, with three girls he knew, and I borrowed his deodorant, Old Spice, and his hair gel, and before we left, standing in front of the hall mirror, he folded up the sleeves of the black-and-white checked shirt I was wearing, which was like the one The Edge in U2 wore in many pictures, and adjusted the lapels of the suit jacket. We met the girls in one of their flats, they found it very funny that I was only sixteen, and thought I should be holding hands with one of them as we walked past the doorman, which I also did the first time I had been to a place where you had to be eighteen to gain admittance. The following day we went to Café Opera and Café Galleri, where we met Mom as well. She was living with her Aunt Johanna in Søndre Skogveien, whose flat Yngve took over later, and that was where I visited him when I was next in Bergen. Once, the year after, I went with a tape recorder to interview the American band Wall of Voodoo who were playing at a club, Hulen, that night. I didn't have an appointment, I went in during the sound check with my press card, and we stood by the stage entrance waiting for them, I was wearing a white shirt and a black boot-lace tie with a large shiny eagle, black pants, and boots. But when the band appeared, suddenly I didn't have the nerve to speak to them, they looked intimidating, a gang of thirty-year-old dopeheads from Los Angeles, and it was Yngve who saved the day. *Hey, mister!* he called, and the bass player turned and came over, and Yngve said, *This is my little brother, he has come all the way from Kristiansand, down south, to do an interview with Wall of Voodoo. Is that okay with you?*

Nice tie! said the bass player, whom I immediately followed into the band's room. He was dressed all in black, had huge tattoos on his arms, long, black hair and cowboy boots, and was extremely friendly; he gave me a beer and answered in great detail all the school newspaper-type questions I had written down. Another time in Bergen, I interviewed Blaine Reininger, who had just left Tuxedomoon, on one of the soft leather sofas at Café Galleri. I never entertained a moment's doubt that this was where I would move, to this metropolis with all its cafés, concert venues, and record shops, after I finished school.

After the Wall of Voodoo gig we sat in Hulen and decided to start up a band when I came: Yngve's friend Pål could play bass, Yngve guitar, and I could play drums. We would find a singer eventually. Yngve would write the music, I would write the words, and one day, we told each other that night, we would play here, at Hulen. Going to Bergen, then, for me was like stepping into the future. I left my current life and spent some days in my next life before having to return. In Kristiansand I was alone and had to fight for everything; in Bergen I was with Yngve and whatever he had, also belonged to me. Not only clubs and cafés, shops and parks, reading rooms and auditoria, but also all of his friends who not only knew who I was when I met them but what I was doing, I had my own music program on local radio and reviewed records and concerts in *Fædrelandsvennen*, and after these meetings Yngve always told me what had been said about me, it was usually girls who had something to say, that I was good-looking or mature for my age and so on, but boys did too, one comment particularly stuck in my mind, Arvid's, that I looked like the young man in Visconti's *Death in Venice*. I was someone for them, and that was thanks to Yngve. He took me with him to Vindilhytta, a cabin where all his friends gathered every New Year's Eve, and one summer when I was selling cassettes on the street in Arendal and financially flush, we went out almost every night, and on one of the nights, I can remember, Yngve was surprised but also proud that I could drink five bottles of wine and still more or less behave. The summer ended with me getting together with the sister of Yngve's girlfriend. Yngve took loads of photos of me with his Nikon SLR, all in black and white, all dreadfully posey, and once we went together to a photographer's, the idea was to give each of our grandparents a photo of us for Christmas, and we did do that, but the photo also turned up in the photographer's display case in the foyer of the Kristiansand Cinema, where anyone who wished could see us posing in our eighties clothes complete with eighties hairstyles. Yngve in a light-blue shirt with leather bracelets around one wrist, long hair down his neck, short on top, me with my black-and-white plaid shirt, my black jacket with rolled-up sleeves, my nail belt and my black trousers, with hair longer at the back and even shorter on top than Yngve's, and with a cross hanging from one ear. I went to the cinema a lot in those days, mostly with Jan Vidar or some others from Tveit, and when I saw the photograph exhibited there, in the illuminated display case, I could never quite associate it with me, that is, with the life I was living in Kristiansand, which had a certain external, objective quality to it, in the sense that it was tied to particular places, such as school, the sports hall, the town center, and to particular people, my friends, classmates, teammates, while the photograph was connected in quite a different way with something intimate and hidden, first and foremost the core family, but also the person I would become once I got away from here. If Yngve ever talked about me to his friends I never mentioned him to mine.

It was confusing and annoying that this internal space should be exhibited for external appraisal. But apart from a couple of isolated comments no one gave it a second thought, since I was not someone to be given a second thought.

When at last I left school in 1987, for some reason, I didn't move to Bergen after all, instead I went to a little village on an island in northern Norway, where I worked as a teacher for a year. The plan was that I would write my novel in the evenings, and with the money I saved travel in Europe for a year; I bought a book which described all sorts of possible and impossible short-term jobs in European countries and that was what I had imagined, traveling from town to town, country to country, working a bit, writing a bit, and living a free and independent life, but then I was accepted by the new Academy of Creative Writing in Hordaland for some work I had done that year and, immensely flattered at this acceptance, I changed all my plans and headed, nineteen years old, for Bergen where, despite all my dreams and notions of an itinerant life in the world outside, I stayed for the next nine years.

And it started well. The sun was shining as I alighted from the airport bus in the fish market, and Yngve, who was working as a receptionist at Hotel Orion on weekends and over the holidays, was in a good mood when I entered the reception area. He had to work another half an hour and then we could buy some shrimp and beer and celebrate the beginning of my new life. We sat on the steps in front of his flat drinking beer with music by the Undertones belting out to us from the stereo in the sitting room. By the time night fell we were already a bit drunk, we ordered a taxi and went to Ola's, one of Yngve's friends, had a bit more to drink, then went on to Café Opera where we remained until closing time at a table to which a stream of people kept coming. This is my little brother, Karl Ove, Yngve said again and again, he's moved to Bergen to study at the Academy of Creative Writing. He's going to be a writer. Yngve had organized a studio for me in Sandviken – the girl who lived there was going to South America for a year – but until it became free I would be sleeping on a sofa at his place. Where he told me off for minor transgressions, as he always had on the few occasions we had lived together for more than a few days, right from his Alrek days when I got into hot water for slicing the cheese too thickly or not putting records back where I had found them, and it was the same level of reprimand this time: I didn't dry the floor well enough after I had showered, I dropped crumbs on the floor while eating, I wasn't careful enough with the stylus when putting on a record, until, standing by his car and being told how I had banged the car door too hard the last time I got in, I suddenly had had enough. Furious, I shouted that he should stop telling me what to do. And he did, after that he never corrected me again. But the balance in the relationship stayed the same, it was his world I had stepped into, and in it I was, and would remain, the younger brother. Life at the academy was complicated, and I didn't make any friends there, partly because everyone was older than me, partly because I simply could not find anything in common with them, so that meant I was frequently running after Yngve's heels, calling him up and asking if he had anything happening over the weekend, and of course he invariably did, could I tag along? I could. And after wandering around town for a whole Sunday or lying in bed at home reading, the temptation to drop by in the evening, even if I told myself I shouldn't, that I had to make my own life, was too great for me to resist, so often I wound up on the sofa in front of his television.

Eventually he moved into a collective, and for me that was bad news because then my dependence on him became so visible; hardly a day passed without my appearing at their door, and when he wasn't at home I sat in their living room, either dutifully entertained by one of the collective's members, or alone, leafing through a music magazine or a newspaper, like a poster child of a failed human being. I needed Yngve, but Yngve didn't need me. That was how it was. I might be able to chat with one of his friends when he was present, there was a framework, but on my own? Go up to one of them on my own? That would just seem weird and forced and obtrusive, that was not on. And in fact my behavior was not very good, to put it mildly, I was getting drunk too often, and I did not flinch from harassing someone if I got the idea into my head. Usually something to do with their appearance or silly, small mannerisms that I might have observed.

The novel I wrote while studying at the academy was turned down, I started at the university, I studied literary science half-heartedly, couldn't write any longer, and all that was left of my writing career was the desire. That was strong, but how many people at university did not nurture the same desires? We played at Hulen with our band, Kafkatrakterne, we played at Garage, some of our songs were played on the radio, we had a couple of fine reviews in music papers, and that was good; however, I knew all the while that the sole reason I was there was because I was Yngve's brother, I was a terrible drummer. When I was twenty-four I had a flash of insight: that this was in fact my life, this is exactly what it looked like and presumably always would. That one's studies, this fabled and much-talked about period in a life, on which one always looked back with pleasure, were for me no more than a series of dismal, lonely, and imperfect days. That I had not seen this before was due to the constant hope I carried around inside me, all the ridiculous dreams with which a twenty-year-old can be burdened, about women and love, about friends and happiness, about hidden talents and sudden breakthroughs. But when I was twenty-four I saw life as it was. And it was okay, I had my small pleasures too, it wasn't that, and I could endure any amount of loneliness and humiliation, I was a bottomless pit, just bring it on, there were days when I could think, I receive, I am a well, I am the well of the failed, the wretched, the pitiful, the pathetic, the embarrassing, the cheerless, and the ignominious. Come on! Piss on me! Shit on me too if you want! I receive! I endure! I am endurance itself! I have never been in any doubt that this is what girls I have tried my luck with have seen in my eyes. Too much desire, too little hope. Meanwhile Yngve, who had had his friends all this time, his studies, his work, and his band, not to mention his girlfriends, got everything he wanted.

What did he have that I did not? How come he was always lucky while the girls I spoke to seemed either horrified or scornful? Whatever the reason, I stayed close to him. The only good friend I had during these years was Espen, who started at the academy the year after me, and whom I met through the literature course – he asked me to look at some poems he had written. I knew nothing about poetry, but I looked at them, gave him some baloney he didn't see through, and then little by little we became friends. Espen was the type who read Beckett at school, listened to jazz, and played chess, who had long hair and a somewhat nervous and anxious disposition. He was closed to gatherings of more than two people, but intellectually open, and he made his debut with a collection of poems a year after we had met, not without some jealousy from my side. Yngve and Espen represented two sides of my life, and of course they did not get along.

Espen probably didn't know this himself, since I always pretended to know most things, but he pulled me up into the world of advanced literature, where you wrote essays about a line of Dante, where nothing could be made complex enough, where art dealt with the supreme, not in a high-flown sense because it was the modernist canon with which we were engaged, but in the sense of the ungraspable, which was best illustrated by Blanchot's description of Orpheus's gaze, the night of the night, the negation of the negation, which of course was in some way above the trivial and in many ways wretched lives we lived, but what I learned was that also our ludicrously inconsequential lives, in which we could not attain anything of what we wanted, nothing, in which everything was beyond our abilities and power, had a part in this world, and thus also in the supreme, for books existed, you only had to read them, no one but myself could exclude me from them. You just had to reach up.

Modernist literature with all its vast apparatus was an instrument, a form of perception, and once absorbed, the insights it brought could be rejected without its essence being lost, even the form endured, and it could then be applied to your own life, your own fascinations, which could then suddenly appear in a completely new and significant light. Espen took that path, and I followed him, like a brainless puppy, it was true, but I did follow him. I leafed through Adorno, read some pages of Benjamin, sat bowed over Blanchot for a few days, had a look at Derrida and Foucault, had a go at Kristeva, Lacan, Deleuze, while poems by Ekelöf, Björling, Pound, Mallarmé, Rilke, Trakl, Ashbery, Mandelstam, Lunden, Thomsen, and Hauge floated around, on which I never spent more than a few minutes, I read them as prose, like a book by MacLean or Bagley, and learned nothing, understood nothing, but just having contact with them, having their books in the bookcase, led to a shifting of consciousness, just knowing they existed was an enrichment, and if they didn't furnish me with insights I became all the richer for intuitions and feelings.

Now this wasn't really anything to beat the drums with in an exam or during a discussion, but that wasn't what I, the king of approximation, was after. I was after enrichment. And what enriched me while reading Adorno, for example, lay not in what I read but in the perception of myself while I was reading. I was someone who read Adorno! And in this heavy, intricate, detailed, precise language whose aim was to elevate thought ever higher, and where every period was set like a mountaineer's cleat, there was something else, this particular approach to the mood of reality, the shadow of these sentences that could evoke in me a vague desire to use the language with this particular mood on something real, on something living. Not on an argument, but on a lynx, for example, or on a blackbird or a cement mixer. For it was not the case that language cloaked reality in its moods, but vice versa, reality arose from them.

I didn't articulate that for myself, it didn't exist as in thought, barely even as inklings, more as a kind of hazy lure. I kept this entire side of me hidden from Yngve, first of all because he wasn't interested, and didn't believe in it either, he had taken Media Studies, and was in full agreement with the tenet of his subject that objective quality did not exist, that all judgments were relative, and that of course what was popular was just as good as what was not popular, but soon this difference, and whatever I held back, was charged with much more for me, it began to be about us as people, about the distance between Yngve and me actually being large, and I didn't want that, I didn't want that for anything in the world, and I systematically played it down. If I suffered a defeat, if I failed at something, if I had misunderstood something vital, I never hesitated to tell him, for anything that could drag me down in his eyes was good, while on those occasions I achieved something of significance, I often opted not to tell him.

In itself, this was perhaps not a serious matter, but when the consciousness of it reared its head, it became worse because I thought about it when we were together, and I no longer behaved in a natural, spontaneous manner, no longer chatted away as I had always done with him but started brooding, calculating, and reflecting. It was the same with Espen, except in reverse, I toned down the easygoing, entertainment-focused lifestyle. At the same time I had a girlfriend with whom I had never been in love, not really, which of course she must have known herself. We had been together for four years. So there I was, playing roles, pretending this and pretending that. And as if that were not enough, I was working at an institution for the mentally impaired as well, and not content with fawning on the other staff there, who were trained nurses, I was also joining them at their parties, which were held in the part of town that students shunned, the down-homey bars with pianists and singalongs, to tune into their opinions and attitudes and perceptions. The few I had of my own I repudiated or kept to myself. There was consequently something furtive and dubious about my character, nothing of the solid, pure traits which I encountered in some people during this period, people whom I therefore admired. Yngve was too close for me to be able to judge in this way, for thoughts, whatever good one can say about them, have a great weakness, namely, that they are dependent on a certain distance for effect. Everything inside that distance is subject to emotions. It was because of my emotions that I was starting to hold things back. He wasn't allowed to make mistakes. My mother could, and I wasn't bothered, my father and my friends could, and of course I could, I didn't give a shit, but Yngve was not allowed to fail, he was not allowed to make a fool of himself, he was not allowed to show weakness. When, however, he did, and I was watching, shame-filled, the shame on his behalf still was not the crux; the crux was that he mustn't notice, he mustn't find out that I harbored such emotions, and the evasive looks in such circumstances, emerged to conceal feelings rather than show them, must have been conspicuous, albeit not easy to interpret. If he said something stupid or glib it did not change my attitude to him, I didn't judge him differently for that reason, so what went on inside me was based exclusively on the possibility that *he* might believe I was ashamed of him.

Such as the time we were sitting in Garage late one night discussing the journal we had long been planning to launch. We were surrounded by people who could write and take photographs, who were all as au fait with the Liverpool team of the 1982–83 season as they were with the members of the Frankfurt school, with English groups as Norwegian writers, with German expressionist films as American TV series. Starting a news-oriented magazine that took this broad range of interests seriously – soccer, music, literature, film, philosophy, and art – had long seemed a good idea. That night we were with Ingar Myking, who was the editor of the student newspaper *Studvest*, and Hans Mjelva, who aside from singing in our band, had been Ingar's predecessor. When Yngve started talking about the magazine I suddenly heard what he was saying with Ingar's and Hans's ears. It sounded flat and unsubtle, and I looked down at the table. Yngve glanced at me several times as he was speaking. Should I say what I was thinking, correct him, in other words? Or should I turn a blind eye, deny myself, and support what he was saying? Then Ingar and Hans would believe I stood where he did on this. I didn't want that either. So I opted for a compromise and said nothing, in an attempt to let the silence affirm Yngve and the assessment of his opinions, which is what I assumed Ingar and Hans were doing.

I was often this cowardly, I didn't want to upset anyone, and held back what I thought, but this time the circumstances were heightened both because it concerned Yngve, who I wanted to keep above me, where he belonged, and because there was some vanity involved, that is, listeners, and I couldn't talk my way out of that.

Most of what Yngve and I did together was on his terms, and most of what I did alone, such as reading and writing, I kept to myself. But every now and then these two worlds met, it was inevitable, for Yngve was also keen on literature although he wasn't interested in the same things as I was. When I had to interview the writer Kjartan Fløgstad for a student magazine, for example, Yngve suggested we do it together, and I agreed without a murmur. Fløgstad, with his mixture of down-to-earth talk and intellectualism, his theories about all things high and low, his undogmatic and independent, almost aristocratic, left-wing views, and, not least, his wordplay, was Yngve's favorite author. Yngve was himself infamous for his wordplay and corny puns, and his core intellectual claim was the notion that a work of art's value was created in the receiver, and not in itself, and that authentic artistic expression was just as much a question of form as inauthentic artistic expression. For me Fløgstad was the great Norwegian writer. The interview with him had been arranged by the tiny Nynorsk student newspaper TAL, for whom I had previously interviewed the poet Olav H. Hauge and the prose writer Karin Moe. I did the Hauge interview with Espen, and Ingve's friend Asbjørn, who took the photos, so it was only natural for Yngve to be in on this one. The interview with Hauge had gone well, after a terrible start it must be said, because I hadn't told him there would be three of us, so as our car swung into his drive he had been expecting one person and refused to let us into his house. *They came in force*, he said in the doorway in sculpted West Coast dialect, and I suddenly felt like a happy, frivolous, stupid, overeager, impulsive, red-cheeked Eastern Norwegian. Hauge was a permanent resident of the intellectual planet, he didn't budge for anything, I was a tourist, and had brought my friends along to examine the phenomenon more closely. That was my feeling, and judging by his severe, almost hostile, expression, apparently also his. But, in the end, he said *Well, you'd better come in*, and lumbered into the living room ahead of us, where we put down our bags and photographic equipment. Asbjørn removed his camera and lifted it to the light, Espen and I took out our notes, Hauge sat on a bench by the wall inspecting the floor. *Perhaps you could stand by that window*, Asbjørn said, *the light's good there. Then we can take a few pictures.* Hauge looked up at him, with his gray bangs hanging over his forehead. *You're not taking any goddamn pictures here,* he said. *All right,* said Asbjørn. *My apologies.* He withdrew to the side and discreetly placed his camera in its bag. Espen was sitting beside me flicking through some notes and holding a pen in one hand. I knew him, and it was clear that it was hardly likely to be concentration that was impelling him to read them through now. An eternity passed without anyone saying anything. Espen looked at me. Then looked at Hauge. *I have a question,* he said. *Would it be all right if I asked you?* Hauge nodded, and pushed back his drooping curls with a movement that was surprisingly light and feminine compared with his otherwise masculine impassivity and silence. Espen started on his question, he read from his notepad, it was long and intricate and contained a brief analysis of a poem. When he had finished, Hauge said, without looking up, that he wasn't going to talk about his poems.

I had read Espen's questions, which all focused closely on Hauge's poems, and if Hauge was not of a mind to talk about his poems, they were all useless. The ensuing silence was protracted. Now Espen was as dark and brooding as Hauge. They were poets, I thought, that is how they are. Compared to their heavy gloom I felt like a lightweight, a dilettante with no understanding of anything, just drifting across the surface, watching soccer, who recognized the names of a few philosophers and liked pop music of the simplest variety. One of the songs I had written for our band, which was the closest I got to poetry, was called "Du duver så deilig" (You Sway so Sweetly). I had to step into the breach because it was obvious that Espen was not going to say any more in the course of this interview, so I began to ask questions about the municipality of Jølster where my mother lived, because the artist Astrup came from there, and Hauge had been interested in him, he had even written a poem about him. There was obviously an elective affinity between them. But he didn't want to speak about this. Instead he talked about a trip he'd made ages ago, some time in the sixties, or so it sounded, and all the names he mentioned, while contemplating the floor, he mentioned in a confidential way as if everyone knew them. We had never heard of them, and this all seemed, if not cryptic, then at least to have no special meaning other than a private one. I asked a question about translation, Asbjørn another, they were answered in the same way, in immensely casual tones, as though he were simply sitting there and talking to himself. Or to the floor, rather. As an interview it was a disaster. But then, after perhaps an hour of this procedure, another car turned into the drive. It was NRK Hordaland, local Radio & TV, they wanted Hauge to read a few poems. They started, but they had forgotten a cable, and had to return for it, and when they resumed, Hauge changed, he was suddenly friendly with us, made jokes and smiled, now it was us against NRK, and the ice was broken, for when NRK had finished recording and had gone on their way his friendliness continued, he was present in quite a different way, and open. His wife came in with a freshly made apple pie for us, and after we had eaten he showed us around the house, took us up to the library on the first floor where he also worked, I saw a notebook on the desk with "Diary" written on the cover, and there he pulled books off the shelves and talked about them, among others one by Julia Kristeva, I remember, because I thought, *you definitely haven't read that one*, Hauge had never been to university, and if you have, you definitely didn't understand it, and then, as we went downstairs, he said something enormously charged and meaningful about death, the tone was resigned and laconic, but not without irony, and I thought I will have to remember this, this is important, I'll have to remember this for the rest of my life, but by the time we were in the car on our way home along the Hardanger fjord I had forgotten. He was walking a few steps behind me, Espen and Asbjørn were already out, it was photo time. While Hauge sat on the stone bench with legs crossed, gazing into the distance, and Asbjørn was taking shots from several angles, crouching one second, standing the next, Espen and I were smoking a few meters away. It was a wonderful autumn day, cold and bright; as we drove inland from Bergen in the morning, frozen mist was lying over the fjord. The trees on the mountainsides were displaying red and yellow leaves, the fjord below was like a millpond, the waterfalls immense and white. I was happy, the interview was over, and it had gone well, but I was also agitated, something about Hauge filled me with unease. Something that would not rest, and I was unsure of the source. He was an old man, wore old man's clothes, a flannel shirt and old man's trousers, slippers and a hat, and had an old man's gait, yet there was nothing old mannish about him, such as there was with my grandfather or my father's uncle, Alf; on the contrary, when he suddenly opened up to us and wanted to show us things, it was in a kind of artless, childlike way, infinitely friendly, but also infinitely vulnerable, the way a boy without friends might behave when someone showed some interest in him, one might imagine, unthinkable in the case of my grandfather or Alf, it must have been at least sixty years since they had opened up to anyone like that, if indeed they ever had. But no, Hauge hadn't really opened himself to us, it was more as if it had been his natural self which his rejection had been protecting when we arrived. I saw something I didn't want to see because the person showing us was unaware of how it looked. He was more than eighty years old, but nothing in him had died or calcified, which actually makes life far too painful to live, that's what I think now. At the time it just made me uneasy.

"Can we do some by the apple trees as well?" Asbjørn said.

Hauge nodded, got up, and followed Asbjørn to the trees. I bent down and stubbed out my cigarette on the ground, cast around for a place to put it as I straightened up, I couldn't just flick it onto his drive, but couldn't see anywhere suitable so put it in my pocket.

Surrounded by mountains on all sides, it felt as if we were standing in an enormous vault. There was still a warm, gentle waft to the air, as there often is in autumnal Vestland.

"Do you think we can ask him if he would read some poems for us?" Espen said.

"If you dare," I said, and noticed that Asbjørn was smiling. If Hauge was a poet for Espen, he was a legend for Asbjørn, and now he was standing there photographing him with permission to take all the time he needed. Once we had finished we went into the living room to fetch our things. I took out the book I had bought in a shop on the way, Hauge's collected poems, and asked him if he would write a line for my mother in it.

"What's her name?" he said.

"Sissel," I said.

"Anything else?"

"Hatløy. Sissel Hatløy."

"*To Sissel Hatløy with best wishes from Olav H. Hauge*," he wrote, and passed it back.

"Thank you," I said.

He escorted us to the door as we left. Espen had his back to him, getting the book ready, then suddenly turned with a face shining with embarrassment and hope.

"Would you mind reading us a poem?"

"Not at all," Hauge said. "Which one would you like to hear?"

"Perhaps the one about the cat?" Esben said. "On the drive? That would be fitting, ha ha ha."

"Let me see," Hauge said. "There it is."

And he read.

The cat is sitting
out front
when you come.
Talk a bit with the cat.
He is the most sensitive one here.

Everyone was smiling, even Hauge.

"That was a short poem," he said. "Would you like to hear another one?"

"We'd love to!" Espen said.

He thumbed through, then began to read.

TIME TO GATHER IN

These mild days of sun in September.
Time to gather in. There are still tufts
of cranberries in the wood, the rose hips redden

along the stone dykes, nuts fall at a touch,
and clumps of blackberries gleam in thickets,
thrushes poke about for the last red currants
and the wasp sucks away at the sweet plums.
In the evenings I set my ladder aside and hang
up my basket in the shed. Meager glaciers
already have a thin covering of new snow.
Lying in bed, I hear the throb of the brisling fishers
on their way out. All night, I know, they'll glide
with staring searchlights up and down the fjord.

Standing there on the drive and looking down at the ground while he read, I was thinking that this is a great and privileged moment, but not even this thought had time to settle, for the moment occupied by the poem, which its originator read in its place of origin, was so much greater than us, it belonged to infinity, and how could we, so young and no brighter than three sparrows, receive it? We could not, and at any rate, I squirmed as he read. It was almost more than I could endure. A joke would have been apposite, at least to lend the everyday life in which we were trapped some kind of form. Oh, the beauty of it, how to deal with it? How to meet it?

Hauge raised his hand in salute as we departed, and he had already gone into the house by the time Asbjørn started the car and was on the road. I felt the way you do after a whole day in the summer sun, worn out and sluggish, despite the fact that all you have done is lie on a rock somewhere with your eyes closed. Asbjørn stopped by a café to pick up his girlfriend, Kari, who had been waiting there while we interviewed Hauge. After we had discussed what had happened for a few minutes, the car went quiet, we sat in silence peering out of the windows, at the shadows lengthening, the colors deepening, the wind coming off the fjord and tousling the hair of those outdoors, the newspaper pennants outside the kiosks flapping, children on their bicycles, those eternal village children on their bicycles. I began to write up the interview from the recording as soon as I came home because I knew from experience that the resistance to the voices and questions and all that had happened would increase quickly over time, so if I did it there and then while I was still relatively close to it, my doubts and the shame would be manageable. The problem I realized at once was that all the good exchanges had taken place beyond the range of the tape recorder. The solution was to write it as it had been, to present everything, our first impressions, the mumbling introvert he had been, the sudden change, the apple pie, the library. Espen wrote an introduction to Hauge's authorship, and several small analytical passages in between, which contrasted well with what else had gone on. From the editor of TAL, the philosophy student, disciple of Professor Georg Johannesen, and Nynorsk speaker, Hans Marius Hansteen, we heard that Hauge had enjoyed it, he had told Johannesen that it was one of the best interviews he had experienced, although it probably wasn't, we were only twenty years old, and as far as Hauge's evaluations of others were concerned, courtesy always triumphed over veracity, but what he liked, and what prompted his wife to ask us for more copies for their friends and acquaintances, was, I reflected after reading his diaries, that it may have given him a picture of himself that was not mere flattery. Of course Hauge was well aware of his hostile, old-man aspects, but people held him in such high esteem that this was always overlooked, a matter which, hidden deep behind layers of politeness and decency, and with him being the truth-loving person he was, he cannot always have appreciated.

Six months later it was Kjartan Fløgstad's turn. He had read the interview with Hauge, and would be happy to be interviewed by TAL, he said when I called him. If I had been on my own I would, out of sheer nervousness and respect, have read all his books, neatly jotted down enough questions for a conversation lasting several hours and recorded everything, for even though my questions might have been foolish his answers would not have been, and if I had them taped, his tone would carry the interview, however deficient my contribution. But, with Yngve along, I was not nervous in the same way, I leaned on him, I didn't read all the books, jotted down less carefully worded questions, I also took account of the relationship between Yngve and myself,

I didn't want to be seen as a corrective presence, I didn't want him to think I could do this better than he, and when we went to Oslo to meet Fløgstad – it was a gray spring day, the end of March or beginning of April, outside a café in Bjølsen – I was less prepared than I had ever been, before or since, and on top of everything Yngve and I had decided that we wouldn't use either a Dictaphone or a tape recorder or take notes at the interview, that would make it stiff and formal, we had figured, we wanted it to be more like a conversation, impressionistic, something that developed on the spot. My memory was nothing to brag about, but Yngve was like an elephant, he never forgot a thing, and if we wrote down what had been said straight after the interview, we could fill in each other's gaps and together complete the whole picture, or so we thought. Fløgstad led us politely into the café, which was of the dark, beer-dispensing variety, we sat down at a round table, hung our jackets over the backs of the chairs, took out our question sheets, and when we said that we were going to run the interview without notes or a tape recorder, Fløgstad said that commanded respect. Once, he added, he had been interviewed by the Swedish newspaper *Dagens Nyheter* by a journalist who hadn't taken any notes, and the report had been impeccable, something he found very impressive. As the interview progressed I was as focused on what Yngve said as on Fløgstad's reactions, not only how he answered, the tone of his voice and body language but also the content of the conversation. My own questions addressed what was going on around the table as much as what went on in Fløgstad's books, in the sense that they tended to complement or compensate for something in the situation. The interview took an hour, and after we had shaken hands and thanked him for his willingness to talk to us, and he had set off for what we assumed was where he lived, we were excited and happy, because it had gone well, hadn't it? We had been talking to Fløgstad! We were so excited that neither of us was in the mood to sit down and write a report about what had been said, we could do that the following day, now it was Saturday, the weekly soccer pools match would soon be on TV, we could watch it in a bar, and then go out, we weren't in Oslo that often after all . . . the train went the next day, so there wasn't any time to write anything down then, and when we arrived in Bergen we went to our own places. And if we had already waited three days, we could wait three more, couldn't we? And three more, and three more? When, at last, we did sit down to write, we could not remember much. We had the questions of course, they were a great help, and we had a vague idea of what he had answered, partly based on what we actually remembered, partly on what we thought he would have answered. It was my responsibility to write the report, I was the one who had been given the commission and did this sort of work, and after I had cooked up a few pages I realized this would not do, it was too vague, too imprecise, so I suggested to Yngve that we should phone Fløgstad and ask him whether we could ask a few supplementary questions over the phone. We sat down at a table in Yngve's flat in Blekebakken and scrawled down some new questions. My heart was thumping as I dialed Fløgstad's number, and the situation was not improved when his reserved voice answered at the other end. But I managed to explain what I wanted and he agreed to give us another half an hour, although I could detect from his voice that he was beginning to put two and two together. While I asked the questions and he answered, Yngve was sitting in the adjacent room with the headphones, like a secret agent, writing down everything that was said. With that, we had it in the bag. Between all the inaccuracies and vagueness, I inserted the new sentences, which were genuine in quite a different way and also gave a touch of authenticity to the rest. After I added a general introduction to Fløgstad's work, as well as more factual or analytical insertions, it didn't look too bad. In fact, it looked quite good. Fløgstad had asked to read the interview before it went to press, so I sent it to him with a few friendly words. I had no idea whether he insisted on reading all such reports in advance or just ours, as we had been foolhardy enough to do the interview without taking notes, but since I had managed to pull it off in the end I didn't much care. I admit, I did have a vague sense of unease about the imprecise parts, but I dismissed it, to my knowledge there was no requirement for interviews to be recorded verbatim. So when Fløgstad's letter fluttered into my mailbox some days later and I held it in my hands, I was blissfully unsuspecting, although my palms were sweaty and my heart was pounding. Spring had come, the sun warmed, I was wearing sneakers, a T-shirt, and jeans and was on my way to the music conservatory where a pal of my cousin's, Jon Olav, was going to give me drum lessons. It might have been wiser to leave the letter unopened because time was tight, but curiosity got the better of me, and, ambling toward the bus, I opened it. Held the printout of the interview. It was covered with red marks and red comments in the margin. "I never said this," I saw, "Imprecise," I saw, "No, no, no," I saw, "???," I saw. "Where did you get that from?" I saw. Almost every sentence had been commented on in this way. I stood stock-still, reading. I could feel myself falling. I plummeted into the darkness. He had attached a short note, I read it as quickly as I could, in feverish haste, as if the humiliation would be over when the last word had been read. "I think it's best this never appears in print," it concluded. "Best wishes, Kjartan Fløgstad." When I set off, dragging my feet, looking at his red marks again and again as I walked, my insides were in turmoil. Hot with shame, on the verge of tears, I stuffed the letter in my back pocket and waited by the bus which had arrived at that moment, boarded, and sat in a window seat at the rear. The shame burned through me as the bus went at a snail's pace towards Haukeland, and the same thoughts churned around my brain. I wasn't good enough, I was not a writer and never would be. What had made us happy, talking to Fløgstad, was now just laughable and painful. On arriving home I called Yngve, who to my surprise took it all quite lightly. That's a pity, he said. Are you sure you can't shuffle it around a bit and send him a new version? Once the worst despair was past, I read the comments and the accompanying note again and saw that Fløgstsad had commented on my comments, for example, the epithet "Cortazar-like." Surely he wasn't allowed to do that. To meddle with my opinions of his books? My evaulations? I wrote this in a letter to him, agreeing that the interview did have inaccuracies in a few places, as he had pointed out, but he had in fact said some of it, I knew this because I had taken notes during the telephone interview, and what was more he had raised objections to my – the journalist's – comments, and that was going beyond his remit. If he wanted, I could use his corrections and suggestions as a basis, perhaps do another interview, and then send him a revised version? A polite but firm letter came some days later, in which he conceded that some of his comments had related to my interpretations, but that did not change the main thrust, which was that the interview should not appear in print. After I had shaken off the humiliation, it took about six months, a period in which I could not see Fløgstad's face, his books or articles without feeling profound shame, I turned the episode into an anecdote for general merriment. Yngve didn't like the fact that it was at our expense, he didn't see anything comical in being humiliated, or to be more accurate, he didn't see any humiliation. Our questions had been good, the conversation with Fløgstad meaningful, that was what he wanted to take from the experience.

My life in Bergen was more or less becalmed for four years, nothing happened, I wanted to write, but couldn't, and that was about it. Yngve was collecting points from his university courses and living the life he wanted, at least that was how it looked from the outside, but at some stage that too stagnated, he was never going to finish his dissertation, he wasn't working very hard at it, perhaps because he was living off past achievements, perhaps because there was so much else going on in his life. After his dissertation, which dealt with the film star system, was finally delivered he was briefly unemployed while I was working on student radio, as alternative military service, and slowly moving into a different milieu from his, not to mention meeting Tonje with whom I got together that winter, head over heels in love. My life had taken a radical new turn, although I hardly understood it myself, I was stuck in the image I had developed during the first years in Bergen when Yngve suddenly left town, he had been offered a job as cultural consultant on Balestrand Council, that may not have been precisely what he had had in mind, but there was no one above him in the administration, so in practice he was the cultural head, and there was a jazz festival in Balestrand, which he would be in charge of and soon his friend Arvid followed him, he too was employed by the council. He met Kari Anne, whom he knew superficially from Bergen, she was working as a teacher there, they got together and had a child, Ylva, and moved to Stavanger a year later where Yngve plunged headfirst into an unfamiliar profession for him, graphic design. I was pleased he did that, but was also uneasy: a poster for the Hundvåg Days and a flyer for a local festival, was that enough?

We never touched, we didn't even shake hands when we met, and we rarely looked each other in the eye.

All of this existed inside me as we stood there on the veranda outside Grandma's house on this mild summer evening in 1998, I had my back to the garden, he was in a deckchair by the wall. It was impossible to determine from his expression whether he was thinking about what I had just said, that I would take charge of all this, also the garden, or whether he was indifferent.

I turned and stubbed out my cigarette against the underside of the wrought-iron fence. Flakes of ash and sparks showered down on the concrete.

"Are there any ashtrays out here?" I said.

"Not that I know of," he said. "Use a bottle."

I did as he said and flicked the butt down the neck of a green Heineken bottle. If I suggested that we should hold the funeral here, which I was pretty certain he would say was impossible, the difference between us, which I did not want to be visible, would become obvious. He would be the realistic, practical person; I would be the idealistic, emotion-driven one. Dad was father to both of us, but not in the same way, and my wanting to use the funeral as a kind of resurrection could, along with my tendency to cry all the time whereas Yngve had not yet shed a tear, be interpreted as evidence that my relationship was more heartfelt and, I suspected, as a covert criticism of Yngve's attitude. I did not perceive it as such, I did fear the possibility that it might be understood in that light, though. At the same time the proposal would cause a clash of wills. Over a bagatelle, it was true, but in this situation I did not want there to be *anything* between us.

A thin wisp of smoke rose from the bottle by the wall. So the cigarette could not have been completely extinguished. I looked around for something to put over the top. The plate Grandma had used to feed the seagull perhaps? There were still two scraps of rissole on it, and some thick gravy, but that would have to do, I thought, balancing it carefully.

"What *are* you doing?" Yngve said, looking at me.

"Making a little sculpture," I said. "It's called *Beer and Rissole in the Garden*. Or *Des boulettes et de la bière dans le jardin*."

I straightened up and took a step back.

"The pièce de résistance is the smoke spiraling up," I said. "In a way, this makes it environmentally interactive. It's not your everyday sculpture. And the leftovers represent decay, of course. That, too, is interactive, a process, something in flux. Or flux itself. A counterpoint to stasis. And the beer bottle is empty, it no longer has any function, for what is a container that does not contain anything? It is nothing. But nothing has a form, don't you see? The form is what I'm trying to emphasize here."

"Aha," he said.

I took another cigarette from the packet on the fence, although I didn't feel like one, and lit up.

"Yngve," I said.

"Yes?" he said.

"I've been thinking about something. Quite a lot, in fact. About whether we should hold the wake here. In this house. We can get the house into shape in a week, if we get going. I have this sense that he ruined everything here, and we're not obliged to put up with that. Do you understand what I mean?"

"Of course," Yngve said. "But do you think we can do it? I have to go back to Stavanger on Monday night. And I can't make it back before Thursday. Wednesday at a pinch, but probably Thursday."

"That's alright," I said. "Are you with me on this?"

"Yep. The question, however, is how Gunnar will take the news."

"It's none of his business. He's our father."

We finished smoking without a word. Beneath us the evening had begun to soften the landscape; its sharp edges, which also included human activity, were gradually being toned down. A few small boats were on their way into the bay, and I thought of the smells on board: plastic, salt, gasoline; they made up such an important part of my childhood. A passenger plane flew in over the town so low that I could see Braathen's SAFE logo. It vanished from sight leaving behind a low rumble. In the garden some birds were twittering under cover of the leaves of an apple tree.

Yngve drained his glass and got to his feet.

"One more shift," he said. "And we can call it a day."

He looked at me.

"Have you made any progress downstairs?"

"I've done all the laundry area, and the bathroom walls."

"Great," he said.

I followed him in. Hearing the loud but muffled sounds of the television, I remembered that Grandma was indoors. I couldn't do anything for her, no one could, but I thought that it might be a tiny relief for her to see us, and to be reminded that we were there, so I went over and stood beside her chair.

"Anything you need?" I said.

She glanced up at me.

"Ah, it's you," she said. "Where's Yngve?"

"He's in the kitchen."

"Mm," she said, returning her gaze to the television. Her vivacity had not gone, but it had changed with her scrawny figure, or was apparent in a different way, tied to her movements, not to her personality as before. Before, she had been lively, cheerful, sociable, never short of a response, often with a wink, to clarify when she was being ironical. Now there was a somberness inside her. Her soul was somber. I could see that; it struck you straightaway. But had the somberness always been there? Had she always been filled with it?

Her arms were stretched along the seat rests, with her hands gripping the ends as if she were traveling at breakneck speed.

"I'm going down to clean the bathroom," I said.

She turned her head to me.

"Ah, it's you," she said.

"Yes," I answered. "I'm going down to clean the bathroom. Is there anything you need?"

"No, thank you, Karl Ove," she said.

"Okay," I said, about to go.

"You don't happen to take a little dram in the evening, do you?" she asked. "You and Yngve?"

Did she imagine that we drank as well? It wasn't just Dad who ruined his life but also his sons?

"No. Absolutely not."

Grandma didn't appear to want to say anything else, and I went downstairs to the cellar floor, which still stank to high heaven, even though the source of the stench had been removed, rinsed the red bucket, filled it with fresh, scalding hot water and started to wash the bathroom. First the mirror, on which the yellow-brown coating was proving stubborn to shift, and only came off when I used a knife, which I ran upstairs to fetch from the kitchen, and a coarse scouring pad, next it was the sink's turn, then the bathtub, then the windowsill above, then the narrow, rectangular, frosted window, then the toilet bowl, then the door, the sill, and the frame, and finally I scrubbed the floor, poured the dark gray water down the drain and carried the bag of garbage onto the steps where I stood for a few minutes gazing into the murky summer dusk, which was not really dark, more like defective light.

The rise and fall of loud voices on the main road beyond, probably a group of people out on the town, reminded me that it was a Saturday night.

Why had she asked if we drank? Was it just Dad's fate that had prompted her, or was there something else underlying it?

I thought of my graduation celebrations, ten years ago, of how drunk I had been in the procession, my grandparents standing in the crowds along the route and shouting to me, their strained expressions when they realized the state I was in. I had started drinking seriously that Easter at the soccer training camp in Switzerland, and just continued through the spring, there was always an occasion, always a gathering, there were always others who wanted to join in, and dressed in prom gear everything was allowed and forgiven. For me this was paradise, but for Mom, with whom I lived on my own, it was different, in the end she threw me out, which did not concern me too much, finding somewhere to sleep was the easiest thing in the world, whether it was a sofa in a friend's cellar or on the prom bus or under a bush in the park. For my grandparents this partying period was the transition to academic life, as it had been for my grandfather and his sons, there was a solemnity about it which I degraded by drinking myself senseless and getting stoned, and by being the editor of the student newspaper, which had illustrated the lead story, a deportation case from Flekkerøya, with a picture of Jews being deported from the ghettos to concentration camps. There was also the matter of tradition; my father had in his turn been the editor of the student magazine in the final school year. So I dragged everything into the dirt.

I didn't give this a moment's thought, however, which the diary I was keeping at the time made absolutely clear, the only thing I attached any importance to was a feeling of happiness.

Now I had burned all the diaries and notes I'd written, there was barely a trace left of the person I was until I turned twenty-five, perhaps for the better; no good ever came of that phase.

The air had become cooler now, and being so hot from work, I was aware of it enveloping me, pressing against my skin, and wafting into my mouth. Of it enveloping the trees in front of me, the houses, the cars, the mountain sides. Of it streaming somewhere as the temperature fell, these constant avalanches in the sky which we could not see, drifting in over us like enormous breakers, always in flux, descending slowly, swirling fast, in and out of all these lungs, meeting all these walls and edges, always invisible, always present.

But Dad was no longer breathing. That was what had happened to him, the connection with the air had been broken, now it pushed against him like any other object, a log, a gasoline can, a sofa. He no longer poached air, because that is what you do when you breathe, you trespass, again and again you trespass on the world.

He was lying somewhere in town now.

I turned and went in, someone opened a window on the other side of the street, and music and loud voices poured out.

Although the second bathroom was smaller, and not quite as filthy, it took me just as long to clean it. When I had finished I took the detergents, cloths, gloves, and the bucket and went up to the second floor. Yngve and Grandma were sitting by the kitchen table. The wall clock showed half past nine.

"You must have finished washing by now!" Grandma said.

"Yes," I said. "I've finished for the evening."

I glanced at Yngve.

"Did you talk to Mom today?"

He shook his head.

"I did yesterday."

"I promised to call today. But I don't think I have the energy. Perhaps it's a bit late too."

"Do it tomorrow," Yngve said.

"I do have to talk to Tonje, though. I'll do it now."

I went into the dining room and closed the kitchen door behind me. Sat in the chair for a moment to collect myself. Then I dialed our home number. She answered at once, as though she had been sitting by the phone, waiting. I knew all the cadences of her voice, and they were what I was listening to now, not to what she was saying. First the warmth and the sympathy and the longing, then her voice seemed to contract into something small, as if it wanted to snuggle up to me. My own was filled with distance. She came closer to me, and I needed that, but I didn't go closer to her, I could not. Briefly I described what had been happening down here, without going into any detail, just said it was awful, and that I was crying all the time. Then we talked a little about what she had been doing, although at first she was reluctant, and then we discussed when she should travel down. After hanging up I went to the kitchen, which was empty, and drank a glass of water. Grandma was back in the TV chair. I went over to her:

"Do you know where Yngve is?"

"No," she said. "Isn't he in the kitchen?"

"No," I said.

The stench of urine tore at my nostrils.

I stood there not knowing what to do. The evacuation was easy to explain. He had been so drunk he had lost control of his bodily functions.

But where had she been? What had she been doing?

I felt like going over to the television and kicking in the screen.

"You and Yngve don't drink, do you?" she said out of the blue, without looking at me.

I shook my head.

"No, that is, it does happen on the odd occasion, but just a drop. Never much more."

"Not tonight then?"

"No, are you out of your mind!" I said. "No, that would be unthinkable. For Yngve as well."

"What would be unthinkable for me?" Yngve said from behind me. I turned. He walked up the two steps that separated the lower living room from the upper.

"Grandma's asking if we drink."

"I suppose, it does happen now and then," Yngve said. "But not often. I've got two small children now, you know."

"Have you got *two*?" Grandma exclaimed.

Yngve smiled. I smiled.

"Yes," he said. "Ylva and Torje. You've met Ylva, haven't you. You'll meet Torje at the funeral."

The flicker of life that had risen in Grandma's face died. I met Yngve's eyes.

"It's been a long day," I said. "Time to hit the hay?"

"I'm going outside first," he said. "Want to join me on the veranda?" I nodded. He went into the kitchen.

"Do you usually stay up late?" I asked.

"What?"

"We were thinking of going to bed soon," I said. "Are you going to stay up?"

"No. Oh no. I'll go too," Grandma said.

She looked up at me.

"Are you boys sleeping downstairs, in our old bedroom? It's free."

I shook my head and arched my eyebrows in apology.

"We were thinking of sleeping upstairs," I said. "In the loft. We've already unpacked our things there."

"Well, that's fine too," she said.

"Are you coming?" Yngve said, standing in the lower living room with a glass of beer in one hand.

When I went out to the veranda Yngve was sitting on a wooden seat by a matching table.

"Where did you find it?" I said.

"Hidden under here," he said. "I seemed to remember seeing it at some point."

I leaned against the railing. The ferry to Denmark was glittering in the distance. It was on its way across. The few small boats I could see all had lanterns lit.

"We'll have to get hold of one of those electric scythes or whatever they're called," I said. "A standard lawn mower won't be any good here."

"We'll find a rental firm in the Yellow Pages on Monday," he said. Looking at me.

"Did you talk to Tonje?"

I nodded.

"Well, there won't be many of us," Yngve said. "Us, Gunnar, Erling, Alf, and Grandma. Sixteen including the children."

"Nope, it won't exactly be a state funeral."

Yngve put his glass down and leaned back in his chair. High above the trees, a bat careered around the gray, shadowy sky.

"Have you thought any more about how we should do it?" he asked.

"The funeral?"

"Yes."

"No, not really. But I certainly don't want any damned humanist funeral."

"Agreed. Church then."

"Yes, there aren't any alternatives, are there? But he wasn't a member of the Church of Norway."

"Wasn't he?" Yngve said. "I knew he wasn't a Christian, but not that he had left the church."

"Yes, he said so once. I left the church on my sixteenth birthday and then I told him at some dinner he was giving on Elvegata. He was furious. And then Unni said *he* had left the church, so he couldn't be angry at me for doing the same."

"He wouldn't have liked it," Yngve said. "He didn't want anything to do with the church."

"But he's dead," I countered. "And, anyway, I like it. I don't want to be part of some trumped-up pseudoritual with poetry readings. I want it to be decent. Dignified."

"I agree," Yngve said.

I turned around again and surveyed the town, a constant hum in the background, sometimes drowned by the sudden revving of an engine, often from the bridge where kids amused themselves racing up and down at this time of night, also on the long stretch along Dronningens gate.

"I'm off to bed," Yngve said. He went into the living room without closing the door behind him. I stubbed out my cigarette on the ground and followed. When Grandma realized we were going to bed she struggled to her feet and wanted to find us some bed linen.

"We'll sort it out," Yngve said. "No problem. You go to bed as well!"

"Are you sure?" she asked, standing small and bowed in the doorway to the stairs.

"Of course," Yngve said. "We can manage."

"Alright then," she said. "Good night."

And slowly she made her way downstairs, without a backward glance.

I shuddered with unease.

There was no water on the top floor, so we fetched our toothbrushes from upstairs, cleaned our teeth in the kitchen sink, taking turns to lean forward to the tap and rinse, as though we were children again. On summer holidays.

I wiped the toothpaste off my lips with my hand and dried it on my thigh. It was twenty to eleven. I hadn't gone to bed so early for several years. But it had been a long day. My body was numb with exhaustion, and my head ached from all the crying. Now, however, that was a distant memory. Maybe I had become immune. Maybe I had already gotten used to this.

Once upstairs, Yngve opened the window, fastened it with the catch, and switched on the small lamp above the bedhead. I did the same on my side, and turned off the ceiling light. There was a stale smell, and it didn't come from the air but from the furniture and carpets that had been gathering dust for a couple of years, perhaps longer.

Yngve sat on his side of the double bed and undressed. I did the same on mine. Sleeping in one bed was a little too intimate, we hadn't done that since we were small boys and close, in a very different way, to each other. But at least we each had our own duvet.

"Has it struck you that Dad never had a chance to read your novel?" Yngve said, turning to me.

"No," I said. "I hadn't given it a thought."

I had sent Yngve the manuscript when it was finished, at the beginning of June. The first thing he had said after reading it was that Dad would sue me. In precisely those words. I was in a telephone booth at the airport on my way to Turkey for a holiday with Tonje, unaware of whether he would be furious or supportive, I had no idea if what I had written would have any effect on those close to me. "I haven't a clue whether it's good or bad," he had said. "But Dad's going to sue you. Of that I am sure."

"But there's a sentence in the book that comes up again and again," I said now. "*My father's dead*. Do you remember it?"

Yngve flipped the duvet to the side, swung his legs onto the bed and lay back. Sat up and straightened the pillow.

"Vaguely," he said, lying back down.

"That's when Henrik flees. He needs an excuse, and that's the only one that occurs to him. *My father's dead*."

"That's right," Yngve said.

I took off my jeans and socks, and found a comfortable position. At first on my back, with my hands folded over my stomach, until it occurred to me that I was lying like a corpse, and rolled onto my side, horrified, looking straight down at the pile of my clothes on the floor. What a damned mess, I thought, and lowering my feet to the floor, I folded my jeans and T-shirt and laid them on the nearby chair with the socks on top.

Yngve switched off the light on his side.

"Are you going to read?" he asked.

"No, no chance," I said, fumbling for a pull switch. There wasn't one as far as I could feel. Was it on the lamp then? Yes, there it was.

I pressed it, hard, because the old mechanism was stiff. The lamps must have been from the 50s. From the days when they moved into the house.

"Good night then," Yngve said.

"Good night," I said.

How glad I was that he was here. If I had been alone my head would have been filled with images of Dad as a corpse, I would have thought only of the physicality of death, his body, the fingers and legs, the unseeing eyes, the hair and nails that were still growing. The room where he was lying, perhaps inside a drawer-like thing they always had in morgues in American films . But now the sound of Yngve's breathing and his many little twitches calmed me. All I had to do was close my eyes and let sleep come.

I woke up a couple of hours later with Yngve standing in the middle of the floor. At first he peered around, irresolute, then grabbed the duvet, rolled it up and carried it through the room and out the door, turned, and came back. As he was about to do the same again I said:

"You're sleepwalking, Yngve. Lie down and go back to sleep."

He looked at me.

"I am not sleepwalking," he said. "The duvet has to cross the threshold three times."

"Okay," I said. "If you say so, fine."

He crossed the floor twice more. Then he lay down and spread the duvet over himself. Tossed his head from side to side, mumbling something or other.

This wasn't the first time he had sleepwalked. When we were boys Yngve had been notorious for it. Once Mom had found him in the bathtub, naked with the tap running; on another occasion she had just managed to grab him on the road outside the house heading for Rolf's to ask if he wanted to come and play soccer. He could suddenly throw his duvet out of the window and lie on his bed freezing for the rest of the night without knowing why. Dad also walked in his sleep. Wearing only his underpants, he had once come into my room in the middle of the night, opened a cupboard, peeped in and glanced at me without any sign of recognition in his eyes. Sometimes I had heard him banging around in the living room, moving furniture this way and that. Once he had gone to sleep under the living room table and hit his head so hard when he sat up that it bled. When he wasn't walking in his sleep, he talked or shouted, and when he wasn't doing that, he ground his teeth. Mom used to say it was like being married to a merchant seaman. As for me, I had peed in the wardrobe one night, otherwise my nocturnal activities did not amount to any more than talking in my sleep until I reached my teenage years when there was a flurry of activity at certain periods. The summer I was selling cassettes on the streets in Arendal and living in Yngve's studio, I had taken his pencil case and walked across the lawn naked, standing in front of every window and peering in, until Yngve had managed to get through to me. I denied that I had been sleepwalking, the proof was the pencil case, look here, I had said, here's my wallet, I was going shopping. How many times had I stood by the window watching the ground disappear or rise, walls fall down or water surge upward! Once I had stood holding the wall, yelling to Tonje that she should make a run for it before the house collapsed. Another time I had got it into my head that she was in the wardrobe and I had thrown out all the clothes while looking for her. If I had to spend the night with anyone else apart from her I would warn them in advance, in case anything happened, and two years before, traveling with Tore, a friend, we had rented what was called a writer's flat in a large manor house on the outskirts of Kristiansand to write a screenplay, and this precautionary measure had saved the situation: we had beds in the same room and in the middle of the night I had got up, gone over, torn the blanket off him, grabbed his ankles and, as he stared up at me in shock, told him: *You're just a doll*. But the most frequently recurring delusion was that an otter or a fox had crawled into the duvet, which I then threw onto the floor and stomped on until I was sure the creature was dead. A year could pass without anything happening, then suddenly I had phases when hardly a night went by without my sleepwalking. I woke up in the loft, in corridors, on lawns, always busy doing something or other that seemed utterly meaningful but which, upon waking, was always utterly meaningless.

The strange thing about Yngve's nocturnal life was that on occasion he could be heard speaking eastern Norwegian dialect in his sleep. He moved from Oslo when he was four and had not spoken dialect for close to thirty years. Yet it could pass his lips when he was asleep. There was something spooky about it.

I watched him. He was lying on his back with one leg outside the duvet. It had always been said that we were identical, but that must have been an overall impression, our aura, because if you took us feature by feature there was very little similarity. The only thing was possibly the eyes, which both of us inherited from Mom. Yet when I moved to Bergen and met Yngve's more peripheral acquaintances they would sometimes ask: "Are you Yngve?" That I was not Yngve was obvious from the formulation of the question, because if they had thought I was, they clearly would not have asked. They had just found the similarity striking.

He twisted his head to the side of the pillow, as if sensing he was being observed and wanting to escape. I closed my eyes. He had told me often that Dad had totally crushed his self-esteem on a number of occasions, humiliated him as only Dad could, and that had colored periods of his life when he felt he was incapable of doing anything and was worthless. Then there were other periods when everything went well, when there were no hitches, no nagging doubts. From the outside, all you saw was the latter.

Dad had also affected my self-image, of course, but perhaps in a different way, at any rate I never had periods of doubt followed by periods of self-confidence, it was all entangled for me, and the doubts that colored such a large part of my thinking never applied to the larger picture but always the smaller, the one associated with my closer surroundings, friends, acquaintances, girls, who, I was convinced, always held a low opinion of me, considered me an idiot, which burned inside me, every day it burned inside me; however, as far as the larger picture was concerned, I never had any doubt that I could attain whatever I wanted, I knew I had it in me, because my yearnings were so strong and they never found any rest. How could they? How else was I going to crush everyone?

The next time I woke, Yngve was standing in front of the mirror buttoning up his shirt.

"What time is it?" I said.

He turned.

"Half past six. Early for you?"

"Yes, you can say that again."

He had put on a pair of light khaki shorts, the type that reach down to below the knees, and a gray-striped shirt with the shirttails hanging out.

"I'm going downstairs," he said. "You coming?"

"Yep," I said.

"You're not going back to sleep?"

"No."

As his steps receded on the staircase, I swung my feet onto the floor and grabbed my clothes from the chair. Looked down with displeasure at my stomach where two rolls of fat still protruded at the sides. Pinched my back, no excess flesh there yet, fortunately. Nevertheless, I would definitely have to start running when I got back to Bergen. And do sit-ups every morning.

I held the T-shirt to my nose and sniffed.

Hm, probably wouldn't make another day.

I opened the suitcase and pulled out a Boo Radleys' T-shirt which I had bought when they played in Bergen a couple of years ago, and a pair of dark blue jeans with the legs cut off. It might not have been sunny outside, but the air was warm and close.

Downstairs, Yngve had put on coffee, set out bread and sliced meats and so on from the fridge. Grandma sat at the table in the same dress she had been wearing the previous day, smoking. I wasn't hungry and made do with a cup of coffee and a cigarette on the veranda before grabbing the bucket, the cloths and the detergents to start work on the ground floor. First, I went into the bathroom to inspect what I had done. Apart from the stained, sticky shower curtain, which for some reason I had not thrown out, it all looked pretty good. Run-down, of course, but clean.

I removed the pole that ran from wall to wall above the bath, pulled off the curtain and threw it into a garbage bag, washed the pole and the two grips, and put them back up. So the question was: what next? The laundry room and the two bathrooms were done. On this floor there was Grandma's room, the hall, the corridor, Dad's room and the big bedroom left to do. I wouldn't touch Grandma's room now, it would have felt like a transgression, because it would be obvious to her we could see the state she was in, and because she would have been deprived of her independence, the grandchild cleaning the grandmother's bedroom. I couldn't bring myself to start on Dad's room either, also because there were papers and much besides we would have to sort through first. The corridor with the wall-to-wall carpet would have to wait until we had contacted a carpet cleaner. So it would have to be the staircase.

I filled the bucket with water, took a bottle of Klorin, a bottle of green soap and a bottle of Jif scouring cream and started on the banisters, which could not have been washed for a good five years. There were all sorts of filth between the stair-rods, disintegrated leaves, pebbles, dried-up insects, old spiderwebs. The banisters themselves were dark, in some places almost completely black, here and there, sticky. I sprayed Jif, wrung the cloth and scrubbed every centimeter thoroughly. Once a section was clean and had regained something of its old, dark golden color I dunked another cloth in Klorin and kept scrubbing. The smell of Klorin and the sight of the blue bottle took me back to the 1970s, to be more precise, to the cupboard under the kitchen sink where the detergents were kept. Jif didn't exist then. Ajax washing powder did though, in a cardboard container: red, white, and blue. It was a green soap. Klorin did too; the design of the blue plastic bottle with the fluted, childproof top had not changed since then. There was also a brand called OMO. And there was a packet of washing powder with a picture of a child holding the identical packet, and on that, of course, there was a picture of the same boy holding the same packet, and so on, and so on. Was it called Blenda? Whatever it was called, I often racked my brains over mise en abyme, which in principle of course was endless and also existed elsewhere, such as in the bathroom mirror by holding a mirror behind your head so that images of the mirrors were projected to and fro while going farther and farther back and becoming smaller and smaller as far as the eye could see. But what happened behind what the eye could see? Did the images carry on getting smaller and smaller?

A whole world lay between the trademarks of then and now, and as I thought about them, their sounds and tastes and smells reappeared, utterly irresistible, as indeed everything you have lost, everything that has gone, always does. The smell of short, freshly watered grass when you are sitting on a soccer field one summer afternoon after training, the long shadows of motionless trees, the screams and laughter of children swimming in the lake on the other side of the road, the sharp yet sweet taste of the energy drink XL-1. Or the taste of salt that inevitably gets into your mouth when you dive into the sea, even if you pinch your lips as your head sinks below the surface, the chaos of currents and rushing water beneath, but also the light playing on the seaweed and the sea grass and the bare rock face, clusters of mussels and fields of barnacles that all seem to radiate a still, gentle glow, for it is a cloudless midsummer day, and the sun is burning down through the high, blue sky and sea. The water streaming off your body as you haul yourself up using hollows in the rock face, the drops left on your shoulder blades for a few seconds until the heat has burned them off, the water in your trunks still dripping long after you have wrapped a towel around yourself. The speedboat skimming over the waves, stuttering and disharmonious, the bow thrust upward, the buffeting of the waves that is heard through the roar of the engine, the unreality of it, since the surroundings are too vast and open for the boat's presence to leave an impression.

All of this still existed. The smooth, flat rocks were exactly the same, the sea pounded down on them in the same way, and also the landscape under the water, with its small valleys and bays and steep chasms and slopes, strewn with starfish and sea urchins, crabs and fish, was the same. You could still buy Slazenger tennis rackets, Tretorn balls, and Rossignol skis, Tyrolia bindings and Koflach boots. The houses where we lived were still standing, all of them. The sole difference, which is the difference between a child's reality and an adult's, was that they were no longer laden with meaning. A pair of Le Coq soccer boots was just a pair of soccer boots. If I felt anything when I held a pair in my hands now it was only a hangover from my childhood, nothing else, nothing in itself. The same with the sea, the same with the rocks, the same with the taste of salt that could fill your summer days to saturation, now it was just salt, end of story. The world was the same, yet it wasn't, for its meaning had been displaced, and was still being displaced, approaching closer and closer to meaninglessness.

I wrung out the cloth, hung it from the edge of the bucket and studied the fruits of my labors. The gleam in the varnish had come to the fore although there was still a scattering of dark dirt stains as though etched into the wood. I suppose I must have done a third of the woodwork up to the first floor. Then there were the banisters and railings to the third floor as well.

Yngve's footfalls echoed in the corridor above.

He appeared with a bucket in his hand and a roll of garbage bags under his arm.

"Have you finished downstairs?" he asked, on seeing me.

"No, I haven't. Are you out of your mind? I've done just the bathrooms and the laundry room. I was thinking of waiting to do the others."

"I'm going to start on Dad's room now," he said. "That's the biggest job, it seems."

"Is the kitchen done?"

"Yes. Pretty damn close. Have to clean out a couple of cupboards. Otherwise it looks good."

"Okay," I said. "I'm going to take a break now. A bite to eat. Is Grandma in the kitchen?"

He nodded, and went past. I rubbed my hands, which were soft and wrinkled from the water, against my shorts, cast a last glance at the railings and went up to the kitchen.

Grandma was sitting in her chair brooding. She didn't even look up as I entered. I remembered the sedatives. Had she taken one? Probably not.

I opened the cupboard and took out the packet.

"Have you taken any today?" I said, holding it up.

"What is it?" she said. "Medicine?"

"Yes, the tablets you took yesterday."

"No, I haven't."

I fetched a glass from the cupboard, filled it with water, and passed it to her with a tablet. She put it on her tongue and washed it down. She didn't seem to want to say anymore, so to avoid being forced by the silence into talking, I grabbed a couple of apples, instead of the sandwiches I had planned, plus a glass of water and a cup of coffee. The weather was mild and gray, like yesterday. A light breeze blew off the sea, gulls screamed in the air above the harbor, metallic blows sounded from close by. The constant hum of urban traffic from below. A crane, high and fragile, steepled above the rooftops a couple of blocks from the quay. It was yellow with a white cabin or whatever the thingy the crane driver sat in at the top was called. Strange I hadn't seen it before. There were few things I found more beautiful than cranes, the skeletal nature of their construction, the steel wires running along the top and bottom of the protruding arm, the enormous hook, the way heavy objects dangled when being slowly transported through the air, the sky that formed a backdrop to this mechanical provisorium.

I had just eaten one apple – seeds, stalk, and all – and was about to sink my teeth into the second when Yngve walked through the garden. He was holding a fat envelope.

"Look what I found," he said, passing me the envelope.

I undid the flap. It was full of thousand-krone notes.

"There's about two hundred thousand in there," he said.

"Wow," I exclaimed. "Where was it?"

"Under the bed. It must be the money he got for the house on Elvegata."

"Oh, shit," I said. "So this is all that's left?"

"I guess so. He didn't even put the money in the bank, just kept it under his bed. And then he drank it, no less. Thousand-note by thousand-note."

"I don't give a shit about the money," I said. "The life he had here was just so sad."

"You can say that again," Yngve said.

He sat down. I put the envelope on the table.

"What shall we do with it?" he asked.

"No idea," I said. "Share it, I suppose?"

"I was thinking more about inheritance tax and that kind of thing."

I shrugged.

"We can ask someone," I said. "Jon Olav, for example. He's an attorney."

The sound of a car engine carried from the narrow street below the house. Even though I couldn't see it, I knew it was coming here by the way it stopped, reversed, and drove forward again.

"Who could that be?" I wondered.

Yngve got up, took the envelope.

"Who's going to look after this?" he asked.

"You," I said.

"Anyway, the problems regarding funeral expenses have been solved now," he said, walking past me. I followed him in. From the downstairs hall we could hear voices. It was Gunnar and Tove. We were standing between the hall door and the kitchen door, physically ill at ease when they came up, as though we were still children. Yngve was holding the envelope in one hand.

Tove was as suntanned and as well-preserved as Gunnar.

"Hello there!" she exclaimed with a smile.

"Hello," I said. "Long time, no see."

"Yes, that's true," she said. "Shame we should have to meet under such circumstances."

"Yes," I agreed.

How old could they have been? Late forties?

Grandma came out of the kitchen.

"So it's you," she said.

"Sit down, Mother," Gunnar said. "We just thought we should give Yngve and Karl Ove a hand with all this."

He winked at us.

"You've got time for a coffee, I suppose?" Grandma inquired.

"No coffee for us," Gunnar said. "We'll be off soon. The boys are alone at the cabin."

"All right," Grandma said.

Gunnar poked his head into the kitchen.

"You've already done a lot," he said. "Impressive."

"We were thinking of having the get-together here, after the funeral," I said. He looked at me.

"You'll never make it," he said.

"We will," I said. "We've got five days. It'll be fine."

He looked away. Perhaps because of the tears in my eyes.

"Well, it's your decision," he said. "So if you two think it's fine, then that's how we'll play it. But we'll have to get a move on!"

He turned and went into the living room. I followed him.

"We'd better toss out everything that's broken. There's no point in saving anything here. The sofas, what state are they in?"

"One of them's OK," I said. "We can wash that one. The other, I think, . . ."

"Then we'll take it," he said.

He stood in front of the large, black, leather three-seater. I went to the other end, bent down, and grabbed hold.

"We can carry it through the veranda door and out that way," Gunnar said. "Can you open it for us, Tove?"

As we carried it through the living room Grandma was standing in the kitchen doorway.

"What are you doing with the sofa?" she cried.

"We're getting rid of it," Gunnar said.

"Are you crazy!" she said. "Why are you getting rid of it? You can't just get rid of my sofa."

"It's ruined," Gunnar said.

"That's none of your business!" she said. "It's my sofa!"

I stopped. Gunnar looked at me.

"We have to, can't you see that?!" he said to her. "Come on, Karl Ove, and we'll get it out."

Grandma advanced toward us.

"You can't do that!" she said. "This is my house."

"Oh, yes, we can," Gunnar countered.

We had reached the steps down to the living room. I edged sideways without giving Grandma a look. She was standing beside the piano. I could feel her iron will. Gunnar didn't notice. Or did he? Was he struggling with it too? She was his mother.

He went backward down the two steps and slowly moved through the room.

"This is not right!" Grandma shouted. Over the last few minutes she had completely changed. Her eyes were shooting sparks. Her body, which earlier had been so passive and closed in on itself, was now opening outward. She stood with her hands on her hips, snarling.

"Oohh!"

Then she turned.

"No, I don't want to see this," she said, and returned to the kitchen.

Gunnar sent me a smile. I walked down the two steps, onto the floor and stepped sideways to reach the doorway. There was a draft coming from it, I could feel the wind against the bare skin on my legs, arms, and face. The curtains were flapping.

"Are you alright?" Gunnar asked.

"I think so," I said.

On the veranda we put down the sofa and rested for a few seconds before lugging it the last stretch, down the stairs and through the garden towards the trailer outside the garage door. Once it was loaded and in position, with one end sticking out perhaps a meter, Gunnar fetched a blue rope from the trunk and started lashing it tight. I didn't know quite what to do and stood there watching, in case he needed help.

"Don't take any notice of her," he said, while tying. "She doesn't know what's good for her right now."

"Right," I answered.

"You've probably got a better overview of things here than me. What else has to be thrown out?"

"Quite a bit from his room. And hers. And the living room. But nothing big. Not like the sofa."

"Her mattress maybe?" he wondered.

"Yes," I said. "And his. But if we get rid of hers we'll have to find her a new one."

"We can take one from their old bedroom," he said.

"We can do that," I agreed.

"If she complains when you boys are alone with her, don't take any notice. Just do what you have to do. It's for her own good."

"Okay," I said.

He coiled the remaining rope and tied it firmly to the trailer.

"That should hold," he said, straightening his back. He looked at me.

"Have you checked the garage, by the way?"

"No," I replied.

"He's got all his stuff in there. A whole truckload. You'll have to take it with you. But go through it now. Probably a lot of it can be thrown away."

"Okay," I said.

"There's not much room for anything else on the trailer, but we'll take what we can and drive to the dump. So bring out some more stuff in the meantime, and we can do another trip. And then I think that's it. If there's anything else, I can come during the week maybe."

"Thanks," I said.

"It's not easy for you kids," he said. "I understand that."

When our eyes met he held mine for a few seconds before looking away. In his tanned face his eyes seemed almost as clear and blue as Dad's.

There was so much he didn't want to engage with. All the emotions I was overflowing with, for example.

He laid his hand on my shoulder.

Something snapped in me. I sobbed.

"You're good kids," he said.

I had to turn away. I bent forward and covered my face with my hands. My body shook. Then it was over, I stood up, took a deep breath.

"Do you know anywhere that rents machinery? You know, floor polishers, industrial lawn mowers, that sort of thing?"

"Are you going to polish the *floor*?"

"No, no, that was just an example. But I was thinking of tackling this grass. And you can't do that with a standard lawn mower."

"Isn't that a bit ambitious? Isn't it best to concentrate on inside the house?"

"Yes, maybe it is. But if there's any time left over."

He bowed his head and scratched his scalp with a finger.

"There's a rental firm in Grim. They should have something suitable. But look in the Yellow Pages."

The white plinth of the house beside us began to shimmer. I looked up. There was a break in the clouds and the sun was shining through. Gunnar went up the steps and into the house. I followed. On the hall floor outside Dad's room were two garbage bags, full of clothes and junk. Beside them was the soiled chair. From inside the room Yngve stood looking at us. He was wearing yellow gloves.

"Perhaps we should throw out the mattress," he said. "Is there room?"

"Not on this run," Gunnar said. "We can take it on the next."

"By the way, we found this under the bed," Yngve said, gripping the envelope he had left on the wall shelf and passing it to Gunnar.

Gunnar opened the envelope and peered inside.

"How much is it?" he asked.

"About two hundred thousand," Yngve said.

"Well, it's yours now," he said. "But don't forget your sister when you divvy it up."

"Of course not," Yngve said.

Had he thought of her?

I hadn't.

"Then you'll have to decide whether you're going to declare the money or not," Gunnar said.

Tove stayed behind to clean when Gunnar drove off a quarter of an hour later with a full trailer. All the windows and the doors in the house were open, and that, the movement of air inside plus the sunlight falling over the floors and the overpowering smell of detergent on at least the second floor, allowed the house to open up, in a sense, and become a place the world flooded through, which, deep in my emotional gloom, I noticed and liked. I continued with the staircase, Yngve with Dad's room while Tove took care of the upstairs living room, the one where he had been found. The windowsills, the panels, the doors, the shelves. After a while I went upstairs to the kitchen to change the water. Grandma looked up as I emptied the bucket, but her eyes were vacant and uninterested and soon returned to the table. The water whirled slowly around the sink as it dwindled, gray-brown and turbid, until the last white suds were gone and a layer of sand, hair, and miscellaneous particles was left, matte against the shiny metal. I turned on the tap and let the jet run down the sides of the bucket until all the dirt was gone and I could fill it up with fresh, steaming hot water. As, straight afterward, I went into the living room, Tove turned to me with a smile.

"My God, this is something!" she commented.

I stopped.

"It's progressing, anyway," I said.

She put the cloth down on the shelf and ran a hand through her hair.

"She's never been one for cleaning," she said.

"It used to look fairly decent here, didn't it?" I asked.

She chuckled and shook her head.

"Oh, no. People might have had that impression, but no . . . as long as I have known this house it's always been filthy. Well, not everywhere, but in the corners. Under the furniture. Under the carpets. You know, where it can't be seen."

"Is that right?"

"Oh, yes, she's never been much of a housewife."

"Perhaps not," I said.

"But she deserved better than this. We thought she could enjoy some good years after Grandfather died. We got her some home-help, you know, and they took care of the whole house for her."

I nodded. "I heard about that," I said.

"That was some help for us too. Before that, it was always us who helped them. With all sorts of things. They've been old for a long time, of course. And with your father being the way he was, and Erling in Trondheim, everything fell on us."

"I know," I said, raising my hands and eyebrows in a gesture that was supposed to show that I sympathized with her, but could not have done anything myself.

"Now, though, she'll have to go into a home and be taken care of. It's terrible to see her like this."

"Yes," I said.

She smiled again.

"How's Sissel?"

"Fine," I said. "She lives in Jølster, she seems to love it there. And she's working at the nursing college in Førde."

"Give her my love when you see her," Tove said.

"Will do," I said and smiled back. Tove picked up the cloth again, and I went down to where I had reached on the stairs, about halfway, put down the bucket, wrung the cloth and squirted a line of Jif over the banister.

"Karl Ove?" Yngve called.

"Yes?" I answered.

"Come down here a minute."

He was standing in front of the hall mirror. A huge stack of papers on the oil-fired heater beside him. His eyes were shiny.

"Look at this," he said, passing me an envelope. It was addressed to Ylva Knausgaard, Stavanger. Inside was a piece of paper on which *Dear Ylva* was written but otherwise it was blank.

"Did he write to her? From here?" I asked.

"Seems like it," Yngve said. "It must have been her birthday or something. And then he gave up. Look, he didn't have our address."

"I didn't think he'd registered that she existed," I said.

"But he had," Yngve said. "He must have thought about her as well."

"She *is* his first grandchild," I said.

"True," Yngve said. "But this is Dad we're talking about. It doesn't have to mean a thing."

"Shit," I said. "It's all so sad."

"I found something else," Yngve said. "Look at this."

This time he passed me a typed, official-looking letter. It was from the State Educational Loan Fund. It was a statement to say his study loan had been repaid in full.

"Look at the date," Yngve said.

It was June 29.

"Two weeks before he died," I said, and met Yngve's eyes. We started laughing.

He laughed.

And I laughed. "So much for freedom."

We laughed again.

When Gunnar and Tove left an hour later, the atmosphere in the house changed again. With only us and Grandma at home, the rooms seemed to close around what had happened, as though we were too weak to open them. Or perhaps we were too close to what had happened and were a greater part of it than Gunnar and Tove. At any rate, the flow of life and movement abated, and every object inside, whether the television, the chairs, the sofa, the sliding door between the living rooms, the black piano, or the two baroque paintings hanging on the wall above it, appeared for what it was, heavy, immovable, laden with the past. Outside, it had clouded over again. The grayish-white sky muted all the colors of the landscape. Yngve sifted through papers, I washed the staircase, Grandma sat in the kitchen, immersed in her own gloom. At around four o'clock Yngve took the car and went to buy some lunch, and, conscious of the whole house around me, I fervently hoped that Grandma would not set out on one of her rare peregrinations and join me, for it felt as if my soul, or whatever it is other people, with such ease, leave their impressions on, was so fragile and sensitive that I would not be able to bear the strain that her grief and gloom-stricken presence would impose. But this hope was in vain, for after a while I heard the scrape of table legs upstairs, and soon afterward her footsteps, first into the living room, then on the staircase.

She held the rail tight, as though on the brink of a precipice.

"Is that you?" she asked.

"Yes," I said. "But I'll soon have finished."

"Where's Ynge then?"

"He's gone shopping," I said.

"Yes, that's right, yes," she said. She stood watching my hand, which, with the cloth held between my fingers, was moving up and down the banister. Then she looked at my face. I met her gaze, and a chill ran down my spine. She looked as though she hated me.

She sighed and flicked the lock of hair that kept falling over one eye to the side.

"You're working hard," she said. "You're working very hard."

"Ye-es," I said. "But now that we've started it's great to make some progress, isn't it?"

There was the sound of a car engine outside.

"There he is," I said.

"Who?" she asked. "Gunnar?"

"Yngve," I said.

"But isn't he here?"

I didn't answer.

"Oh, that's right," she said. "I'm beginning to unravel too!"

I smiled, dropped the cloth in the turbid water, and grabbed the handle of the bucket.

"We'd better make something to eat," I said.

In the kitchen, I poured out the water, wrung the cloth dry, and hung it over the rim of the bucket while Grandma sat in her place. As I removed the ashtray from the table she moved the lowest part of the curtain aside and peered out. I emptied the ashtray, walked back, took the cups, put them in the sink, wet the kitchen rag, sprayed the table with a detergent and was washing it when Yngve came in with a grocery bag in each hand. He set them down and began to unpack. First, what we would have for lunch, which he laid out on the counter, four vacuum-packed salmon steaks, a bag of potatoes stained dark with soil, a head of cauliflower, and a packet of frozen beans, then all the other goods, some of which he stowed in the fridge, some in the cupboard next to it. A 1.5 liter bottle of Sprite, a 1.5 liter bottle of CB beer, a bag of oranges, a carton of milk, a carton of orange juice, a loaf. I switched on the stove, took a frying pan from the cupboard under the counter and some margarine from the fridge, cut off a slice and scraped it in the pan, filled a large saucepan with water and placed it on the rear burner, opened the bag of potatoes, spilled them into the sink, turned on the tap, and started washing them, as the dollop of margarine slowly slid across the black frying pan. Again it struck me how clean and, for that reason, heartening the presence of these purchases was, their bright colors, the green and white of the frozen beans bag, its red writing and red logo, or the white paper around most of the loaf, though not all, the dark, rounded, crusty end peeped out like a snail from its shell, or, so it appeared to me, like a monk from his cowl. The orange tint of the fruit bulging through the plastic bag. Together, one globular shape hidden behind the other, they almost resembled a textbook model of a molecule. The scent they spread through the room as soon as they were peeled or cut open always reminded me of my father. That was how the rooms he had been in smelled: of cigarette smoke and oranges. Entering my own office and smelling the air there, I was always filled with good feelings.

But why? What was it that constituted the "good?"

Yngve folded up the two grocery bags and put them in the bottom drawer. The margarine was sizzling in the pan. The jet from the tap was broken by the potatoes I was holding beneath it, and the water that ran down the sides of the sink was not powerful enough to remove all the soil from the tubers and so formed a layer of mud around the plughole until the potatoes were clean and I removed them from the jet, which then swept everything with it in a second, to reveal once again the spotless, gleaming metal base.

"Hmm," Grandma said from the table.

Her deep eye sockets, the darkness in her otherwise bright eyes, her bones visible all over her body.

Yngve was drinking a glass of Coke in the center of the floor.

"Anything I can do to help?" he asked.

He set the glass down on the counter and belched quietly.

"No, I'm fine," I said.

"I'll go for a walk then," he said.

"You should," I said.

I placed the potatoes in the water, which was already coming to a boil; small bubbles were rising. Found the salt, it was on the hood of the stove, in a small silver Viking ship with spoons as oars, sprinkled a little into the water, cut up the cauliflower, filled another pan with water and put it on, then sliced open a packet of salmon with a knife and took out the four filets which I drizzled with salt and laid on a plate.

"It's fish tonight," I said. "Salmon."

"Oh, yes," Grandma said. "I'm sure it'll be good."

Her hair needed washing, and she needed a bath. And a fresh change of clothes. I was almost dying for it to happen. But who would take charge of that? It didn't look as if she would do anything on her own initiative. We couldn't tell her. That was out of the question. And what if she didn't want to? We couldn't force her either.

We would have to ask Tove. At least it wouldn't be quite so humiliating for her if it came from someone of the same sex. And who was a generation closer.

I placed the filets in the pan and switched on the fan. In seconds the undersides lightened, going from a deep, reddish pink to pale pink and I watched the new color slowly permeate the flesh. Turned down the potatoes, which were boiling over.

"Ohh," said Grandma.

I looked at her. She was sitting exactly as before and was probably not aware that a groan had escaped her lips.

He had been her firstborn.

Children were not supposed to pre-decease their parents, they weren't supposed to. That was not the idea.

And to me, what had Dad been to me?

Someone I wished dead.

So why all these tears?

I snipped open the bag of green beans. They were covered with a thin layer of downy frost and had a grayish appearance. Now the cauliflower was boiling as well. I turned down the burner and glanced at the wall clock. Eighteen minutes to five. Four more minutes and the cauliflower would be ready. Or six. Maybe another fifteen for the potatoes. I should have cut them in half. After all, this was no banquet we were having.

Grandma looked at me.

"Do you boys ever drink beer with your meals?" she said. I saw that Yngve had bought a bottle.

Had she seen it?

I shook my head.

"It has happened," I said. "But it's rare. Very rare, in fact."

I turned the filets. There were a few brownish-black patches here and there on the light flesh. But they weren't burned.

I emptied some beans into the pan, added salt, and poured out the excess water. Grandma leaned forward and looked out of the window. I took the frying pan off the heat, turned down the temperature, and joined Yngve on the veranda. He was sitting in a chair and gazing out.

"Food'll soon be ready," I said. "Five minutes."

"Good," he said.

"The beer you bought. Was that for the meal?" I asked.

He nodded and glanced over at me.

"Why?"

"It's Grandma," I said. "She asked if we ever had beer with meals. I was thinking that perhaps we don't have to drink when she's there. There's been so much boozing here. She doesn't need to see anymore. Even if it's only a glass with food. Do you see what I mean?"

"Of course. But you're going too far."

"Possibly I am. But this is not exactly a huge sacrifice."

"No," Yngve said.

"Are we agreed then?"

"Okay!" he said.

The irritation in his voice was unmistakable. I didn't want to leave with that hanging in the air. At the same time I couldn't think of a way to smooth things over. So after a few seconds of indecision, with my arms hanging limply down by my sides and tears in my throat I went back to the kitchen, set the table, emptied the water from the saucepan of potatoes and let them steam themselves dry, lifted the salmon filets onto a dish with the spatula, sliced the cauliflower and put it and the beans on the same dish, then found a bowl to put the potatoes in, and set everything on the table. Pink, light-green, white, dark-green, golden-brown. I filled a jug of water and was putting it on the table with three glasses just as Yngve came in from the veranda.

"That looks really good," he said and sat down. "But a knife and fork might come in handy."

I grabbed some cutlery from the drawer, passed it to them, sat down, and started to peel a potato. The hot skin burned my fingers.

"Are you peeling them?" Yngve said. "But these are new potatoes."

"You're right," I said. Impaled another potato with my fork and transported it to my plate. It crumbled as I pressed my knife in. Yngve raised a sliver of salmon to his mouth. Grandma sat dividing it up into small chunks. I got up for some margarine from the fridge, put a blob on the potato. From force of habit I breathed through my mouth as I chewed the first mouthful. Yngve appeared to have a more normal, adult relationship with fish. He even ate lutefisk now, which at one time had been the worst of the worst. In my head I could hear him saying *In fact it's really nice with bacon and all the trimmings*, while he sat beside me eating in silence. Lutefisk lunches with friends, well, that wasn't a world I inhabited. Not because I couldn't force down lutefisk but because I wasn't invited to that kind of gathering. Why not, I had no idea. I didn't care anymore anyway. But there had been days when I had cared, days when I had been on the outside and had suffered. Now I was only on the outside.

"Gunnar said there was a tool rental in Grim," I said. "Shall we go there tomorrow after seeing the undertaker? It would be good to get this done before you go. While we have a car, I mean."

"Fine," Yngve said.

Also Grandma was eating now. A pointed, rodent-like expression came over her face. Every time she moved I caught a whiff of pee. Oh, we were going to have to get her into the bathtub. Get her into clean clothes. Get some food into her. Porridge, milk, butter.

I raised the glass to my lips and drank. The water, so cool in my mouth, had a faint metallic taste. Yngve's cutlery clattered against the plate. A wasp or a bee buzzed around the dining room, behind the half-open door. Grandma sighed. And she twisted sideways in her chair as though the thought that had occurred to her had passed not only through her consciousness but also her body.

In this house they had even eaten fish on Christmas Eve. When I was small it seemed outrageous. Fish on Christmas Eve! But Kristiansand was a coastal town, the tradition well-established and the cod on sale in the fish hall during the Christmas run-up carefully selected. I had been there once with Grandma, I remembered the atmosphere that met us in the hall, the darkness after the blinding sunshine outside in the snow, the large cod swimming calmly around in their tanks, their brown skin, which was yellowish in places, greenish in others, their mouths opening and closing so slowly, the beard beneath the soft, white chin, the rigid yellow eyes. The men working there wore white aprons and rubber boots. One of them cut off the head of a cod with a large, almost square knife. The next moment, after moving the heavy head to the side, he sliced open the stomach. The intestines oozed out between his fingers. They were pale and wet, and thrown into a large waste drum beside him. Why were they so pale? Another man had just wrapped a fish in paper and was stabbing a till with one finger. I noticed that he treated the keys quite differently from the way they were treated in other shops, as though two distinct worlds, one tidy and the other rough, one indoors and the other outdoors, were brought together here in the fish vendor's brusque yet unpracticed fingers. The hall smelled of salt. Fish and shrimp were bedded in ice on the counters. Grandma, who was wearing a fur hat and a dark, floor-length cloak queued in front of one of the counters while I wandered over to a wooden crate full of live crabs. From the top they were dark-brown like rotten leaves, underneath yellowish-white bones. Their black, pinlike eyes, antennae, claws that made clicking sounds when the crabs crawled up on one another. They were like a kind of container, I thought, containers of meat. It was a marvelous adventure that they came from the deep, and had been hauled up here, as all live fish had. A man was hosing down the concrete floor; the water flowed towards the grille. Grandma leaned forward and pointed to a completely flat fish, greenish with rust-red spots, and the assistant lifted it from the ice-bed and put it on some scales, then onto paper, and wrapped it up. He put the packet into a bag, handed the bag to Grandma who, in turn, passed him a banknote from her little purse. But the sense of adventure that surrounded the fish here was gone as soon as they were on my plate, white, quivering, salty and full of bones, the same as with the fish that Dad and I caught in the sea off Tormøya, or in the sound by the mainland, with a jig, trolling line, or pole, that sense left them as soon as they had been prepared for the table and lay on one of our brown lunch plates at home in Tybakken in the seventies.

When had I accompanied Grandma to the fish hall?

I hadn't stayed with my grandparents on many weekdays when I was growing up. So it must have been the winter holiday that Yngve and I had spent there. When we caught the bus on our own to Kristiansand. That meant Yngve must have been with us on that day as well. But in my memory he wasn't. And the crabs could not have been there; the winter holiday was usually in February when you couldn't buy live crabs. If it had been February they wouldn't have been in a wooden crate. So where did this image, so distinct and detailed, actually come from?

Could have been anywhere. If my childhood was full of anything, it was fish and crabs, shrimp and lobsters. Many was the time I had seen Dad fetch cold leftovers of fish from the fridge, which he ate standing in the kitchen at night, or on weekend mornings. He liked crab best, though; when late summer came and they began to fill out he used to go to the fish wharf in Arendal after school and buy some, if for once he didn't catch them himself, in the evening or at night, on one of the islets in the skerries, or by the rocks on the far edge of the island. Sometimes we joined him, and there is one special occasion that sticks in my memory, one night by Torungen lighthouse under the bluish-black August sky, when the gulls launched themselves at us as we were leaving the boat to make our way across the islet, and afterward, with two buckets full of crabs, we lit a fire in a hollow. The flames licked at the sky. The sea around us was immense. Dad's face shone.

I set down the glass, cut off a piece of fish, and stuck my fork into it. The dark gray, oily meat separated by the three prongs was so tender that I could break it up with my tongue against my palate.

After eating we resumed the cleanup. The stairs were finished, so I took over where Tove had left off while Yngve began in the dining room. Outside, it was raining. A fine layer of drizzle fell against the windows, the veranda wall was slightly darker, and at sea, where presumably it would have fallen with greater force, the clouds on the horizon were striped with rain. I wiped the dust off all the small ornaments, the lamps, the pictures and the souvenirs that littered the shelves, and put them on the floor piece by piece in order to clean the shelves themselves. An oil lamp that looked like something from *One Thousand and One Nights*, both cheap and precious, with ornate, gilt decorations, a Venetian gondola that gleamed like a lamp, a photograph of my grandparents in front of an Egyptian pyramid. As I examined it I heard Grandma get up in the kitchen. I wiped the glass and frame and put it down, reached for the little stand holding old-fashioned 45 rpm records. Grandma stood with her hands behind her back, watching me.

"No, you really don't need to do *that*," she said. "You don't need to be *so* thorough."

"It won't take a second," I said. "Might as well while I'm at it."

"Fair enough," she said. "It's looking nice."

After wiping the stand down I put it on the floor, piled the records beside it, opened the cupboard and removed the old stereo player.

"You don't take a little drop in the evening, do you?" she asked.

"No," I said. "Not during the week anyway."

"I guessed as much," she said.

In the town on the other side of the river the lights had started to shine more brightly. What could the time be? Half past five? Six?

I cleaned the shelves and replaced the stereo. Grandma, who must have gathered that there was nothing more to be gained here, turned with a sigh and went down to the second living room. Immediately afterward I heard her voice, and then Yngve's. On entering the kitchen to get some newspaper and a window spray I noticed through the open door that she had taken a seat at the table to chat with Yngve while he was working.

Drink really had gotten a hold on her, I was thinking, as I took the spray from the cupboard, tore a few pages from the newspaper on the chair under the wall clock, and returned to the living room. Not exactly a surprise. He had been systemically drinking himself to death, no other way of explaining it, and she had been here to witness it. Every morning, every afternoon, every evening, every night. For how long? Two years? Three years? Just the two of them. Mother and son.

I sprayed the glass door of the bookcase, crumpled up the newspaper, and rubbed it over the runny liquid a few times until the glass was dry and shiny. Looked around for more to do while I had the spray in my hand, but saw nothing apart from the windows, which I had determined to save till later. Instead, I went on with the bookcase, cleaned up everything, starting with its contents.

In the meantime the air in the harbor basin was streaked with rain. The next moment it beat against the window in front of me. Large, heavy drops that ran down and formed tremulous patterns across the whole pane. Grandma walked past behind me. I didn't turn, but her movements were still engaging my mind as she stopped, picked up the TV remote control, pressed it, and sat in the chair. I put the duster on the shelf and went to see Yngve.

"They're full of bottles as well," he said, nodding toward the line of cupboards along one entire wall. "But the dishes are fine."

"Has she asked you if we usually take a drink?" I said. "She must have asked me ten times since we arrived. At least."

"Yes, she certainly has," he said. "The question is whether she should have a little drink. She doesn't need our permission, but that's what she's asking for. So . . . what do you think?"

"What?"

"Didn't you understand?" he asked, looking up again. With a tiny mirthless smile on his lips.

"Understand what?" I replied.

"She wants a drink. She's desperate."

"Grandma?"

"Yes. What do you think? Is it okay for her to have one?"

"Are you sure that's what it is? I was thinking the opposite."

"That was my first thought too. But it's obvious when you think about it. He lived here for a long time. How else could she have stood it?"

"Is she an *alcoholic*?"

Yngve shrugged.

"Thing is she wants a drink now. And she needs our permission."

"Shit," I said. "What a mess this is."

"It's fine, but surely it wouldn't hurt to have a little drink now, would it? She is in shock, kind of."

"So what do we do?" I said.

"Well, we can ask her if she wants a drink? Then we can have one with her."

"Okay, but not right now, surely?"

"Let's finish up for the evening. And then ask her. As though it were nothing out of the ordinary."

Half an hour later I had finished the bookcase and went onto the terrace, where it had stopped raining and the air was full of fresh fragrances from the garden. The table lay under a film of water; the seat covers were dark with moisture. Plastic bottles lying on their sides on the brick floor were dotted with raindrops. The bottlenecks reminded me of muzzles, as if they were small cannons with their barrels pointing in all directions. Raindrops hung in clusters along the underside of the wrought-iron fence. Now and then one let go and fell onto the wall beneath with an almost imperceptible plop.

That Dad had been here only three days ago was hard to believe. That he had seen the same view three days ago, walked around the same house, seen Grandma as we saw her and thought his thoughts only three days ago was hard to grasp. That is, I could grasp that he had been here recently. But not that he couldn't see this now. The veranda, the plastic bottles, the light in the neighbor's windows. The flakes of yellow paint that had peeled off and now lay on the red terrace by the rusting table leg. The gutter and the rainwater still running down it into the grass. I could not grasp that he wouldn't see any more of this, however hard I tried. I did grasp that he wouldn't see Yngve or me again, that had something to do with our emotions, in which death was interwoven in a completely different way from the objective, concrete reality that surrounded me.

Nothing, just nothing. Not even darkness.

I lit a cigarette, ran my hand over the wet chair seat a couple of times and sat down. I only had two left. So I would have to go to the newsstand before it closed.

A cat slunk along the fence at the end of the lawn. Its coat was a grizzled gray and it looked old. It stopped with one paw raised, staring into the grass for a while, then went on. I thought about our cat, Nansen, on which Tonje lavished her affections. It was no more than a few months old and slept under her duvet with its head just peeping out.

I hadn't given Tonje a single thought during the day. Not one. What did that mean? I didn't want to call her because I had nothing to say, but I would have to for her sake. If I hadn't thought about her, she would have thought about me, I knew that.

In the air high above the harbor a seagull was flying toward us. It was heading for the veranda, and I felt myself smile, it was Grandma's seagull on its way for supper. But with me sitting there it didn't dare approach and landed on the roof instead, where it leaned back and squawked its seagull squawk.

Bit of salmon wouldn't go amiss, would it?

I stubbed the cigarette out on the veranda, put it in a bottle, stood up, and went to Grandma, who was watching TV.

"Your gull's here again," I said. "Shall I give it some salmon?"

"What?" she said, turning toward me.

"The gull's here," I said. "Shall I give it some salmon?"

"Oh," she said. "I can do that."

She got to her feet and walked with her head hunched into the kitchen. I grabbed the TV remote control and lowered the volume. Then I went into the dining room, which was empty, and sat by the telephone. I dialed home.

"Hello, Tonje here."

"Hi. Karl Ove here."

"Oh *hi* . . ."

"Hi."

"How's it going?"

"Not wonderfully," I said. "It's hard going here. I'm in tears almost all the time. But I don't really know what I'm crying about. Dad being dead, of course, but it's not just that . . ."

"I should have gone with you," she said. "I miss you so much."

"It's a house of death," I said. "We're wading through his death. He died in the chair in the room next door, it's still there. And then there's everything that happened here, I mean, a long time ago, when I was growing up, all that's here too, and it's surfacing. Do you understand? I'm somehow very close to everything. To the person I was when I was younger. To the person Dad was. All the feelings from that time are resurfacing."

"Poor Karl Ove," she said.

Grandma came through the door in front of me, carrying a dish of cut-up salmon. She didn't see me. I waited until she was in the other room.

"No, don't feel sorry for me," I said. "It's him we should feel sorry for. His life was so awful at the end you wouldn't believe it."

"How's your grandmother taking it?"

"I don't quite know. She's in shock, she seems senile. And she's so damn thin. They just sat here drinking. Her and him."

"Her as well. Your grandmother?"

"Absolutely. You wouldn't believe it. But we've decided to clean everything up and have a wake here after the funeral."

Through the glass door to the veranda I could see Grandma putting down the dish. She stepped back and peered around.

"That sounds like a good idea," Tonje said.

"I don't know," I said. "But that's what we're going to do now. Clean the whole damn house and then fix it up. Buy tablecloths and flowers and . . ."

Yngve stuck his head through the door. When he saw I was on the phone he raised his eyebrows and withdrew, just as Grandma came in from the veranda. She stood in front of the window and looked out.

"I was thinking of coming down a day before," Tonje said. "Then I can give you a hand."

"The funeral's on Friday," I said. "Can you get a day off work?"

"Yes. So, I'll come in the morning. I miss you so much."

"What have you been doing today?"

"Mm, nothing special. Had lunch with Mom and Hans. Love from them, they were thinking about you."

"Mm, that was nice of them," I said. "What did you have to eat?"

Tonje's mother was a fantastic cook; meals in her house were an experience, if you were the foodie type. I wasn't, I didn't give a rat's ass about food, I was just as happy to eat fish fingers as baked halibut, sausages as fillet of Beef Wellington, but Tonje was, her eyes lit up when she started talking about food, and she was a talented cook, she enjoyed working in the kitchen; even if it was only pizza she was making, she put her heart and soul into it. She was the most sensuous person I had ever met. And she had moved in with someone who regarded meals, home comforts, and closeness as necessary evils.

"Flounder. So it's just as well you weren't there."

I could hear her grinning.

"But, oh, it was fantastic."

"That I don't doubt," I said. "Were Kjetil and Karin there too?"

"Yes. And Atle."

A lot had happened in her family, as in all families, but this was not something they talked about, so if it was manifest anywhere, it was in each of them, and the atmospheres they created collectively. One of the things Tonje liked best about me, I suspected, was that I was so fascinated by precisely that, by all the contexts and potential of various relationships, she wasn't used to that, she never speculated along those lines, so when I opened her eyes to what I saw she was always interested. I had this from my mother, right from the time I went to school I used to carry on long conversations with her about people we had met or known, what they had said, why they might have said it, where they came from, who their parents were, what kind of house they lived in, all woven into questions to do with politics, ethics, morality, psychology, and philosophy, and this conversation, which continued to this day, had given my gaze a direction, I always saw what happened between people and tried to explain it, and for a long time I also believed I was good at reading others, but I was not, wherever I turned I only saw myself, but perhaps that was not what our conversations were about primarily, there was something else, they were about Mom and me, that was how we became close to each other, in language and reflection, that was where we were connected, and that was also where I sought a connection with Tonje. And it was good because she needed it in the same way that I needed her robust sensuousness.

"I miss you," I said. "But I'm glad you aren't here."

"You must promise you won't exclude me from what's happening to you now," she said.

"I won't," I said.

"I love you," she said.

"I love you too," I said.

As always when I said this, I wondered if it was actually true. Then the feeling passed. Of course I did, of course I loved her.

"Will you call me tomorrow?"

"Of course. Bye now."

"Bye. And give my love to Yngve."

I hung up and went into the kitchen where Yngve was standing over the counter.

"That was Tonje," I said. "She sends you her love."

"Thanks," he said. "Same to her."

I sat down on the edge of the chair.

"Shall we call it a day?"

"Yes. I couldn't do much more, anyway."

"I've just got to run down to the newsstand. So we can . . . well, you know. Is there anything you need?"

"Could you get me a pouch of tobacco? And maybe some chips or something?"

I nodded and got up, went downstairs, put on my coat, which was hanging in the wardrobe, checked that my bank card was in the inside pocket, glanced at myself in the mirror, and left. I looked exhausted. And even though it was quite a few hours since I had been crying you could see it in my eyes. They weren't red; it was more that they were swollen and watery.

I stopped for a moment on the steps. It struck me that there were a lot of things to ask Grandma. We had been too circumspect so far. When, for example, had the ambulance come? How quickly? Had there still been a life to save when they arrived? Had it been an emergency call?

Up the drive it must have come, lights flashing, siren blaring. The driver and doctor jumped out and dashed up the steps with the equipment to the door, which must have been locked. This door was always locked. Had she had the presence of mind to come down and unlock it before they arrived? Or did they stand here ringing the bell? What did she say to them when they came in? *He's over there?* And did she lead them to the living room? Was he sitting in the chair? Was he lying on the floor? Did they try to revive him? Heart massage, oxygen, mouth-to-mouth? Or did they immediately confirm that he was dead, beyond help, and lay him on the stretcher and take him away, after exchanging a few words with her? How much had she understood? What did she say? And when did this happen: in the morning, in the middle of the day, or in the evening?

Surely we couldn't leave Kristiansand without knowing the circumstances of his death, could we?

I set off with a sigh. Above me the entire sky had opened. What a few hours earlier had been plain, dense cloud cover now took on landscapelike formations, a chasm with long flat stretches, steep walls, and sudden pinnacles, in some places white and substantial like snow, in others gray and as hard as rock, while the huge surfaces illuminated by the sunset did not shine or gleam or have a reddish glow, as they could, rather they seemed as if they had been dipped in some liquid. They hung over the town, muted red, dark-pink, surrounded by every conceivable nuance of gray. The setting was wild and beautiful. Actually everyone should be in the streets, I thought, cars should be stopping, doors should be opened and drivers and passengers emerging with heads raised and eyes sparkling with curiosity and a craving for beauty, for what was it that was going on above our heads?

However, a few glances at most were cast upward, perhaps followed by isolated comments about how beautiful the evening was, for sights like this were not exceptional, on the contrary, hardly a day passed without the sky being filled with fantastic cloud formations, each and every one illuminated in unique, never-to-be-repeated ways, and since what you see every day is what you never see, we lived our lives under the constantly changing sky without sparing it a glance or a thought. And why should we? If the various formations had had some *meaning*, if, for example, there had been concealed signs and messages for us which it was important we decode correctly, unceasing attention to what was happening would have been inescapable and understandable. But this was not the case of course, the various cloud shapes and hues meant *nothing*, what they looked like at any given juncture was based on chance, so if there was anything the clouds suggested it was meaninglessness in its purest form.

I entered the main road, which was deserted of people and traffic, and followed it to the intersection, where the Sunday atmosphere also prevailed. An elderly couple was walking on the opposite sidewalk, a few cars passed slowly on their way to the bridge, the traffic lights didn't change to red for anyone. A black Golf was parked by the bus stop beside the newsstand, and the driver, a young man in shorts, clambered out, wallet in hand and darted into the shop, leaving the car idling. I met him in the doorway as he was coming out, this time holding an ice cream. Wasn't that a bit infantile? Leaving the car running to buy an *ice cream*?

The sportily dressed shop assistant from the previous day had been replaced by a girl in her early twenties. She was plump with black hair, and from her facial features, about which there was something Persian, I guessed she came from Iran or Iraq. Despite the round cheeks and full figure, she was attractive. She didn't so much as give me a glance. Her attention was held by a magazine on the counter in front of her. I slid open the fridge door and took out three half-liter bottles of Sprite, scanned the shelves for chips, found them, grabbed two bags and put them on the counter.

"And a pouch of Tiedemanns Gul with papers," I said.

She turned and reached down for the tobacco from the shelf behind her.

"Rizla?" she inquired, still without meeting my eyes.

"Yes, please," I answered.

She put the orange cigarette papers under the fold of the yellow tobacco pouch and put it on the counter while entering the prices on the till with her other hand.

"One hundred and fifty-seven kroner fifty," she said in broad Kristiansand dialect.

I passed her two hundred-notes. She entered the amount and selected the change from the drawer that slid out. Even though I had my hand outstretched she placed it on the counter.

Why? Was there something about me, something she had noticed and didn't like? Or was she just slow on the uptake? It is quite usual for shop assistants to register eye contact at some point during a transaction, isn't it? And if you have your hand outstretched, surely it is bordering on an insult to put the money anywhere else? At least demonstratively.

I looked at her.

"Could I have a bag as well?"

"Of course," she said, crouching down and pulling a white plastic bag from under the counter.

"Here you are."

"Thank you," I said, gathering the items and leaving. The desire to sleep with her, which manifested itself more as a kind of physical openness and gentleness than lust's more usual form, which of course is rougher, more acute, a kind of contraction of the senses, lasted all the way back to the house, but it was not in complete control because grief lay all around it, with its hazy, gray sky, which I suspected could overwhelm me again at any moment.

They were sitting in the living room watching TV. Yngve was in Dad's chair. He turned his head when I came in and got up.

"We thought we would have a little drink," he said to Grandma. "Since we've been slogging away all day. Would you like one as well?"

"That would be nice," said Grandma.

"I'll mix you one," Yngve said. "Then perhaps we can sit in the kitchen?"

"Fine," Grandma said.

Did she walk a touch faster across the floor than she had before? Had a little light lit her otherwise dark eyes?

Yes, indeed.

I put one bag of chips on the counter, emptied the contents of the second into a bowl, which I placed on the table while Yngve took a bottle of Absolut Blue from the cupboard – it had been among the food items when we were pouring all the alcohol we could find down the sink and we missed it – three glasses from the shelves above the counter, a carton of juice from the fridge and started mixing drinks. Grandma sat in her place watching him.

"So you like a bit of a stiffener in the evenings as well," she said.

"Yes," Yngve said. "We've been at it all day. It's good to relax a bit too!"

He smiled and gave her a glass. So, there we were, sitting around the table, all three of us, drinking. Outside, it had begun to get dark. There was no doubt that the alcohol was doing Grandma some good. Her eyes soon had their previous glint back, some color came into her wan, pale cheeks, her movements were gentler, and after she had finished the first drink and Yngve had given her a second it was as though she was able to unburden herself, for soon she was chatting away and laughing like in the old days. During the first half-hour I sat as if paralyzed, rigid with unease, because she was like a vampire that had finally gotten a taste of blood, I saw, that was how it was: life was returning to her, filling her limb by limb. It was terrible, terrible.

But then I felt the effect of the alcohol, my thoughts mellowed, my mind opened, and her sitting here, drinking and laughing, after having found her son dead in the living room no longer seemed creepy, there was no problem, she clearly needed it; after spending the whole day sitting motionless on the kitchen chair, interrupted only by her wanderings through the house, restless and confused, ever silent, she livened up, and it was good to see. And, as for us, we really needed it too. So there we sat, with Grandma telling stories, us laughing, Yngve adding his bit, and us laughing some more. They had always found a wavelength with their sense for wordplay but seldom better than on this evening. Every so often Grandma wiped tears of laughter from her eyes, every so often I met Yngve's gaze, and the pleasure I saw there, which at first contained an element of apology, was soon back to its initial state. This was a magic potion we were drinking. The shiny liquid that tasted so strong, even diluted with orange juice, changed the conditions of our presence there, by shutting out our awareness of recent events and thus opening the way for the people we normally were, what we normally thought, as if illuminated from below, for what we were and thought suddenly shone through with a luster and warmth and no longer stood in our way. Grandma still smelled of pee, her dress was still covered with grease and food stains, she was still frighteningly thin, she had still lived the last few months in a rat's nest with her son, our father, who had still died here of alcohol abuse and was still barely cold. But her eyes, they were gleaming. Her mouth, smiling. And her hands, which so far had remained motionless in her lap, unless they had been busy with her perpetual smoking, were beginning to gesticulate now. She was transforming before our very eyes into the person she had been, easy, razor-sharp, never far from a smile and laughter. We had heard the stories she told, but that was the point of them, at least for me, because hearing them took me back to the grandmother she had been, to the life that had been lived here. None of these stories was amusing in itself; it was the way Grandma told them that elevated the anecdotes to stories, and the fact that she found them amusing. She always had an eye for the drollness of everyday life and laughed just as much every time. Her sons were part of it, inasmuch as they kept telling her snippets from their lives, she laughed and, if they were to her taste, assimilated them and included them in her repertoire. Her sons, especially Erling and Gunnar, were also partial to wordplay. Wasn't it Gunnar they had sent to the shop to buy elbow grease? And an overhead cable? Wasn't it Yngve they had tricked into thinking that "exhaust pipe" and "carburettor" were the filthiest words in existence, and had made him promise he would never use them? Dad would also participate in these shenanigans, but I never associated it with him; when he did I generally reacted with surprise. The very idea that he would indulge in storytelling and laugh the way Grandma did was inconceivable.

Even though she had told the stories hundreds of times before, her telling of them was so vivid that it seemed to be the first. So the ensuing laughter was therefore utterly liberating: there wasn't a scrap of artificiality about it. And after we had drunk a bit, and the alcohol had brightened all the darkness that may have been in us, in addition to eradicating the observing eye, we had no compunction about joining in the party. One chorus of laughter led to another. Grandma drew from her profusion of anecdotes, collected over the eighty years of her life, but she did not stop there, for as her inebriation grew her defenses weakened, and she extended the familiar stories, told us more about what had happened in such a way that the point of them changed. For example, in the early 1930s she had worked as a chauffeur, we knew that already, it was part of the family mythology, there weren't many women with a driver's license at that time or, for that matter, who worked as chauffeurs. She had answered an advertisement, she said, she read the *Aftenposten* at home in Åsgårdstand and had spotted the position vacant, written a letter, accepted the job, and moved to Oslo. She worked for an elderly, eccentric, and wealthy woman. Grandma, who was in her early twenties then, had a room in her mansion and drove her wherever she wanted to go. She had a dog that used to hang its head out of the window and bark at passersby, and Grandma laughed when she described to us how embarrassed she had been. But there was another incident she used to mention to exemplify how eccentric and presumably senile the elderly lady had been. She kept her money all over the house. There were wads of banknotes in kitchen cupboards, in saucepans and teapots, under rugs, under pillows. Grandma used to laugh and shake her head as she was speaking, we were reminded that she had just left home, that she came from a small town, and this was her first experience of not only the world outside but of the finer world outside. This time, sitting around the lit kitchen table, with the shadows of our faces on the darkening windows, and a bottle of Absolut vodka between us, she suddenly asked, rhetorically: "So what was I to do? She was stinking rich, you know, boys. And she had her money lying around everywhere. She wouldn't notice if some disappeared. Surely it wouldn't make any difference if I took a bit?"

"You took her money?" I probed.

"Yes, of course I did. It wasn't much, it meant nothing to her. And if she didn't notice, what was the problem? And she was a cheapskate. Yes, she was, the wages I got were a pittance. Because I did more than drive for her, I was responsible for everything else too, so it was only right that I should be better paid!"

She banged the table with her fist. Then she laughed.

"But that dog of hers! What a sight we were, driving through Oslo. There weren't many cars at that time, as you know. So we were noticed. We certainly were."

She chuckled. Then she sighed.

"Oh well," she said. "Life's a pitch, as the old woman said. She couldn't pronounce her *b*'s. Ha ha ha."

She raised her glass to her lips and drank. I did the same. Then grabbed the bottle and refilled my empty glass, glancing at Yngve, who nodded, and I poured.

"Would you like some more?" I said, looking at Grandma.

"Please," she said. "Just a finger."

After I had attended to her glass, Yngve poured in some juice, but it ran out before the glass was half-full, and he shook the carton a few times.

"It's empty," he said, looking at me. "Didn't you buy some Sprite in the shop?"

"I did," I said. "I'll get it."

I went to the fridge. As well as the three half-liters I had bought there was a 1.5 liter bottle Yngve had picked up earlier in the day.

"Had you forgotten this one?" I said, holding it up.

"Oh yeah," Yngve said.

I put it on the table and left the room to go downstairs to the toilet. The darkened rooms lay around me, large and empty. But with the flame of alcohol burning in my brain I took no notice of the atmosphere that otherwise would have affected me, for although I wasn't outright happy, I was elated, exhilarated, motivated by the desire to continue this, which not even a direct reminder of Dad's death could shake, it was just a pale shadow, present but of no consequence, because life had taken its place, all the images, voices and actions that drinking alcohol conjured up at the drop of a hat and gave me the illusion that I was somewhere surrounded by a lot of people and merriment. I knew it wasn't true, but that was how it felt, and it was feeling that was leading me, also when I stepped on the stained wall-to-wall carpeting on the ground floor, illuminated by the dim light seeping in through the front door pane, and entered the bathroom that hissed and whistled as it had done for at least thirty years. On my way out I heard their voices above and hurried upstairs. In the living room, I took a few steps inside to see the place where he had died while I was in a different, a more carefree frame of mind. I was given a sudden sensation of who he had been. I didn't see him, it wasn't like that, but I could sense *him*, the whole of his being, the way he had been during his final days in these rooms. It was uncanny. But I didn't want to linger, nor could I perhaps, for the sensation lasted only a few moments, then my brain sank its claws into it and I went back to the kitchen where everything was as I had left it, except for the color of the drinks, which were shiny and full of small, grayish bubbles now.

Grandma was talking more about the years she had lived in Oslo. This story too was part of the family mythology, and this too she gave an unexpected, and for us new, twist at the end. I already knew that Grandma had been in a relationship with Alf, our grandfather's elder brother. At first they had been a couple. Both the brothers had been studying in Oslo, Alf natural science, while Grandad studied economics. When the relationship with Alf finished Grandma married Grandad and moved to Kristiansand, as did Alf, but with Sølvi as his wife. She had had TB in her youth, one lung was punctured and she was sickly all her life, she couldn't have children, so at a relatively late age they had adopted an Asian girl. When I was growing up most of our get-togethers were with Alf plus family, and Grandma and Grandad plus family, they were the ones who visited us, and the fact that Alf and Grandma had once been a couple was often mentioned, it was no secret, and when Grandad and Sølvi were dead, Grandma and Alf met once a week, she visited him every Saturday morning, at the house in Grim, no one considered this strange, but there were a few kindly smiles, for was this not how it should have been?

Grandma told us about the first time she had met the two brothers. Alf had been the extrovert, Grandad the more introverted one, but both apparently showed an interest in the girl from Åsgårdstrand, for when Grandad saw which way the wind was blowing with his brother, who was charming her with his good humor and wit, he whispered to her: *He's got the ring in his pocket!*

Grandma was laughing as she spoke.

"What was that?" I asked, despite having heard what he said. *He's got the ring in his pocket!* he repeated. *What kind of ring?* I asked. *An engagement ring!* he answered, boys. He thought I hadn't understood!"

"Was Alf already engaged to Sølvi at that time?" Yngve asked.

"Indeed he was. She lived in Arendal and was sickly, you know. He didn't expect it to last. But they made it in the end!"

She took another sip from the glass and licked her lips afterward. There was a silence, and she withdrew into herself as she had done so many times in the last two days. Sat with her arms crossed, staring into the distance. I drained my drink and poured myself a fresh one, took out a Rizla, laid a line of tobacco, spread it evenly to get the best possible draw, rolled the paper a few times, pressed down the end and closed it, licked the glue, removed any shreds of tobacco, dropped them in the pouch, put the somewhat deformed roll-up in my mouth and lit it with Yngve's green, semitransparent lighter.

"We were going to travel south to the sun the winter Grandad died," Grandma said. "We had bought the tickets and everything."

I looked at her as I blew out the smoke.

"The night he collapsed in the bathroom, you know . . . I just heard a crash inside and I got up, and there he was on the floor, telling me to call for an ambulance. When I'd done that I sat holding his hand as we waited for it to come. Then he said, *We'll still go south*. And I was thinking, *It's a different south you're heading for*."

She laughed, but with downcast eyes.

"It's a different south *you're* heading for!" she repeated.

There was a long silence.

"Ohh," she said then. "Life's a pitch, as the old woman said. She couldn't pronounce her *b*'s."

We smiled. Yngve shifted his glass, looked down at the table. I didn't want her thinking about either Grandad's or Dad's death, and I tried to change the subject by returning to her previous subject.

"But did you come here when you moved to Kristiansand?" I asked.

"Oh, no," she replied. "We were farther down Kuholmsveien. We bought this house after the war. It was a wonderful location, one of the best in Lund because we had a view of course. Of the sea and the town. And so high up that no one can look in. But when we bought the plot there was another house here. Although to call it a house is a bit of an exaggeration. Ha ha ha. It was a real hovel. The people who lived here, two men as far as I remember, yes, it was . . . you see, they drank. And the first time we came to see the house, I remember it well, there were bottles everywhere. In the hall where we entered, on the stairs, in the living room, in the kitchen. Everywhere! In some places it was so thick with bottles you couldn't set a foot inside. So we got it quite cheap. We demolished the house and then we built this. There hadn't been a garden, either, just rock, a hovel on rock, that was what we bought."

"Did you put a lot of work into the garden?" I asked.

"Oh yes, you can imagine. Oh yes, yes, I did. The plum trees down there, you know, I took them from my parents' house in Åsgårdstrand. They're very old. They're not that common anymore."

"I remember we used to take bags of the plums home," Yngve said.

"Yes," I said.

"Do they still bear fruit?" Yngve asked.

"Yes, I think so," Grandma said. "Perhaps not as much as before, but . . ."

I reached for the bottle, which was nearly half-empty now, and poured myself another glass. Not so strange perhaps that it had not struck my grandmother that the wheel had come full circle with what had gone on here, I mused. Wiped a drop from the bottleneck with my thumb and licked it off while Grandma, on the other side of the table, opened the tobacco pouch and placed a fingerful in the roller machine. However extreme life had been for her over recent years, it barely constituted a tiny part of all the things she had been through. When she had looked at Dad she had seen the baby, the child, the adolescent, the young man; the whole of his character and all of his qualities were contained in that one look, and if he was in such a drunken state that he shat his pants while lying on her sofa, the moment was so brief and she so old that it would not, compared with all the immense span of time together that she had stored, have had enough weight to become the image that counted. The same was true of the house, I assumed. The first house with the bottles became "the house of the bottles" whereas this house was her home, the place where she had spent the last forty years and the fact that it was full of bottles now could never be what the house meant to her.

Or was it just that she was so drunk she couldn't think straight any longer? In which case she hid it well, for apart from her obvious blossoming there were few signs of drunkenness in her behavior. On the other hand, I was not the right person to judge anyone. Spurred on by the alcohol's ever brighter light, which was corroding more and more of my thoughts, I had begun to knock back the drinks almost like juice. And the pit was bottomless.

After pouring Sprite into my glass I took the Absolut bottle, which was obscuring my view of Grandma, and stood it on the windowsill.

"What are you doing?!" Yngve asked.

"You've put the bottle in the window!" Grandma cried.

Flushed and confused, I snatched the bottle and returned it to the table.

Grandma began to laugh.

"He put the bottle of booze in the window!"

Yngve laughed too.

"Of course. The neighbors have to see us sitting here and drinking," he said.

"Okay, okay," I said. "I wasn't thinking."

"No, you weren't. You can say that again!" Grandma said, wiping tears of laughter from her eyes.

In this house where we had always been so careful to prevent others from prying, where we had always been so careful to be beyond reproach in everything that could be seen, from clothes to garden, from house front to car to children's behavior, the closest you could come to the absolutely unthinkable was to exhibit a bottle of booze in a brightly lit window. That was why they, and eventually I too, laughed as we did.

The light in the sky above the hill over the road, which could just be glimpsed through the reflection in the kitchen window, with us three resembling underwater figures, was a grayish-blue. This was as dark as the night sky ever got. Yngve had started to slur. To someone who didn't know him this would have been impossible to detect. But I noticed because he always slipped the same way when he drank, at first a touch unclear, then he slurred more and more, until toward the end, the moment before he passed out, he was almost incomprehensible. In my case the lack of clarity that went hand in hand with drinking was primarily an inner phenomenon, it was only there that it was manifest, and this was a problem because if it was not visible from the outside how utterly plastered I was, since I walked and talked almost as normal, there was no excuse for all the standards that at a later point I might let slip, either in language or behavior. Furthermore, my wild state always became worse for that reason, as my drunkenness was not brought to a halt by sleep or problems of coordination, but simply continued into the beyond, the primitive, and the void. I loved it, I loved the feeling, it was my favorite feeling, but it never led to anything good, and the day after, or the days after, it was as closely associated with boundless excess as with stupidity, which I hated with a passion. But when I was in that state, the future did not exist, nor the past, only the moment and that was why I wanted to be in it so much, for my world, in all its unbearable banality, was radiant.

I turned to look at the wall clock. It was twenty-five to twelve. Then I glanced at Yngve. He looked tired. His eyes were slits and slightly red at the margins. His glass was empty. I hoped he wasn't thinking of going to bed. I didn't want to sit there alone with Grandma.

"Do you want some more?" I asked, nodding to the bottle on the table.

"Well, maybe just a drop more," he said. "But it'll have to be the last. We need to get up early tomorrow."

"Oh?" I said. "Why's that?"

"We have an appointment at nine, don't you remember?"

I smacked my forehead. I doubted if I had performed this gesture since I left school.

"It'll be fine," I said. "All we have to do is turn up."

Grandma looked at us.

Please don't let her ask where we're going! I thought. The words "funeral director" would certainly break the spell. And then we would be sitting here again like a mother who has lost her son and two children who have lost their father.

However, I didn't dare ask her if she wanted anymore. There was a limit, it had something to do with decency, and it had been crossed ages ago. I reached for the bottle and poured a drop into Yngve's glass, then my own. But after I had done that, her eyes met mine.

"One more?" I heard myself ask.

"A little one perhaps," she replied. "It's late."

"Yes, it's late on earth," I said.

"What do you mean?" she asked.

"He said it was late on earth," Yngve explained. "It's a quote from a famous Swedish poem."

Why did he say that? Did he want to put me in my place? Oh, what the hell, I suppose it was a stupid thing to say. "Late on earth" . . .

"Karl Ove's going to have a book published soon," Yngve said.

"Are you?" Grandma asked.

I nodded.

"Yes, now that you mention it, someone must have told me. Was it Gunnar, I wonder? Goodness. A book."

She raised the glass to her mouth and drank. I did the same. Was it my imagination, or had her eyes darkened again?

"So you didn't live here during the war then?" I said, before taking another sip.

"No, after the war, it was a few years after when we moved here. During the war we lived over there," she said, pointing behind her.

"What was it like actually?" I asked. "During the war, I mean?"

"Well, it was almost the same as before, you know. A bit harder to get hold of food, but otherwise there wasn't such an enormous difference. The Germans were normal people, like us. We got to know a few of them, you see. We went down to visit them after the war as well."

"In Germany?"

"Yes. And when they were leaving, in May 1945, they gave us a call and said we could go and help ourselves to some things they had left behind, if we wanted. They gave us the finest drinks. And a radio. And a lot of other things."

I hadn't heard that they had been given presents by the Germans before they capitulated. But then the Germans had been to their homes.

"Things they'd left behind?" I echoed. "Where?"

"By some cliff," Grandma said. "They called to tell us exactly where we could find them. So we went out that evening, and there they were, precisely as they had said. They were kind, no doubt about that."

Had Grandma and Grandad clambered around a cliff one May evening in 1945 hunting for the bottles left by the Germans?

The light from a pair of car headlights flitted across the garden and shone on the wall under the window for a few seconds, then the car was around the bend and slowly glided past along the alley below. Grandma leaned toward the window.

"Who could that be at this time of night?" she wondered.

She sighed and sat back down, with her hands in her lap. Looked at us.

"It's good you're here, boys," she said.

There was a silence. Grandma took another sip.

"Do you remember when you lived here?" she said suddenly, looking at Yngve with warmth in her eyes. "Your father came to pick you up and he had a beard. And you ran upstairs shouting 'He's not my dad!' Ha ha ha! 'He's not my dad!' We had so much fun with you, my goodness."

"I remember that very well," Yngve said.

"And then there was the time we were listening to the radio, and they were talking to the owner of Norway's oldest horse. Do you remember that? 'Dad, you're the same age as Norway's oldest horse!' you said."

She leaned forward as she laughed and rubbed her eyes with the knuckles of her index fingers.

"And you," she said, focusing on me. "Can you remember the time you came with us to the cabin on your own?"

I nodded.

"One morning we found you sitting on the steps crying, and when we asked why you were crying you said 'I'm so lonely.' You were eight years old."

It had been the summer Mom and Dad had gone on vacation to Germany. Yngve had been in Sørbøvåg with Mom's parents, and I had been here, in Kristiansand. What did I remember of that? That the distance between me and Grandma and Grandad had been too great. Suddenly I was just one part of their everyday lives. They were strangers to me more than ever, as there was no one or nothing to bridge the gap between us. One morning there had been a bug in the milk, I didn't want to drink it, and Grandma told me not to be so fussy, I just had to take it out, that's how it was in nature. Her voice had been sharp. And I drank the milk, queasy with disgust. Why had that memory of all memories stuck? And no others? There must have been others. Yes: Mom and Dad sent me a postcard with a picture of the Bayern Munich soccer team. How I had longed for that, and how happy I had been when it finally arrived! And the presents when they finally came home: a red-and-yellow soccer ball for Yngve, a red-and-green one for me. The colors . . . oh, the feeling of happiness they brought . . .

"Another time you were standing on the stairs here shouting for me," Grandma said, looking at Yngve. "*Grandma, are you upstairs or downstairs?* I answered *downstairs* and you shouted *Why aren't you upstairs?*"

She laughed.

"Yes, we had lots of fun . . . When you moved to Tybakken you just knocked on the neighbors' doors and asked if there were any children living there. *Are there any children living here?* you asked them." She broke into laughter again.

After the laughter had died down, she sat chuckling while forming another cigarette in the roller machine. The tip of the roll-up was empty and flared up when she lit it with the lighter. A tiny fragment of ash floated down to the floor. Then the flame reached the tobacco and shrank to a glow, which shone brighter every time she puffed on the filter.

"But now you've grown up," she said. "And that's so strange. It seems like only yesterday you were boys here . . ."

Half an hour later we went to bed. Yngve and I cleared the table, tucked the vodka bottle away in the cupboard under the sink, emptied the ashtray, and put the glasses in the dishwasher while Grandma watched. When we had finished she got up too. Some pee was dripping from the seat of the chair, but she paid it no attention. She leaned against the door frame on her way out, first in the kitchen, then on the landing.

"Good night!" I said.

"Good night, boys." She smiled. I watched her and saw the smile fade the moment she turned her head and began to go downstairs.

"Oh well," I said when, a minute later, we were upstairs. "That was that."

"Yup," Yngve said. He pulled off his sweater, laid it across the back of the chair, and took off his pants. Warmed by the alcohol, I felt like saying something kind to him. All the differences of opinion had been straightened out, there were no problems and everything was simple.

"What a day," he said.

"Mm, you can say that again."

He lay back in bed and pulled up the duvet.

"Good night," he said, closing his eyes.

"Good night," I said. "Sleep tight."

I went to the door and turned off the main light. Sat down on the bed. Didn't feel like sleeping. For one insane second it occurred to me that I could go out. There were still a couple of hours before the bars closed. And it was summer, the town was full of people, some of whom I probably knew.

But then the tiredness hit me. Suddenly all I wanted to do was sleep. Suddenly I could barely lift my arms. The thought of having to undress was unbearable, so I lay back in bed with all my clothes on and descended into the soft, inner light. Every tiny movement I made, even the stirring of my little finger, tickled my stomach, and when I fell asleep the very next second it was with a smile on my face.

Even in deepest sleep, I knew something terrible awaited me beyond. As I approached a quasiconscious state, I tried to go back and would certainly have succeeded, had it not been for Yngve's insistent voice and the knowledge that we had an important meeting that morning.

I opened my eyes.

"What time is it?" I asked.

Yngve was standing in the doorway, fully dressed. Black trousers, white shirt, black jacket. His face seemed puffy, his eyes were narrow and his hair tangled.

"Twenty to ten," he said. "Get up."

"Shit," I said.

I struggled into a sitting position and could feel the alcohol still in my body.

"I'll be downstairs," he said. "Hurry."

Still wearing the clothes from yesterday made me feel very uneasy, a feeling that grew as the memory struck me of what we had actually done. I pulled them off. There was a heaviness about all the movements I made, even getting up and standing on two feet took energy, not to mention what raising my arm and reaching for the shirt on the clothes hanger over the wardrobe door did to me. But there was no option, it had to be done. Right arm through, left arm through, do up the buttons on the sleeves first, then at the front. Why the hell had we done it? How could we have been so stupid? It wasn't what I had wanted, in fact it was the very last thing I had wanted, to sit drinking with her, here of all places. Yet that was *precisely* what I had done. How was that possible? How the hell had that been possible?

It was shameful.

I knelt in front of the suitcase and unpeeled layers of clothes before finding the black trousers, which I put on while sitting on the bed. And how good it was to sit! But I had to get to my feet again, to hoist my trousers, to find the jacket and put it on, to go down to the kitchen.

After pouring myself a glass of water and drinking it, my forehead was damp with sweat. I leaned forward and sprinkled water over my head from the running tap. It cooled me down and made my hair, which was short but untidy, look better.

With water dripping from my chin and my body as heavy as a sack, I lurched down to the hall and onto the steps where Yngve was waiting for me with Grandma. He was rattling the car keys in one hand.

"Got any chewing gum or something?" I said. "I didn't have time to clean my teeth."

"You can't skip cleaning your teeth today of all days," Yngve said. "You'll be fine if you hurry."

He was right. I probably smelled of alcohol, and that was not how you should smell at the undertaker's. But hurrying was beyond me. I had to pause on the second-floor landing and hang over the banister; my will seemed to be drained. After getting my toothbrush and toothpaste from the bedside table I cleaned my teeth as fast as I could over the kitchen sink. I should have left the toothbrush and tube there and dashed down, but something in me said that was not right, they didn't belong in the kitchen, they had to be taken back to the bedroom, and so two further minutes were lost. It was four minutes to ten by the time I was standing on the front steps again.

"We're off," Yngve said, turning to Grandma. "It won't take long. Back soon."

"That's fine," she answered.

I got into the car, strapped myself in. Yngve plumped down in the seat beside me, inserted the key in the ignition, twisted it, craned his head and began to reverse down the little slope. Grandma was standing on the top step. I waved to her, she waved back. As we reversed into the alley and could no longer see her I wondered if she was still waiting, as she had always done, because when we moved forward again we could see each other for a last time and wave a final goodbye, then she would turn to go in and we would enter the road.

She was still there. I waved, she waved, and then she went in.

"Did she want to come along today as well?" I asked.

Yngve nodded.

"We'll have to do what we said. Be quick. Although I wouldn't mind sitting in a café for a while. Or visiting some record shops."

He touched the indicator with his left index finger as he down-shifted and looked to the right. Nothing coming.

"How are you feeling?" I asked.

"Absolutely fine," Yngve said. "And you?"

"I can still feel it," I said. "Think I'm still a bit drunk in fact."

He glanced at me as he set off.

"Oh dear," he said.

"Wasn't such a great idea," I said.

He smiled thinly, changed down again, came to a halt behind the white line. A white-haired, elderly man, stick-thin with a large nose, crossed in front of us. The corners of his mouth drawn down. His lips dark red. He first looked up at the hills to my right, then to the row of shops across the road before lowering his gaze to the ground, presumably to be sure where the coming curb was. All of this he did as though completely alone. As though he never took any account of other eyes. This was how Giotto painted people. They never seemed to be aware that they were being watched. Giotto was the only painter to depict the aura of vulnerability this gave them. It was probably something to do with the era because succeeding generations of Italian painters, the great generations, had always interwoven an awareness of watching eyes in their pictures. It made them less naïve, but they also revealed less.

On the other side of the street, a young, redhaired woman with a stroller bustled up. The pelican crossing lights changed from green at that moment, but she was watching the traffic lights, which were still on red, and she ventured across, dashing past us the very next second. Her child, about a year old, with chubby cheeks and a small mouth, sat upright in the stroller, looking around, slightly disorientated, as they rushed past.

Yngve released the clutch and carefully accelerated into the intersection.

"It's two minutes past," I said.

"I know," he said. "If we can find a place to park quickly, that's not too bad."

As we came to the bridge, I looked up at the sky above the sea. It was overcast, so light in some places that the white had taken on a touch of blue, as though a semitransparent membrane had been stretched over it, in other places it was heavier and darker, gray patches, their outer edges drifting across the whiteness like smoke. Wherever the sun was, the cloud cover had a yellowish tinge, though not so strong that the light beneath was anything but muted and seemed to come from all directions. It was one of those days when nothing casts a shadow, when everything holds on tight.

"It's tonight you're going, isn't it?" I said.

Yngve nodded.

"Ah, there's one!" he said.

The very next moment he pulled up to the curb, switched off the engine, and yanked the hand brake. The undertaker's was on the other side of the street. I would have preferred a slower transition, one in which I could have prepared myself for what was awaiting us, but there was nothing to be done, we just had to throw ourselves into it.

I got out, closed the door, and followed Yngve across the street. In the waiting room the woman behind the counter sent us a smile and said we could go straight in.

The door was open. The stout funeral director got up from behind his desk when he saw us, came over, and shook hands with a courteous but, in the circumstances, less than cordial a smile on his lips.

"So, here we are again," he said, motioning to the two chairs with his hand. "Please take a seat."

"Thank you," I said.

"I'm sure you've given the funeral some thought over the weekend," he said, sitting down, reaching for a thin sheaf of papers on the desk in front of him and flicking through them.

"We have, yes," Yngve said. "We've decided on a church burial."

"I see," said the funeral director. "Then I can give you the phone number of the priest's office. We'll deal with the practical side, but it would be good if you could have a word with him yourselves. As you know, he has to make a little speech about your father and it would be helpful if you could pass on some information."

He looked up at us. The folds of skin around his neck hung, lizardlike, over his shirt collar. We nodded.

"There are many ways to do this," he continued. "I have a list here of the various options. Such things as whether you would like music, for example, and if so in what form. Some people like to have live music, others prefer recorded music. But we do have a church singer whom we use a great deal and he can also play several instruments . . . Live music, of course, has a special atmosphere, a solemnity or dignity . . . I don't know, have you considered what you would like?"

My eyes met Yngve's.

"That might be good?" I offered.

"Yes," Yngve replied.

"Shall we go for it then?"

"I think so."

"So we're agreed then?" probed the funeral director.

We nodded.

He stretched across the desk to hand Yngve a sheet of paper.

"Here are a few options regarding the choice of music. But if you have any particular wishes not on the list it's not a problem, so long as we know a few days in advance."

I leaned over and Yngve moved the sheet to allow me to see.

"Bach might be good," Yngve suggested.

"Yes, he was very fond of Bach, wasn't he," I said.

For the first time in close to twenty-four hours I started to cry again.

Damned if I'm going to use one of his Kleenex tissues, I thought, wiping my eyes on the crook of my arm, took a deep breath, and slowly released it. I noticed Yngve sending me a quick glance.

Was he embarrassed by my tears?

No, he couldn't be.

No.

"I'm fine," I said. "Where were we?"

"Bach would be good," Yngve said, looking at the funeral director. "The cello sonata, for example . . ."

He faced me.

"Do you agree?"

I nodded.

"So that's agreed then," the funeral director said. "There are usually three musical items. And one or two hymns that everyone sings."

"*Deilig er jorden*," I said. "Can we have that one?"

"Naturally," he said.

Ohhh. Ohhh. Ohhh.

"Are you alright, Karl Ove?" Yngve asked.

I nodded.

We chose two songs that the church singer would perform, as well as a hymn everyone would sing, plus the cello piece and *Deilig er jorden*. We also agreed that no one would give a speech by the coffin, and with that the funeral was planned, for the other elements were part of the liturgy and fixed.

"Would you like flowers? Apart from the wreaths and so on? Many people think it lends atmosphere. I have a small selection here if you would like to see . . ."

He passed Yngve another sheet of paper. Yngve pointed to one option, glanced at me and I nodded.

"That's that then," the funeral director said. "That leaves the coffin . . . We have a variety of pictures here . . ."

Another piece of paper crossed the desk.

"White," I said. "Is that okay with you? That one."

"Fine by me," Yngve said.

The funeral director retrieved the sheet and made a note. Then he peered up at us.

"You requested a viewing today, didn't you?"

"Yes," Yngve said. "Preferably this afternoon, if that's possible."

"That's fine, of course. But . . . erm, you are aware of the circumstances he died in, aren't you? That his death was . . . alcohol-related?"

We nodded.

"Good," he said. "Sometimes it's just as well to be prepared for what might await one in such situations."

He shuffled his papers and tapped them on the table.

"I'm afraid I won't be able to receive you myself this afternoon, but my colleague will be there. At the chapel by Oddernes Church. Do you know where it is?"

"I think so," I said.

"Four o'clock. Is that convenient?"

"Yes, that's fine."

"So let's say that then. Four o'clock at the chapel by Oddernes Church.

And if there's anything else that occurs to you, or if you wish to change anything, just ring me. You have my number, don't you?"

"Yes, we do," Yngve said.

"Fine. Oh, there is one more matter. Would you like a funeral announcement in the newspaper?"

"I suppose we would, wouldn't we?" I said, looking at Yngve.

"Yes," he said. "We've got to do that."

"But it might be best to spend a bit of time on it," I said. "To decide what we should say and what names we should mention and all that . . ."

"No problem," said the funeral director. "You can just drop by or give a call when you've given it some thought. But don't leave it too late. The newspaper usually needs a couple of days' notice."

"I can call you tomorrow," I said. "Is that alright?"

"Excellent," he said, standing up with another sheet of paper in his hand. "Here's our telephone number and the priest's address. Which of you would like to hold on to it?"

"I will," I said.

Standing outside on the pavement, Yngve produced a packet of cigarettes and offered me one. I nodded and took it. Actually the thought of smoking was repugnant, as it always was the day after drinking because the smoke, not so much the taste or smell as what it stood for, created a connection between the present day and the previous one, a kind of sensory bridge across which all kinds of things streamed so that everything around me, the grayish-black tarmac, the light gray curbstones, the gray sky, the birds flying beneath it, the black windows in the rows of houses, the red car we were standing beside, Yngve's distracted figure, were permeated by terrifying internal images; at the same time there was something in the sense of destruction and desolation that the smoke in my lungs gave me that I needed, or wanted.

"That went well," I said.

"There are a few things we still have to sort out," he said. "Or rather you will have to sort out. Like the funeral announcement, for example. But you can just call me while I'm heading back."

"Mm," I said.

"Did you notice the word he used, by the way?" Yngve commented. "Viewing?"

I smiled.

"Yes, but then there is something estate agent–like about this industry. Their job is to make things look as good as possible and pocket as much as they can. Did you see how much the coffins cost?"

Yngve nodded.

"Hm, and you can't exactly be a tightwad when you're sitting there," he said.

"It's a bit like buying wine in a restaurant," I said. "If you're not a connoisseur, I mean. If you've got a lot of money you take the second-most expensive. If you haven't, you take the second-cheapest. Never the most expensive, nor the cheapest. That's probably the way it is with coffins as well."

"By the way, you expressed a very firm opinion there," Yngve said. "The coffin having to be white, I mean."

I shrugged and threw the glowing cigarette onto the road.

"Purity," I said. "I suppose that was what I must have been thinking."

Yngve dropped his cigarette on the ground, stepped on it, opened the car door, and got in. I followed.

"I'm dreading seeing him," Yngve said. He buckled the seat belt with one hand while putting the key in the ignition and twisting with the other. "Are you?"

"Yes. But I have to do it. Unless I do I will never comprehend that he's really dead."

"Same here," Yngve said, checking the mirror. Then he signaled and drove off.

"Shall we go home now?" he asked.

"The machines," I said. "The carpet cleaner and the lawn mower. Would be great if we could get them before you leave."

"Do you know where the shop is?"

"No, that's just it," I said. "Gunnar said there was a place to rent them in Grim, but I don't know the precise address."

"Okay," Yngve said. "We'll have to find a telephone directory. Do you know if there's a phone booth nearby?"

I shook my head.

"But there's a gas station at the end of Elvegata, we can try there."

"That's a good idea," Yngve said. "I have to fill up before I go tonight anyway."

A minute later we pulled up under the roof of a gas station. Yngve parked beside the pump and while he filled I went into the shop. There was a payphone on the wall and below it three boxed directories. After finding the address of the rental firm and memorizing it I went to the till to buy some tobacco. The man ahead of me in the queue turned around as I went up.

"Karl *Ove*?" he said. "Is it you?"

I recognized him. We had been at gymnas together. But I couldn't remember his name.

"Hello, it's been a long time," I said. "How's it going?"

"Great!" he said. "How are you?"

I was surprised by the genuine tone. During the prom period I had had a party at home and he had come, turned nasty, and kicked a hole in our bathroom door. Afterward he had refused to pay and there had been nothing I could do. Another time he had been driving a prom bus, with Bjørn I think it must have been and me sitting on the roof, we were going to the recreation center, and all of a sudden, on the hill after the Timenes intersection, he stamped on the accelerator and we had to spreadeagle and hold on tight to the bars, he was doing at least seventy, probably eighty, and just laughed when we arrived, even when we gave him a hard time.

So why the friendly overtures now?

I met his gaze. His face was perhaps a bit more fleshy, otherwise he hadn't changed at all. But there was something stiff about his features, a kind of fixedness, which the smile reinforced rather than softened.

"What are you doing now?" I asked.

"Working in the North Sea."

"Ah," I said. "So you're earning tons of money!"

"Yep. And I get lots of time off. So that's good. And you?"

While he was talking to me he looked at the shop assistant and pointed to a grilled sausage and hoisted one finger in the air.

"Still studying," I said.

"What subject?"

"Literature."

"Mm, you always did like that," he said.

"Yes," I said. "Do you see anything of Espen? Or Trond? Or Gisle?"

He shrugged.

"Trond lives in town so I see him now and then. Espen when he comes home for Christmas. And you? Do you have any contact with any of the others?"

"Just Bassen."

The assistant put the sausage in a bun and placed it on a napkin.

"Ketchup and mustard?" he asked.

"Yes, please, both. And onions."

"Raw or fried?"

"Fried. No, raw."

"Raw?"

"Yes."

After the order had been completed and he had the sausage in his hand, he turned back to me.

"Nice to see you again, Karl Ove," he said. "You haven't changed!"

"Nor you," I said.

He opened his mouth, bit off a chunk of the sausage and passed the assistant a fifty-krone note. There was a moment of embarrassment as he waited for his change because we had already concluded the conversation. He mustered a faint smile.

"Okay," he said as he closed his hand around the coins he was given. "See you around maybe!"

"Yeah, see you around," I said. I bought some tobacco and stood in front of the newspaper stand pretending I was interested, because I didn't want to bump into him again outside. Yngve came to pay and did so with a thousand-krone note. I looked away as he drew it from his wallet, didn't want to show that I knew it was Dad's money, just mumbled something about going out, and headed for the door.

The smell of gasoline and concrete, in the half-light beneath a gas station roof, is there anything more charged with associations? Engines, speed, future.

But also hot dogs and CDs by Celine Dion and Eric Clapton.

I opened the car door and got in. Yngve came soon after, started up, and we left without a word.

Up and down the garden I walked, cutting the grass. The machine we had hired consisted of a device you strapped to your back and a rod with a rotating blade on the end. I felt like a kind of robot as I walked around, wearing large, yellow ear protectors and attached, as it were, to roaring, vibrating machinery and methodically cutting down all the sapling trees, all the flowers and all the grass I came across. I was crying nonstop. Sob after sob surged through me as I worked, I didn't fight it any longer, I just let the tears come. At twelve Yngve called me from the veranda, and I went in to eat with them, he had set out tea and rolls, as Grandma had always done, heated on a gridiron over a burner so that the usually soft crust went crispy and sprinkled crumbs as you sank your teeth in, but I wasn't hungry and soon left to continue my work. It was liberating to be outside and alone, satisfying too, because you could see the results so quickly. The sky had closed over, the grayish-white clouds lay like a lid beneath, with the effect that the dark surface of the sea contrasted with greater clarity, and the town, which under an open sky was a small, insignificant cluster of houses, a speck of dust on the ground, was lent greater weight and solidity. This is where I was, this is what I saw. Mostly my gaze was focused on the rotating blade and the grass falling like soldiers being mown down, more yellow and gray than green, mixed with the red of foxtail grass and the yellow of black-eyed Susan, but occasionally I did raise my eyes to the massive, light-gray sky roof and the massive, dark-grey sea floor, to the jumble of hoods and hulls, masts and bows, containers and rusting junk by the quay, and to the town vibrating like a machine with its colors and activity, as tears flowed down my cheeks without cease, for Dad, who had grown up here, he was dead. Or perhaps that was not why I was crying, perhaps it was for quite different reasons, perhaps it was all the grief and misery I had accumulated over the last fifteen years that had now been released. It didn't matter, nothing mattered, I just walked around the garden cutting the grass that had grown too tall.

At a quarter past three I turned off the infernal machine, stowed it in the shed under the veranda, and went in for a shower before leaving. Went to get clothes, towel, and shampoo from the loft, laid them on the toilet seat, locked the door, undressed, clambered into the bathtub, adjusted the shower head away from me, and started the water. When it had run warm I twisted the shower head back and the hot water streamed down over me. Usually this was followed by a good feeling, but not this time, not here, so after I had hastily washed my hair and rinsed it, I turned off the water and got out, dried myself, and got dressed. Smoked a cigarette on the steps waiting for Yngve to come down. I was dreading the next stage, and as he unlocked the car, I could see from his face across the roof that he was too.

The chapel was adjacent to the gymnas I attended, located diagonally behind the large sports hall, and we drove the same route I had walked for the six months I had lived in Grandma's and Grandad's flat on Elvegata, but the sight of familiar places evoked nothing in me, and perhaps I was seeing them for the first time as they actually were, meaningless, devoid of atmosphere. A picket fence here, a white nineteenth-century house there, a few trees, some bushes, a bit of grass, a road barrier, a sign. Statutory cloud movement in the heavens.

Statutory human movement on earth. The wind lifting branches, making the thousands of leaves shake in patterns that are as unpredictable as they are inevitable.

"You can drive in here," I said as we passed the school and saw the church behind the stone wall in front of us. "It's in there."

"I've been here before," Yngve declared.

"Really?" I said.

"A confirmation ceremony. You were there too, weren't you?"

"I don't remember one," I said.

"But I do," Yngve said, leaning forward to be able to see farther ahead.

"Is it behind the parking lot?"

"Has to be, I suppose," I answered.

"We're early," Yngve said. "It's only a quarter to."

I scrambled out of the car and closed the door. A lawn mower came toward us on the other side of the stone wall, pushed by a man with a bare chest. After the machine had passed, no more than five meters away, I saw that he was wearing a silver chain around his neck with what looked like a razor blade suspended from it. To the east, above the church, the sky had darkened. Yngve lit a cigarette and took a few steps across the parking lot.

"Yeah, well," he said. "We're here anyway."

I glanced at the chapel. A lamp was lit over the entrance, barely visible in the daylight. A red car was parked nearby.

My heart beat faster.

"Yes we are," I said.

Some birds circled high above us, under the sky, which was still a pale gray. The Dutch painter Ruisdael always painted birds high in his skies, to create depth, it was almost his signature, at any rate I had seen it in picture after picture in the book I had about him.

The undersides of the trees beyond were black.

"What's the time now?" I asked.

Yngve jerked his arm forward so that his jacket sleeve slid back and he could see his watch.

"Five to. Shall we go in?"

I nodded.

When we were ten meters from the chapel, the door opened. A young man in a dark suit looked at us. His face was tanned, his hair blond.

"Knausgaard?" he said.

We nodded.

We shook hands in turn. The skin around his nostrils was red and inflamed. The blue eyes absent.

"Shall we go in?" he suggested.

We nodded again. Entered a hall at first, where he stopped.

"It's in there," he explained. "But before we go in I should perhaps prepare you a little. This is not a very pleasant sight, there was a lot of blood, you see, so . . . well, we did what we could, but it's still visible."

The blood?

He looked at us.

I shivered.

"Are you ready?"

"Yes," Yngve said.

He opened the door and we followed him into a larger room. Dad was lying on a bier in the middle. His eyes were closed, his features composed.

Oh God.

I stood beside Yngve, in front of my father. His cheeks were crimson, saturated with blood. It must have got caught in the pores when they tried to wipe it away. And the nose, it was broken. But even though I saw this, I still didn't see it, for all the detail disappeared into something other and something greater, into both the aura he gave off, which was death and which I had never been close to before, and also what he was to me, a father and all the life that lay therein.

It was only when I was back in Grandma's house, after seeing Yngve off for Stavanger, that the matter of the blood came back to me. How could it have ended like that? Grandma said she had found him dead in the chair, and on the basis of this information it would have been natural to assume his heart had given out while he was sitting there, probably while he was sleeping. The funeral director, however, had said there was not only blood but a great deal of it. And Dad's nose had been broken. So, some form of mortal combat must have taken place? Had he got up, in pain, and fallen against the chimney breast? To the floor? But if so, why wasn't there any blood on the wall or the floor? And how come Grandma hadn't said anything about the blood? Because *something* must have happened, he could *not* have died peacefully in his sleep, not with all that blood there. Had she washed it off and then forgotten to say? Why would she? She hadn't washed anything else, it didn't seem to be one of her drives. It was just as strange that I had forgotten so quickly. Or, perhaps not so strange, there had been so many other things I had to attend to. Nevertheless I would have to call Yngve as soon as I got back to Grandma's. We needed to get hold of the doctor who had organized the transfer of the body. He would be able to explain what had happened.

I walked as fast as I could up the gentle slope, along a green wire fence with a dense hedge on the other side, as though I could not arrive soon enough, while another impulse was also working inside me, to drag out the time I was on my own for as long as possible, maybe even find a café and read a newspaper. It was one thing to stay at Grandma's with Yngve and quite another to be there alone. Yngve knew how to handle her. But that light, bantering tone of theirs, which Erling and Gunnar also shared, had never been part of my nature, to put it mildly, and during the year at school in Kristiansand when I had spent a lot of time with them, since I lived nearby, my manner had seemed uncongenial to them, there had been something about me they didn't want to know, which suspicion was confirmed after a few months when one evening my mother told me Grandma had called to say I shouldn't go over there so often. I could handle most rejection, but not this, they were my grandparents, and the fact that not even they wanted to have anything to do with me was so shattering that I couldn't restrain myself and burst into tears, right in front of my mother. She was upset, but what could she do? At the time I didn't understand any of this and simply believed they didn't like me; however, since then I have begun to sense what it was that made my presence uncongenial. I was unable to dissemble, unable to play a role, and the scholarly earnestness I brought into the house was impossible to keep at arm's length in the long run, sooner or later even they would have to engage with it, and the disequilibrium it led to, as their banter never demanded anything at all of me, that was what must have made them call my mother in the end. My presence always made demands on them, either in concrete ways, such as food, for if I went there after school and before soccer practice, I would otherwise have had to last until eight or nine at night without eating, or money because only the afternoon buses were free for schoolchildren, and often I could not pay for the ticket. As far as both food and money were concerned, they didn't mind, in essence, giving me either, but what provoked them was, I assume, the fact that I had to have both, and as such they had no choice: food and bus money were no longer gifts from their hearts but something else, and this other thing impinged on our relationship, created a knot between us, of which they did not approve. I couldn't understand it then, but I do now. My manner, my getting close to them with my life and thoughts, was part of the same pattern. This closeness they couldn't and presumably wouldn't give me; that too was something I took from them. The irony was that during these visits I always considered them, always said what I thought they wanted to hear; even the most personal things I said because I thought it would be good for them to hear, not because I needed to say them.

The worst part of all this, however, I was thinking, as I walked along the avenue towards Lund, past the flow of afternoon traffic, past tree after tree whose trunks were blackened with asphalt dust and car exhaust, so hard and rocklike compared to the expanse of light, green leaves on the branches above, was that at that time I actually regarded myself as a sound judge of character. I had a gift, or so I had deluded myself into thinking, it was something I was good at. Understanding others. While I myself was more of a mystery.

How stupid can you get.

I laughed and glanced up immediately to check whether any of the people sitting in cars in the road alongside had seen me. They hadn't. Everyone was wrapped up in their own thoughts. I might have become smarter over those twelve years, but I still could not pretend. Nor could I lie, nor could I play roles. For that reason I had been only too happy to let Yngve deal with Grandma. But now I would have to stand on my own two feet.

I stopped to light a cigarette. Moving on, I somehow felt heartened. Was it the once white but now polluted houses on my left that had done that? Or was it the trees in the avenue? These motionless, foliage-laden, air-bathing beings with their boundless abundance of leaves? For whenever I caught sight of them I was filled with happiness.

I took an especially deep breath and flicked the silver-gray cigarette ash off as I walked. The unabsorbed memories evoked by my surroundings on the way to the chapel with Yngve now hit me with full force. I recognized them from two periods: the first, when I had been visiting Grandma and Grandad in Kristiansand as a boy and every tiny detail of the town had seemed like an adventure, the second, when I lived here as a teenager. I had been away for a number of years now, and ever since I arrived I had noticed how the stream of impressions the place left you with was partly tied to the first world of memories, partly to the second, and thus existed in three separate time zones at once. I saw the pharmacy and remembered when Yngve and I had been there with Grandma; the snow drifts had been high outside, it was snowing, she was wearing a fur hat and coat, in line, white-coated pharmacists were shuttling back and forth. Now and then she turned her head to see what we were doing. After the first searching glances, when her eyes were, if not cold, then at least neutral, she smiled, and they filled with warmth, as if at the wave of a magic wand. I saw the hill going up towards Lund Bridge and remembered that in the afternoon Grandad used to come cycling from that direction.

How different he seemed outdoors. As though the slight wobble, caused by the incline, said something not only about the bike he was riding but also the person he was: one moment any elderly Kristiansander in coat and beret, the next Grandad. I saw the rooftops in the residential area stretching down the road and remembered how I used to walk among them as a sixteen-year-old, bursting with emotions. When everything I saw, even a rusty, crooked rotary dryer in a back garden, even rotten apples on the ground beneath a tree, even a boat wrapped in a tarpaulin, with the wet bow protruding and the yellow, flattened grass beneath, was ablaze with beauty. I saw the grass-covered hill behind the buildings on the other side and remembered a blue sky and a cold winter's day when we had been sledding with Grandma. There was such a sparkling reflection of sun on snow that the light resembled that in the high mountains, and the town below us seemed so strangely open that everything that happened, people and cars passing in the streets, the man shovelling snow from the assembly room forecourt across the road, the other children sledging, did not appear to be attached anywhere, they were just floating beneath the sky. All of this was alive in me as I walked, and it made me acutely aware of my surroundings, but it was only the surface, only the uppermost layer of my consciousness, for Dad was dead, and the grief this stirred shone through everything I thought and felt, retracting the surface, in a sense. He also existed in these memories, but he was not important there, oddly enough, the thought of him evoked nothing. Dad walking on the sidewalk a few meters in front of me, once at the beginning of the seventies, we had been to the newsstand and bought pipe cleaners and were going to Grandma and Grandad's, the way he lifted his chin and raised his head while smiling to himself, the pleasure I felt at that, or Dad in the bank, the way he held his wallet in one hand, ran the other through his hair, catching a reflection of himself in the glass in front of the teller's window, or Dad on his way out of town: in none of these memories did I perceive him as important. That is, I did when I was experiencing them, but not at the moment of thinking about them. It was different now that he was dead. In death he was everything, of course, but death was also everything, for while I was walking, in the light drizzle, I seemed to find myself in a zone. What lay outside it meant nothing. I saw, I thought, and then what I saw and thought were withdrawn: it didn't count. Nothing counted. Just Dad, the fact that he was dead, that was all that counted.

All the time I was walking, the brown envelope, which contained the possessions he had on him when he died, was on my mind. I stopped outside the market across the road from the pharmacy, I turned to the wall and took it out. I looked at my father's name. It seemed alien. I had expected Knausgaard. But it was correct enough; this laughably pompous name was the one he had had when he died.

An elderly woman with a shopping bag in one hand and a small white dog in the other looked at me as she came out of the door. I took a few steps closer to the wall and shook the contents into my hand. His ring, a necklace, a few coins, and a pin. That was all. In themselves, as everyday as objects can be. But the fact that he had been wearing them, that the ring was on his finger, the chain around his neck when he died, gave them a special aura. Death and gold. I turned them over in my hand, one by one, and they filled me with disquiet. I stood there and was frightened of death in the same way that I had been when I was a child. Not of dying myself but of the dead.

I put the items back in the envelope, put the envelope back in my pocket, ran across the road between two cars, went to the newsstand and bought a newspaper and a Lion bar, which I ate while walking the last few hundred meters to the house.

Even after all that had happened, there were still echoes of the smell I remembered from childhood. As a young boy I had already wondered at the phenomenon: how every house I had been in, all the neighbors' and the family's houses, had a specific smell all of their own which never changed. All except for ours. It didn't have a specific smell. It didn't smell of anything. Whenever Grandma and Grandad came they brought the smell of their house with them; I remembered one particular occasion when Grandma had surprised us with a visit, I knew nothing about it, and when I came home from school and detected the aroma in the hall I thought I was imagining things, because there was no other evidence to support it. No car in the drive, no clothes or shoes in the hall. Just the aroma. But it wasn't my imagination: when I went upstairs Grandma was sitting in full regalia in the kitchen, she had caught the bus, she wanted to surprise us; so unlike her. It was odd that, twenty years later, after so much had changed, the smell in the house should be the same. It is conceivable that it was all to do with habit, using the same soaps, the same detergents, the same perfumes and aftershave lotions, cooking the same food in the same way, coming home from the same job and doing the same things in the afternoons and evenings. If you worked on cars, there would be traces of oil and white spirit, metal and exhaust fumes in the smell, if you collected old books, there would be traces of yellowing paper and old leather in the smell, but in a house where all previous habits had stopped, where people had died off, and those left were too old to do what they used to do, what about the smell in these houses, how could it be unchanged? Were the walls impregnated with forty years of living, was that what I could smell every time I stepped inside?

Instead of going to see her right away, I opened the cellar door and ventured down the narrow staircase. The cold, dark air that met me was like a concentrate of the usual air in the house, just as I remembered it. This was where they had stored the crates of apples, pears, and plums in the autumn, and combined with the stench of old brick and earth their exhalations lay like a sub-smell in the house, to which all the others were added and with which they contrasted. I had not been down there more than three or four times; like the rooms in the loft, this had been a forbidden area for us. But how often had I stood in the hall watching Grandma come up from the cellar with bags full of juicy, yellow plums or slightly wrinkled and wonderfully succulent red apples for us?

The only light came from a small porthole in the wall. Since the garden was lower than the house entrance you could see straight into it. It was a disorientating perspective, the sense of spatial connection was broken, for a brief moment the ground seemed to have disappeared beneath me. Then, as

I grabbed the banister, everything became clear to me again: I was here, the window was there, the garden there, the house entrance there.

I stood staring out of the window without registering anything or thinking of anything in particular. Then I turned and went up to the hall, hung my jacket on one of the clothes hangers in the wardrobe, and glanced at myself in the mirror by the stairs. Tiredness lay like a membrane over my eyes. When I ascended the stairs it was with heavy footfalls so that Grandma would hear me coming.

She was sitting as she had when we left her a few hours before, at the kitchen table. In front of her was a cup of coffee, an ashtray, and a plate full of crumbs from the roll she had eaten.

When I entered she glanced up at me in her alert, birdlike way.

"Ah, it's you," she said. "Did everything go alright?"

She had probably forgotten where I had been, though I could not be sure, and I answered with the gravity that such an occasion demanded.

"Yes," I nodded. "It went well."

"That's good," she said, looking down. I stepped into the room and put the newspaper I had bought on the table.

"Would you like some coffee?" she asked.

"Yes, please," I answered.

"The pot's on the stove."

Something in her tone made me look at her. She had never spoken to me like that before. The strange thing was that it didn't change her as much as it changed me. That was how she must have spoken to Dad of late. She had addressed him not me. And that was not how she would have addressed Dad if Grandad had been alive. This was the tone between mother and son when no one else was there.

I didn't think that she had mistaken me for Dad, only that she was talking out of habit, like a ship continuing to glide through the water after the engines had been switched off. It chilled me inside. But I couldn't let that affect me, so I helped myself to a cup from the cupboard, went over to the stove, felt the coffeepot with my finger. It was a long time since it had been warm.

Grandma whistled and drummed her fingers on the table. She had done that for as long as I could remember. There was something good about seeing it, for so much had changed about her otherwise.

I had seen photos of her from the 1930s, and she had been attractive, not strikingly so, but enough to mark her out, in the typical way for that era: dark, dramatic eyes, small mouth, short hair. When, toward the end of the fifties, as a mother of three, she had been photographed in front of some tourist sights on their travels, all of those characteristics were still there, if in a softer, less distinct yet not undefined way, and you could still use the word "attractive" to describe her. When I was growing up, and she was in her late sixties, early seventies, I couldn't see any of this of course, she was just "Grandma," I knew nothing about her characteristic traits, the things that told you who she was. An older woman, middle class, who was well-conserved and dressed elegantly, that must have been the impression she gave at the end of the seventies, when she took the unusual step of catching a bus to visit us and sat in our kitchen in Tybakken. Lively, mentally alert, vigorous. Right up until a couple of years ago that was how she was. Then something happened to her, and it was not old age that had her in its grip, nor illness, it was something else. Her detachment had nothing to do with the gentle otherworldliness or contentedness of old people, her detachment was as hard and lean as the body in which it resided.

I saw that, but there was nothing I could do, I could not build a bridge, could not help or console her, I could only watch, and every minute I spent with her I was tense. The only thing that helped was to keep moving and not to let any of what was present, in either her or the house, find a foothold.

With her hand, she wiped a flake of tobacco off her lap. Then looked at me.

"Shall I make you a cup as well?" I offered.

"Was there anything wrong with the coffee?" she said.

"It wasn't that hot," I said, taking the pot to the sink. "I'll put some fresh on."

"Wasn't that hot, did you say?"

Was she reproving me?

No. For then she laughed and brushed a crumb from her lap.

"I think my brain's unravelling," she said. "I was sure I'd only just made it."

"It wasn't *that* cold," I said, turning on the tap. "It's just that I like my coffee boiling hot."

I rinsed out the dregs and sprayed the bottom of the sink with the water until it had all gone down the drain. Then I filled the pot, which was almost completely black on the inside and covered with greasy fingerprints on the outside.

"Unravelling" was our family euphemism for senility. Grandad's brother, Leif, his brain "unravelled" when, on several occasions, he wandered from the old people's home to his childhood home, where he hadn't lived for sixty years, and stood shouting and banging on the door all through the night. His second brother, Alf, his mind had started unravelling in recent years; it was most obvious in his merging of the present and the past. And Grandad's mind also started unravelling at the end of his life when he sat up at night fiddling with an enormous collection of keys, no one knew he had them, let alone why. It was in the family; their mother's mind unravelled eventually, if we were to believe what my father had said. Apparently the last thing she did was climb into the loft instead of going down into the cellar when she had heard a siren; according to my father, she fell down the steep loft staircase in her house and died. Whether that was true or not, I don't know, my father could serve up all manner of lies. My intuition told me it wasn't, but there was no way of finding out.

I carried the pot to the stove and put it on the burner. The ticking of the safety device filled the kitchen. Then the damp pot began to crackle. I stood with folded arms, peering at the top of the steep hill outside the window, at the imposing white house. It struck me that I had stared at that house all my life without ever seeing anyone in or around it.

"Where's Yngve then?" Grandma asked.

"He had to go back to Stavanger today," I said, addressing her. "To his family. He'll be back for the f . . . for Friday."

"Yes, that was it." She nodded to herself. "He had to go back to Stavanger."

As she grasped the pouch of tobacco and the small, red-and-white roller machine, she said, without looking up: "But you're staying here?"

"Yes," I said. "I'll be here all the time."

I was happy that she so clearly wanted me to be here, even though I gathered that it was not me especially that she wanted here, anyone would do.

She cranked the handle of the machine with surprising vigor, flipped out the freshly filled cigarette and lit it, brushing a few flakes from her lap again and sat staring into space.

"I thought I would carry on cleaning," I said. "And then I'll have to work a bit later this evening and make a few phone calls."

"That's fine," she said and looked up at me. "But you aren't so busy that you don't have time to sit here for a while, are you?"

"Not at all, no," I answered.

The coffeepot hissed. I pressed it down harder on the burner, the steam hissed louder, and I removed it, sprinkled in some coffee, stirred with a fork, banged hard, once, on the stovetop and placed it on the table.

"There we are," I said. "Now it'll just have to brew for a bit."

The fingerprints on the pot, which we hadn't washed off, must have included Dad's. I visualized the nicotine stains on his fingers. There had been something undignified about doing this. Inasmuch as the trivial life it demonstrated did not go together with the solemnity death evoked.

Or that I wanted death to evoke.

Grandma sighed.

"Oh dear," she said. "Life's a pitch, as the old woman said. She couldn't pronounce her *b*'s."

I smiled. Grandma smiled too. Then her eyes glazed over again. I racked my brain for something to say, found nothing, poured coffee in the cup even though it was more a golden color than black, and tiny coffee grains floated to the surface.

"Do you want some?" I asked. "It's a bit thin, but . . ."

"Please," she said, nudging her cup a few centimeters along the table.

"Thank you," she said when it was half-full. Grasped the yellow carton of cream and poured.

"Where's Yngve then?" she asked.

"He's gone to Stavanger," I answered. "Home to his family."

"That's right. He had to go. When's he coming back?"

"On Friday, I think," I said.

I rinsed the bucket in the sink, ran the tap, poured in some green soap, put on rubber gloves, grabbed the cloth on the table with one hand, lifted the bucket with the other, and went to the back of the living room. Outside, darkness was beginning to fall. A faint bluish glimmer was visible in the light at ground height, around the foliage on the trees, their trunks, the bushes as far as the fence to the neighbor's plot. So faint was it that the colors were not muted as they would gradually become in the course of the evening, on the contrary, they were strengthened because the light no longer dazzled, and the dulled background allowed their fullness to come to the fore. But to the southwest, where you could just see the lighthouse in the sea, daylight was still unchallenged. Some clouds had a reddish glow, as though powered by their own energy, for the sun was hidden.

After a while Grandma came in. She switched on the TV and sat down in the chair. The sound of commercials, louder than the program, as always, filled not only the living room but also reverberated against the walls.

"Is the news on now?" I asked.

"I suppose so," she said. "Don't you want to see it as well?"

"Yes, I do," I said. "I'll just finish up here first."

After washing all the paneling along one wall I wrung out the cloth and went into the kitchen, where the reflection of my figure, in the form of vague, lighter and darker patches, was visible in the window, poured the water into the sink, draped the cloth over the bucket, stood motionless for a second, then opened the cupboard, pushed the paper towels to the side and pulled out the vodka bottle. I fetched two glasses from the cupboard above the sink, opened the fridge and took out the Sprite bottle, filled one glass with it, mixed the other with vodka and carried both into the living room.

"I thought we might allow ourselves a little drink," I smiled.

"How nice," she smiled back. "I think we might too."

I passed her the glass with the vodka, took the one with the Sprite, and sat down in the chair beside her. Terrible, it was terrible. It tore me apart. But there was nothing I could do about it. She needed it. That's the way it was.

If only it had been cognac or port!

Then I could have served it on a tray with a cup of coffee, and that would have given, if not a completely normal impression, then at least one not as conspicuous as clear vodka and Sprite.

I watched her opening her aged mouth and swallowing down the drink. I had been determined that this would not happen again. But now, there she was, sitting with a glass of alcohol in her hand. It cut me to the quick. Fortunately she didn't ask me for more.

I got up.

"I'll go and make some phone calls."

She turned her head toward me.

"Who are you going to call at this hour?" she asked.

Again she seemed to be addressing someone else.

"It's only eight o'clock," I said.

"It's not later?"

"No. I thought I would call Yngve. And then Tonje."

"Yngve?"

"Yes."

"Isn't he here then? No, of course, he isn't," she said. Then she focused her attention on the TV as though I had already left the room.

I pulled out a chair from under the table, sat down, and dialed Yngve's number. He had just walked in the door, everything had gone fine. In the background I could hear Torje screaming and Kari Anne hushing him.

"I was wondering about the blood," I said.

"Yes, what *was* that?" he said. "There must have been more going on than Grandma told us."

"He must have fallen or something," I said. "On a hard surface because his nose was broken. Did you see that?"

"Of course."

"We ought to have a word with someone who was here. Preferably, with the doctor."

"The funeral director probably has his name," Yngve said. "Do you want me to ask him?"

"Yes, could you?"

"I'll call tomorrow. It's a bit late now. Then we can talk about it."

I had thought of talking more about all the things that had happened here, but detected a certain impatience in his voice, and that was not so surprising. His daughter, Ylva, who was two years old, had waited up for him. And, of course, it was hardly more than a few hours since we had seen each other. However, he didn't make a move to end the conversation, so I had to do it myself. After hanging up I dialed Tonje's number. She had been waiting for me to call; I could hear it in her voice. I said I was very tired, that we could chat more the following day and that in a couple of days she would be down here very soon anyway. The conversation lasted only a few moments, nonetheless I felt better afterward. I fished out my cigarettes, snatched a lighter from the kitchen table, and went onto the veranda. The bay was full of returning boats. The mild air was filled with the town's smell of timber, as always when the wind came from the north, the scent of plants from the garden below and the faint, barely detectable, tang of the sea. In the room inside, the light from the TV flickered. I stood by the black wrought-iron gate at the end of the veranda, smoking. I extinguished the cigarette against the wall, and the glowing ash fell like tiny stars into the garden. Again I checked that Grandma was sitting in the living room before going upstairs to my bedroom. My suitcase lay open beside the bed. I picked up the cardboard box containing the manuscript, sat down on the edge of the bed, and tore off the tape. The thought that this had actually become a book which would soon be published struck me with full force when I saw the title page, set out so differently from the proof version to which I had become accustomed. I quickly put it at the bottom, couldn't spend time thinking about that, found myself a pencil from the pocket in the suitcase, picked up the sheet with a key to the proofreader's marks, slipped into bed with my back to the headboard and rested the manuscript on my lap. This was urgent, so I had planned to go through as much as I could during the evenings here. So far there hadn't been any time. But with Yngve in Stavanger and the evening still young I had at least four hours in front of me, if not more.

I started reading.

The two black suits, each one hanging on a half-open wardrobe door by the wall, disrupted my concentration, for while I was reading I was aware of them, and even though I knew they were only suits the perception that they were real bodies cast a shadow over my consciousness. After a few minutes I got up to move them. I stood with a suit in each hand, looking around for somewhere to hang them. From the curtain rod above the window? They would be even more visible there. From the door frame? No, I would have to walk through. In the end I walked into the adjacent loft drying room and hung them on separate clotheslines. Hanging freely, they looked more like people than before, but if I closed the door at least they were out of sight.

I went back to my room, sat down on the bed, and continued reading. In the streets below a car accelerated. From the floor below came the noise of the TV. In the otherwise quiet, empty house it sounded absolutely insane, there was a madness in the rooms.

I looked up.

I had written the book for Dad. I hadn't known, but that was how it was. I had written it for him.

I put down the manuscript and got to my feet, walked to the window.

Did he really mean so much to me?

Oh, yes, he did.

I wanted him to see me.

The first time I had realized what I was writing really was something, not just me wanting to be someone, or pretending to be, was when I wrote a passage about Dad and started crying while I was writing. I had never done that before, never even been close. I wrote about Dad and the tears were streaming down my cheeks, I could barely see the keyboard or the screen, I just hammered away. Of the existence of the grief inside me that had been released at that moment, I had known nothing; I had not had an inkling. My father was an idiot, I wanted nothing to do with him, and it cost me nothing to keep well away from him. It wasn't a question of keeping away from something, it was a question of the something not existing; nothing about him touched me. That was how it had been, but then I had sat down to write, and the tears poured forth.

I sat down on the bed again and placed the manuscript on my lap.

But there was more.

I had also wanted to show him that I was better than he was. That I was bigger than he was. Or was it just that I wanted him to be proud of me? To acknowledge me?

He hadn't even known I was having a book published. The last time I met him face to face before he died, eighteen months previously, he had asked me what I was doing with myself, and I had answered that I had just started writing a novel. We had been walking up Dronningens gate, we were going to eat out, sweat was running down his cheeks even though it was cold outside, and he asked, without looking at me, obviously to make conversation, if anything would come of it. I had nodded and said that one publishing house was interested. Whereupon he had glanced at me as we were walking, as though from a place in which he still was the person he had once been, and perhaps could be again.

"It's good to hear you're doing well, Karl Ove," he had said.

Why did I remember this so well? I usually forgot almost everything people, however close they were, said to me, and there was nothing in the situation that suggested this would be one of the last times we would meet. Perhaps I remembered it because he used my name; it must have been four years since I had heard him last use it, and for this reason his words were so unexpectedly intimate. Perhaps I remembered it because only a few days earlier I had written about him, and with emotions that were in stark contrast to those he had evoked in me by being friendly. Or perhaps I remembered because I hated the hold he had over me, which was clear from how I became so happy about so little. Not for anything in the world would I lift a finger for him, nor be forced into anything for his sake, neither in a positive nor a negative sense.

Now this show of will was worth nothing.

I placed the manuscript down on the bed, stuffed the pencil back in the suitcase pocket, leaned forward and reached for the cardboard box on the floor nearby, tried to squeeze the manuscript back in, but it wouldn't fit, so I laid it in the suitcase as it was, right at the bottom, carefully covered with clothes. The box, perched on the bed now, which I stared at for a long time, would remind me of the novel whenever I saw it. My first impulse had been to carry it downstairs and dispose of it in the kitchen trash can, but, upon reflection, I decided I didn't want to do that, I didn't want it to be become part of the house. So I parted the clothes in the suitcase again, put the box beside the manuscript, covered it with clothes, closed the suitcase lid, zipped it up, and then I left the room.

Grandma was in the living room watching TV. A talk show. It made no difference to her what was on, I supposed. She watched children's programs on TV2 and TV Norge in the afternoon with as much pleasure as late-night documentaries. I had never understood what appealed to her in this insane youth reality TV, with its endless cravings, of which even news and talk shows were full. She, who was born before the First World War and came from the really old Europe, on the outer perimeter though, it is true, but nevertheless? She, who had her childhood in the 1910s, her adolescence in the 1920s, adulthood in the 1930s, motherhood in the 1940s and 1950s, and was already an elderly woman in 1968? There had to be something, for she sat here watching TV every evening.

Beneath her chair there was a yellow-brown puddle on the floor. A dark patch down the side showed where it had come from.

"Yngve sends his love," I said. "He got back okay."
She threw me a brief glance.
"That's good," she said.
"Is there anything you need?" I asked.
"Need?"
"Yes, food, and so forth. I can easily make you something if you want."
"No, thanks," she said. "But you help yourself."

The sight of Dad's dead body had put me off any thought of food. But I could hardly associate a cup of tea with death, could I? I heated a pan of water on the stove, poured it, steaming, over a tea bag in a cup, watched for a while as the color was released and spread in slow spirals through the water until it was a golden tint everywhere, and I took the cup and carried it onto the veranda. A long way out, at the mouth of the fjord, the Danish ferry was approaching. Above it the weather had cleared. There were still traces of blue in the dark sky, which made it seem palpable, as though it were really one enormous cloth and the stars I could see came from the light behind, shining through thousands of tiny holes.

I took a sip and put the cup down on the windowsill. I remembered more from the evening with my father. There had been a thick layer of ice on the sidewalk; an easterly wind had been sweeping through almost deserted streets. We had gone to a hotel restaurant, hung up our coats, and taken a seat at a table. Dad had been breathing heavily, he wiped his brow, picked up the menu, and scanned it. Started again from the top.

"Looks like they don't serve wine here," he said and got up, went over and said something to the head waiter. When he shook his head, Dad turned on his heel and came back, almost tore his jacket off the chair and was putting it on as he headed for the exit. I hurried after him.

"What happened?" I asked when we were outside on the sidewalk again.

"No alcohol," he said. "Jesus, it was a temperance hotel."

Then he looked at me and smiled.

"We have to have wine with our food, don't we? But that's fine. There's another restaurant down here."

We ended up in Hotel Caledonien, sat at a window table, and ate our steaks. That is, I ate; when I had finished, Dad's plate had barely been touched. He lit a cigarette, drank the last dregs of red wine, leaned back in the chair and said he was planning to become a long-distance truck driver. I didn't know how to react, just nodded without saying a word. Truckers had a great time, he said. He had always liked driving, always liked traveling, and if you could do that and get paid for it at the same time, why hang around? Germany, Italy, France, Belgium, Holland, Spain, Portugal, he said. Yes, it's a fine profession, I said. But now it's time for us to go our separate ways, he said. I'll pay. You just go. I'm sure you have a lot to do. It was good to see you. And I did as he suggested, got up, took my jacket, said goodbye, went out through the hotel reception area, onto the street, wondering briefly whether to get a taxi or not, decided against it and ambled toward the bus station. Through the window I saw him again, he was walking through the restaurant toward the door at the far end that led to the bars, and once again his movements, despite his large, heavy body, were hurried and impatient.

That was the last time I saw him alive.

I had the distinct impression that he had pulled himself together. That in those two hours he had summoned all his strength to stay in one piece, to be sensitive and present, to be what he had been.

The thought of it pained me as I paced back and forth on the veranda staring at the town and then the sea. I considered whether to go for a walk into town, or perhaps to the stadium, but I couldn't leave Grandma on her own, and I didn't feel like walking either. Besides, tomorrow everything would look different. The day always came with more than mere light. However frayed your emotions, it was impossible to be wholly unaffected by the day's new beginnings. So I took the cup to the kitchen, put it in the dishwasher, did the same with all the other cups and glasses, plates, and dishes, poured in powder and started it, wiped the table with a cloth, wrung it, and draped it over the tap, even though there was something obscene about the meeting between damp, crumpled rag and the tap's shiny chrome, went into the living room and stopped beside the chair where Grandma was sitting.

"I think I'm going to bed," I said. "It's been a long day."

"Is it so late already?" she asked. "Yes, I'll be off soon as well."

"Good night," I said.

"Good night."

I started to leave.

"Karl Ove?" she called.

I turned back.

"You're not thinking of sleeping up there tonight too, are you? It would be better for you downstairs. In our old bedroom, you know. Then you've got the bathroom next door."

"That's true," I said. "But I think I'll stay where I am. We've got all our things up there."

"Alright," she said. "You do as you like. Good night."

"Good night."

It was only when I was upstairs in the bedroom undressing that I realized it had not been for my sake that she had suggested I sleep down below, but for hers. I put my T-shirt back on, lifted the sheet, rolled the duvet into a ball, put it under one arm, grabbed the suitcase with the other, and made my way downstairs. I bumped into her on the first-floor landing.

"I've changed my mind," I explained. "It would be better downstairs, as you said."

"Yes, good," she said.

I followed her down. In the hall she turned to me.

"Do you have everything you need?"

"Everything," I answered.

Then she opened the door to her little room and was gone.

The room I was going to sleep in was one of those we had not tackled yet, but the fact that her things, such as hairbrushes, rollers, jewelery and jewelery box, clothes hangers, nightgowns, blouses, underwear, toilet bags, cosmetics lay scattered around on bedside tables, the mattress, shelves in the open wardrobe, on the floor, on the windowsills did not bother me in the slightest, I just cleared the mattress with a couple of sweeps of my hand, spread out the sheet and duvet, undressed, switched off the light and got into bed.

I must have fallen asleep at once for the next thing I remember is that I woke up and switched on the bedside lamp to look at my watch, it was two o'clock. On the staircase outside the door I heard footsteps. Still drowsy with sleep, the first thing that occurred to me, and presumably connected with something I had dreamed, was that Dad had returned. Not as a ghost, but in the flesh. Nothing in me refuted this notion, and I was frightened. Then, not right away, but somehow following up on this notion, I realized the idea was ridiculous and went into the hall. The door to Grandma's room was ajar. I looked in. Her bed was empty. I ascended the staircase. She was probably getting herself a glass of water, or perhaps she hadn't been able to sleep, and had gone up to watch TV, but I would check there anyway, to be on the safe side. First, the kitchen. She wasn't there. Then, the living room. Nor there. So she must have gone to the special occasion living room.

Yes, she was by the window.

For some reason I didn't make my presence known. I paused in the shadow of the dark sliding door, watching her.

It was as though she were in a trance. She was standing motionless, staring into the garden. Occasionally, her lips moved, as though whispering to herself. But not a sound emerged.

Without warning, she whirled around and came toward me. I didn't have the wit to react, just watched her coming toward me. She passed by half a meter away, but although her eyes flitted across my face she didn't see me. She walked straight past, as if I were just a piece of furniture.

I waited until I heard the door downstairs shut before following.

Once back in my bedroom, I was afraid. Death was everywhere. Death was in the jacket in the hall, where the envelope containing my father's possessions was, death was in the chair in the living room, where she had found him, death was on the stairs, where they had carried him, death was in the bathroom, where Grandad had collapsed, his stomach covered with blood. If I closed my eyes it was impossible to escape the thought that the dead might come, just like in my childhood. But I had to close my eyes. And if I succeeded in ridiculing these childish notions, there was no getting past the sudden image of Dad's dead body. The interlaced fingers with the white nails, the yellowing skin, the hollow cheeks. These images accompanied me deep into my light sleep, in such a way that I couldn't say whether they belonged to the world of reality or dreams. Once my consciousness had opened in this way, I was sure his body was in the wardrobe, and I checked, rummaged through all the dresses hanging there, checked the next, and the next, and having done that, I went back to bed and continued sleeping. In my dreams he was sometimes dead, sometimes alive, sometimes in the present, sometimes in the past. It was as if he had completely taken me over, as if he controlled everything inside me, and when at last I awoke, at around eight o'clock, my initial thought was it had been a nocturnal visitation, and then, that I had to see him again.

Two hours later I closed the door to the kitchen, where Grandma was sitting, went to the phone, and dialed the funeral director's number.

"Andenæs Funeral Parlor."

"Ah, hello, this is Karl Ove Knausgaard. I was at your office the day before yesterday, with my brother. About my father. He died four days ago . . ."

"Ah yes, hello . . ."

"As you know, we went to see him yesterday . . . But now I was wondering if it would be possible to see him again? A final visit, if you understand . . ."

"Yes, of course. When would be convenient?"

"We-ell," I said. "Some time this afternoon? Three? Four?"

"Shall we say three then?"

"Three's good."

"Outside the chapel."

"Okay."

"Okay, so it's set then. Excellent."

"Thank you very much."

"Not at all."

Relieved that the conversation had been so unproblematic, I went into the garden and continued cutting the grass. The sky was overcast, the light gentle, the air warm. I finished at around two o'clock. Then I went back in to see Grandma and said I was going to meet a friend, changed clothes, and headed for the chapel. The same car was by the front door, the same man opened up when I knocked. He acknowledged me with a nod, opened the door to the room where we had been the day before, did not enter himself, and I stood in front of Dad again. This time I was prepared for what awaited me, and his body – the skin must have darkened even further in the course of the previous twenty-four hours – aroused none of the feelings that had distressed me before. Now I saw his lifeless state. And that there was no longer any difference between what once had been my father and the table he was lying on, or the floor on which the table stood, or the wall socket beneath the window, or the cable running to the lamp beside him. For humans are merely one form among many, which the world produces over and over again, not only in everything that lives but also in everything that does not live, drawn in sand, stone, and water. And death, which I have always regarded as the greatest dimension of life, dark, compelling, was no more than a pipe that springs a leak, a branch that cracks in the wind, a jacket that slips off a clothes hanger and falls to the floor.

We would like to acknowledge the generous involvement of the following individuals:

Jennifer Acker, Cameron Ackroyd, Anonymous (4), Taylor Davis-Van Atta, Terry Atwater, David Auerbach, Jeremy Austin, Andy Bankin, Holt Barnitz, Alisa Bayes, Michael Bedrick, Jeanne Begley, Sherwood Belangia, Aaron Bell, Matt Bell, Stuart & Caitlin Benton, Nadia Ben-Youssef, Timothy Berge, Susan Bernofsky, Trevor Berrett, Sumit Bhardwaj, Black Mountain Institute, Penelope Boehm, James Boice, Alexander Brock, Parker Brown, Matthew Buell, David & Pamela Bullen, John Carmichael, Margaret Carson, Sonia & Roger Celestin, The Abbott Chalew Family, Mieke Chew, Jessica Chia, Jon Chodosh, David Christensen, Zenia Chrysostomidis, Steve Connell, Susan Cooke, Alex Cox, Sean Cronin, Moyra Davey, Susan DeWitt Davie, Colin Dickey, Darby M. Dixon III, Nicholas During, Erin Edmison, Kevin Elliott, Joshua Ellison, Karen Emmerich, Scott Esposito, Joshua Evans, Will Evans, Marc Feder, Bill Fitzgerald, Kelsey Ford, Kathryn Fox, Katharine Freeman, Mark Fried, Amos Friedland, Sarah Gaddis, Erika Goldman, Todd Goldwasser, Graydon Gordian, Sara Gore, Julia Grawemeyer, Nick Greene, Jessica Griffiths, Kyle Gross, Yannick Guillemot, David Haan, Daniel Hahn, Donavan Hall, Chris Hammer, Wendy Hardenberg, Elizabeth Harris, Susan Harris, Laura Hauther, Justin Haviland, Michael Heald, Mark Hendel, Jim Hicks, Susan Hight, David Hobson, Leslie Hodgkins, Geoffrey C. Howes, Nicholas Hudson, Brigid Hughes, Neil Hume, Laird Hunt, Christopher Iacono, James Jacobo-Mandryk, Matthew Jacobs, Kristin Jensen Storey, Sandra Johnson, Morgan Karr, Chris Kauffman, Mezan Khaja, Rafay Khalid, Cari Kilbride, Brandon Korch, Stephen Korpi, Jed Lackritz, Callan Lamb, Joseph Langdon, Sean LaRiche, Todd Lester, Cressida Leyshon, Todd Lieber, Michael Lin, Michael Lindgren, Andrew Linscott, Stefan Lorenzutti, Florence Lui, Irene Lui, Matthew Lundin, Dan Luu, Erling Maartmann-Moe, Elizabeth Macklin, Darlene Mazzone, Victor Mazzone, Tom McCarthy, Colin Meloy, Tony Messenger, Fredi Milberg, Josh Milberg, Lynda & Breon Mitchell, Brett Mizelle, Toril Moi, Honor Moore, Gabriel Munoz, Ragnar Naess, Kestutis Nakas, Alexander Neher, Mary Ann Newman, Tiffany Nichols, Patrick O'Hara, Zachary Pace, Ilaria Papini, Timothy Paulson, Emily Perper, Jim Petersen, Joy Pierce, Gerald Pirog, Jill Propst, Francine Prose, Jeff Purdue, Marcia Lynx Qualey, Wilder Ramsey, Red Hen Press, Brian Rogers, Rooftop Films, Steven Salardino, Ryan Schofield, Gloria Schoolman, Hugh Schoolman & Franci Diniz, Hank Scotch, Barbara Schulman, Marian M. Shear, Zach Shoup, Katherine Silver, Jacob Silverman, Russell Snowden, Harris Sockel, Sprucedale, Tim Stokes, Matt Storey, Miranda Tedholm, Justin TerAvest, Karen Tiefenwerth, Susan Tomaselli, Stephen Twilley, Maximiliano Udenio, Vaughn, Peter von Ziegesar & Hali Lee, Thomas Walker, Ted Warin, Ivan Webster, Evan Weingarten, Sasha Weiss, Brad Weslake, Rick Whitaker, Diane & Richard White, Richard Wiley, Christopher Winks, Bram Wispelwey, Alexander & Vanessa Wolff, Ingebjorg Wollo, Ryan Woodsmall, Ben Yarde-Buller, Steven Yit, Lila Azam Zanganeh, Anne Zinsser

archipelago books
is a not-for-profit literary press devoted to
promoting cross-cultural exchange through innovative
classic and contemporary international literature
www.archipelagobooks.org